OVERTIME

Marsha,
Always keep
fighting.

OVERTIME

THE ASSASSINS SERIES

TONI ALEO

Edited by Silently Correcting Your Grammar, LLC
Interior designed and formatted by

www.emtippettsbookdesigns.com

The Bellevue Bullies Series
Boarded by Love
Clipped by Love
Hooked by Love (late 2015)

The Assassins Series
Taking Shots
Trying to Score
Empty Net
Falling for the Backup
Blue Lines
Breaking Away
Laces and Lace
A Very Merry Hockey Holiday
Overtime

Standalone
Let it be Me

Taking Risks Series
The Whiskey Prince
Becoming the Whiskey Princess

This book is for anyone who is fighting to better themselves.
Fighting the battle of addiction.
Fighting the battle of depression.
Fighting the battle of abuse.
Know that this book is for you.
You can do it.
I believe in you.
As Jared Padalecki says:
JUST KEEP FIGHTING!

Chapter ONE

J ordie Thomas knew he was screwed.

There were two things that he didn't want, ever, in his life.

Herpes, and to be called into Elli Adler's office.

Everyone knew that it wasn't good to be called into the office of the owner of the professional hockey team he played for, the Nashville Assassins. If it was something good, usually she just called to chitchat, as she called it, and dote on her players. But when she called them into her office, ten out of ten times, they were screwed.

And today, Jordie must be screwed.

As his good leg bounced from the nerves, Jordie waited for the door to open to Elli's office. His shoulders were taut, his other knee ached, and his heart was pounding. Ever since he got the call that she wanted him to fly from Colorado to Nashville for a meeting, he had been replaying every single scenario in his head. He hadn't been making the greatest decisions lately, and he was pretty damn sure this had to do with his spur-of-the-moment vacation to Louisiana.

He should have just stayed home.

That whole trip was a clusterfuck. That's the only way he could describe it. He hadn't acted like himself, he kept trying to forget a certain someone, and he really should have just stayed home and healed. Not only had it pushed him back a week in PT but now he was worried that something he did there may be back to haunt him. As he replayed the weekend, which consisted of a lot of alcohol, a lot of women, and a good long visit in the ER that resulted in

1

even more great sex, he couldn't find anything out of the ordinary that could have brought him here. Then again, Elli didn't like when her players' whore-like tendencies hung out, but still, she usually called and warned them to clean it up.

Hell, he had gotten that call plenty of times. Maybe that's why he was here? She was done with his ways? Damn it. Hopefully, that wasn't it though. He was on the road to recovery after a really nasty hit into the boards last year, and nothing was going to keep him off the ice.

Well, except Elli Adler, that is.

Maybe she didn't want to wait for him to heal? The draft was coming up; maybe she had her eyes on someone to replace him. Shit. Did he want to go to another team? He had already been to so many, and he was convinced this was the team he was going to retire from. He loved the Assassins. They were his brothers, his friends, and he was invested in this team. He couldn't leave…but then the nagging voice inside of him kept reminding him that his career could be over. Yeah, the doctors felt good and were optimistic about a full recovery from snapping his leg in two, but what if he didn't play like he used to? Maybe Elli knew that and wanted to cut ties now? If she knew that, then that meant everyone must know.

Fuck. Was he in denial?

Slowly running his hand through his hair that he really needed to cut, he wondered what he would do if he didn't play hockey? Hockey was his life. It's all he'd ever wanted to do. It's all he knew how to do. It was his saving grace, the one thing that kept him going when life seemed to be over. Which, growing up, was a lot of the time. He didn't have it easy like some kids. While his mom always married guys for money, it didn't mean that any money went to Jordie like it should have. While she was decked out in Gucci, Jordie rocked Goodwill, but he really didn't mind. She made sure he had his hockey gear, and that was all he cared about.

Nothing mattered but hockey. Because of that, during school, all the girls did his homework for his attention and he was glad to provide it, so it wasn't like he was book smart. Street smarts, sure, he could get by with no problem, but his math and his spelling were a little suspect, and he was pretty sure he would need those to do any job a normal person would do.

Stroking his beard to keep his hands from shaking from the nerves that were rapid-firing through his body, Jordie bit into his lip. He wasn't good at anything but hockey. Oh, well, and sex. He was damn good at that. He loved it too. Come to think of it, he was hung like a horse too, so maybe he could become a porn star? Hey, that wasn't a half-bad idea.

Before he could even entertain that idea, the door opened to Elli's office and she filled the doorway, looking killer in a pair of green heels that should have been illegal. Her auburn hair flowed down her shoulders, curled to perfection, her green eyes piercing and her skirt tight, wrapping around her thick thighs. No one would ever assume that Mrs. Adler was a mommy of five; she was too hot for that. She may be his boss and even his captain's wife, but Jordie had always had a soft spot for her. It was probably because she'd always been on the chunky side from having so many babies. Jordie loved kids, and he really loved her kids. But as he drank her in, he noticed that Mrs. Adler looked mighty fine and a little leaner.

Grinning at her, he slowly stood. "Have you lost weight, boss? Shea not feeding you?"

She giggled. "Oh hush, I'm watching what I eat."

"Well, you can tell, and that Shea Adler is a lucky man, boss."

As she smiled back at him, his heart slowed a bit. If she was smiling, that was a good thing. Maybe he'd overthought this? "Thanks, Jordie. Come on in," she said in her thick accent that always made him feel like she was ten seconds away from serving him a big, buttered biscuit.

Hobbling over, he passed by her, her intoxicating mango scent making him dizzy as she asked, "How's the leg?"

Regrouping, Jordie nodded his head. "Healing. I'll be brand-spanking-new for next season," he answered, holding her gaze. But when she shut the door, he looked up and saw that not only was his agent Charles Bolster sitting by Elli's desk but so was the other owner of the Assassins, Bryan Fisher.

Double fuck.

Swallowing loudly, he went for an aloof approach and said, "Hey, guys. Didn't know you were coming too."

"I didn't know either," Charles said, annoyed, and that had Jordie's stomach sinking.

"Elli wanted us here," Bryan answered, and Jordie's chest clenched. Ignoring the need to flee, he dropped slowly into the seat that was in front of Elli's desk and glanced nervously over at Charles. He was working his lip, looking over some paperwork in front of him. When he looked at Jordie, he knew he was fucked to the max.

His heart started to slam into his ribs as Elli came around her desk, lowering into her big, puffy teal chair with black trim. Behind her was a massive museum-like display of pictures of her and her family. The sweet faces of her five children—that Jordie could honestly say were the greatest kids ever—smiled back at him in different poses and shots. There was even a picture with all the kids and him, along with some of the other guys from the team. When his eyes settled on that picture, he saw Elli's oldest, Shelli, was wrapped around him like a koala. She had always been his favorite. She loved to braid Jordie's beard and paint his nails. He never told her no since she was a mini Elli and, really, he didn't mind. He loved kids.

He also hoped that kids were in his future, but he couldn't be dwelling on that right now. Not when his boss was looking at him like he was one of her five children and he'd been caught busting the windows out with a hockey puck.

"You're probably wondering why you're here," she started and he shrugged, leaning back in the plush teal chair that was a smaller version of hers.

"I've narrowed it down to assuming I've done something wrong," he joked, trying to break the tension in the room. But when her green eyes cut to his, he snapped his lips shut.

"You've assumed right," she said, sliding a piece of paper toward him. Picking it up, the first thing he saw was *Suspended* written below his name. His heart stopped as his brows shot up, and soon he was unable to catch a breath.

"Suspended?" he croaked out before looking up to meet her gaze.

Lacing her fingers together, she slowly nodded her head. "We don't tolerate drug use, Jordie. You know that."

He did, and he hadn't touched a single drug because of it. He wasn't into them anyway, so what the hell was this... And then it was like the whole room went still as it dawned on him that he'd never told her about Louisiana like he'd meant to.

"Your last blood test came back with high amounts of MDMA, and also, your trainer is saying you are drinking a lot more than usual."

He was, but he had always been a drinker.

Dropping the paper, he held his hands up as he scooted to the edge of his seat. "Okay, I forgot to call you and tell you about the Molly when I was in Louisiana. I was drugged, and you can call the nurses and doctors down there and they'll vouch for me."

"I already have," she said and his brow furrowed.

"Okay? Then why is this an issue? Why am I being suspended?" he asked, completely confused.

"Because you put yourself in that position, Jordie. Everyone has heard about your wild weekend in Louisiana. Even the girls you were with have done interviews, saying how you hurt your leg trying to have sex with them."

He grimaced; it wasn't the most flattering blog post either. The only good thing about it was that they said his cock was huge. Points for him, but he was sure that didn't matter to his boss. "Yeah, but—"

She shook her head, cutting him off. "No, you've been making some really, excuse me, but shitty choices lately. Your drinking is getting you in trouble. Now, usually I let it go, but you went down to Louisiana, got shit-faced drunk, high out of your mind, and screwed anything with tits. You are all over the blogs about your wild nights, and you're making our team look bad. You've been doing this for a while and I've been turning my cheek to it because you're a good guy, a great player. But the drug use, voluntary or not," she added when he went to interrupt her, so he swallowed his retort as she went on, "is the straw that broke the camel's back. Things are gonna change, or I will not be renewing your contract in October."

What? That was bullshit!

"Are you serious right now? I'm being punked, right?" he demanded, turning to Charles. "I'm not that bad. I have fun, I do what I want, but I've always been a team player. And my extracurricular activities have never interfered with my game play. Never."

Looking over at him, Charles shook his head as Elli went on, "You're right, Jordie. But you're supposed to be healing, not going out getting trashed and hurting yourself all over again."

Meeting Elli's gaze, he shook his head. "I know that wasn't the best choice for me, but I wanted to have fun. I was going stir-crazy," he said, which was a total lie.

He'd wanted to forget a certain someone and thought partying down in Louisiana was the way to go. Actually, it was the worst idea ever, and he still hadn't forgotten her. If anything, his feelings for her had only gotten stronger, which meant that his weekend that had now resulted in him getting suspended was for absolutely nothing.

Scary shit, feelings were. Trouble too.

"Which is completely understandable, Jordie. But the one bad decision snowballed into a mess. Now we have trainers wondering if you're even worth working with because you're drinking all the time and coming up hot on a drug test. And then the blogs are going nuts with this. Questioning Elli's and my next move. I mean, what we should do is let you go now. But you're lucky that Elli fights for the people she believes in and did the research needed. Because, if it was me, you'd be gone," Bryan said, and Jordie's eyes met Elli's. She looked sad and stressed out, and he hated that his actions caused her eyes to be filled with all that. "The only thing you should be doing is sleeping and working on rehabbing that leg."

"You're right," Jordie decided, looking from Elli to him. "I'm sorry."

"Sorry isn't enough, buddy," was his answer and Jordie looked away.

Jordie didn't know what to say. He didn't want to be suspended; he'd worked hard to stay in the good graces of his owners, and this wouldn't help him when it was time to renew his contract. He'd always kept his party life separate from his hockey game. Before, yeah, he drank, but he only drank when he wasn't playing. And even then, it wasn't much. But when he busted his leg, he drank to dull the pain that was eating him alive. Between not being able to play and being away from his team, he was also dealing with all the feelings he had for her. He was a mess and, now, it was about to get worse.

Swallowing loudly, he looked back up at his owners and nodded. "Then tell me what is enough. I don't want to be suspended."

Slowly unclasping her hands, Elli crossed her arms over her chest, leaning back in her chair. "We don't want to suspend you, Jordie, but it's the only way we can show you we mean business."

"I understand that."

"Good, so now we need to see that you mean business too. We have enrolled you in a rehab facility back in Colorado for ninety days. Your PT will come to you and work with you."

There was silence as what she had just said slowly sank in, and when it did, Jordie came unglued.

"What the fuck! Rehab? There is nothing wrong with me! I don't want people thinking I'm a fucking druggie. Or an alcoholic! I like to drink. There is nothing wrong with that!" he yelled, unable to fathom why they thought he needed rehab.

Elli's eyes went wide as Bryan shook his head at Jordie's outburst. Soon Charles was talking fast. "It isn't a real rehab place, Thomas. It's private and residential—no one will ever know you are there. You can even keep your phone. But when people come to see you, they will be searched, and you can't leave until your time is up."

"That is fucking stupid!"

"Those are our terms," Elli said. "When you are done, you will go to group therapy two times a week and one-on-one therapy once a week. All your therapists and PT have to clear you before you can come home."

Looking between each of their faces, Jordie's mind was reeling. Surely, they were joking… But their faces were like ice, and he didn't understand why this was happening. "I don't need rehab," he reiterated, and he truly believed that. "This is extreme. You haven't even given me the chance to clean up my act."

"Because I don't think you can," she answered and his face scrunched up. "What?"

"You've changed, Jordie. The injury has really messed you up."

It isn't only the injury, he thought, but he didn't say that. "Yeah, it hurts, but I'm fine!" he said, his voice rising. "I'm still me."

"No," she said, shaking her head. "I can hear it in your voice when I speak to you weekly. You are hurting and becoming so withdrawn. People are saying you aren't returning calls and texts. You've gone to PT drunk more times than sober. You've changed. You aren't my Jordie, and we all really feel this will help."

He wasn't?

He wasn't.

He knew he wasn't.

Looking into Elli's green eyes, he could see the truth staring back at him.

His face was reflected in her eyes, and he almost didn't recognize the man looking back. Usually a confident, carefree person, he was now scared. Carried the weight of the world on his shoulders. Scared his career was hanging in the balance. Scared that his feelings for her meant more than he thought. He was confused and he was hurting and, yeah, he was using alcohol to help that. It numbed everything. But he honestly saw no problem with that. If he wanted to stop, he could.

"I can clean up, I promise."

Looking up at them, he could see the doubt in their eyes as Elli said, "Fine, humor me then."

"I don't want to humor you. I don't want to go."

"It will be good for you. They are really good there, and this will nip it in the bud before it blossoms into something that can't be fixed."

Looking away, he ran his hands through his hair. It had gotten longer. Usually, he kept it pretty clean and cut short since his beard was so long, but lately he didn't care. Which was very unlike him. He was letting himself go and, fuck, what was he doing? God, he was stressing out, he could really use a… Shit.

Letting out a long breath, he shut his eyes tightly and sucked in a new breath before opening them again. "And then the suspension will be lifted?"

"It will be lifted as soon as you do the ninety days," she informed him and he nodded. "But I'll put you right back on if you don't honor the therapy agreement."

Squeezing his eyes shut, he honestly wanted to scream. He wasn't a share-your-feelings kind of guy, and he knew what therapy consisted of. He'd gone for four years when he was younger. They dissected you and wanted to know your deepest, darkest thoughts. He wasn't one to share them then, and he really wasn't in the mood to share them now. He'd probably needed to back then, but now, he had no inclination to do that. He was fine. Maybe he had gotten off track, but this was a bit extreme in his opinion. He could quit drinking if he wanted to.

He just didn't want to.

Looking up, he met her pleading eyes and asked, "I don't have a choice, do I?"

"Not really," she answered slowly. "But I want you to know I'm doing this for you."

Holding her gaze, he knew that was a fact. Elli loved him.

"Yeah, I know that, Elli, and you know I love you for it. You've always taken good care of me," he said and she smiled.

"I have and I always will. You need this, Jordie. I don't think you are dealing with your feelings right. I swear, it's like you're changing in front of my eyes, and it's killing me. Honestly…" she started, her voice breaking. When her eyes filled with tears, he had to look away. "You're like a brother to me, Jordie."

"I know," he said softly, and she *was* the sister he'd never had. "I'll go."

"Good," Bryan said.

"You'll come back a billion times better," Charles informed him. "This is for the best."

He could dispute that, but maybe he was the wrong one here. That was his MO lately. Always being wrong.

"You're making the right choice," Elli said, and he looked up at her then as she wiped a stray tear away. He didn't want to make her cry; he didn't want to make her worry. Elli was very special to him, not only as his boss but as his friend. There wasn't a dinner he wasn't invited to, a holiday he couldn't crash, and a place he couldn't sleep. She mothered him and was ten times the mother he'd had. The slow burn of guilt filled his chest, and he had to look away once more.

He had consistently been making bad decision after bad decision. Each one was staring back at him from behind his closed lids, and he wished he could make them all go away. But still they flashed in his face, demanding his attention.

Going in for the puck when he knew there was a goon of a player behind him and ending with his leg in two. Which resulted in his career being up in the air.

The drinking. Fuck, the drinking.

Getting involved with his best friend's sister.

Falling in love with said sister, and then pushing her away, like he always did with everyone.

And all of Louisiana.

It was time to make the right choice for once.

He had to, because he had already lost the one person who meant everything to him, and he couldn't lose hockey too.

That couldn't happen.

"Ma, I don't know, maybe I should wait. I don't actually have to be there till August for summer training."

Kacey King watched as her parents packed her belongings into her little Civic. She was about to embark on the sixteen-hour drive to Nashville from her home in Wausau, Wisconsin. She grew up in the gorgeous town and to leave it was a little scary. She had friends here, and she knew the town like the back of her hand. She grew up playing on the frozen ponds and all her memories were here, but with her parents moving to Nashville and the new job that Karson, her older brother, had gotten her, Kacey knew there was no other choice. She had to go.

I want to go, she told herself for the hundredth time.

Karl King looked back at her and shrugged, his brow furrowed as he stuffed her comforter into the backseat. "We can't go until the house sells, Kace. So you go, help your brother and Lacey with the new baby, work out with the guys to get to know them before you start, live life. You've been a zombie lately. It's weird," he essentially barked at her as her mother came up and wrapped her arms around her.

"A pretty zombie though. Like, the prettiest," she commented, moving a piece of hair out of Kacey's eyes, eyes that were the exact shade of caramel as hers. "If you don't want to go, you don't have to."

"It's not that I don't want to go," she informed them. "It's just that I don't want to impose on Kar and Lacey. The baby will be here in no time."

Karl stood up straight, his hands on his hips. "You aren't imposing; they want you there, Karson said it himself. It's stupid for you to get an apartment when: one, you're broke and haven't started getting paid yet, and two, we will be there soon."

He was right, but still.

"I'm not that broke," she commented softly and he scoffed. After clearing her debts by using the money from her endorsements from winning the gold at the Olympics, she may have been a little low on funds. But still, she could manage. The thought of living with her brother and new sister-in-law and niece gave her the shakes. She didn't want to bother them, but everyone was so insistent.

"We know, love, but this is for the best. With the Olympics and everything, you know, you haven't had time to relax and figure out your next move. This will give you the chance to do that," her mother reminded her, like she had been doing for the last few weeks once they decided they wanted to pick up and move to be closer to their new grandbaby. "Plus, with Lacey being so fragile lately, she could use you there."

Kacey knew that too. Her sister-in-law wasn't very stable, even with all the groups and counseling she and Karson had gone through. Lacey was still a nervous wreck that her baby girl would develop breast cancer like she had. Everyone tried to ease her concerns, but poor Lacey couldn't think any other way. Add in the fact that she was running three lingerie stores, dealing with a family from hell, and the constant worry for her child, and Kacey's sister-in-law was one step away from needing to be in a padded room. She probably did need Kacey there. Especially since they had become best friends over the course of the last year.

But she was still hesitant and she knew why.

Letting out a long breath, she pushed him out of her mind and nodded. "Yeah, I know. I'm going," she said. "Plus, you're right, Daddy. Working out with the guys will help me get to know them and work them harder for the start of the season." Her father nodded his head, looking as if he knew he was always right. She rolled her eyes before breaking away from her mother and going into the house.

Reaching the mantel, she slowly grasped the box that held her gold medal. A small smile covered her lips as pride burst in her chest. She'd worked hard for her medal. Years upon years, she'd worked for one thing and that was the gold. She knew it was hers, and when they'd put it around her neck, words couldn't describe the feelings she'd felt. It was as if she had been almost flying. It was perfect, except that the person she'd wanted there, craved to be there to celebrate with her, wasn't.

Even though they had decided to stop sleeping together, Kacey couldn't fathom why he would do her like that. Didn't she mean something to him? If not in love, at least as friends. Instead, Jordie Thomas cut off all ties with her, acting as if their relationship that lasted a good four months didn't matter. That the nights they sat up talking about everything, the way they made love, and the way he made her feel were all a lie. She hadn't spoken to him in over six months. Hadn't seen him or even heard from him. Every time she asked her older brother about his best friend, he just said he was fine. Nothing more and nothing less. Since Karson wasn't supposed to know that she was in love with his best friend, she never asked more and it killed her inside.

She missed him. Greatly.

But when he didn't show up for the Olympics, that's when she knew she needed to let him go. But she was having a really hard time with that. She wanted so desperately to be in love with someone who loved her back. She was almost thirty, still a good two years away, but she figured by now, she'd at least be in a relationship, ready to get married once she brought the gold home. That was her plan, at least. Instead, she brought her gold home to her parents' house, along with a broken heart.

But Nashville was a new start. Karson had gotten her a job as a trainer with the Nashville Assassins. Something that was hard to get into. She was the first woman trainer in their club, and it only made sense since they had just drafted the first woman on to their team and into the NHL. That Elli Adler was making history for sure. Kacey was excited about this opportunity, knew that she would get along with the guys since they all loved her anyway. Then she'd find someone who wanted what she wanted, who would love her the way she needed to be loved, and she would be happy.

She wouldn't allow Jordie to consume her soul any longer. So what? It didn't work out. She knew going in that Jordie Thomas wasn't into relationships and he couldn't love anyone. It wasn't in his DNA. That was fine. It was her fault for falling for him. If she saw him, she'd be cordial. She knew what she was getting into when she went to bed with him. She had to forget him and maybe even forgive him. Because this was her new beginning. It was time to let go of him, the pain and the rejection she felt, and find someone who would never cause her to feel like that again.

That was her plan, at least.

Chapter TWO

After saying goodbye to her parents, Kacey placed her gold medal in the front seat and drove out of her parents' driveway for the last time. The next time she would be back, she'd be there to help them move, which they all hoped would be before Karson and Lacey's baby came. Lacey wasn't due for another month and a half, and her parents had already had a few bites on the house that Karson had bought her family so long ago. It was sad to see her home go, but she was excited to be closer to her new niece.

As her home disappeared in the rearview, she let out a breath and prepared herself, not only for the sixteen-hour drive but also for what Nashville could hold. Brushing her hair off her shoulders, she drove with her knee as she pulled it up into a mini ponytail. Growing her hair out from her pixie cut had been a pain, but she liked the result. Maybe now Karson would stop calling her a lesbian, not that she really cared what he thought. Having short hair was easy when she was wearing her helmet, and Kacey liked convenience. Now that she was done with hockey professionally, she was ready to look more like a girl. Maybe it would finally attract a good guy, since before, all she could get were douches or a lot of attention from women.

But it was so hard! Everyone talked about how great single life was, but Kacey found it really lonely. She wanted someone to come home to. Someone to hold her at night and tell her she was pretty, even when she wasn't. Her life partner. The Lacey to her Karson. Unfortunately though, the last three guys she'd dated had been duds. All of them only looking for sex, no one wanting the white picket fence and kids thing like she had.

She had always wanted that. When she was little, there wasn't a moment she wasn't playing house. Usually, she made Karson be the dad to her many baby dolls, but that got weird quick when he told her they were supposed to kiss. No way in hell was she kissing her older brother. So then she moved to Barbie dolls, and when she wasn't kicking ass on the ice, she was in her room, making little worlds with her dolls. It was great and she always knew she was going to be a wife and a mommy.

Hockey got in the way though, not that she minded much. She was good, damn good, and soon that's all she cared about. She'd always idolized Karson, wanted what he did. And to be able to play the sport he did, she felt, brought them closer. And it had, but while his sights were on the Cup, hers were on the gold medal. Ever since she saw her first Olympics at the age of six, she knew that was what she wanted. Since then, she had worked hard to get to the Games, and when she was finally there, she felt like all her dreams had come true.

Except for the personal aspect. She'd always dated, always had a boyfriend going through school, but for some reason, it never worked. She never clicked with anyone because she would admit she was a little hard to deal with. She didn't have the normal girl personality; she was ruined by her years of playing hockey with Karson and his friends. She was a little rough around the edges, had a mouth on her that would make a classy woman cry, and didn't take shit from anyone. She was an act now, think later kind of girl, and that always seemed to get her in trouble.

Especially when Jordie put the moves on her.

She knew it was a bad idea, but she'd had a thing for Jordie Thomas since she was eighteen. The first time she'd met him was at Karson's apartment when he was playing for the University of Wisconsin. Jordie was on his team; they weren't roommates but still friends. And when she saw him, he was a clean-shaven young guy who made her heart race. She doubted he remembered the first time they met. He was drunk, but she'd never forget the way those dark eyes held hers, the way his mouth curved in the most sinful grin, or how his hand felt in hers. Ugh, she got tingles along her arm just thinking about it. But Karson must have known that the air was crackling around them because he quickly removed Kacey from the room and wouldn't let her out of his room until the party was over, despite her protests.

She never got a chance to see Jordie again though. She and Karson both transferred to Chicago on full-ride scholarships, but she knew that Jordie and Karson had stayed friends. It wasn't until they were both sent to the Assassins seven years later that Kacey saw him again. He came home for Christmas with Karson and, boy, had he changed. No longer the clean-shaven young guy, he was rugged, bulky, and oh so gorgeous. He had a beard growing, nothing like it was now, but it was thick then, and she'd never realized she had a thing for beards until that moment.

When he spoke to her, butterflies went nuts in her belly but she was completely comfortable around him. He made her laugh, made her feel pretty with only a look, and he appreciated her game. Anytime they all got together, they were outside smacking the puck around and it was great. She was feeling him and was sure he was feeling her, but she never acted on her desires and neither had he. Karson had told her that Jordie didn't do relationships, and since that's what Kacey wanted, she stayed clear, keeping him at arm's length.

But that all changed when she was home for Thanksgiving last year. Karson and Lacey had just gotten married without telling anyone until afterward, Jordie had just suffered an injury, and she didn't know why she gave in, but soon she was flat against the sink, taking it from behind. They had always flirted, but this time their flirting got out of hand and there was no saying no to him. She desired him. She was sure it wouldn't happen again—one time and, bam, they were good. But then it wasn't a one-time thing. It turned into an every-day thing. Then she was staying with him in Colorado, helping him with his PT, and being there on the nights he felt most alone. She was sure that she was his girlfriend, but he kept reminding her that they were just friends.

And somehow she still fell in love with him.

She had never been in full-out, head-over-heels, smack-dab-in-the-heart kind of love, but she was with him. How could she not be? He was everything she wanted and more, but for some reason, he wouldn't recognize that. He didn't see that he was sweet and had a good heart. He had been abused, hurt, had a bit of a drinking problem. And still knowing all that, she went in, heart wide open for him. She thought she could change him, fix him, make him love her, but she wasn't enough. And then he completely stopped talking to her and that made the rejection even harder to swallow.

Blinking away the tears, she hated that she allowed him to still invade her thoughts, to continually break her heart over and over again. She just wanted to know why though. Had he found someone else? Was she honestly not enough for him? There were so many questions, but he didn't give her any answers. He cut her out of his life and it wasn't fair. She was there, holding his hand, holding him to keep him from drinking. He never admitted to having a problem, and maybe there wasn't one, but that was the first thing he always went to when things got tough. Except, when he was with her, she was his drink.

But it wasn't only about sex. It was real. It had to be.

Or at least she thought it had been.

Wiping her face free of the tears, she shook her head as she settled into her seat. No, it was only sex, and the sooner she accepted that, the sooner she'd get over him. It was coming up on seven months without any communication; he didn't want her. Fine. There was someone out there for her. She just had to find him.

And she would.

"You got in late?"

Kacey looked up from her cup of coffee as her sister-in-law wobbled to the sink to wash some potatoes. Her growing belly pushed against the front of the cabinets, and Kacey couldn't help grinning despite how dog-tired she was. She just couldn't wait to meet her niece, to cuddle her and be her best friend. She'd always thought that Karson would have started earlier in making a family—he was always cut out to be a dad—but then he didn't get Lacey back into his life until recently. Kacey had always known that Lacey was going to be her sister-in-law after meeting her almost nine years ago. She was everything that Karson needed, his other half, and they always just fit.

Kacey could still remember the first time she met Lacey. Karson was completely head over heels for her, his eyes glassy anytime she was near, and Kacey just knew her brother would marry no one but her. And man, Lacey was beautiful. She'd had short hair from when she was going through chemo back then, but now she had long, gorgeous blond hair that went to her butt. Her eyes were still the same beautiful green that was brought out by her long, dark lashes. She had gained weight only in her stomach, the rest of her thin and lean, and that drove Kacey crazy. Kacey was convinced when she had a kid, she'd blow up. She loved food more than life, and the thought of feeding two instead of one gave her the giggles. She could eat what she wanted and no one could say anything to her about it. She would be growing a life. And looking at Lacey, she realized she wanted that more than ever.

She needed a man first, though.

Unfortunately.

"Three a.m."

"Jesus," she muttered. "Why are you awake now?"

Kacey had no clue, but she was pretty sure it was because the last time she'd slept in her bed here, Jordie had been on top of her. Not that she was going to tell her sister-in-law that.

"Not sure," she sighed before taking a long pull of her coffee. Meeting Lacey's knowing gaze, Kacey smiled. Lacey knew all about Jordie, but they didn't speak of it when Karson could be in hearing distance. It wasn't that Karson hated Jordie, he loved him, but Jordie wasn't good enough for Kacey. No one was, in the eyes of her older brother, but if he found out how Jordie had basically cut off all communication with her and everything else, she was sure that Karson would kill him. So before Lacey could ask anything, Kacey said, "You look gorgeous, Lace."

"Please." She scoffed, waving her off. "I'm as big as a house."

"Whatever." Kacey laughed. "Pregnancy looks good on you, sister."

Lacey grinned before looking down at her belly, her chest rising and falling before glancing back over at Kacey. Her eyes were full of worry, something Kacey had seen a lot of since they announced the baby was coming. "Yeah. I guess I just feel big."

"It's all in the belly," Kacey promised, and it wasn't a lie.

"Yeah, that's for sure," she said, rubbing her belly in a very protective way. "I wish she could stay in there, y'know?" she whispered, almost so low that Kacey didn't hear her. Thankfully, she did though.

Biting into her lip, Kacey reached over, taking Lacey's hand in hers. "Lacey, she's gonna be perfect and healthy. Don't worry so much."

"I try not to," she said honestly, looking over at Kacey and squeezing back. "But it's so damn hard. I worry that she'll go through what I did, and I don't want that for her."

"None of us do, Lacey, but the good thing is she'll always have us. Between me, Ma, Dad, and you guys, that little buttercup will never be alone through the fight. But I promise you don't have to worry about that right now. If ever. Let's be positive about it."

Lacey's lip started to wobble, and before a tear could even fall, Kacey was up and around the island, her arms around her sister-in-law, holding her tightly. She knew that Lacey's past with breast cancer still weighed heavy on her beautiful heart. Despite the support groups, Lacey just couldn't shake the worries that ate her alive. It worried Kacey, but Karson had said one of the main things was reassuring her that it wouldn't happen, to stay positive. Holding her tightly, Kacey kissed her cheek. "It's okay, Lacey, don't worry. Enjoy this. You are having a baby, a little you and Karson. What a blessing!"

Lacey wrapped her arms around Kacey's middle since she was so much taller than her, nodding her head against her arm as her body shook with small sobs. "I know. I want to be happy and excited like Karson and you guys are, but I'm just so nervous."

"Don't be," Kacey urged against her hair. "Enjoy it."

"I am. Really, this is the most amazing thing in the world," she said, and Kacey knew it was more for herself than for her. Sending her a grin, she slowly parted from Lacey. "But the nerves do eat me alive. And that's why I'm so glad you're here, 'cause when Karson isn't around, I get a little crazy."

Kacey grinned. "You, crazy? Please."

Lacey smacked her playfully before turning to mix the potato salad. She looked perfect doing it too, if that were possible. She made being a wife look so damn good, and Kacey hated how jealous she was of her. "I want your life, Lacey."

Lacey scoffed. "Say what? You have a great life; you're a gold medalist."

She nodded. "Oh yeah, I know and it's awesome, but I want to be the successful wife making potato salad while my kiddo grows inside me."

"One day, don't worry," Lacey said with a wink. "Then I can sit there and tell you what to expect and warn you of the sleepless nights and scare the shit out of you. Man, the team's wives don't hold back."

Kacey laughed. "Um, I bet! Especially with Elli—I'm pretty sure she's been through everything."

"She has and, good Lord above, it's scary."

Grinning, Kacey nodded. "I bet, but I'll sit back and watch you. Learn from your mistakes," she added with a wink and Lacey laughed.

"I'm sure there will be a ton!" she groaned as she added the pickles.

"Doubt it."

Lacey grinned before she shrugged. "So, no new man in your life?"

Kacey looked up and made a face. "I've been dating nothing but idiots for the last year."

"Eh, not all of them were that bad," she said with a knowing look.

"Ha. Please."

"So you haven't spoken to him?"

They both shared a long look. It didn't take a genius to know exactly whom her sister-in-law was speaking of. Shaking her head slowly, she picked at a hangnail as she answered. "Not since I walked out of his cabin seven months ago."

"I'm sorry, Kacey. I really hoped that something could have happened between you two."

Kacey shrugged, trying to act indifferent about it. She didn't want Lacey to know how much she was hurting. "Eh, it wasn't meant to be, I guess."

"Yeah, I guess not," she said slowly.

Biting her lip, Kacey watched her for a moment and then finally asked what she had wanted to know for months. "Have you spoken to him?"

She knew that Lacey had. Karson and Jordie were best friends to the extreme, basically holding each other's dicks when the other peed, but still no one had spoken about him in months. Maybe something had changed?

When Lacey shrugged slowly, she reached for the salt and pepper before biting the inside of her cheek. "Yeah, of course, we have."

"About me?" she urged and Lacey looked away.

"No, Kacey, I wouldn't do that in front of Karson, and I've only seen or talked to Jordie with Karson."

"Oh," Kacey said sadly. She wasn't hoping for a different answer. She should have known better. It wasn't as if Lacey would betray her and talk about her in front of her brother, but she sort of hoped that Lacey had been able to get Jordie alone. Because she wanted to know something, anything. Maybe that he missed her. Or that he even talked about her. But it seemed that she didn't matter to him, something she needed to accept. "So he hasn't asked about me?"

Looking up, Lacey slowly shook her head. "No, I'm sorry. I thought maybe he was talking to you on the sly."

"Nope, nothing."

"That really sucks," she said softly. "He could really benefit from having you in his life."

Her statement sounded really loaded, but before Kacey could ask, Karson strolled into the kitchen. "Hey, people are getting here. You ready, love? Ew, Kacey, you gonna fix your hair or something? The team is starting to show up."

"Fuck you," Kacey shot back as she redid her ponytail, looking her brother over. He had gained a little weight over the summer, probably sympathy eating with Lacey, which was just too damn cute. But nonetheless, Karson was basically her male twin. Despite the two-year age gap, they looked so much alike it was scary. Both with caramel eyes and dark hair, tall and broad shouldered with lean, strong bodies. There wasn't a summer where they didn't work out or spend the day playing hockey. While Karson was an ass and drove her insane, he was her best friend and she loved him more than words could describe. She knew he loved her more than that and was disgustingly overprotective. Hence why he didn't know that there had been a relationship between her and Jordie. He thought they'd only slept together once, and he was still very unhappy about that. But despite all the love between the two siblings, they fought like cats and dogs. "I am supposed to be in bed."

"Then why aren't you? I told you we were having this party today. You should have come in tomorrow," he said, coming up behind Lacey and cuddling her close to him.

"I didn't want to drive on the Fourth of July, and Ma and Dad basically pushed me out the door. Dad wants me to start training with you guys on Monday."

"True," he said with a nod. "Well then, go put on your party shoes and drink a few more cups of coffee, 'cause it's time to party!"

"You're an idiot," was her decision as she downed the rest of her cup. "Where is the dee to your dum?"

"What?" he asked confused as Lacey giggled softly.

"Jordie," she said, acting as if she was bored.

His shoulders dropped, his grin gone as he looked away, reaching for the bowl that Lacey has pushed to the side. "He won't be here."

"Really? Why? That's weird," she said, watching her older brother, who was obviously uncomfortable. "What's wrong with you?"

"Nothing. He can't come." He then disappeared, and Kacey looked across the island at Lacey.

"What the hell was that about?"

"I don't know," Lacey lied with a shrug. But the thing about Lacey was that she couldn't lie for shit.

"You're lying to me," Kacey said, surprised. "Why?"

"I don't know," she said again, still ignoring eye contact. Before Kacey could ask anything else, the side door opened and Kacey promptly forgot her next question. Because in walked a freaking Greek god of sexiness. Tall, very tall, taller than her, and that didn't happen much since she was almost 6'1". He was carrying a couple cases of beer with ease, his shoulders flexing as the tank he wore pulled to the side due to the cases against his chest, showing off one hell of a pec. It would be a great place for a tattoo, but he was bare, his virgin bronze skin only covered in light blond hair. His eyes were the color of the ocean, his blond hair brushed to the side, his face full of sharp lines that were surprisingly beautiful. His nose was a bit crooked, but that was a hockey player for you, and at least he had all his teeth. Fake, yes, because they were bright as hell and blinding her as he set down the cases, grinning over at Lacey.

"Hey, Lacey, where do you want me to put these?"

Lacey didn't even smile at him, obviously still thinking of their previous conversation. But Kacey has already forgotten it and was consumed with Mr. Tall, Light, and Hot. "Over here, please. Sorry, my head is running a billion miles a second."

"No problem," he said in a low tenor of a voice, lifting the cases and taking them to the cooler Lacey had opened. "Almost ready for that baby, yeah?"

She smiled up at him as he placed them in the cooler. "Almost."

"You look beautiful, as always."

Reaching over, she squeezed his arm with a grin pulling at her lips. "Thanks, Liam." She then looked over at Kacey and her brow rose. A slow, Cheshire cat grin covered her lips and she asked, "Hey, Liam, have you met my sister-in-law Kacey yet? You know, she is the new athletic trainer for the Assassins and also a gold medalist."

God bless her. Free babysitting was in Lacey's future, anytime she needed it.

Liam's eyes then moved over to Kacey, and an appreciative grin came over his face. Oh, yes, nice smile.

"Kace, this is Liam, he plays for the Assassins."

"Wow, hey, Liam Kelly," he said, reaching out to take her hand. They shook slowly, their eyes locked.

"Kacey King."

He grinned sheepishly, almost in a boy next door way, and it hit Kacey square in the gut. "Wow, you are like King's twin. Way prettier, of course."

She got that all the time and wasn't offended. The way he said it too made her belly warm with desire. He had a sexy voice, low, but still not raunchy the way she had come to love. He didn't look like the kind of guy who would flip her upside down and eat her out, but he did look like the kind of guy who wanted a wife and family. And since that's what she wanted, she smiled sweetly at him, batting her eyes as Lacey grinned. He seemed like a clean-cut, stand-up guy, maybe not the type she usually went for—but the type she had been going for had been screwing her over lately. Plus, he played hockey and that was a win in her book. No ring and he wasn't glued to his phone yet—while most guys would have put the cases down and pulled it right out—and he had great eye contact.

Hmm. He could be the one.

Chapter
THREE

"Jordie, how are you feeling?"

Looking up from where he was staring at the crack in the floor, Jordie's brow rose. His stance probably told the poor little mousy therapist, whose name he still didn't know, that he was bored. That he hated this place with all the passion in his soul. That he would rather be face first in a beehive but, yet, she was still grinning at him. He leaned back in his chair, one leg up on the rung of the chair beside him while the other hung to the side. His arms were across his chest in a very aggressive pose and he was working his lip, praying for the time to pass. It was easy to say that rehab blew big donkey dick and Jordie was ready for it to be over.

But in case she didn't know that, he figured he better remind her.

"Feel great. I hate this place and I'm ready to go."

A few people nodded in agreement. It was mostly men, fellow athletes who were too far gone and needing to clean up. Jordie was nothing like these guys and didn't understand why he was in here with pill poppers and true alcoholics.

"We still have about an hour left."

"Yeah, I know, but I mean out of this place."

Her brows came in. She was a cute little thing, nice legs and okay tits. She had sweet little green eyes though and a small little mouth that resulted in a small little meditative voice. "You have forty-five days left, Jordie."

"Don't remind me," he groaned, leaning back and letting his head drop.

"In the forty-five days we've been together, you have shared absolutely

OVERTIME

nothing with me and nothing with the other therapist before me at your group meetings."

"Because there isn't anything to share."

"Sure, there is. You're an alcoholic."

"No, I like to drink," he said, still with his head hanging. "That doesn't constitute an alcoholic."

"It does when you drink to *not* feel something."

He glared. "I mean, what's the point of drinking if it's not to forget? Everyone does it."

"In moderation. Before you entered here, you'd gone to PT drunk five out of the six sessions, according to your physical therapist. And you also went drunk to your group meetings that were planned while we waited for a spot to open up here."

He shrugged. "Hey, those are good odds in my opinion. And plus, they all drove me to drinking because I hate them so much."

She tsked while a few of the guys laughed. "You shouldn't be going drunk at all."

"Sure, and I won't ever again," he said, sitting up then. "Now, can I leave?"

Her eyes narrowed and she crossed her arms. "The answer is still no."

"There isn't anything for me here. This place isn't going to magically fix me. I'm not going to be ready for a sober life once I leave. I'm good. I don't want to talk, I don't even want to drink anymore, so maybe it has worked. I don't fucking know. I just want to play hockey and be out of here."

"There is a lot wrong with you," she countered without missing a beat.

Jordie scoffed, rolling his eyes before setting her with a dark, challenging look. The whole time he had been here, she had hounded him for information, trying to get him to open up about shit he didn't even want to speak about. He was good having all his past secrets deep inside him. And plus, they had nothing to do with the fact that he liked to drink. He drank because it numbed the pain.

The pain of his career hanging in the balance.

The pain of not knowing the future.

Most of all, the pain of letting Kacey go.

Therapist Lady knew none of this. She knew nothing, only what was on paper. And he didn't think it was any of her business about anything else. She wanted to know about his past? Read his file and leave him the fuck alone, was his opinion.

But yet, she continued to come at him. It was time to shut her up. "Oh, yeah? Please enlighten me, Ms. Therapist Lady."

Glaring, she held his gaze for a moment and then looked down at her file, clearing her throat. His chest seized up right as he realized what she was about

22

to do. Before he could stop her though, she was talking.

"Well, let's see, shall we?" she said very slowly. "But first, you're okay if I share?" she asked, her eyes challenging, and he shrugged. He refused to be weak in front of these wack-jobs and her stuffy ass.

"Do you, lady."

She smiled coyly. "Okay, well, your mother has been married ten times in the course of your life. When you were four, you were raped by her third husband, more than once. You were found on the bed bleeding and unresponsive from multiple areas after he beat you almost to death—"

"I don't see how this has to do with anything. I don't even remember it."

"Fuck, man, did the fucker rot for it?" Manny, a tight end for some pro football team, asked and Jordie shrugged, not wanting to shed any light on that drama.

"Oh yes, he's still in jail. But he is up for parole this year," she said, her eyes meeting his. "I understand that you don't remember this, and that's fine, but your drinking started up more than usual this year. Such a coincidence that the year Gary Davis goes up for parole is the year you're forced to go to rehab."

Sucking in a breath at the sound of his abuser's name, Jordie shook his head. "That's not the reason I drink."

"Then what is?"

"I don't know," he answered quickly.

"Fine then, but this is part of your history, and I am reviewing it to remind you why you are here. Now, please allow me to finish. I let you talk when you want to complain and moan about being here, now allow me to finish," she snapped, and Jordie glared as the stares from his fellow group members made the room feel as if it were closing in. So mousy therapist lady had a tough side. Good to know, not that he fucking cared. Sucking in another breath, he crossed his arms tightly over his chest for protection as she went on. "Now, after years of therapy, they deemed you to have extreme trauma from the episode, which was expected—it was a very horrifying experience. You didn't speak to anyone for two years, but somehow, your therapist writes that you recovered when you started playing hockey. He says you were a different child, that hockey healed you. It does say that you did shut down whenever anyone said his name or even brought up what happened. They feared you had suppressed the tragedy and suggested more therapy, but your mother pulled you."

God, this was torture. Of course, he had suppressed the whole thing. It was horrible and he could still, to this day, hear his mother bitching from the bedroom about all the trials and how fucked up he had been. Hockey saved him because Lord knows his mom was too consumed with her own issues to worry about him. He loved his mother...but only because he had to. She didn't make his life easier to say the least, and she may have been the reason for a lot of the discrepancies in that file. Their relationship had always been strained, especially in his older years. He was more a problem to her than her child.

"But then the ADHD and anxiety started when you turned fourteen, which resulted in more therapy and meds. They said the anxiety was brought on by the multiple men that your mother married and divorced during your childhood. But when they suggested you be removed from the home, you fought it because you didn't want to leave your mom."

He'd thought maybe if he stayed, she'd love him, but it never happened. She cared more about the different men that were "Daddy" each year than she did about him. Sad, yeah, but he'd hardly call that a reason to drink. Letting out a long breath, he watched as the therapist met his gaze and she shook her head.

"And then came the death of Robbie Lincoln."

Hearing that name made all the hairs on Jordie's arms stand at attention. His chest seized, his breathing became labored, and he had to look away. He didn't think of Robbie much because he wouldn't allow himself to. He wanted to tell her to stop but she was proving a point, and he refused to let her know that she was slowly but surely killing him from the inside.

"He was your best friend who was stabbed by a boy when he tried to stop three other boys from killing you, according to what the report says. After that, you didn't show up to therapy anymore, and then the drinking started. You were arrested for DUI and public intoxication twice before you were eighteen. Your coach told you to clean up or you would lose your scholarship to Wisconsin."

"And I did. The end," he said when she paused, clapping his hands. "All that says is that I've had a shitty past. It doesn't define me now."

"It does," she said, meeting his heated and embarrassed gaze. "All that is the foundation of the reason why you drink. It started young—when something bad happens, you shut down and check out of this world. This time, it was your injury, I'm sure. But then something is telling me it's more. A woman, maybe? Because the last girl you were with that you considered a girlfriend was the one who almost got you killed. Since then, you've jumped from bed to bed, never allowing anyone in."

He shook his head, slowly taking in breaths through his nose and letting them out of his mouth. "You don't know shit."

"I know a lot. And, Jordie, the thing is, I'm here to help you. How are you going to really learn how to deal with your feelings if you won't share them with me? Are you scared?"

"Fucking shit, I'm not scared of anything," he said, but even he didn't hear conviction in his voice. He knew it was a lie. There was something—no, *someone*, that he was scared of.

Himself.

"The point of my job is to help you, and I think you forget that I'm the signature you need to get out of here."

His brows crashed together as he sat up higher in his seat. "Are you threatening me?"

She chuckled softly. "I don't threaten—I remind. And I suggest that you open up to me before it's too late. Only forty-five days left."

Yeah, forty-five days of fucking hell, he thought as he shook his head, looking down at the ground. He hated hearing his past; it needed to stay where it belonged—in the past. But he also hated how right she was. What happened to his boy Robbie was what started the drinking. It was the way he got rid of the feelings and fear. There wasn't a time when he did allow himself to think about Robbie that he didn't wish it was he who had died. Robbie was a good guy and the only other person, along with Angie, whom he'd trusted. But then Angie betrayed him and Robbie was dead, so all he had was the bottle since his mom was too busy looking for another man to love her. She was constantly fighting for love and looking for it that it scared Jordie to even try for it. It never seemed to be attainable. So why try for something that would never be his?

Running his fingers through his hair, he couldn't believe he hadn't seen this before. Hearing his past wasn't easy, knowing the sure signs of his issues didn't settle in his stomach right. Maybe he wasn't a full-blown alcoholic, but he was tiptoeing along the line and he wasn't sure what side he'd end up on. He did know that he didn't want to end up facedown in a ditch, suffocating on his own vomit, before losing his life to the sickness. He also didn't want to be like his mother, so unhappy by herself that she needed a man.

Was he doing that with the bottle? Because he couldn't trust women, he only used them for sex, but a part of him was getting so tired of that. He had really wanted to try with Kacey; a part of him had felt like love was actually realistic when he was with her. But the other part of him knew he wasn't ready for that. He wanted to trust her fully, or trust anyone for that matter. He wanted to allow himself to truly love someone. He wanted more from his life, but he didn't know how to get it.

Something had to change.

He had to change.

But did he want to?

And could he?

Jordie didn't say anything else during the group meeting.

As he sat there, reevaluating his life, he couldn't be more disgusted. He hadn't lived the life he wanted, minus the hockey, and he really didn't have any good memories.

Except Kacey.

Kacey was every good memory he had in his whole damn life, but then he did the dumb-ass thing of letting her go. Letting go of the light in his life. Another bad choice. As he walked back to the closet they said was his room, each bad choice he'd made stared back at him and he hated it. It was like he was living a lie. Everything he did wasn't what he wanted, and most of the time all he thought about was drinking. How pathetic. He couldn't name one good thing in his life at that moment. No, wait, his game was good when he actually got to play it. But off the ice, what did he have?

Nothing except his Jack.

Fuck. Maybe he was an alcoholic.

Man, that therapist had really gotten to him because all he could do was think of his life thus far. He hated the pain he'd caused people, the people he'd lied to, and most of all, the love he'd thrown back in so many people's faces. He honestly didn't understand why Karson was still his friend. He was the only one who stood strong beside him, no matter what. For the first year of their friendship, all Jordie did was drink and Karson was the one picking him up to take him home. Covering up why he didn't go to practice. It took a month of that before Karson shook him hard and told him to clean it up before he didn't make the draft, something they both wanted. So he did, but that only lasted until he was in the NHL. Then most the time he slept because he was so tired, only binge drinking on the weekend.

Then there were three years that Jordie ignored Karson's calls. All because he called Karson on a drunken night and spilled the beans about everything. The rape, Robbie's murder, and all the other craptastic things that he had done. The nights when he would make himself puke just to get the alcohol out of him so that he could get on the ice the next morning. Or how he would sell his roommate's things to get money for booze.

Shit, he was an alcoholic.

Slamming his door, he wobbled over to his bed and slowly lifted his leg onto the mattress. It was rehabbing great but, for some reason, being here, the pain was overwhelming. Since he was trying to prove that he wasn't an addict, he was forgoing his pain meds, though he still craved a drink. Just a small one, something to take the edge off. Closing his eyes tightly, he shook his head.

What the fuck was wrong with him?

Before he could analyze anymore, his phone rang. Not looking at where he was grasping on his nightstand, he finally took his phone in his hand and brought it out so he could see who was calling.

It was Karson.

Hitting Talk, he brought it to his ear. "What's up, bro?"

"Hey, how ya doing?" he asked in his carefree way. Karson had the life. Beautiful wife, great home, and a baby on the way. The American dream. Something that, at this point, Jordie was convinced he couldn't have.

"This day has quickly gone to shit," he admitted as he closed his eyes. Karson, Lacey, Elli, and her husband Shea were the only ones who knew he was in rehab. Like everyone promised, it was very quiet. No one knew he was here, and he wanted to keep it that way. This place was for failures, people who couldn't get their shit together, and he didn't want to seem that weak.

Jordie Thomas was not fucking weak.

"The damn therapist is on me like you wouldn't believe. Wanting me to open up and shit."

"Couldn't hurt you," Karson suggested. "Maybe it could help?"

"Eh, I don't know," Jordie grumbled as he rolled to his side. "I just want out."

"I know, man. We want you home, but you gotta get better."

"I'm fine."

He didn't answer right away, and Jordie knew it was because he didn't agree. "Are you trying?"

"Not at all," Jordie admitted and Karson let out a long breath.

"Man, I need you to."

"I know, so does everyone else. But I'm fine, really."

"No, *really*," Karson stressed, and Jordie's brow came up.

"No really, what? I'm telling you the truth, man."

He paused and Jordie waited on edge as his friend got his words together. "I want my best friend back." Something about that sentence just gutted Jordie. Closing his eyes, he covered them with his hand, feeling every bit guilty. "You've changed, Jordie. You've always been a bit of an asshole, and always been busy with the ladies, but lately it's been so bad. You aren't you, and I don't get it. I get the injury hurt you, man—it did all of us. But you're supposed to bounce back, not drink yourself stupid."

Swallowing around the lump in his throat, he nodded because Karson was completely right and it scared the shit out of Jordie. "I know."

"Please fix you. I'll do anything I can to help."

"I know, Kar," Jordie whispered. "But I gotta be the one to fix this. I gotta want it."

He may not have acted like he was listening to Therapy Lady, but he did. He knew what he needed to do; no one could help him but him. This place wouldn't do anything for him if he didn't want it.

"You do," Karson added, and then he cleared his throat. "Because we don't want anyone else to be the godfather of our baby girl but you."

"What?" Jordie whispered, trying to catch his breath because surely he had heard him wrong.

"We want you to be the baby's godfather, but I can't ask you to take on the role unless you are healthy, Jordie. Not just for our baby, but for you. I want you to be happy."

"Are you sure you want that? Me?" he gasped, still unable to catch his breath.

"Yeah, Uncle Jordie, you're it for our little baby girl."

Fear settled in his chest where pride should have been. This was a great honor, something he knew he wanted, but would he be enough for the precious baby that his best friend's wife was carrying? He knew he wouldn't be if he stayed in the mind-set he was in right now. If the drinking was more important than anything else. Hell, he wouldn't trust himself with a baby. He wouldn't even let himself near one. He was too fucked up.

He had to change.

"I got you, Kar," he croaked out and Karson chuckled.

"I know, bro, that's why this wasn't hard choice. It's you and that's it. You'll fix this, I know you will. You're too damn stubborn to allow it to defeat you."

Such blind faith Karson had in him. Jordie wished he could borrow some of it. Tears stung his eyes as he closed them tightly. He never cried. Never, and at this moment, he wanted to cry. "I haven't been the greatest best friend to you."

"No, you haven't, not all the time. But when you are, you're the best."

Not all the time...

Jordie cleared his throat, sitting up slowly. "I'm sorry for all the wrong I've done you, man."

"Forgiven," Karson said without even thinking. "Just get healthy and that'll be your apology to me, okay?"

"I will, I promise."

"Good, I'm holding you to it. So is Little-Bit-who-still-has-not-been-named."

As a tear rolled down his cheek into his beard, he smiled. "Jordie is a good middle name."

Karson laughed before yelling out, "Jordie said his name is a good middle name for Baby Unnamed."

"The hell," he heard Lacey say. "No way, but it will be a J name for sure. And an M name for Kacey."

"Kacey?" he croaked out.

"Yeah, she's going to be the godmother."

His heart sped up in his chest. "So if you two keel over, we play Mom and Dad to Little Bit?"

Karson laughed. "In retrospect, yes."

"So I get to bang your sister?" he teased and Karson groaned.

"Such a great conversation until that moment. I'll call you tomorrow, asshole," Karson laughed.

"Bye, bro," Jordie sang with his first true grin in months, before handing up and letting his phone drop between his legs. Looking up at the ceiling, he sucked in a deep breath as the nerves ate away at him.

This was not going to be easy, but he could do it. He was stronger than this; he was a beast of a man, nothing could get him down. How could he allow his need for a drink to ruin his life? The signs were everywhere, blinking in his face and blinding him. He had to stop. This place opened his eyes, and he just couldn't do it anymore. He had a baby girl to be a godfather to, and he wouldn't let Lacey and Karson down.

Definitely not the baby they were about to have.

It was time to be the man he wanted to be.

It was time to live the life he wanted.

And maybe, just maybe, he could get the love he wanted too.

Because her being the godmother to his godfather wasn't enough.

He wanted Kacey to be his.

Chapter FOUR

Liam Kelly really had dreamy eyes and a wonderful bod.

But holy crap, he was boring.

Leaning on her hand, Kacey tried to pay attention as he talked about his cat, but really? This was her life right now? Greek god of a man was a cat guy? What the ever-loving fuck was going on here, and why didn't she see this at the barbecue? He was funny there, full of wit, and good Lord, dreamy. So of course, she jumped at the chance of a date when he asked if she wanted to get together. What she didn't expect was for him to text her the next morning and to set something up the following night. She was cool though, she was ready. But now that she was here, she wished she would have done another group setting with him.

She just didn't get it. Why couldn't she find a dude that was her match? He'd seemed so cool at the barbecue, but now, now he was awkward. Was it really that hard to find someone who wanted a dog, a white picket fence, and some kids, while keeping her completely and utterly satisfied in bed and also making her laugh? That was a requirement. Of course, thinking of laughing made her think of Jordie, and then she was instantly depressed. Jordie was a hoot. He could have her crying from laughter in two seconds flat, and for the stupidest reasons too. His crude humor got her every time, and sometimes she knew that a sweet, classy girl shouldn't find that kind of thing funny, but she sure did.

But Liam was not being funny.

Blinking to keep from falling asleep, she focused on his mouth, which was downright sinful, as he went on.

"Her name is Buttons because, when I first got her, she ate all the buttons off my shirts," he said with a laugh and she smiled.

"How adorable."

He smiled. "Stupid, I know. I'm kind of a boring guy. It's hockey and my cat, that's it."

Which wasn't a bad thing, Kacey! Straighten up! He was boring, which was good—bad guys had drama that broke girl's hearts! Liam Kelly was not a heartbreaker.

"No, it's sweet. I'm more of a dog gal though."

"Oh yeah, I love dogs. But when I'm gone, it's hard on a dog. Cats are easy, they don't need as much attention," he agreed with a nod before taking a pull of his beer. "When I find someone who wants to marry me, then I'll get a dog."

Kacey sat up a bit straighter. "Why aren't you married yet, Liam? You're how old, thirty-three?"

He nodded which was good because, for a second there, she thought she was being a bit rude. "I got married young, twenty, but when I got drafted, she started cheating on me. I tried to make it work, but she didn't want to be with me," he said softly with a shrug. "Really sucked, but that was eons ago. Now, it's hard to find a woman around my age who doesn't have kids already. I don't want to deal with baby daddy issues."

"True that," she said, tipping her drink to him.

"But also a woman who wants a long-term relationship with a hockey player. It's tough being married to someone who's gone most of the year."

"I'm used to it," she commented and he smiled. Man, he really was pretty. If only he would stimulate her more than her just wanting to bang him. Because, even though he was saying everything she wanted, she was bored. He was too clean-cut. That was the problem. She wanted to reach over and mess his hair up. Paint some tattoos on him and grow him a beard. Maybe have him cuss a bit more. He was just too nice.

"Yeah, I bet, growing up with hockey all your life."

"Yeah, it's in my blood."

"Which is so awesome. I watched you in the Olympics, but I didn't know how gorgeous you were," he said and then he blushed.

Fucking blushed.

She wanted to sigh, but instead, she asked, "Are you nervous?"

His brow came up and he asked, "A little, why?"

She smiled sweetly, hoping that she didn't come off as too much of a bitch, but she was sure she was about to. "Because you're being kinda boring, not like you were at the party."

He laughed. "Yeah, I guess I'm more nervous than I thought."

"Sorry if that's rude," she said quickly at his defeated look.

"No, not at all," he said, waving her off. "It's just...well... Karson is my friend, and I asked him if it was okay—"

"You asked my brother if you could take me out?" she deadpanned.

She should think that was sweet. She should.

"Yeah, I mean, he's your brother, my friend, and teammate. I don't want bad blood between me and him if I started dating you without his permission."

His permission? What the fuck?

"It doesn't matter what he thinks though. He doesn't control me, or own me, for that matter," she added and he nodded.

"Oh, I know, but I just wanted to make sure he wasn't gonna freak out on me."

Yup, too clean-cut for her. She wanted a man who wanted her and didn't care about anything else.

"You're mad," he observed and she looked up to meet his apologetic gaze.

"No," she lied, tucking her hands in her lap to keep from clenching them. "I've always been Karson's little sister, the girl no one wants to date because they are scared of him. It gets to be annoying."

"Oh, I want to date you. I wasn't lying when I said you are gorgeous, Kacey. But I did that for damage control. If he would have said no, then I probably still would have taken you out."

That perked her interest. "Karson said yes?"

"Yeah, he was really for it, actually. Calmed my nerves a bit. But when I picked you up and, man, you're really lovely, I guess my nerves got the best of me."

Karson said yes? To a guy?

"You're still mad."

She was staring at him. Her brows were pulled together while she chewed on her lip.

Karson said yes?

"Sorry, I'm still caught up on the fact my brother said yes. He never agrees to anyone dating me."

A dazzling grin curved Liam's lips, and Kacey found herself breathless as he said, "He knows I'm a good guy and I won't hurt you."

She wanted to drop her face flat on the table and moan. She knew that too, so why was she fighting this? He wanted a dog, he was looking for a woman to marry him, and he was nice. Plus, he was nervous, so that was the reason he wasn't as funny as she liked. Liam Kelly was a good guy. Karson thought so and she needed to trust that.

She needed to try.

Leaning on her hand, she smiled. "Good, 'cause I'm in the market for a good guy who won't hurt me."

Grinning ever so sinfully, he said, "Then I'm thinking I'm that guy."

Matching his grin, she smiled up at him, and before she could say something along the lines of she hoped so, her phone rang. "Oh shit, sorry. I should have turned it off," she said as she dug it out of her purse. She went to turn the ringer off but saw that it was Karson. She declined the call, but as she went to put it back in her purse, he called back. She eyed her phone and then looked across the table at Liam. "I'm sorry, let me make sure everything is okay."

"Of course," he said sweetly and she smiled as she answered the phone.

"Karson, I'm on a—"

"Lacey went into labor and we are at the hospital. Get your ass up here now," he barked and then he hung up.

Stunned, she looked up at Liam and his eyes narrowed. "Everything okay?"

"No, Lacey went into labor. She's early. I gotta go," she said, throwing her phone in her purse and standing up. Then she realized that Liam had driven her. "Fuck, can you drive me to Vandy? If not, I'll get a cab," she said frantically.

"No, I got you. Let's go," he said, throwing a twenty on the table. As they started for the door, his hand fell to the middle of her back and he said, "Don't worry, I'm sure everything will be fine."

Nodding, she prayed he was right.

Looking down at the little bundle of pink, Kacey could hardly see her brand-spanking-new niece with her tear-filled eyes. As the baby looked up at her through her goo-filled brown eyes that had a slight blue tint around the middle, Kacey decided that Mena Jane King was by far the most gorgeous baby she had ever seen. Moving her finger down Mena Jane's sweet curve of a cheek, a tear slowly rolled down her own cheek.

"Hello, my sweet Mena Jane. I'm your auntie, and I'm gonna be your best friend," she said softly as she looked down at her, her eyes full of all the goodness in the world. The baby looked just like Karson, spitting image, with basically nothing of Lacey. But it was still early. Kacey was sure she would favor her momma in no time. Or the King genes were so strong that this was the product and, man, what a product. She was perfect, and Kacey wanted a little baby of her own so damn badly.

Glancing up at where Karson was moving Lacey's hair behind her ears, looking at her like she'd just given him the world, which she had, his eyes were so full of love it hit Kacey square in the chest. She wanted that. She wanted all this. The birth was magical and her sister-in-law was a beast, that's all she could say. Karson, ever the doting husband, was amazing during the birth, and Kacey prayed she gave some support too. Just from the grin on Lacey's face as she met her gaze told her she did, or that the drugs were working very well. She was going to take her first assumption and run, though.

"She's perfect, guys."

"She is," Lacey agreed as Karson still stared at her.

"You're perfect. You did so great, baby," he whispered against her cheek and Kacey smiled, looking back down at her sweet niece.

"I'm gonna make sure you are always protected," Kacey whispered. "You have so many people who love you."

Mena Jane just kept staring at her and it warmed her soul. This little girl had Kacey completely wrapped around her finger and nothing would ever hurt her. Not while her aunt was around.

"Sorry to pull you from your date," Lacey said then and Kacey waved her off, cuddling Mena Jane closer to her.

"This was way more important," she assured her, and then she glanced over at Karson. She knew this probably wasn't the place for this, but she had to hear it from him. "You told Liam yes to dating me?"

Lacey smiled as Karson shrugged. "He's a good dude. He would be good for you."

Hearing it from his mouth seemed almost as if he were speaking Klingon. "Really?"

He nodded. "He's a supernice guy, Kace. Really."

"He is," Lacey agreed just as a knock came at the door. All three looked at the door as it opened and Liam poked his head in.

Speak of the devil and he shall appear. But Liam wasn't the devil, he was more an angel because in his hand was the biggest bouquet of yellow and pink roses she had ever seen.

"Company, okay?" he asked and Lacey nodded.

"Yes, come on in. You haven't been waiting all this time have you?"

He smiled sheepishly as he nodded. "I wasn't sure if Kacey would need to go home, and I was her ride," he said as he carried the flowers to her little tray table and Kacey's heart kicked up in speed a bit.

"You didn't have to do that," she called to him and he grinned.

"It's no big deal. My phone lasted the whole six hours."

She smiled as he shot her a playful grin before looking back over at Lacey. "These are for the momma," he said before leaning over to kiss her cheek. "Congrats."

"Aw, thank you, Liam."

He grinned as he reached over, handing Karson a flask. "For Daddy."

Karson laughed before taking a long pull. "Thanks, bro."

Then he made his way to Kacey, pulling a single rose out from behind his back and handing it to her. "For the other birthing coach," he said with a wink as she took it. Her heart was beating out of her chest as she grinned up at him, laying the rose beside her.

"Thank you."

"Of course," he said, looking closer at Mena Jane. "She's beautiful, guys," he called back at Lacey and Karson, but they were staring into each other's eyes, not paying the least bit of attention. He then looked down at Kacey and smiled that sweet grin of his. "You look good with a baby in your arms."

She smiled down at Mena Jane and then back up at him. Their eyes met and she prayed for the sparks, but they weren't there. He was sweet and nice, he'd had no reason to wait for her or even get her a rose, but he did. He also was very interested in her. Not sex. Her. But did he want kids?

Holding his gaze, she said, "I can't wait for my turn."

He didn't even hesitate; he nodded and said, "Yeah, I can't wait to have some of my own too."

Right there was what she needed to hear. He wanted what she wanted and he really was nice. Totally different from the douchebags she was used to. Yeah, there weren't sparks or fireworks, but he wanted what she did and he liked her. You didn't find men like Liam Kelly every day. She needed to take him and run. He was everything she needed.

What else could she ask for?

"So Jordie, how are you feeling?

Jordie looked up from where he was staring down at his hands, trying to forget everything that he had just heard. Jon, a defenseman from the Lightning, was battling some crazy cocaine addiction that sometimes Jordie wasn't sure he would overcome. He had just been caught with his girl bringing some in, and they were six seconds away from kicking him out. Portia, the therapist, fought for him to stay though. She fought for everyone. She was a good girl. But every time Jon starting talking about his past, the things he'd done which really should have led to him being committed or arrested, it always made Jordie uncomfortable. He hated how much the guy suffered and, most of all, hated all the bad in the world. It was just shitty.

Nodding his head at Portia, Jordie smiled. "I'm good. No need for a drink at all."

"Good," she said with a grin. "Is the guitar playing helping with the late-night cravings?"

"Yeah," he said with a nod. "A lot. Keeps my mind off everything."

In the last week, they'd discovered that when he was alone with nothing to do was when he craved a drink the most. She suggested playing an instrument, and since he had some experience with the guitar, he chose that. He was happy he did too; he loved playing and it really did help him at night.

"I saw you in church this weekend. That was nice."

He smiled sheepishly as most of the guys looked over at him. The whole time he had been there, he had fought tooth and nail about going to church. When he was a kid, religion was forced on him constantly by his mother, and he never really wanted anything to do with that. But Portia's thing was to pray on it. It was easy to say that Jordie had been praying a lot and figured that going to church was the next step. He didn't hate it, didn't love it, but he went.

"I mean, don't get ahead of yourself, Portia. I won't be turning into some damn holy roller. I like sex and cussing way too much."

She smiled as she shook her head. "Wouldn't expect you to stop those things, of course."

"Never," he said with a wink.

"So you feel you need sex then?"

Ah, sneaky little shit. Rolling his eyes, he leaned back in the chair, crossing his arms over his chest. "I don't need sex, I love it, and I'm damn good at it."

A couple of the guys laughed while the others, who were holy rollers, rolled their eyes. Portia, still with a small grin on her face, asked, "When was the last time you had sexual intercourse?"

He grinned. He knew what he expected him to say and he wouldn't lie, but he was excited to see her little face filled with shock once she heard his answer. The thing about Portia was she was a save-the-world kind of girl. She wanted to diagnose everyone and fix 'em. She'd had the inkling that Jordie was addicted to sex since he'd first gotten there. There was a huge difference between being addicted and just liking it. He was addicted to alcohol in some sense, in that he went for it to stop feeling what he was feeling. He had sex because he wanted to. Minus his trip to Louisiana, he had never had sex to get rid of what he was feeling. He'd tried to fuck his feelings for Kacey out of himself, which was very stupid, but the whole time he was drunk. He was pretty sure he wouldn't have made a lot of those decisions if he hadn't been drunk through it all.

"February was the last time."

"February?!" she almost shrieked.

"Yup," he said proudly, which really that wasn't something to be proud of, but small victories, he guessed. "When I was in Louisiana."

"Really? That surprises me, honestly," she admitted and he grinned. "Why is that?"

"Sex means nothing to me anymore if it can't be with the person I want it to be with," he said slowly, avoiding eye contact. He felt the gazes of everyone on him, but he ignored them, sucking in a deep breath as flashes of Kacey's gorgeous naked body appeared. As much as he wouldn't mind plowing into a female at the moment, he wanted more. He wanted Kacey, and he was cleaning up to be the man she needed. Not just for him, but also for her and for Karson's child. There was a huge possibility that she had moved on—he fully expected her to—but he needed something to get him through this fight. Knowing that he soon would be a man worthy of her love did that for him. It made him fight as hard as he could against his sickness.

"Not the answer I expected," she said, and he looked up at her. "So your visitor, Natasha Gallagher?"

Where was she going with this? "Yeah?"

"Are you two in a relationship?"

Natasha, the doctor he'd slept with in Louisiana, had been visiting him since he was admitted. She was doing a work-study up in Colorado and she wanted to support him. He hadn't expected her to, or even asked her; she just started coming every Saturday. If he was honest, it was nice to talk to someone who wasn't trying to pry his head open and find out all the bad inside. Despite her offering her body to him every single time, their visits were the highlight of his week.

"No, she's just a friend."

"You don't have friends."

He grinned. "I have a few, but really, just a friend."

"But you've slept with her?"

"Yup, she's got killer tits," he said before laughing along with his group while Portia just stared at him.

"But not in the last six months?"

"No, it was a one-time deal."

"But you stayed friends?"

He shrugged. "Yeah, I guess."

She eyed him slowly and then shook her head. "You are a very confusing man, Mr. Thomas. One minute I think I have you pegged, but then you hit me with that. How is it that you don't do relationships, but you are friends with a girl you've slept with? You aren't having sex until it can be with someone you want it to be with, which is very uncharacteristic of your personality. You give off a very careless, playboy image that I have slowly but surely discovered is just an act that is covering the real you."

Jordie grinned, sliding to the edge of his seat. "And that is, Ms. Portia?"

Portia smiled. "A very decent guy with a past that has you hiding yourself."

She let that sink in as everyone watched for his next response, but there wasn't one. He didn't know what to say, and soon she was talking again.

OVERTIME

"You want so badly to keep everyone at arm's length so that they can't hurt you, because you see no happiness in your life. You choose only the people you know won't leave you. But, even with them, you don't let them completely in on purpose. Yet, you want happiness. Just in this last week, you've opened up about wanting children and a part of you wants a wife. But I had seriously pegged you to be alone the rest of your life because you won't allow anyone in. And then you say that—that you aren't having sex because it means nothing if it can't be with the person you want it to be with. So, Jordie, who is that person? I have a feeling you know her, but you're scared to let her in. To trust her."

His skin was clammy and his heart was pounding, but he never broke their intensely locked gazes. She was challenging him, something he noticed she did when she wanted a straight answer from him. In the short time he'd been there, she had figured him out. Normally that would make him want to run, but in some odd, twisted way, Jordie trusted Portia.

Something he didn't do much.

But before he could answer her, the timer went off behind her, signaling that group was over and visiting hours had started. It was Saturday and he knew that Natasha was waiting for him, so he got up quickly and hightailed it out of there before Portia could stop him to probe him some more about Kacey. He heard her call his name and figured he was dooming himself for tomorrow, but he didn't care. He had to adjust to the idea of talking about Kacey, and tomorrow, maybe.

Probably not.

When he reached the meeting room for visitors, he saw Natasha sitting on the patio, her long brown hair flowing in the evening breeze. The sun was setting behind the mountains, the sky a pretty pink as he closed the distance between them. When he had almost reached her, she looked up, grinning her dazzling grin as she stood too, hugging him tightly. She was wearing short shorts and a tank that showed off her chest in the most revealing way. Her tits and mouth were what had attracted him back in Louisiana, but now as he hugged her, he felt nothing but friendship for her.

Because Kacey consumed him. Everything inside him was hers. He just wished he had realized how in love with her he was before he pushed her away.

"How ya feeling?"

He smiled. "Alive. Sober."

"Good," she said, tapping his arm before they both sat down. Soon refreshments were served, along with a light dinner. Nothing that raised the skirt, but it was good and the conversation was easy. They spoke about her work-study and how she was heading back to Louisiana in four weeks.

"So right around the time I get out, then?"

She nodded. "Guess so. Works out."

"Yeah."

"Will you go straight back to Nashville?"

"Gotta get cleared by my PT. He feels like it'll be another week or two to see how I do out of here before they send me back. I'm ready to get on the ice. It's killing me here."

"I bet," she agreed. "I'm proud of you, though."

"Thanks." He shot her a grin before taking a long sip of his iced tea. Usually, he wished there was Jack in it but not for the last week. This last week he'd tried. He wanted to get better. He had to get better.

"Maybe I could come to Nashville?"

He looked over at her, his brow raised. "For? You have a job there?"

She smiled sheepishly, her brown eyes sparkling in the falling sunlight as she held his gaze. She really was a pretty girl and deserved someone who could handle all of her. But she wasn't into relationships, just as he hadn't been. Though, after this stint in rehab, Jordie was ready to sing a different tune. Life was so short, and the things he'd heard while being here had made him realize he needed to be healthy and sober to live the life he wanted. He had been so close to losing everything, and he couldn't allow that to happen.

"For us."

Say what?

"Us?" he asked, confused.

"Yeah, I could get a job at Vandy. I have some friends there who could get me in without any problem. They've actually been asking me to move there. Nothing worth moving for until now. But yeah, maybe we can give it a go, an actual relationship instead of just hanging out at rehab. Ha, what a story to tell the kids one day."

He eyed her and then shook his head. Surely he was hearing her wrong. "Wait, huh? You don't do relationships."

She laughed nervously, looking down at her perfectly manicured nails. Everything about her was so put together. The only time she didn't look like a billion bucks was when she was under him. What a sight, but not the sight he wanted for the rest of his life.

"I usually don't, and especially not with a hockey player, but I want to now." She looked up at him. "With you," she said slowly. Her eyes were wary as they held his and he was a little taken aback.

Yeah, they had become close, but nowhere in there had he ever expected her to say that. Sex, yes—he was irresistible to say the least. But a relationship? No way, but wait, shit... Was this his fault?

Leaning forward, he held her hopeful gaze as he said, "Please say I didn't lead you on, because I never meant to."

"No, you haven't, but I thought maybe you wanted the same thing."

He shook his head. "Natasha, I'm sorry, but I don't want to start something with you when my heart wouldn't be in it."

"It could be," she suggested, not looking the least bit derailed. But he shook his head.

"It won't."

"Because of her?" she asked, her eyes never leaving his, and he nodded.

"Yeah, she's important to me. She matters."

"I'm sure we can fix that. She was obviously not enough to keep. You did leave her and fucked me."

"She was more than enough. More than I deserved," he countered, their eyes burning into each other's.

Looking away finally, she let out a breath. "You could at least give me a chance."

"It wouldn't be fair to you," he said, reaching out to take her hand with his. "You deserve someone who will want you from the beginning. That's not me. I wanted you for sex, and I'm sorry if that made us a bit messy. I understand if you don't want to come hang out with me anymore."

Removing her hand from his, she folded her hands in her lap and shook her head. "It was a stupid idea anyway," she said, still not looking at him, but he could see the tears welling up in her eyes. "We are good in bed, not out of it."

When he didn't answer, because he wasn't sure how, she glanced over at him. "Thanks for being honest though."

"I wouldn't lie to you," he promised just as his phone went off. It was a text from Karson.

Karson: Meet your goddaughter, Mena Jane King.

And then there was a picture of the sweetest little bundle of pink Jordie had ever seen. Gasping, he covered his mouth as he took in his new goddaughter, his heart pounding in his chest.

Love. Love at first sight.

"What?" Natasha asked, a little annoyed.

"My goddaughter was just born," he said as he typed back a quick congratulations. Karson wrote back that he'd call in a bit, and Jordie was excited to hear from him. He was sure to get an earful; Karson's biggest fear about having the baby was the birth. Jordie was glad it seemed to have gone well. Figured if something were wrong, Karson would have said something. Opening a text to Lacey, he typed.

Jordie: Congratulations, Mama. She's just as gorgeous as her mama. Can't wait to see you guys. 38 more days hopefully!

She wrote back almost immediately, the little text bubble taunting him with her unspoken words.

> *Lacey: Thanks, we wish you were here! She is perfect! She has all of us wrapped around her sweet little finger.*
> *Jordie: Mena Jane? Love it, but what happened to naming her after me? Lol.*
> *Lacey: Mena for Kacey Marie, since there are already too many K's in my opinion. And then Jane for you, Jordie.* ☺

Jordie grinned as his eyes started to itch. Stupid allergies.

> *Jordie: Awesome. I can't wait to get home.*
> *Lacey: We can't wait to have you home. Check out this picture. It's my favorite so far.*

He waited as the picture came in, and when it did, it was as if he took a puck shot by Shea Adler himself square in the chest. Kacey sat in all her beautiful glory with Mena Jane in her arms. She had grown her hair out, lost a little weight in her face, but her eyes… God, they were filled with all the love in the world. He knew those eyes well; they used to stare back at him just like that. Seeing her holding Mena Jane did something to his chest, and soon, he was fighting back the tears.

How could he have been so stupid? This girl was it for him, his winning goal, his heart, and he let her go. Choking back the tears, he typed back.

> *Jordie: It's my new favorite picture.*
> *Lacey: So you miss her?*
> *Jordie: There isn't enough character space to tell you how much.*
> *Lacey: Come home, Jordie. Healthy.*
> *Jordie: That's the plan.*

And then Kacey Marie King would be his.

Chapter FIVE

"**H**e just told me he loves me."

Kacey leaned against the bathroom counter, her brows pulled together as she held her phone to her ear while looking at her reflection as Lacey sputtered on the other line.

"Say what?" Lacey exclaimed.

"Exactly!" Kacey agreed, still unable to fathom how Liam could love her. "Tell me I'm not the only one who thinks that is batshit insane! We've only been technically dating for a month, I think? We haven't even slept together! You can't love someone when you haven't seen them naked. What if I had an elephant vagina or something?"

Lacey paused. "Um, what? I'm sorry, but what is an elephant vagina?"

"You know, like big lips that kind of look and hang like elephant ears."

"Wow. That's a new one."

"Focus!" Kacey exclaimed.

"Anyway, you know that everyone is different and falls at different times," Lacey suggested like the practical person she was, but Kacey was internally freaking the hell out. She thought when she finally heard someone say those words to her, it would be the person she really wanted. She'd never expected Liam to fall for her. She liked the idea of it, but when he said those three words, it didn't feel right. It felt fake. Unreal and, ugh, it was killing her. She should be shitting rainbows and sunshine! Riding on a unicorn of love, but instead, she felt like she wanted to punch something. Or cry, and she really hated crying.

"No, normal people don't fall that quickly for someone they hardly know!"

"I don't know what to say here, Kacey. Where are you?"

"In the bathroom."

"Where is he?"

"At the table!"

"What? You ran!" she shrieked.

"No! He said it. I said, oh, okay, and then that I had to pee and… Yeah, I did run."

"Oh my goodness, Kacey. He probably feels like shit now," she complained, and Kacey did feel a bit bad about that, but it freaked her out. Flight was her only option at that point.

"What do I do, Lacey?" she whined as her head fell back. "I don't want to go out there and say it, because I don't feel it. I don't want to lead him on."

"Do you even want to date him? You don't seem very invested here."

"I do, he's great, but I don't want to rush it. I want it to feel real."

But it didn't. Not even in the least. Something was off.

"Maybe I need to sleep with him?" she thought out loud before Lacey could say anything.

"How would that help?"

"I don't know. I just don't feel that soul-deep connection with him, and maybe if he is deep inside me, I'll feel something," she added and Lacey snorted.

"You're insane," she laughed. "Like you said, you don't want to rush this. So don't make him a notch on your bedpost to find that soul-deep connection. If he isn't the one, he isn't."

"But don't you think I should give him time? I mean, feelings develop over time."

"You're right, they do. But I don't know, I don't feel you're 100 percent committed to this."

She wasn't. Maybe fifty percent, but that was pushing it.

"He's a good guy though," she said, letting out a long breath. "I'm so tired of all the shit guys. The ones who continually hurt me or are emotionally unavailable. I have this good guy, who apparently loves me, and I feel like, if I throw that away, I'll regret it. And plus, I don't want to hurt his feelings. He's a sweet guy."

And he was. She truly enjoyed spending time with him. They worked out together every day, went to the movies, hung out with Karson and Lacey. It was nice, but she knew something was missing. The thing was, she didn't know how to find it. And every time she thought of "it," Jordie came crashing into her mind, slamming into her like the defenseman he was. With him, "it" was there. Everything was there. They fit and it was what she wanted. She felt like she fell in love over and over, every single moment she was with him.

But he was emotionally unavailable and had thrown her away.

Story of her fucking life.

Liam was everything that Jordie wasn't, but Jordie still held her heart. Was it wrong of her to continue this relationship when she wasn't all there? Was she the one who was emotionally unavailable now? And really, how stupid of her! It had been eight months; he wanted nothing to do with her, and now this great guy did. She needed to try. She just had to. Or she really did feel she'd end up alone—the crazy aunt who watched *Notting Hill* over and over again, hoping for her own William to come and sweep her off her feet. Since the chap was nowhere in sight, she'd better open her eyes and see what was in front of her.

Liam.

"I think you should be honest," Lacey said, stealing her attention back. "Tell him the truth, that you've been screwed over left and right before, and that you don't love him, but maybe one day you would."

"Good idea," she decided, pushing off the counter.

"But then you only give him one more month. If, in that month, you don't feel that soul-deep connection, then please let him go. Don't grasp for something that isn't there because it's easy. You have to remember, if it isn't worth fighting for, then it isn't worth your time."

"You're right. Okay, I'll be home sometime, I guess."

As she reached for the door, Lacey said, "Okay, but please don't sleep with him tonight just to see if something is there."

Kacey laughed. "I'm gonna take it slow, let it happen when it does. But really, why hasn't he tried anything?"

"Because he is a nice guy and he respects you."

She thought that through. It felt very foreign to her, but hey, there was always a first time for everything. "Oh. Okay, call you later."

Lacey laughed. "Bye, Kace."

Hanging her phone up, she left the bathroom and made her way through the crowded pub toward the corner table where Liam sat. He was sitting there, cool as a cucumber, not even playing on his phone. That was one thing that drove her insane about Jordie. He was constantly on his phone, and she was always sure it was so that he could hook up with girl after girl. She wanted to say he hadn't slept with anyone else but her when he was with her, but she didn't believe that for a second. Jordie was a wanderer and she didn't need that.

When Liam spotted her, he smiled and stood up, pulling her chair out for her.

Smiling up at her, he said, "I thought you fell in. I was about to send in a rescue party."

She smiled. "I had to call Lacey."

"Everything okay?" he asked, his grin falling.

"Yeah, just you kinda freaked me out," she said and his brow rose. "The whole 'I love you' thing."

He nodded and then looked away, the tops of his ears turning red. "I meant every word, Kacey. I do love you. It's fast, I know, but I'm not gonna hide my feelings from you. I want to be honest."

She nodded as she held his gaze. "That's what I want, but it caught me off guard is all. It's only been a month, and I really do think you're great—"

"But you don't feel the same," he supplied for her, leaning back in his chair, one arm resting on the back of her chair.

"Yeah, I don't. But I'm not saying that I won't, one day," she added and he nodded. "It's just I've been continually hurt by guys in the past. I guess I always choose the shitty ones. And I always fall first because I want to be in a relationship with someone who's gonna love me and cherish me, but none of those guys ever did. The shitty thing is, most of the time I knew they were just in it for the sex, but I still hoped and dove in with them."

"Because you thought you could change 'em," he supplied and she nodded.

"Yeah, I really did. I thought I was enough to do that."

"You are," he said, taking her hand in his.

She smiled, moving her thumb with his. Staring down at his hand, she admitted, "The last guy I was with still weighs heavy on my heart. I wanted so much for him to love me, but he never did, and then he just cut off all communication with me. That hurt, and I still wonder why I wasn't enough. It sucks," she said, looking up at him. "But it's in the past. I'm over him and I'm ready to move on," she said, waving her hand nonchalantly, even though she knew her statement was a complete lie. There was no way she could ever get over Jordie. He did something to her. Branded her without her even knowing it and she felt bad for lying to Liam, but then she was pretty sure she was trying to tell herself the same thing. The right thing. That she was over Jordie and he was a thing of the past.

But she could still see his crooked grin and his dark brown eyes clear as day. As if he were standing in front of her, beckoning her in for a kiss.

Come here, sugar thighs, let me get a kiss.

Ugh, she could still feel his voice against her throat, the feel of his hands on her thighs as he kissed her senseless. As much as she wanted to be rid of him, she held tightly to those memories as a little girl did her favorite doll. Or, in her case, the way she held her stick when she hit the ice. She couldn't let it go because that's how she scored. That's how she won.

But she lost with Jordie.

And she still hadn't recovered.

"But you loved him?"

"Oh yes. More so than anyone else."

His brow came up as he slowly nodded. "When did you two break up?"

"We were never together."

"Huh?"

She shrugged. "He made it very clear that we were only fucking, but I caught feelings hard. But I guess, to answer your question, we stopped talking about eight months ago."

"Oh, okay," he said, still holding her gaze. "Are you sure you want to move on?"

Chewing her lip, she didn't allow her gaze to avert. She didn't want to move on, but she had to. Or she would lose it. She stayed locked with Liam's sweet gaze and slowly nodded. "I am. I want to be with someone who wants what I want."

"Completely understandable. Thank you for being honest with me," he said before leaning over and kissing the side of her mouth. "And it's fine that you don't love me yet. Just means I have to work hard to get you to fall for me," he whispered against her mouth, his blue eyes burning into hers. He then pressed his thin lips to hers and she instantly missed the feel of hair. The smell of the coconut oil that Jordie used for his beard. She missed him. When Liam pulled back, he held her chin by his thumb, his eyes searching his, and she hoped she didn't look as pained as she felt. And as she stared into his eyes, she begged the sparks to fly. The fireworks to burst or, hell, anything. Something.

But she felt nothing for Liam.

And everything for Jordie.

Jordie watched as Jim poked and prodded at his knee, his brow up in his hairline as he bent it one way and then another. "You feel good?" he asked and Jordie nodded.

"Great."

"Good, it looks great, and you've been really dedicated these last six weeks."

Jordie smiled. "Ready to go home," was his answer, and Jim nodded as he slowly laid his leg down.

"Good, 'cause I have paperwork saying you are released from me," he said, reaching for a stack of papers and handing them to Jordie. "You look good, son, hoping that it stays that way. You've done very well. I'm proud of you; you're a completely different person than the one I met nine months ago."

Yeah, he was sober and healthy.

That could definitely change a person.

"I feel great. Ready to hit the ice with my boys back home," Jordie said, hopping off the table without even a cringe. He really did feel brand-spanking-new.

"Just stay clean, Jordie, and healthy. If it hurts, nurse it. Don't try to hide it because you want to keep playing."

"Gotcha," Jordie agreed with a nod. "Won't happen."

"And stay away from the bottle."

He didn't hesitate. "Will do."

Jim held his gaze for a little longer and then nodded. "I believe in you, son. Now, believe in yourself."

He then turned and left the room with no other words. Jordie and Jim didn't always get along, mostly because Jordie was a selfish, drunken bastard—Jim's words, of course. But the last two weeks had been good. They were clicking and had developed a certain kind of respect between them. He would miss the old coot, but he was ready to go home.

Heading outside to go back to his cabin he had rented for his belongings, he called Karson first. He needed to call to get an airline ticket, but his excitement had to be shared with his best buddy.

"Hey, bro, what's up?" Karson asked, breathing hard into the phone.

Jordie grinned, almost bouncing as he made his way to the car. "Guess what?"

"What?"

"Been cleared! Coming home!"

"No shit! That's awesome, bro!"

"I know," he said, letting out a long breath. "Longer than I wanted, but I'm excited to get home, start training with you guys."

"For sure, just in time too. Camp starts Monday. Must have been meant to be. Get clean and healthy; come home right in time to show off."

"I know," he said, getting in and starting the car he had rented. "Praying I can keep up. I've only been on the ice for the last two weeks."

And oh, how perfect it had been. Jordie couldn't help himself, he'd found himself face first in the ice, just to smell it. He'd wanted to immerse himself in it, become one with it. He had missed it so much. He'd stayed out for hours, skating and just playing around. While guitar playing had helped with not wanting to drink, when he was on the ice, alcohol was nowhere in his mind. It was only him, the ice, his stick, and the puck. It was perfect.

He was home.

"You'll be fine. No worries at all."

"Hope so," he said, turning onto the highway to get out to his place. "So you are still cool with me staying with you guys till we know my fate?"

Karson laughed. "Don't be so dramatic. Elli lifted the suspension, you aren't going anywhere."

"But I haven't signed anything, so you never know," he said, his heart sinking a bit. He hadn't heard from Elli since he went into rehab—only a text saying to call her once he was released, which was something he needed to do. The only reason he knew that his suspension had been lifted was because his agent had sent him an email saying so. Everything was still up in the air though; he went up for free agency in October. Would he be let go, or would she sign him? He wasn't sure, but he had to keep his nose clean, that was for sure.

"Yeah, yeah, she'll sign you. She loves you, but yeah, you're good. Are you flying in tonight?" he asked. He then huffed before yelling, "Damn it, Dad, that was my foot!"

"What are you doing?"

Karl hollered something unintelligible and Karson huffed out another breath. "My parents are selling their house so they can move to Nashville to be close to us and Mena Jane. So I'm up here doing some home improvements to meet the demands on the offer sheet."

"Oh, so you aren't even home?"

"No, but Lacey and Mena Jane are. Are you flying in tonight?"

"Yeah, I was going to, but I can wait."

"No, go. I won't be back till Sunday and neither will Kacey. BJ sent her to a trainers' convention down in Chattanooga."

"Kacey? Trainers? Huh?"

"Oh, did I not tell you? Kacey got a job with the trainers. She's our work-out trainer now. She won't travel with the team, which is good 'cause Lacey can't be alone right now. But that's why you going home tonight would be ideal because Kacey just left today."

Kacey worked for the Assassins now? She was his trainer? Ha. That was gonna be awesome….once he got her to forgive him.

Unable to say that, his next concern was Lacey. "What's wrong with Lacey? Why can't she be alone?"

"She's got a touch of postpartum depression, and she is deathly scared that Mena Jane is gonna get breast cancer or die or something. I really didn't want to leave them, but she was scared to put Mena Jane on a plane with sick people."

"Oh shit, dude," Jordie said, worried about her. He had known about her being nervous, but he didn't know she had basically lost her shit.

"Yeah, as much as I wanted kids, I sorta wish, for her sake, we would have waited a bit longer. She isn't handling everything well."

"I'll talk to her. She has a soft spot for me," he said and Karson laughed.

"Never would have thought that would happen. She used to hate you."

"I grow on people."

Karson scoffed. "Sure, you do."

Jordie laughed and then paused before asking the question that had been burning in his soul since Karson brought her up. "So Kacey is living at your place too?"

"Yeah, until Ma and Dad get in. Then she is moving in with them, unless she gets her own place or whatever. We are praying that Lacey gets better before the season starts because, if she doesn't, then Kacey will stay until she does."

Oh. Wow. He had all the intentions in the world of finding Kacey and talking to her, but he thought he'd have some time before that. Now he was being thrown in a house with her, and he wasn't sure if he should be excited or learn to sleep with one eye open. He hadn't done her right and fully expected her to lose her shit on him. After all that though, he planned on schmoozing her back into his life. He missed her, more than he could describe, and he truly believed that it was she and Mena Jane who helped him get his shit together and make it through rehab. He had not only done it for himself, but he'd done it for them.

His girls.

"Is it really that bad?"

"Yeah, man, she won't go on antidepressants because she doesn't think she needs them. I was worried to say something 'cause it will hurt her feelings and she'll start crying. I think that's all she does, hold Mena and cry. It's driving me insane. She's got me all kinds of nervous and fucked up, but knowing you are going home and staying with her will ease some of my concerns."

"For sure. Shit, dude, I'm sorry I haven't been around to be there."

"No biggie. You're here now, and she'll be excited to know you're coming home healthy."

"Yeah," he said with a nod before pulling up into his drive. "And there is space? 'Cause I can get a hotel when you come back."

"Of course. It's a huge house. It will be fine. No worries."

"Okay, cool, bro. So I'll see you Sunday?"

"Yeah, call me if you think Lacey needs me. According to her, she is fine. I'm not gonna call her and tell her you are coming. Just show up and tell me what you find."

"Will do. Thanks again, bro."

"Anything for you, Jordie," he said and then he hung up. Jordie let his phone rest in his lap and sucked in a deep breath. He felt like shit for not being there for Karson and Lacey. He had always known that the cancer that had taken a lot more than just her breasts weighed heavy on Lacey, but he'd assumed having their sweet girl would help with that. Knowing it hadn't really hurt him, and he was ready to get home in the hopes that he could somehow help Lacey out. They didn't start out as friends, but she was his sister now and he loved her.

He would help fix this.

Picking his phone back up, he called for an airline ticket and then rushed inside to pack, since the first flight out was in two hours. Once he was packed, he loaded the car up and headed for the airport. He figured he had put off calling Elli for long enough and fished his phone out of his pocket before finding her number and calling.

She answered on the fourth ring, her thick Southern drawl full of happiness as she said, "Hey!"

Oh, thank God, she was happy. Maybe she didn't recognize the number though?

Cautiously, he said, "Hey, Elli. It's Jordie. How are you?"

"I'm good, and I know who it is! But sorry, jeez, I'm out of breath! I was chasing the twins outside. How are you?"

Jordie grinned. That was another reason he was excited to get home; he missed the Adler clan. "Good, I got released today. Flying out in a little over two hours."

"Oh my goodness! Yay! I'm so happy! How do you feel?"

"Wonderful. Ready to hit the ice and be with my team."

"We are ready to have you home. I'm so glad that you got cleared. Jim feels good about everything? How about Portia?"

"Yeah, he's good. And Portia is finding me a therapy group in Nashville and also referred me to a therapist for my weeklies," he said, still not too keen on the idea of furthering his therapy. But Portia was very adamant about it, and he figured whatever made her release him, he'd do. He wanted to be home. He was ready to be home.

"Awesome. Oh my God, Jordie, you sound so damn good. I can't wait to see you and squeeze you," she squealed, and Jordie blushed as he smiled.

"I can't either," he admitted.

"Come to dinner next weekend?"

"I'll be there."

"Good," she decided. "Okay, so text me when your plane lands, and I'll see you Monday morning before y'all start training. Did you hear that Karson's sister is the new trainer? I heard she's been kicking our boys' asses over the summer."

Jordie's heart went dead in his chest as he sucked in a deep breath. He would be spending a lot of time with her in the future, and he prayed that it would continue out of the club gym too. But he had some big-time fixing to do. Getting Kacey to trust him again wouldn't be easy. Swallowing, he nodded. "I did hear that."

"Yeah, Shea says she has the hands of a god, and I wanted to be jealous of her for that. But I'm pretty sure she could kill me with those god-like hands, so I just threatened to kill Shea if he left me with his clan of children. Told him he had to at least take the twins."

Jordie scoffed. "Elli, Shea isn't going anywhere without you."

"I know," she said with a sweet giggle. "Gotta keep him on his toes though. And it doesn't help that Kacey is just gorgeous with the body of a damn goddess."

Jordie closed his eyes for a brief second, the vision of her beautifully naked body covering his filling his mind before he let out a long breath. "Again, Shea won't leave you."

"Yeah, that's what he said. But thanks, makes her rubbing out his tight muscles a little less bothersome."

Jordie laughed. "Good to know. Don't worry, I'll keep an eye on things for you," he teased and she laughed.

"I knew I loved you for a reason," she said warmly. "You know, now that I think about it, you two would be adorable together. She's tall like you, built like an ox. She needs a strong, burly dude. You could so pull that off."

"You think?" Jordie asked and his grin grew.

"Yes, I do. It's now my sole purpose in life to get you two together. I need you to settle down."

"You sound like a mom, Elli, and I'm too old to be your son," he said, very careful not to add that she sounded like *his* mom. She didn't, because his mom was too busy finding a new husband since hers died two months ago. The only reason he knew that was because of Facebook. She didn't even know that Jordie was in rehab, probably didn't care either. He hadn't heard from her in months. He tried not to let that bother him, but it still stung. It would have been nice to have his mother fuss over him, but she never did.

"Well, I wear that title proudly, but are you telling me to butt out in a nice way?"

Jordie laughed. "No, play the matchmaker. I'm sure Kacey would love that," he said, knowing damn well she wouldn't.

Elli didn't say anything for a moment and then said, "In some weird way, I feel like you have a thing for Ms. King."

"Me? Never. That's my best friend's sister."

"Which answers how you know each other," she added and he laughed.

"Oh look, I just got to the airport. I'll text you later."

She laughed. "Have a safe flight, Jordie."

"Thanks, Elli."

As he hung up the phone, his grin was erased. Because Jordie didn't have a thing for Kacey King. No, he was madly in love with her. And the sooner she knew that, the better.

Chapter SIX

When Jordie pulled into the driveway of Karson and Lacey's exquisite home, he let out a sigh of relief. He was home. Their home had always been a second home of his. He and Karson had roomed together for as long as he could remember, and when Karson moved in with Lacey, there wasn't a time that Jordie didn't feel comfortable stopping by just to hang with them. He was always welcomed there, and when he got hurt, Lacey volunteered to care for him. Which was why he didn't hesitate on coming in early to help her out while Karson was gone.

The house was huge. Mansion-size almost, but it fit them. It was very country chic but modern. Once Lacey got ahold of it, it became their home and very inviting. Jordie had a designated room, one that was attached to the room that Kacey would sleep in when she visited, which was probably what had led to them sleeping together. Okay, that was a lie; he wanted her from the beginning and had to have her. The easy access was key, plus neither of them was able to say no. His room was down the hall from Karson and Lacey's, and he figured that Mena Jane would be in the big room at the end of that hall. The room had huge French doors and windows for days. It would suit a newborn just perfectly, especially since Lacey's walk-through closet connected to it. She had been using it as her office. But he was sure that would have changed since she had opened Lacey's Lace, her lingerie store that accommodated women who'd had mastectomies, here in Nashville.

Gathering his bags, he headed toward the house, noticing that only the living room light was on—the rest of the house dark. It was late, but it wasn't that late, he noted as he reached the back door, using his key to get in. Once he entered, he threw his bags down as he relocked the door. When he turned though, Lacey was standing there, looking like roadkill run over twice, a baby held close to her chest and a gun pointed at him.

"Shit, Lacey!" he hollered, holding up his hands. "When did you start packing?"

"Jordie?" she asked, her gun still trained on him.

He wanted to laugh and cry at the same time. He had never seen her look so crazed—her hair was a bird's nest, she was wearing clothes that had been thrown up on and even shit on. Her eyes were dark with tears and she just looked like a hot mess. But at the same time, this was a story for Mena Jane when she got older, for sure.

"Yeah, put the gun down, Annie, and come here," he said, holding his arms out before he started for her.

She laid the gun on the counter and just started to cry, holding Mena Jane close to her chest. Swallowing past the lump in his throat, he wrapped them both up in his arms, kissing Lacey's temple as her heart pounded against his chest.

"I thought you were a burglar," she cried, her hand snaking around his waist as he hugged her closer. Mena Jane slept soundly, unaware that her momma had almost killed her godfather.

"Sorry I didn't call. I flew in right after I got clearance. I think Karson forgot to call," he said, covering for his buddy.

"Or he wanted you to make sure I wasn't a basket case," she said as she pulled back, and Jordie hid his grin. "Which I am not, for your information."

They knew each other too well.

"Either way, surprise! I'm here!" he said, waving his hands in the air, but Lacey didn't even crack a grin.

"Why does your head look like that?"

"Like what?" he asked, confused as she squinted up at him like he stunk.

"You're usually cleaner about your beard and hair. You look like Jesus hanging from the cross, Jordie."

He made a face, running his fingers through his beard. "So you're saying I look angelic or like shit?"

"Like shit," she deadpanned, and he laughed as she gathered Mena Jane in closer. "Angelic and Jordie Thomas do not go in the same sentence. You need a haircut."

"Yeah, I'm gonna make an appointment Monday," he said, chucking her under the chin. "You, too, look like roadkill, my darling."

She nodded. "I feel like it," she said on a sigh.

Reaching out to take Mena Jane, he didn't even take offense when she hesitated to give her to him. Finally, she gave her up and Jordie cuddled the sweet baby in his arms. Walking into the light, he drank in the sight of his gorgeous goddaughter and smiled. She had a roundness to her face, her dark lashes kissing her cheeks. Her lips were bright red, a little chapped, and she had a head full of dark brown hair. He had seen this face before. Loved this face, and it honestly knocked the air out of him when he realized who she looked like.

Moving his finger along her rosy cheeks, he whispered, "She looks just like Kacey."

"Striking resemblance, for sure. Thankfully, she has my chin or I would be convinced Karson and Kacey made her."

Jordie grinned. "Yeah," he whispered before leaning over to kiss Mena's nose. "Must be why I love you so much already, huh?"

When he looked up, Lacey was watching him, her eyes dark with wonder, and he promptly looked away. "Don't read into that," he said and she laughed without humor.

"Yeah, sure," she said. "Because hearing that you love my daughter because she looks like your ex isn't something to read into?"

"Nope, not at all," he said, flashing her a grin. But he knew Lacey, she wasn't going to let go that easily.

"Whatever. So you still love her, then?"

"You know I do," he answered simply. He was tired of holding back how he felt. If rehab did anything, it taught him that he had to be open with his feelings. No matter how badly he wanted to keep all his vulnerability locked up tight, he had done that for way too long. And that's what had often led to his drinking since he couldn't handle all his feelings. As much as he hated that place, he was thankful for it. Thankful that Elli knew what he needed. That woman really was a gem.

Shea Adler had really hit the jackpot with her.

Lacey eyed him, not that he was paying attention to her because Mena Jane had stolen all his interest. She really was a pretty baby. He usually said that about all babies to make the mommies happy, even though most of the time, those other babies came out looking like hairless rats. But this one, man, she was a gorgeous little thing. Tears stung his eyes as he looked her over, her little hand grasping his finger. He was her godfather. He got to love her for the rest of her life, and he never had to be all disciplinarian with her like her parents had to. He could be the cool dad, the one she could come to whenever she needed anything. The one who would kill anyone that hurt her. A huge, overwhelming feeling of protectiveness washed over him as she slowly opened her eyes, the same color as Kacey's, and he vowed that no one would even come close to hurting her while on his watch.

Clearing her throat, Lacey said, "I do, but it's still crazy hearing you say it."

He looked over at her and shrugged. "It's the truth."

"So what's your plan? Gonna try to get back with her?"

"If she'll have me," he said, finally looking over at her. He shrugged again, his eyes held hostage by her inquisitive ones. "I don't deserve her though."

"No, you don't. Not after what you did," she said, a little apprehension in her voice.

He nodded, completely in agreement with her. He knew good and well that he could see Kacey and she could tell him to fuck off. He deserved it, but unlike before, when he would have gone to get drunk and let her go, he wouldn't let go this time. He was going to fight and he would get her back. No matter what. For the last ninety days, he'd gone over and over all the ways he planned to win her back. He even got some ideas from his buddies in rehab. He also had to come clean to Karson, which was going to be hard, but she was worth it. He needed her. It was that simple. He had already apologized to Karson, Lacey, and Karson's family for all the wrong he'd done over the years, but Kacey would take more than a simple apology, he knew that.

"I was fucked up, Lacey, and I regret it every single day. You don't need to remind me."

"She's still hurt," she said, moving her hair out of her face. His heart cracked a bit, so he snuggled into Mena Jane for a little extra support.

"I know, but that also gives me hope. A little push that she still thinks of me."

"But it doesn't mean she won't try to kill you."

"She won't," he said with a grin. "She loved me at one time."

"I think she still does," she admitted and Jordie nodded, his heart pumping faster in his chest.

"That's all well and good, and I pray to Jesus you're right, Lacey, but that's an issue I need to fix. Because only I can do it," he said simply. "But enough about me. When was the last time you showered?"

She made a face. "Why?"

"Because you stink, and you have baby shit on your shirt along with something crusty and white in your hair. Since Karson isn't home, I'm gonna guess it's not what it should be, so you need a shower."

He said it to make her laugh, but she wasn't laughing. Instead, her lips pressed together as her eyes started to fill with tears and he shook his head. "What the hell is going on, Lacey? I've never seen you like this."

She looked away sheepishly as he turned to look at the disaster that was her living room. Tissues were everywhere, dirty diapers, little circle pads, bottles of soda, and clothes littered the floor.

"You're drinking Coke now?"

She was a clean eater, something she believed in since having breast cancer. She always told him, "You've got one body. Keep it healthy." Apparently, she wasn't living by that anymore.

She shrugged. "I guess. It keeps me awake."

"Lacey, what's going on?"

She looked up at him, tears rolling down her cheeks, and her little lip wobbled. His heart broke for her. He didn't understand what she was feeling. Hell, no one probably did. This girl was fighting an internal battle that only people in the same boat with her would understand. It killed him, but he had to help.

"I'm scared twenty-four seven, Jordie. I know Karson is freaking out and trying to think of ways to help me, but all I can think is that she's gonna die. My sweet little Mena Jane will be taken from me, and I can't handle it. It's like I have this weight on my chest and I'm struggling to breathe, to get out from underneath it to save her. I don't know what to do. I won't leave her and I won't take her anywhere because I'm so scared. I just don't know what to do. People call all the time to come and visit, and I make up excuse after excuse. Half the time I don't even answer the phone. I'm a train wreck, and I don't know how to make it better."

She started to sob and Jordie couldn't take it. As much as he wanted to just hold Mena Jane, he knew that he needed to hold Lacey. Laying Mena Jane in the bassinet by the couch, he turned, taking Lacey in his arms, hugging her in close to his chest and almost squeezing her too hard. Snuggling her nose into his chest, she let out a sob that rattled his soul.

He hated when women cried; it always made him feel an inch tall. It used to kill him to watch him mom cry over all her failed marriages. It would make him so mad because he would want to rattle her, scream at her that she didn't need anyone, that he was enough, but he never did. He just comforted her. Why he did, he still didn't understand. She never loved him enough to just be good with only having him, but this was different. Lacey loved Jordie for Jordie. Maybe because she had to, but she did and that was enough to make him want to do anything to help her.

Kissing the top of her head, he fought back his own tears as she just sighed again, her eyes fluttering shut. She was exhausted. "When was the last time you slept the whole night?"

She shook her head under his lips. "I don't even remember. I can't sleep. I'm always worried something will happen."

"Didn't they prescribe you something for that?"

"They did," she said with a nod. "But I'm so worried that I won't wake up to tend to her and Karson is such a heavy sleeper. And I don't want to depend on Kacey to care for her."

"Okay, well, I'm here now," he said, pulling her back by her shoulders so she could look up at him. "You depend on me. You've gone above and beyond to help me. Now let me help you. Take the meds tonight. Sleep, Lacey, you need it. Me and Mena will chill in the living room. I'll sleep on the couch. Then tomorrow, I want you to take your anti-anxiety meds."

Her brows pulled together, and he hadn't noticed how bloodshot her poor eyes were. "Why? I'm—"

"Don't say fine. We both know that's not true. You need them."

"But—"

"No, give them a chance. You need them, and I know Karson hasn't said that to you or even Kacey 'cause they are worried about your feelings and they love you. And I love you too, but I won't sugarcoat shit. You're tiptoeing on the line between batshit crazy and sane. We both know you need them."

Her lip wobbled a bit more, and then she nodded and sounded oh so defeated as she whispered, "I do."

"You do."

"I just feel so weak taking them. I should be strong for her."

"But you can't be. They can help you; everyone else can help you. Just take the help, Lacey."

She nodded slowly. "Okay."

"Okay," he said with a triumphant smile. "Now go shower and take the meds. Sleep."

She nodded again, looking toward where Mena Jane was sleeping. "Are you sure?"

His head fell to the side, holding her gaze. "Do you trust me?"

She didn't even hesitate. "Yes."

"Then go."

She nodded again and let go of him, heading for the hall that led to her room. When she turned, he smiled. "I'll even clean," he added with a wink.

She smiled, the first true smile since he had been there. "Payback's a bitch, but thankfully those tissues are only full of snot and tears instead of dead little sperms."

Jordie laughed, thinking of his very first interaction with Karson's new wife. It was back when they were living in the apartment and Karson had been gone marrying Lacey, leaving Jordie alone with a stack of porn, some lotion, and a box of tissues. The aftermath of the tissues was downright disgusting and he was the first one to admit it, but being the trooper she was though, she cleaned everything. He was pretty sure that's when he knew Lacey was a good one. How many women would clean up come-filled tissues for their new husband? Not many.

"Thank God. But for you, I'd clean up anything. No more tears, okay?"

She nodded, her eyes watery along with her smile. "I'll try."

"Good, off you go."

She turned and disappeared down the hall. When he heard her door shut, he looked over at his sleeping goddaughter and smiled.

"You sleep, I'll clean, and then we'll get to know each other once you wake up," he whispered to her, but she didn't even stir. As he watched her sleep, he honestly couldn't believe he was standing there in the state he was in. He felt good. He felt alert and healthy, and he was thankful that he wasn't who he was ninety days ago. He was a new Jordie, and he was ready to share himself with the world.

Especially with Kacey.

When Liam suggested that he drive and go to the training convention with Kacey, she was sure that meant they were going to get down and dirty. She was convinced. It had been six weeks, it was time. But apparently, she was the only one who'd thought that. Sitting back in the passenger seat of his Prius, she glanced over at him and just drank him in. They'd had fun in Chattanooga; he was funny and very upbeat when she didn't want to wake up to go to the seminars. She loved training, but she hated waking up early. Wasn't her thing, but apparently Liam was an early riser and wouldn't stop knocking on her door until she answered it.

No, they did not share a room.

It was just wrong, really. Was it her? Did she not wear a revealing enough tank? Were her pants not tight enough? Has she not grazed his dick right? How could someone do that wrong? Ugh, it was stressing her out and giving her a complex. She was actually starting to like him, more than as a friend. Or at least she was telling herself that she needed to. The more time she spent with him, the more she knew she needed to fall for this guy. He always asked about Mena Jane, which she thought was just dreamy. He showed interest when she spoke of her parents and even offered to go help them move. He was a damn good guy and, damn it, she needed good in her life!

As she let out a long breath, he glanced over at her, taking her hand in his. "You all right?"

She smiled as she nodded. "Yeah, tired."

"I bet," he agreed with a nod.

And she was. They trained the shit out of her this weekend. She was pretty up-to-date on the training for athletes but, man, she learned a lot more this weekend. She was ready to get back home and start on her plans. She had to turn them in to BJ on Monday morning to cover the next three weeks. She was excited to start training the guys, but she was also really nervous. They had been nice to her and even joked with her, but that was because she was being nice Kacey. When trainer Kacey came out, it might be a different story. At least Shea Adler loved her, and Karson had to love her, oh, and apparently Liam loved her…that she still couldn't fathom. If he loved her, why didn't he want to poke her with his dick?

When her phone sounded, she looked down to see it was from Lacey.

> *Lacey: Did you guys do it? I haven't heard from you all weekend. I'm figuring so.*
> *Kacey: lol, no, not at all and I'm sorry. They worked me like a dog this weekend.*
> *Lacey: No biggie, but really? Why?*
> *Kacey: No clue. It's weird.*
> *Lacey: It is.*
> *Kacey: Yeah, I'm ready to get home, make some plans, and get to work tomorrow. Maybe even think this through because I really don't understand him.*
> *Lacey: Have you asked him? Honesty is not hard for you.*
> *Kacey: True. Maybe I will.*
> *Lacey: Good.*
> *Lacey: So off the wall question, but have you talked to Jordie?*

Kacey made a face as her heart sank. Why would Lacey ask that? Scrunching her face up, she texted her back quickly.

> *Kacey: wtf? No, why would I?*
> *Lacey: No reason, but rumor is, he is back and he'll be there tomorrow.*

Her heart sped up in her chest as her hands went clammy.

> *Lacey: You're not gonna kill him the first time you see him, right?*

Kacey scoffed and Liam looked over at her.
"Lacey is a nut," she said and then looked back down.

> *Kacey: For me to want to kill him means I still care. No, he is the least of my concerns. I'll do my job, no biggie.*
> *Lacey: Good to know.*

Kacey: Who told you he was in town?
Lacey: He did.
Kacey: You've seen him?
Lacey: Yes.
Kacey: Well? How did he look?
Lacey: Like shit.

That made Kacey's lips press together in a straight line.

Kacey: Oh. Okay.
Lacey: Yeah.

Kacey's heart was racing in her chest, but she knew she had to make it stop. Jordie had no control over her anymore. She was over him. He didn't want her, and the quicker she accepted that, the easier her job would be. She couldn't be in the same room with him and still want to be with him. No, she had until tomorrow to get her shit together. Jordie had no control over her. None. She was with Liam now. He was her boyfriend and, damn it, they were going to have sex!

When she saw the sign for Nashville, she knew she couldn't get out of the car until she was sure of that. Looking over at Liam, she let her phone fall to her lap and stared at him as he drove. He had the most delectable jawbone, but she still felt it needed a little hair. Just a dusting. Or a massive beard, ugh! *No!* He was perfect and gorgeous and would make sweet babies with her! He was everything she needed.

He must have felt her staring at him because he glanced over, a goofy smile on his face as he asked, "What?" She smiled as he chuckled, squeezing her hand. "You sure you're okay?"

"Yeah," she said, waving him off. "Are we together?"

He seemed a little surprised by that but recovered quickly. "I thought so."

"So you aren't fucking anyone else?"

He scoffed. "No, Kacey, I'm not."

"So why aren't you fucking me?"

He glanced over at her a little surprised, and really, she probably could have delivered that better, but the thought of seeing Jordie tomorrow had her in knots. Her heart still hadn't slowed to a normal rate, and she felt like she was coming out of her skin. She had to know she was in a relationship with a good guy so she wouldn't falter and fall vagina first on top of Jordie's face when he smiled at her. He had that power over her, but she wasn't a cheater. If she were in a relationship, she wouldn't be interested. She knew she wouldn't. But fuck, was she using Liam?

Damn it.

No. She liked him. He was nice. He was her match. *Cosmo* said so. It also said Jordie was her match too, but that was beside the fucking point! What the hell did *Cosmo* know anyway?

Dumb magazine. Who even read it anymore?

Waiting for his answer, she watched as he looked out at the road and shrugged. "To be honest, I wanted to wait."

"Why?" she asked, and he gave her a sidelong glance.

"Because I don't want to rush this," he finally admitted and she held her breath. "Every time I rush into sex with a girl, she's gone just as fast. I love you, Kacey. I want this to last for, if possible, ever. And the thing is, I know you're not there yet. I know you like me, but you don't love me. Call me old-fashioned, but I want you to get there before I take us to the next step. I want to know that, once we are together, it will be the last time either of us has sex with anyone else."

Whoa.

Who the fuck said that anymore?!

Ugh!

When he glanced over at her, he shrugged. "I've been burned too many times, Kacey."

"No, I got you," she said with a nod, and maybe he was smart to think that way.

So why did she think he was a complete idiot? Maybe she was a slut, because that seemed dumb to her, but then maybe... Okay, yeah, she did think it was sweet. He was sweet. Which is what she wanted.

Or so she kept repeating to herself.

"So yeah, I mean, don't think I don't want you, because I do, Kacey. So damn bad, but I think waiting is what's best for us."

"Not till, like, marriage though, right?" she asked as he turned onto Lacey's street.

He chuckled. "No, gotta make sure we fit before we take that step, but I want to wait. Believe me, it's hard and it honestly might kill me if I have to keep enduring you in those work-out shorts of yours, but I think this is what's best for us."

What about what she thought?

Before she could ask that though, he pulled into the driveway and looked over at her. "Also, while we are being honest, has anyone ever told you you cuss a lot?"

"No," she said simply, unfazed by his statement. "Why? Do I?"

He smiled. "Kinda."

"Oh," she said then paused, eyeing him. "Is that a problem?"

He laughed and shrugged. "My parents don't really like it, so maybe when they come into town, you can watch it a bit?"

She made a face and then shrugged. "Yeah, sure."

"Don't be mad."

"I'm not, but I'm not going to fucking sugarcoat myself… Whoa, hold on," she said, holding up her hand. "I'm tired and pissy—not at you, promise—and horny. So let's put this convo on hold because I'm not sure how to control what will come out of my mouth."

He eyed her skeptically and then nodded. "That's fine with me. I'm sorry."

"No, it isn't your fault. Come here," she said, taking him by his shirt and pulling him to her, smashing her mouth to his. As she kissed him, she prayed to feel something, and maybe she could, but she was mad. Usually when she was mad, she didn't feel anything but rage, which meant she had to get out of that car now. Parting, she smiled a stupid fake smile as he pulled back, fixing his shirt, which bothered her.

He was always so put together.

And he didn't like that she cussed.

Rolling her eyes, she reached for her overnight bag and opened the door.

"Do you want me to carry that in, baby?" he asked, but she shook her head.

"I'm good, thanks though. Thanks for driving and the wonderful weekend," she said sweetly and he smiled.

"Anytime. Call me later?"

"Sure," she answered, but as she slammed the door, she glared at the grass. "If you think I fucking cuss a lot, wait till you meet my daddy."

Grumbling as she made it to the door, she used her key to open it, and as she entered, she hollered out, "It's me, Lacey, don't shoot."

When the door slammed behind her, she heard, "I'd never shoot someone as gorgeous as you."

His rough, naughty voice sent chills down her spine as her eyes locked with his dark-as-night gaze. Her heart jumped up in her throat as Jordie grinned back at her, running his hand shyly through his hair. As he licked his lips, desire shot straight to her gut and she wanted to scream in frustration at the same damn time.

Really? He was here. Really!

"Hey, sugar thighs. Long time, yeah?"

As her eyes burned into his, all she could think was, yeah, she cussed a lot. But Liam couldn't even fathom was she was capable of.

But this asshole was about to find out how damn skilled Kasey King was in the art of cussing.

Chapter SEVEN

Red-hot rage burned through her as their eyes stayed locked. Lacey wasn't kidding, Jordie did look like shit, but Kacey still thought he was every bit as gorgeous as he was when he was all cleaned up. There was something about that beard that got her every time, but he really needed to groom it. She had no clue what he had been doing or what he had been through, but he looked like it had been hellish. Instantly, she was even more pissed. Why couldn't he have allowed her to be there for him? She would have. She'd follow him to the end of the earth. Anywhere. But he didn't want her. He didn't love her. He didn't need her. She was nothing to him.

And she was ready to tell him what she thought about all of that.

Months of anger were about to spew all over him, and she prayed for the safety of the innocent bystanders.

"How dare you!" she hollered and his brows shot up.

"What? I said hi," he said, feigning innocence, but there was nothing about Jordie that was innocent. His name and innocence didn't even belong in the same sentence. What did belong was: Jordie Thomas was a heartbreaking fucking asshole!

"You know damn well that's not what I'm speaking of! I haven't heard from you, seen you in almost nine months, and you have the gall to fucking stand there, looking at me like I'm one of the boys, and say hi to me like I'm nothing? Like I didn't mean anything to you. Like you didn't throw me away for whatever slut of the month. Like you didn't break my fucking heart!"

"That's not how I said it," he said, laying the knife he'd been chopping with down. "I welcomed you and, whoa, can we at least greet each other before you start accusing me of shit?"

"Accusing!" she screamed, and he grimaced a bit. "No! There is no accusing. You did it, and you also don't get to fucking welcome me to my house."

"Our house."

"*What!*"

He smiled before waving in a very annoying way. "Hey, roomie."

"Are you fucking kidding me? You fucking asshole!"

"Whoa, calm down, Kacey," Lacey said from the doorway, Mena Jane cradled in her arms, but Kacey's gaze didn't leave Jordie's.

"No, I don't have to calm down because this asshole used me like a pair of gloves and threw me in the Dumpster without even a reason why. All I did was admit I loved you, and I really did think you loved me back. But no, you completely shut me out. How dare you? After all we went through, after all we shared, after what I did for you. I mean, I was commuting from Minnesota to Colorado for you! So obviously I meant business. So please, Jordie, explain to me why I didn't mean more to you?"

"I didn't use you, Kacey," he said softly, his eyes averting like the coward he was.

"Oh, really? So that's why you answered my calls and my texts after I left your cabin on New Year's?" When he didn't answer, it only made her madder. "I was nothing to you. Just an easy fuck, and when shit got deep, you moved on to the next slut. Like you always do. Can't stay with one person, because they'll fuck you over like every man in the world fucks your mom."

"Kacey Marie!" Lacey scolded, but Kacey rolled her eyes. Lacey didn't know half the shit Jordie had done to her. The heartbreak he caused. When she looked over at him, his eyes met hers and she saw the pain and hurt in his eyes. But she refused to let that affect her. He broke her. She wouldn't be sorry for saying the damn truth.

"No, you were more than that. And don't use my mom to hurt me, that's fucking low," he said, cool as a cucumber to her, but she knew differently. His mom was a low-blow subject and she was wrong to use it, but she couldn't hold it in. She was just so damn mad.

"Really? But it wasn't low or rude that you didn't answer my texts or calls?"

"I was scared, Kacey," he said softly. "You scare the shit out of me."

She only glared. What a fucking stupid thing to say. He didn't say shit like that, because he wasn't scared of anyone! He didn't let anyone in to be scared of them, and she didn't believe him for a second.

"Bullshit. Tell the truth, Jordie. You didn't answer because I made you feel something more than what you were used to."

"That's the same damn thing, Kacey. That's what I fucking meant," he yelled back at her. But that couldn't be true…

"Bullshit! You don't mean that. You rejected me and made me feel like I wasn't worth anything!" she yelled, her eyes clouding with tears. She wouldn't let them fall though. No matter what, she wouldn't. He didn't deserve her tears. It enraged her that he walked in here, assuming they would be cool after all he did. He ruined her.

Honestly broke her.

She knew she should have been smarter and not fallen as hard as she did, but she couldn't control her heart. It did want what it wanted and she just followed it. For some reason, it always led to Jordie. Always.

"You're right," he said, his gaze burning into hers. "And there isn't a day I don't regret it."

She didn't expect that, but then again, that was Jordie. He was quick to say sorry but never owned up to his mistakes. If he meant any of what was coming from his lips, he wouldn't have hurt her the way he did. He wouldn't have let her walk away and ignored her for months. He would have been there for her like she had been for him when he was facedown, lying in his own puke, drunk. She was always there, cleaning up and believing that he would change. It was the injury, it had to be, that had had him so depressed. So she loved him extra hard, and yet, he still tossed her out on her ass.

Her lip started to wobble and she looked away, sucking in a deep breath. Looking back at him, her eyes in slits, she asked, "Really? Well, wanna know what I regret?"

His eyes didn't stray, only stayed on hers as he said, "I'm sure I can guess."

"Nope, it isn't the regular, 'I wish I'd never met you' bullshit, because I don't regret that. No matter how bad you hurt me, I loved you. But instead, it's the 'I wish we would have used condoms the whole time' because, while you checked out on us, Jordie, I wasn't allowed to. I hurt for you, over and over again, and then I found out I was pregnant."

There was no sound once that last word left her lips. She could only hear her heart in her ears, beating ever so loudly as Jordie just stared at her. His mouth dropped open, his eyes widened, and he leaned against the kitchen island for support. He honestly looked as if she had hit him.

Lacey shrieked. "*What!*"

"Pregnant?" he gasped, his knuckles white from holding on to the counter so hard.

Lacey sputtered unintelligible things, coming toward her, but Kacey held up her hand, stopping her.

"But I lost our little bundle of joy three days after finding out," she said, her chest rising and falling as her heart broke all over again.

And the tears started to fall.

When she'd found out she was pregnant two weeks after leaving Jordie's cabin, she was elated and knew that he would be happy. He wanted a kid, and Lord knew she did. She was convinced that a baby would bring them together. That they could work stuff out. And she truly believed that, no matter how idiotic it made her sound. She knew that a baby shouldn't force two people together, but maybe it was the push Jordie needed. Either way, she knew he'd be a good daddy. He loved kids.

But he'd never answered her calls for her to tell him.

No matter her pleas.

And then she'd started bleeding.

A part of her was grateful that it happened so early since it was all so new and she hadn't already picked out names, put pillows under her shirt to see what she would look like, and stuff like that. She knew there were women who went full-term and lost their babies, but that didn't mean her heart would ever be the same. Not only had she been rejected by the man she was convinced was her soul mate but she also lost their child. She felt like a failure on both counts and, honestly, she still didn't know how she pulled it together to play in the Olympics. In a way, she was sure it was because she wasn't even there half the time. Her heart, her soul, were with Jordie and their baby who had its own pair of wings, looking over both of them.

But only one of them cried over it.

Well, that is, until now. Because as the tears rolled down her cheeks, she sucked in a breath as Jordie's eyes clouded with his own tears. It was quite a confusing thing to see. Jordie didn't cry because Jordie felt nothing but the desire for sex and booze. Who was this man standing in front of her?

Clearing his throat, he looked down. For some reason, that made her indescribably mad because she felt she didn't know this man. She had no clue who he was.

"Kacey—"

"No, no words," she barked at him, her fiery gaze meeting his as she wiped away her traitorous tears. "Nothing you can say will fix how badly you fucked me over. I trusted you. I loved you, and you left me high and dry. No reasons, no anything. I was nothing to you."

"If I had known—"

"You would have if you'd called me back, I know."

"I thought you were calling to beg me to come back," he said simply. "I couldn't handle it."

"Couldn't handle it?" she growled as her eyes went to slits. "Really? What about what *I* could handle? You never cared one bit about how I felt or anything. Instead, you just ignored me, threw me to the side. Thanks, it's fucking wonderful to know my worth to you. That it was all a fucking lie."

"Kacey, I was fucked up—"

Glaring, she shook her head. "You're always fucked up, Jordie. Fucked up is your middle name, but I loved you anyway. I believed in the man you could be."

He looked away as Lacey took a step toward her, her hand lacing with Kacey's. "Kace, just calm down and maybe take a breather."

"No! You know what he did to me."

"Yes, but he's been—"

"Let it be, Lacey," he said then, looking up, and Kacey was breathless. His eyes were full of tears, but they still hadn't fallen as he held her gaze. "I fucked up, and Kacey, I'm so—"

"Oh, don't you dare tell me you are sorry unless you mean it, Jordie Thomas!" she snapped.

He looked down at her and nodded. "I do mean it, sugar. I am."

She'd thought that when he admitted it she would feel better, but all the rage was still eating her alive and she didn't know how to handle it. A part of her wanted to swing at him, smash her fist into his nose. But the other part wanted to wrap her arms around his neck and beg him to tell her she meant more than just a fuck. One thing was for sure, that was not the apology she wanted or needed.

"That's not enough," she said, blinking away her tears. "You made me your sappy bitch while you fucked anything with tits, forgetting all about me. The tears I've fucking cried, the feeling of pure defeat… You have no clue what I've been through. And the shitty thing is, I still wanted you there. I wanted you to comfort me, to make it all better because I believed in you. You just didn't believe in me, though."

When he looked up, loss was in his eyes and his shoulders slumped as he worked his lip between his teeth. He really did look like shit and she should have felt bad, but she couldn't forget all those months of crying. Being wrapped up in a ball as she bled out their child. The pain, the hurt, the rejection didn't allow her to feel bad. She wanted him to feel what she did and then make it all better. It was a bipolar feeling, for sure, but she felt it.

"You're right, Kacey, and I wish I would have been there. I wish I would have done right by you."

"Me too," she said simply. "But instead I'm left the fool."

"No," he said, his chest rising and falling as he shook his head. He then looked up at her, knocking the air completely out of her as a lone tear rolled down his beautiful face, getting lost in the curls that were his beard. With his eyes so intense and striking, he whispered, "I didn't fool you, I failed you, and I'm so sorry, Kacey. So sorry."

Before she could say anything, he left the kitchen. When his door slammed down the hall, she jumped, her heart sneaking up into her throat. Closing her eyes, she leaned her head against Lacey's shoulder and let out a long breath. No matter how hard she tried, or how she didn't want them to, tears rushed down her cheeks, landing on Lacey.

Why didn't she feel better? Why didn't she feel like she'd gotten her closure? And most of all, why did she still love him? Why did she want to know the person who was standing in front of her more than she wanted to know what the rest of her life held? Why did looking into his eyes do nothing but make her fall all over again? The pain, she wanted to ease it. She wanted him to love her, and she was fucking stupid for that. Because he may be sorry and he may think he'd failed her, but Jordie Thomas didn't love her.

And that hurt most of all.

Jordie always lived by the saying, "What doesn't kill you, makes you wish you were dead," and at that moment, it had never rung truer.

Kacey's eyes didn't kill him, but he sure did want to be dead after everything she said.

A baby?

Fuck.

As he came barreling out of his room, his heart was thudding so loudly against his ribs, he was sure it was going to break them all. He welcomed the pain, he needed it; he needed to be reminded of the suffering and heartache he'd caused the woman he loved. How did he expect to get her back when he'd essentially ruined her?

He didn't deserve her.

He didn't deserve anyone.

Rushing through the living room, he noticed that Mena Jane was in her bassinet and almost stopped, but he knew he wouldn't leave if he did. He had to get out of there. The walls were closing in on him, his heart hurt, and playing his guitar wasn't helping at all. Nothing was. He wanted to find Kacey, try to apologize again, but like she said, it wasn't enough. The thing was, he didn't know what was enough for her. He had never cared enough to want to figure that out. Even at the moment, he didn't want to know. He just wanted to stop hurting.

When he went to cut through the kitchen, Lacey's voice stopped him. "Jordie, you need to tell her."

He shook his head. "Later, and let me do it."

"Okay."

"I'm serious, Lacey. Don't you tell her anything. I'll do it when I'm ready."

She didn't agree, but he didn't have to look at her to know she'd do what he asked. They'd grown closer over the weekend and he trusted her. When she cleared her throat, he closed his eyes, knowing what she was about to ask.

"Where are you going?

His hand was on the doorknob, he was ready to flee, but he knew he owed her an answer as to whether he'd be back. Still, he didn't turn to look at her. He didn't want her to see the tears in his eyes, the defeat and utter emptiness he felt. "Out."

"Where?"

"I don't know," he said roughly as he let out a long breath. "I need to just go."

"Will you come back?"

He nodded and pulled the door open. "Yeah, I'll text you."

"And you won't go out for a drink?" she asked then, causing him to pause.

He wanted to turn and say he'd never do such a thing.

But that would make him a liar.

Ignoring her last question, he told her bye and slammed the door shut before heading to his truck. Getting in, he went around the two cars in the driveway and ignored Lacey as she tried to wave him down from the porch. Speeding down their street, he hit the main road and couldn't hold back anymore. The tears fell down his face, wetting his beard and splattering all over his black tee. He couldn't believe he had done what he did to her.

She had been pregnant.

And alone.

If he hadn't been so fucked up and trying so hard to forget her, he would have been there for her. He would have married her on the spot so her dad and Karson wouldn't have killed him…and because he loved her. Maybe then she wouldn't have lost the baby. It was probably the stress of him being a complete dick that didn't allow her body to hold on to their child. It was his fault. Everything, her heartache, her anger, their loss, he caused it all. When the hell did he ever do anything right?

He was a fucking screw-up.

Blinking away the tears, he sucked in a breath before turning his music all the way up. Just to get lost. Just to forget what had happened back there, but there was no forgetting the pure hatred in her eyes. Or forgetting the way she said she'd *loved* him. Past tense. No, Kacey didn't love him anymore. How could she? He'd broken her heart because he was a selfish drunk.

And man, he wanted a drink so bad.

Pulling into the liquor store parking lot, he didn't even hesitate. He got out and marched into the store, despite his shaking hands and the erratic beat of his heart. His heart was telling him not to do it, to go get a milk shake instead, but his mind was telling him to forget. He had to forget. This wasn't his first time in this store; it was one of his favorite ones because his drink was right on the counter. Reaching for a bottle of Jack, he threw a twenty down before turning away. For some reason, he didn't want the cashier to judge him. He felt she knew that he was trying to recover, and he didn't want to see the disappointment in her eyes.

Muttering, he said, "Keep the change."

He then marched out to the truck, the bottle heavy in his hand. But he ignored that. He needed that drink. He needed to let go of all his fucked-up feelings. He wanted to just forget everything. Sitting down behind the wheel, he didn't start the car or even open the bottle. He just held it, staring at the black logo, the fiery brown liquid inside. He hated the power it had over him, but he wanted it so bad.

So why hadn't he opened the bottle?

When his phone sounded, he dug it out of his pocket, expecting it to be Lacey. But it was Natasha.

Natasha: Haven't heard from you in a couple days? You good? How's Mena Jane?

Ugh. Mena Jane.

Sucking in a breath, he laid the bottle down and closed his eyes. He said he wanted to be healthy for Mena Jane and Kacey, but then he was sitting here, a bottle in his hand, ready to ruin all the progress he had made. Hadn't he just said that day that he liked being healthy? That he didn't even miss drinking? That he couldn't wait to show the man he had become to Kacey? Was he really ready to ruin that?

When he thought of Kacey balled up on the floor, their child dead inside of her, he felt as if he were drowning. He hated feeling like that. Despised it.

Then a tap came at the window and he looked over, his eyes wide when Elli Adler's eyes bored into his. Her brow rose as she obviously waited for him to roll down the window. He was trying to figure out why she was there, but then he saw that she was holding bags of Chipotle. So he slowly rolled down the window, pushing the bottle off his lap into the seat. Praying the dark night would keep it hidden.

"Oh, hey, Elli."

"Funny to see you here. Did you get Chipotle too? The kids wanted chicken nuggets and I didn't, so I came on out and got me and Shea some Chipotle. I looked over and saw ya, came to say hi. Wanna come on by and eat with us?"

Even though the truck was on big tires, Elli's signature heels gave her the height she needed to look him square in the eyes.

He swallowed loudly and shrugged. "Yeah, um—"

He paused when he saw her eyes dart to the seat beside him.

"Open the door, Jordie," she demanded and he closed his eyes, letting his head hang. Not waiting for him, she reached through the open window and unlocked the door, pulling it open. Laying her bags at his feet, she surprised him when she gathered him in her arms. He went willingly. Burying his face in her neck, he drew in a breath through his nose and then blew it out of his mouth as she rubbed his back like the mother she was.

"What are you doing, Jordie?" she whispered.

But he just shrugged, unable to talk without sobbing like a child.

"I see the bottle. Did you drink it?"

He shook his head, still unable to look at her.

"Why? What happened?"

He squeezed his eyes shut and wrapped his arms tighter around her. He was a second from saying nothing, but he knew that wouldn't help. He had to be honest; he had to own up to his mistakes to fix them. But would Elli even care once she heard how weak he was?

Sitting up, he broke out of her hug and crossed his arms over his chest, swallowing his sob. "I'm not gonna make it," he whispered. "You should just trade me and let me go ruin myself somewhere else, out of your sight."

"No," she said firmly. "Not gonna happen, because you are done ruining yourself."

"Everything I try to do, everyone I love, I fuck over," he breathed and she laced her fingers with his, pulling his attention to hers.

"Then stop. Don't do it anymore. You know what you've done to hurt people, so don't do it. Learn from your mistakes."

Biting into his lip, he looked down before sucking in a breath. "She was pregnant with my baby and she lost it," he whispered, and he heard the little intake of breath from Elli but didn't dare to look up.

"Who?"

"Kacey."

He finally looked up and her eyes were searching his. "But you never knew."

"Nope, 'cause I ignored her. I cut off all ties because I couldn't handle what I felt for her."

She nodded slowly and then squeezed his hand. "Okay, how does that make you feel?"

He gave her a look and she shrugged. "What? Dr. Phil says that all the time."

"Fucking hell," he muttered before shaking his head. "I feel like shit. I feel like I failed her."

"You did," she said and he nodded. "But that was old Jordie. New Jordie needs to show her who he is, own up to his mistakes, and fix them."

"I don't deserve her though," he admitted, but she set him with a look.

"You deserve to be happy, and if she makes you happy, then you deserve her. You've done such great things for yourself. Show her, show the world. But most of all, accept what you've done, be proud, and please don't go back to what you were."

Leaning forward, he rested his forehead on the steering wheel and closed his eyes. He did want to show off who he was now. He wanted Kacey to be proud, to love the better man he had become too. He wanted to make all his wrongs rights. He would listen, he would appreciate her, never lie or ignore her, he would give her the world. And most of all, he would love her more than life itself. He just needed the chance.

"I don't think she'll ever see it," he admitted quietly.

Elli's hand came to rest on the back of his neck and she whispered, "Not if you go back to the man you were."

"I hurt her."

"Yes. But will you do it again?"

He met her gaze and shook his head. "Never."

"Okay, tell her that."

"She won't listen," he said quietly. "She hates me."

"Then show her."

"Yeah," he agreed, unsure how to do that.

"Or go back to the way you were and be wholly incomplete for the rest of your life," she said in a very snippy way that caused him to look at her. Holding his gaze, she shook her head. "Doesn't even seem right, does it?"

He shook his head, his vision blurring with tears. "No. I don't want that."

"Do you think your Mena Jane wants her goddaddy to be a drunk?"

"No."

"And do you want to look in the mirror and see the man you were or the one you are fighting to become?"

His heart ached in his chest as he looked away, sucking in a breath. "I want to keep fighting."

"Good," she said, taking his hand in hers. "Now get out of the truck and grab that bottle."

Unsure what she was doing, he still did as she asked and then looked over at her, embarrassment flooding all his senses. He couldn't believe he'd come here. That he was that pathetic and sad.

Even though he was unable to look at her, she instructed him in her very stern, Mrs. Adler voice. "Now bust the bottle and know that that bottle, that liquid has no power over you. You are breaking that hold because it can't control you."

He glanced over at her and asked, "Did you see this on Dr. Phil?"

"Yes, but the poor, sweet woman, bless her heart, Jordie, she was 600 pounds! She was addicted to food, and he made her smash all these bottles of Coke and bags of chips. I cried like a baby," she said, fanning her face, almost as if she was keeping in her tears. "Ugh, it killed me, but anyway, this is the same thing! Addiction is a nasty, mean disease, but you are so lucky because you have people who love you and want to help you fight it. You just have to allow them and be honest with who you are."

A recovering alcoholic.

He looked away again and swallowed loudly, his shoulders taut and hurting. The bottle was so heavy and almost felt alien to him. He used to live off this stuff, but now it was foreign and he didn't want it. A part of him hoped that he wouldn't have drunk it if Elli hadn't come to his truck, but the other part wasn't so sure.

"Now smash it," she said again and he held the bottle up, looking long and hard at it. It was sort of astonishing how something as simple as a colored liquid could make him neglect everything. It was also pathetic how badly he thought he needed it. Truth was, he didn't. All he needed was the love and support of the people he loved. He knew if he had taken that drink, he would have been failing Kacey all over again and, for the first time, Mena.

And then himself.

He couldn't do that any longer. He wanted to be a good man, he wanted to fight for it, so he slammed the bottle against the curb and it burst, glass flying as the fiery liquor spilled along the road. He stood there, watching as the liquid ran down the side of the road to the gutter and he shook his head. If he'd kept on that path, he'd be the one in the gutter, completely and utterly alone. He couldn't allow that to happen. He didn't want that to happen. He wanted to be healthy. The surprising thing was, as all the Jack ran down into the gutter, he did feel like a weight had been lifted from his shoulders. Weird, but he felt one more step closer to his recovery.

To the man he wanted to be.

Glancing over at Elli, he smiled. "Dr. Phil may have been on to something."

She smiled back, taking his hand in hers. "Yeah, that's why I watch it."

He didn't answer or commit, only watched as the road sucked up the liquid as if it were suffering from the same thirst that Jordie was fighting to get rid of.

When her other hand clasped his, he looked over as she said, "Next Sunday, you'll go to church with us? Then I'll cook lunch and we'll go out to dinner. Spend the day with us. You need a little Jesus and the Adlers in your heart."

Jordie smiled. She was right. He did need those things. "I'll be there."

"Good, Jordie, I'm proud of you."

He nodded slowly as his grin grew. It was really something to have someone

OVERTIME

like Elli Adler be proud of you, and he was grateful for that.

But now, it was time to be the man *he* would be proud of.

Chapter EIGHT

Kacey had no clue how she was going to handle the next day.

How was she supposed to train a team of guys when the guy who broke her in two would be there, along with her boyfriend and her brother? Really, that was her life? She sounded like a damn soap opera! But really, how was she supposed to keep it together when all she wanted to do was cry? How was she supposed to act like Jordie was nothing to her when he was basically everything? How was she supposed to lie and act like everything was fine to Karson and Liam but, more importantly, to herself?

Because she was not okay.

Not even in the least, but she didn't know what to do. She'd thought when she saw him for the first time, she could handle it. But man, how wrong she was. She'd gotten diarrhea of the mouth and let him have it. At least she didn't hit him, but no telling for the future. Once thing was for sure, she knew that she needed to steer clear of Jordie. She needed to ignore him because he was going to hurt her again if she allowed him back in, and she would if she didn't stay away from him. But that just didn't sit well in her heart. Her heart wanted her to rush to him, beg him to let her in, and to forgive him. Her pride though, that was what was holding her back. She just couldn't allow him to hurt her again.

She was better than that.

And Liam was a really nice guy. No reason to ruin that for someone who had no understanding of how to love her the way Liam could. She had to stay where it was safe. No matter how much her heart yearned to go in a direction where nothing was certain, she had to be smart about this. But really, why was she even entertaining this notion? He didn't want her. She was supposed to hate him, wish he were dead. So what was wrong with her? Was she really that big of a glutton for punishment?

It was his eyes.

Those sweet brown eyes that held so much hope but no promise.

Leaning her head against her headboard, she closed her eyes, causing her tears to roll down the sides of her face, falling into her ears. Bringing her hair out from behind her ear, she ran it along her nose as her tears fell, something she always did when she was nervous. She had done it since she was a kid and had thought she was over it, but apparently that was only because her hair had been in a pixie cut. As soon as it had grown long enough for her to rub along her nose, she was doing it again. It was a comfort thing. Something her mom did to her every night before bed.

As her lip trembled, she closed her eyes tightly and wished like hell she hadn't told him about the baby. She hadn't told anyone, not a soul, but in a matter of seconds, not only the father but her brother's wife knew. Of course, Lacey was on her, fishing for information, wanting to fix her. But Lacey really needed to worry about herself. Yeah, she had seemed a lot different than she had been when Kacey left before the weekend, but still. She was in no way, shape, or form in any place to try to talk about feelings. Kacey was probably really wrong for saying that to Lacey too and needed to apologize, but for now, she'd lie alone with her thoughts. Trying to come to terms with how she was going to handle tomorrow and the rest of the season.

A part of her considered quitting, but that would be giving Jordie more power over her. She couldn't let that happen. He already had so much. She needed to take it back, but she was unsure how.

How did you stop loving someone?

Even if they were toxic for you.

When she heard the strum of a guitar, her head popped up in surprise since it was coming from Mena's room. She was supposed to be sleeping; Lacey had put her down hours ago. She glanced at the time to be sure and she was right, so what the hell was going on? Standing up, she opened her door and looked down the hall. Lacey was at the door, the music louder now, and soon Kacey was closing the distance between them to see what she was looking at. Before she could reach the doorway though, Lacey turned, stilling her with a look before pressing her finger to her mouth in a quieting motion.

Perplexed, she looked past Lacey to see Jordie standing beside the crib, a guitar in his arms as he played with ease. She didn't know he could play. How did she not know that? His eyes were closed as he softly sang "You Are My Sunshine" in what was honestly the sweetest way she had ever heard. It was so rustic, his voice blending so beautifully with the music he was making with the strums of his fingers. From where she was standing, she could see Mena Jane through the crib rails and she was just watching Jordie in awe.

Kacey was sure she matched her niece at the moment.

"He has done this for the last two nights. Mena loves it. She gets so quiet and just watches him," Lacey whispered to Kacey, but she couldn't tear her eyes off the sight before her. Something inside her just broke because that was supposed to be his baby he was singing to. She would have been due right around the same time as Lacey. They would have had a new little girl or boy of their own, but that wasn't the case. Instead, they had heartbreak and rejection. Two things that ate Kacey alive daily. When her lip started to wobble, she looked down at the ground, sucking in a deep breath.

Unable to watch any longer, she turned, starting down the hall, but Lacey stopped her with a hand on her arm. "He really has changed."

But Kacey shook her head. "No, that's Jordie. He loves kids, he's good with them, and he's a damn good man. But he'll never love me the way I love him. It isn't in his DNA."

Lacey went to say something, but Kacey stopped her. "Let it be, Lacey. I have to let go or I'll continually set myself up to be hurt by him."

She shook her arm from Lacey's and started for her room. Slamming the door, her tears fell faster as she headed toward her bathroom. Looking in the mirror, her lip quivered at the sight of how pathetic she looked. She looked so heartbroken and defeated. Why did she allow him to hurt her like this?

Turning the water on, she leaned over the sink, her tears mixing with the water that was running as she pulled in shaky breaths. Reaching for the hand towel that rested next to the sink, she wet it before washing her face free of tears. Holding it there, she allowed herself to sob into the warmth of the towel, and she hated herself for imagining it being the warmth of Jordie's arms. He honestly gave the best hugs. The kind of hug that you felt all the way in the depths of your soul. And boy, did it linger. She could still feel his arms around her, suffocating her in the most rewarding way. That was one of her favorite things about him.

His hugs.

But would she ever hug him again?

And why did she yearn to?

He doesn't love you!

That alone had another round of tears filling the towel until she heard the door open. She sucked in her cries as she heard him move into the bathroom. She knew it was him, their rooms were attached by the bathroom and, being the idiot she was proving to be with each passing second, she had forgotten to lock his door before she went in there. How was she supposed to hide the fact that she had been crying over him? Ugh, when were her parents going to be back so she could move in with them? Or maybe she could move in with Liam?

Or not.

She knew she needed to get out of this house though, which made her feel horrible because she was supposed to help Lacey. Instead though, Jordie seemed to be doing way more than she had been and that bothered her even more. She was family, he was only a friend. But even as she thought that, she knew it wasn't true. Her family loved Jordie as their own. That was another reason she loved him so much. Her father thought he was the greatest thing since sliced bread, and Karl King didn't like many people.

When she heard the water turn on in the other sink, she lowered the rag, washing her face free of the tears and snot, trying so damn hard not to look at him. But she failed miserably. He was staring at her as he put toothpaste on his toothbrush, his eyes dark and full of the desire she was sure stayed in his gaze. He always looked at her in such an intense and fulfilling way. Her heart stopped as her stomach clenched just from being under his gaze. Looking away, she folded the towel on the sink, reaching for her own toothbrush. She didn't want him to think he had any effect on her. She wanted to seem strong, but as she started to brush her teeth, she swore she could smell the coconut oil from his beard, and soon tears gathered in her eyes again. It was funny how one little smell or word or image could bring back a billion thoughts and feelings.

Another of her favorite things about Jordie Thomas was his beard.

It was her Achilles' heel.

The feeling of it along her thighs, her throat, her lips…she loved it.

She loved him.

When a lump of a sob formed in her throat, she tried to swallow but it wasn't happening. Spitting quickly, she washed her mouth out and then bent forward to wash her toothbrush, telling herself not to look at him. She could feel his gaze on every inch of her. It felt warm, perfect, but she knew it was bad. Jordie had a way of getting her naked—hell, he could do it to anyone and did, hence why he didn't need her any longer. She refused to be his simple fuck, but as she sat up, her eyes met his and everything went still.

Desire burned between them and soon her lips parted as he asked, "Are you okay?"

She didn't know what to say. She honestly didn't expect him to talk to her.

"No," she answered and she didn't mean to. Her eyes widened at her honesty as he nodded, his gaze holding hers in the mirror.

"Me either," he admitted and then wiped his mouth. "I would like to talk to you." She stared at him blankly, surely imagining this as he continued, "When you're ready, of course."

"Ready?" she croaked out and he nodded.

"You're still mad and probably hate me, with good reason—"

"I don't hate you," she whispered, looking down at the ground. "No matter how much I wish I did, I don't."

When she looked back up, he nodded. "Well, when you're ready to talk, I'd really like that."

Did she want to talk to him? Was this his plan to get in her pants and then break her heart again?

"Yeah, okay," she muttered in a snide way, but that didn't derail him.

"I really am sorry," he whispered but she shook her head.

"Yeah, I'm sure."

"No, really," he said, bringing her attention to his. "I truly am."

She didn't say anything. She didn't know if she could. His eyes held hers and she begged her resolve to stay strong. To ignore his sad brown eyes, his taut shoulders, or the way he looked like he had been through the wringer. She wanted to brush his hair out of his face, she wanted to comb his beard, she wanted to hold him. But she knew she couldn't. No matter how much she wanted to, she couldn't.

He doesn't love you. Snap out of it.

Looking away, she closed her eyes and soon she heard his door shut. Leaning against the counter, she covered her face and shook her head as the tears spilled onto her hands. It wasn't supposed to be this way. He was supposed to love her, she was supposed to be holding their baby, and she was supposed to be fucking happy.

Instead, she was in a heap of tears while her ex-lover, who she was still stupidly in love with, slept in the room next to hers.

Her boyfriend was begging for her love.

And her brother had no clue what the hell was going on.

It was easy to say that her life was a fucking mess.

"When did you start cooking?" Karson chortled as Jordie laid a plate of eggs and bacon in front of him. Lacey smiled as she switched arms with Mena Jane so she could eat. Mena was wide awake and alert, watching everything Jordie did. There was something about their relationship that was special. She loved him as he did her, but since the night before, it was hard for Jordie to look at her without thinking that he could have had a baby that looked just like her.

Just like Kacey.

Turning to put the pan back on the burner, he braced himself against the stove and pulled in a breath through his nose. He didn't sleep any the night before. He stayed up, reliving the last eight months. If he hadn't been so fucked up, he could be a daddy right now. Maybe he would have let Kacey in, maybe he would be married to her. But then, the more he thought about it, the more he knew he had to go through everything he had to be where he was now. He wouldn't have been a good man for Kacey. He might have been a good father, but even that wasn't certain. He needed the help he'd gotten. It was that simple.

Given the chance again, he wouldn't have left Kacey behind; he would have been honest.

But like Elli said, he had learned from his mistakes. Now it was time to make up for them.

Clearing his throat, he picked the pan back up and made Kacey a plate. She was running late this morning. Or avoiding him. In the past, they would share the bathroom, moving around each other, but this morning he didn't hear her door open until his shut. It sucked, but she needed time. As much as he was hurting, she was hurting ten times worse. He hadn't been there for her, she'd had to do it alone, and that really weighed heavy on his heart.

"I cooked a lot in Mountain Care," he said, speaking of the rehab center as he set her plate on the island. "I actually like it."

Lacey smiled. "Then please, cook away."

He sent her a grin, grabbing his own plate and sitting across from her at the island. As he shoveled his eggs into his mouth, out of the corner of his eye, he saw Kacey coming down the hall. That was the thing about Kacey. No matter what, he always knew when she was near. And when he caught sight of her short work-out shorts and black sports bra, he was sure he wasn't going to make it through training.

Not with that hot bod distracting him.

"Hey, Lacey, have you seen my Assassins work-out windbreakers?" she asked, walking through the kitchen, completely ignoring him. But he couldn't ignore her. Not with a body like that. She must have been training more than usual the last eight months because, holy fuck, she was ripped. He didn't remember those abs the last time he had her naked but, boy, did she have them now. Her arms, spectacular, her legs, strong as an ox, and an ass he could bounce a quarter off of. His shorts grew tighter as he drank her in, his fork paused at his mouth as she bent over to look in the dryer.

Thank you, Lord.

"I have no clue. Jordie's been doing the laundry," Lacey said before leaning over to kiss Mena.

"What?" Karson and Kacey both asked, their faces twisted in almost the same way. It sometimes freaked him out how much they favored each other. They were practically twins.

Lacey looked up. "What? He just started doing it."

"They are folded in your basket," Jordie announced, ignoring their stares. "Also, why should Lacey be doing laundry? She's still recovering and also fighting her own demons. You two need to be a little more thoughtful," he said, but he might as well have been growing a second head.

"You did laundry?" Karson asked and then glanced at Lacey. "Plus, I told you I'd do it today."

She shrugged but Kacey was still standing there gaping at Jordie. Snapping her mouth shut, she glared. "Don't wash my clothes."

For some reason, when she glared, she was the cutest.

Jordie grinned. "But I like checking out all your naughty girl panties," he teased, and Karson groaned while Kacey's glare deepened.

"Bro, come on, that's gross," he said, causing Lacey to laugh. It was nice to see her smiling and not crying. She had been taking her meds like she had promised Jordie, and he thought she was doing better.

"That's the only way you get to check them out," Kacey spat back, grabbing her basket.

He knew he should have left it alone. It was too early to tease and pick at her, but he couldn't help himself. He missed their banter, he missed her, and also he liked the little scowl she wore when she was irritated. Plus, Karson wouldn't expect anything else. Until Jordie was honest with him about Kacey, he had to play the part of Kacey's biggest pain in the ass. So, grinning up at her, he said, "For now."

Karson scoffed and Lacey chanced a glance at Kacey, shaking her head. But he could tell he had crossed the line. That she wasn't ready for their banter. Her mouth parted, her eyes went to slits, and he was pretty sure she was ten seconds from throwing the laundry basket at him.

But still, his grin was unstoppable. It felt like old times, and it was so refreshing that soon he was saying, "By the way, I made you breakfast."

Her jaw dropped, but she only faltered for a second. Stomping past him, she yelled out, "Stick it up your ass, JT."

He scoffed and called out to her. "But I made you sausage instead of bacon. I know how much you love my sausage."

She threw her middle finger up and slammed her door with the vengeance of a two-year-old.

"Jordie," Lacey scolded, and he shrugged.

"She's easy to tease," was his answer. But honestly, he couldn't walk on eggshells around her. He'd grieve, he'd apologize, but after that, he was ready to win back his girl. He was going to do everything to show her that he had changed. That he was ready to be the man she deserved, but he wouldn't lose himself. She loved his humor and he loved picking at her. He couldn't stop, no matter how much she didn't like him at the moment. She would get over that;

she would forgive him because he would do everything to earn that forgiveness. He'd never believed in happily ever afters. They hadn't been in his cards, but now, now he was ready for his.

But only if Kacey King was his queen.

"You're an asshole, and I'm pretty sure she's gonna make you pay for that." Karson laughed as he stuffed his face with bacon, and Jordie matched his grin.

"Probably," Jordie agreed, but he wasn't worried. While she may be in the bedroom, cursing him to Hades, at least she was thinking about him. That's what he wanted. He wanted her to remember the good times, and he was going to keep pushing them at her. Then he would beg for her to take him back.

Jordie had never begged a woman for anything, but he wouldn't hold back with Kacey.

He just had to wait for the right time.

When Jordie reached the training center for the Assassins, he was home.

Within moments of walking in the door, all his boys were greeting him, manly hugs were a must, and Jordie couldn't stop smiling if he tried. This was his home and these men were his brothers.

"Great to see you," Tate Odder, the goalie for the Assassins, said in his thick Swedish accent. "Long time."

"Yeah, it's great to be back. How's Audrey and the kiddos?"

Tate's face lit up at the mention of his beautiful family. After their first child, they couldn't get pregnant with the second child they so desperately wanted. But after some fertility treatments, they welcomed a little boy, Phillipe, this past summer. He was a preemie, but from what Jordie saw on Facebook, the little guy was getting stronger every day and everyone was very excited.

"Penny and Philly are good, very good. Audrey is wonderful too," he said, nodding his head, that look of complete bliss on his face. "You, how's the leg?"

"Great, I'm ready to rock," he said just as Phillip Anderson cuffed him hard on the shoulder.

"JT, bro! You look like hell run over twice," he laughed and Jordie grinned.

"I'm hitting up the barbershop after this. You know I don't trust anyone but Billy Ray with this gorgeous mug," he said, flashing his teeth, and Phillip laughed.

"If you can walk. Man, Karson's sister is sadistic," he said in a mock whisper. "She scares me."

"But man, she has hands like a dream. My back's been tweaking, but she rubs it out great," Erik Titov said, and Jordie could definitely get behind that statement. Kacey did have great hands. Strong, and she knew how to work them. A chill ran down his spine at the thought, and he decided that he needed a nice rubdown by her.

"Good to see you, JT," Lucas Brooks called at him and Jordie shook his hand with a nod, but before he could say anything, a large hand came down on his shoulder.

Looking over, he saw his captain and smiled. "Hey, Cap."

Shea Adler nodded, squeezing Jordie's shoulder. "Hey, Thomas, ready for the season?"

He nodded. "Yeah, absolutely."

"Awesome, it's good to have you back. Despite looking like a bird is making a home in your beard, you look good. Healthy."

Jordie smiled as his cheeks grew a little darker. He wasn't sure what Elli had told him about the night before, and it was hard to look into Shea's eyes. But Jordie did it, nodding his head as he said, "Yeah. I feel that way."

"Awesome, Elli said you're joining us at church on Sunday? The boys are excited for Uncle Jordie to show up," he said with a proud grin. Shea loved his kids, probably more than life itself. For sure, hockey, because rumor was that this was Shea's last year. It was really a bummer, but at the same time, Shea wanted to be home with his kids. Elli was busy with the team and raising the whole Adler clan, and she was doing a stellar job at both, but it had to be nice to have some help. As much as no one wanted to see Shea go, they knew where his priorities were.

"Yeah, me too." Jordie beamed.

"Jordie? What, you found Jesus, bro?" Phillip teased and everyone chuckled but Shea and Karson. They both just smiled as Jordie nodded.

"You can say that."

Phillip laughed along with the guys. It wasn't a secret that Jordie wasn't too keen on praising the Lord. All of them had invited him to church on previous occasions and Jordie had quickly declined, so it didn't bother him that they teased him. For the longest time, he was convinced the church would burn down and the roof would open to the good Lord above shaking his finger at him if he ever stepped foot inside. But he soon learned that wasn't the case.

"Crazy," Erik joked as Lucas laughed.

"Busting your leg apparently did you some good, eh?" Phillip asked and Jordie shrugged.

"Guess so."

"Shit, next thing you know, you'll tell me you're sober or something," Lucas said. And the guys all laughed since that was comical; who would ever expect Jordie to stop drinking? Jordie noticed that Karson and Shea had gone mute, both of them looking at Jordie with sympathy in their eyes. Probably waiting for his next move.

"Yeah. I am."

The laughter stopped as they all gaped at him. Again, it was a shocking statement. He was pretty sure he'd been drunk seventy percent of the time he was with the guys. He was the life of the party, they had a good time, but he would have to learn to do that without alcohol.

He could do it.

"Hundred and eight days sober," Jordie said slowly with a nod of his head.

He was proud of that number. It wasn't a year, but he would get there and he would ignore that he had almost ruined it all last night.

"And we are fucking proud, Thomas," Shea said, cupping his shoulder. "Everything in the past is the past. We are looking forward now. Strive to be better than you were yesterday and you'll succeed. Especially with all us busting your chops to be the man we know you can be."

With that statement, he knew that Elli had told Shea about the night before. Instantly, Jordie felt two inches tall, but then, his words were very uplifting too. Shea was the kind of man every man strived to be. No one wanted to be looked down on by Shea, and he hardly ever did it, but when he did, you felt like shit for a day. To know that he was behind Jordie though, it really meant a lot. It told him he wasn't as alone as he'd thought when he first embarked on this journey.

Reaching out, Lucas grasped Jordie's shoulder, shaking it hard. "Way to go, bro. Keep it up."

Soon all the guys were saying the same thing, hugging it out and shaking hands hard. It felt good to know that they knew. He had been wanting to tell them, but first he'd wanted to get out of rehab, get healthy, and he had. Now he was ready to live the life he wanted. For that to happen, he needed Kacey in it.

Where was she anyway?

"Good, come on then, boys," Shea said, smacking his hands together. "Let's get in there. Oh, but first! Let's welcome the rookies," he added, and everyone turned to see where nine guys and a girl stood.

Whoa, wait, a girl?

Shea rambled off names, not that Jordie was listening until he got to her. Baylor Moore. The girl Elli drafted this past summer. Usually, they sent the newbies down to the farm team, so that said something about Baylor. That Elli believed she could hang with the big boys. Jordie was actually excited to see this go down. A lot of the guys looked at her sideways, but that didn't keep Baylor from standing proudly under all the scrutinizing gazes. At that moment, Jordie decided he liked her.

"Everyone ready?" he heard Kacey call, but he couldn't see her through the sea of big hockey players. Even the chick was tall and strong.

"Okay, let's get in the training room. Kacey has some torture to inflict,"

Shea called, and everyone nervously chuckled as they started for the training room while Kacey laughed.

"Only enough to make you puke," she said as everyone gathered around her, and she was all smiles. Well, that was, until she looked at him. Her eyes held something between disgust and hatred and maybe a little desire, but he didn't care. He drank her in with no reservations at all. Karson was used to him checking out his sister; he may not like it, but Jordie did it anyway. She was wearing those naughty shorts and, man, they did something to Jordie's equilibrium.

When she bent over to demonstrate a station of dead lifts, he took notice that she was lifting over a hundred pounds...and then the fact that she really did have a great ass. Watching her, he let out a long breath, trying to rein back in his desire, but then noticed that a lot of the guys were staring at her the way he did. Soon his chest was puffed out and his scowl was deep as he glared at each of the single guys. A few of them noticed and quickly looked away, but one, Liam Kelly, who Jordie was sure was gay, was staring extra hard.

What the fuck?

He decided he needed to have a talk with Kelly, put him in his place, but soon Kacey was releasing them, breaking them up in pairs for each workout. He was put on the dead-lift station with Shea, and like the boss that Shea was, he added some weight to the bar and dead-lifted with ease. When it was Jordie's turn, he went to the bar, scooped it up and then shrugged.

He could do this.

But when he went to lift it, it wasn't budging.

Or maybe not.

He blamed this on the fact that he'd just started lifting again two weeks ago. Before that, he was doing laundry and cooking and trying to stay sober. He ran a lot, but there had been no lifting going on.

"It's fine, Thomas, take some off," Shea said, helping him remove the weights, but then Kacey stopped by the two of them.

"What are you doing? That's only two hundred and five. You can lift that with one hand," she snapped and Jordie looked up at her.

"Not anymore, took some time off," he said offhandedly, dropping it down to the weight she lifted.

"Are you kidding me? That's pathetic," she sneered and Shea glared over at her.

"Hey now, no need for that," he said, but Jordie stopped him.

"Maybe so," he agreed, because it was pathetic. It should have never happened, but he hadn't been strong enough to say no to the bottle. Not that he was going share that with Kacey in a room full of his team.

She took a step toward him, her brown eyes burning into his as her mouth dripped with venom. "No 'maybe so' about it. Maybe if you weren't fucking everything with tits and drinking yourself stupid, you'd be ready for this season. I hope you're ready to work, because my job is to get you ready, and I don't fail at anything I put my mind to. Oh, well, except you. I failed at you, huh?" she said in a low whisper and Jordie just held her gaze. He could feel Shea bursting at the seams, but there was no way he was breaking their intense stare-down.

"I am ready," he said calmly, even though his heart was jackhammering against his chest. "And you didn't fail me, Kacey. It's the other way around."

Her eyes narrowed and she shook her head. "Whatever."

She walked away but then paused, looking back at him. "I know you can do one-fifty. Do that at least."

He nodded. "10-4, boss."

She gave him a snide look and walked away, shaking her head, and he was pretty sure she was two seconds from blowing her top. Shea stole his attention though when he asked, "What the hell is her problem?"

Jordie looked over and scoffed. "I fucked that girl over. I deserve everything she throws at me."

"Are you sure? I can get her fired. I'm sleeping with the boss, and she loves you probably as much as she loves the kids," he reminded him and Jordie smiled.

"I know, and yeah, I'm sure," he decided, bending down to get the bar. He didn't think he could do it at first. But to his surprise, he was able to pull it up and hold it before lowering it down and then back up for the recommended ten reps. As the weights hit the ground, he looked over at Shea. "I'm gonna win her back, and if I get her fired, that might throw a wrench in my plans," he said with a wink, but Shea didn't smile. He made a face, crossing his arms. "What? What's that face?"

He looked around and then glanced back at Jordie. "You know she's dating Kelly, right?"

Jordie moved closer because surely he had heard his captain wrong. "Excuse me?"

"Yeah, they've been dating for a while now," he added and the world closed in.

No. Fucking. Way.

Jordie's heart jumped in his throat as he gasped, "Gay Liam Kelly?"

Shea scoffed. "Obviously he isn't gay since he's screwing her."

Jordie felt as if he had been hit as he whipped his head to where she was standing with Kelly. He watched as Kelly reached out, smacking her butt playfully, and everything went red. Pulling in a deep breath through his nose, Jordie's shoulders went back and his chest puffed out as he turned to find Karson. Surely, Karson wouldn't allow this to happen!

When he found Karson, he walked toward him, but Jordie's eyes never left them as they flirted back and forth. It was way more one-sided on Kelly's part, but Kacey was flirting too. He also didn't miss the way she kept looking back, probably hoping that he was watching. It was such a chick move, but he couldn't blame her. If she had done to whim what he had to her, then he would be pulling all the moves to show her he had moved on. But he knew damn well it wasn't going to work.

Kelly was a damn pussy.

Kacey needed a man who had some rough edges. Someone who could make her laugh and feel beautiful. And also fuck her like a dream. That dude. No. Seeing them together actually made Jordie want to puke. They just didn't go. He was too light, she was too dark, plus she could probably lift him over her head while eating a can of spinach. Liam Kelly was not the man for his girl.

For the simple reason she was *his* girl.

Obviously.

Karson glanced up at him from where he was bench-pressing and gave him a look. "What?"

"You're allowing your sister to date Kelly?" he snapped, and really, it was surprising. Karson didn't let anyone date his sister without throwing a fit, and since Jordie hadn't heard anything until now about Kacey being with that pussy, he knew that Karson was cool with it.

Karson scoffed. "She's a grown-ass woman—"

"Nope, try again," he said, knowing good and well that that was a lie. Karson was the extremely scary, overprotective big brother. God help Mena Jane when she wanted to start dating. Jordie and Karson would constantly be cleaning guns.

Laughing, Karson shrugged. "He's a good guy. He would be good for her."

"Um, no. He's a fucking pussy," he snapped, and Karson laughed along with Lucas.

"Yeah, he is," Lucas agreed and Jordie pointed at him.

"See!"

"Yeah, but he won't hurt her," Karson said then as Lucas took the bar. "She needs a rebound guy. Apparently she's been hitting some duds in the dating pool. Last guy fucked her up, but this dude can show her how she should be treated and then she'll move on. It won't last, believe me."

Jordie's face twisted. "That is the stupidest thing I've ever heard. That dude is a douchecanoe and you know it. He says 'excuse me' when he passes the other team on the ice. He's a girl!"

"Hey!" Baylor said and Jordie grinned.

"My bad," he said quickly. "He's a fucking big mountain of rubber dicks!"

They all laughed, but Jordie didn't find this funny. "So what, Jordie, want me to go break them up?" Karson asked.

"Yes," he said simply. "She deserves someone better."

"Like you?" Lucas laughed and Karson's eyes cut to him.

"Um, no. Jordie knows better," he explained, and it was like a bag of rocks dropped into the pit of Jordie's gut.

Biting the inside of his lip, he knew he did know better, but Jordie rarely followed the rules. He was a rebel and proud of it. He may have cleaned up his act, but this was one thing he couldn't budge on. He sure as hell didn't like lying to his best friend, but like he said, Karson didn't mess around when it came to Kacey. She was his first baby, and Jordie knew his limits. If only he could warm Karson up to the idea. Get him to see that he could be the good guy that Kacey deserved. It wouldn't be easy, but he would succeed.

Because loving and being with Kacey was the one rule of Karson's he made a vow to break the day he left rehab, and he planned to break that rule daily.

No matter who the hell she thought she was going to date.

Because she was his.

And that was final.

Chapter NINE

Jordie was surprised he could move.

Shea wasn't kidding when he said Kacey was going to inflict pain. She had basically killed them, then add in the hour of ice time, and it was easy to say that Jordie's legs were Jell-O. He'd never felt better. It was what he lived for and, man, he loved it. Despite mean mugging Kelly through most of the workout, and maybe slamming him into the boards, he enjoyed his day. Loved it.

But the whole Kacey dating Kelly thing set his teeth on edge. That was probably why he went so hard. Not only was he trying to impress her but he was trying to bottle his hatred and anger toward Kelly. He wished he had been warned. He'd never expected her to stay single—she was a catch, he knew that—but at least knowing she was with someone else would have been nice. Finding out the way he had really fucking sucked. He looked like a dumbass in front of Shea and he didn't like that. He did have his pride, but he knew he had to put all that in the past. It was done, she was with some other prick, and it was time to get his girl back.

And he would win.

As he drove toward Billy Ray's Barbershop, he got out his phone and called Lacey. He couldn't believe she hadn't told him. Shouldn't that have been something worth mentioning to him?

She answered on the second ring, Mena Jane in the background cooing and probably being adorable.

OVERTIME

"Hey, what's up?" Lacey asked. Happily, he might note.

"Oh, nothing much, just the fact that you never told me Kacey was dating someone," he said as calmly as he could, but it had been bothering him since Karson confirmed it. The sick part of him, the hopeful part, kind of wished that she would never find anyone. That she would wait for him. But the realistic part of him knew that was selfish and unfair. She needed to be happy, and maybe if he were honest with himself, maybe he was too late. She could have moved on, and if so, who was he to mess with her happiness? She seemed pretty chummy with puss-face, and if that was who she wanted to be with, maybe he should leave her be.

But why did thinking that make his face scrunch up and his heart drop?

"Oh, about that," she said in a very apologetic way. "I'm pretty darn sure it won't last."

"Didn't think you should tell me about it?"

"Well, you see… What had happened was, you were so gung ho and, like, honest and stuff that I thought, why should I derail you? I really don't think it will last between them. I don't think she is into him. I think she is using him to get over you."

He made a face as he pulled into the parking spot he always parked in. It was the front space, right in front of the window that said "Billy Ray's Barbershop." He had been coming here since he'd first come to Nashville. It was his spot and Billy Ray was known for classy beard care. It also had a very retro feel. There was even a barber's pole, which Jordie thought was supercool.

Turning the truck off, he leaned back in his seat, looking at the roof of the car.

"Not helping, Lacey," he moaned.

"Well, it's true, and honestly, they aren't made for each other."

"I know this, you know this, but she wants it to work. I saw them together."

"And? They aren't cute together. At first I thought so, but the more I watch them together, it doesn't feel right."

"But it might feel right to her," he said sadly, twisting his beard around his finger. "Maybe I should just let her go? She's obviously let me go."

It wasn't as if he had even really done anything to let his feelings be known. For all she knew, he just wanted friendship. Or sex probably, since that's how they started. Yeah, he had messed with her, said he was sorry. But that didn't say I love you. It was just the way he was. He was always apologizing for something, and Lord knew he loved messing with her. But he hadn't been honest with her and he was unsure when he could be. Should he do it now, knowing about Kelly? Or should he wait it out? One thing was for sure, he knew he couldn't rush into this. He had to get her to believe in him again—in them—before he admitted to loving her.

90

Man, why was this so hard?

"No, don't. She hasn't let you go. I know she hasn't."

"Then what do I do?"

"Pursue her! Woo her!"

Jordie's face twisted in confusion. "Okay, first, isn't that wrong when she has a boyfriend?"

"Well, yeah, it's kinda sleazy."

"Which is something I'm trying not to be," he reminded her and she made a little noise. "Been there, done that, trying something new."

"True, but I'm serious, I give them a week at the most. Especially after Karl and Regina come to town. He's coming to dinner, and you know Karl hates all guys but you and Karson. She cares so much about what he thinks. She'll drop him and, boom! You swoop in."

"Those drugs are working well on you," he said dryly and she laughed.

"Yeah, I really do see life in a different light. It's supercool."

"Very true, almost like being sober, I guess," he agreed.

"I bet," she giggled and Jordie grinned.

"But okay, let's say I wait, and I will 'cause she's the girl you wait for. But then, please explain to me, what in the ever-loving fuck do you mean by 'woo her'?"

"Seriously, Jordie?"

"No, really, I have no clue what that is."

"Woo her! Buy flowers and chocolates with little hearts taped to them. Like court her?"

"Lacey, come on. We live in the twenty-first century," he deadpanned. "Do people even woo anymore?"

"The men who want their women do! Karson is great at wooing." She pointed out. "I love his wooing."

"Because he's a pansy-ass," he mumbled, but before she could say anything, he laughed. "No, but really, what do I do?"

"I don't know, like, be romantic and shit."

"What's the shit?" he asked, confused.

Before she could answer him, Mena Jane started to cry and Lacey fumbled with the phone. "Crap, let me call you back. She just exploded shit all over me."

"Joys of motherhood. I'll see you at home," he said before they both said bye and he hung up. He was two seconds from Googling "wooing" when he glanced at the time, noticing that he needed to get inside. It was hard to get an appointment with Billy Ray, and he didn't accept lateness. Rushing out of the truck, Jordie made it inside with the bell ringing, just in time.

Billy Ray looked over at him and grinned. "JT, long time, buddy."

Billy Ray was an older guy in his mid-sixties, but acted as if he was in his early thirties. He was bald with dark black eyebrows and a beard that went to his chest. The guys always teased him for not being able to grow hair on his head but only on his face. He didn't care though. He rocked that beard and nothing held the guy back. He was also an Assassins' season-ticket holder, and everyone went to Billy Ray. He was a good dude and cut hair to perfection.

Wrapping him up in a manly hug, he squeezed Jordie tightly before they parted. "Where ya been? No calls? No flowers? Do I mean nothing to ya?"

Jordie grinned. "Busted leg and then a stint in rehab, hence why I look like Jesus on the cross, as my buddy's wife said," he admitted. And unlike everyone else, Billy Ray wasn't the least bit surprised. He didn't laugh or give him a look of disappointment. He just nodded.

"I always knew you'd end up there. You just had to realize you needed help."

"Wasn't me. Elli made me."

"Or she'd make you," he said with a grin before tapping the seat in front of him. "Ya look like hell."

"True, but I feel good," Jordie said, sitting down. "But yeah, I look like hell 'cause I won't let anyone touch me but you."

"So attached," Billy teased, putting the towel around Jordie's neck. "So ya glad you went?"

"Very much so."

"Good boy, I'm proud of you," he said, running a comb through Jordie's hair. "So tell me everything; I have a lot of hair to cut and shape up."

He then went to work as Jordie told him about his leg, getting healthy, Mena Jane, and moving back home. He left out Louisiana, mainly because he was embarrassed by it. Like the amazing barber he was, Billy Ray commented on some things and just listened to others. As time passed, Jordie watched as the old Jordie soon looked back at him. The only differences were his eyes were brighter, he didn't look like death, and he didn't feel like it either. He was feeling like the person he wanted to be.

Now, he just needed the love of a good woman.

"Just a regular clean hairstyle? Or you feeling frisky?"

Jordie grinned. "Let's do a Mohawk this time."

"Frisky it is," Billy Ray agreed before going to work. "How's that girlie girl of yours?"

Karson made a face. "I told you about Kacey?"

"Um, yeah," he said, looking back at him in the mirror. "Man, were you drunk all the time?"

"Basically," Jordie said with a laugh. "But things are a little up in the air."

"Really? You seemed pretty smitten with her."

"I was, but I lied to myself and pushed her away," he said, closing his eyes. He then explained the whole thing, thankful that the shop was completely empty. It was embarrassing enough to think about his mistakes; admitting them was much worse. When he finished, Billy Ray was standing there, the clipper by Jordie's head as he stared at him in the mirror.

"So you knocked her up and then ignored her?"

Jordie nodded.

"Man, you did mess up," he said, simply shaking his head. "I wouldn't take you back."

"Me either," Jordie agreed and Billy Ray laughed.

"But if she's anything like my Sarah, she'll forgive you and take ya back."

He grinned as he met the old man's wrinkled eyes. "Oh, yeah?"

"Oh, yeah," he agreed. "Sarah, man, she forgave me for the shittiest things. I was a bad guy when I was younger, into those drugs and drinking, bad. I never cheated, but there were a few times where she could have assumed I did. But still, she loved me. Never gave up on me. As soon as our little Amy came into the world, I cleaned up and then loved her extra hard for dealing with me for so long. Now, she says she has the best husband, and in return, I say I've always had the best wife," he said with a little grin that brightened his eyes.

"Sounds like a real strong, good woman you got there."

"The strongest. I asked once what made her stay, and she told me that you never give up on the person you can't go a day without thinking about."

"Wow," Jordie said, a little bit in awe. He wanted that. The undying, stay together through thick and thin kind of love. If he wanted that with Kacey, he had to fight for her. Or woo her, as Lacey said.

Hey. Wait.

"Hey, Billy Ray, you know what wooing is, right?"

Billy's brow rose. "Yeah, I woo the hell out of Sarah. Still to this day."

Jordie's grin grew. "Good. I need some wooing advice."

He laughed. "Hoping to woo her away from the guy she's with and into loving yer sorry ass again?"

"Maybe not woo her away, but rumor is it won't work, they aren't meant for each other. And when that does happen, you're damn right I'm gonna woo the shit out of her. I'll do anything to get her back."

"Have ya thought about just telling her how ya feel?" he asked and Jordie shrugged.

"Figured I've always been about talking and making promises but never following through with them. I thought if I showed her how I felt, wooed her a bit, and *then* told her my feelings, it would work better."

Billy Ray nodded as he brushed the hair off Jordie's shoulder. "Good plan, I like the way you think."

Jordie laughed as he nodded. "Thanks, now hit me with that wooing."

"All righty now, listen closely, boy. I'm about to give you some winning advice, and I won't be repeating myself."

He wouldn't expect him to, but Jordie did pray that Billy Ray's advice would win Kacey back. It was honestly killing him knowing that she was with Kelly and not him. Yeah, he understood that he was late to the game, only realizing now that Kacey was it. But surely she hadn't given up on him fully. So Jordie would wait, because good things come to those who wait. But he hoped it didn't take long.

Because Jordie wasn't known for being patient.

Kacey dragged herself into the house after a long day of training and massages and then an evening of meetings. When she'd started this job, she'd thought it was going be an eight-to-noon job, but she soon realized that the Assassins' training team worked seven-to-eight in the weeks before the season started. It was intense, but she'd be lying if she said she didn't love it. She loved the guys, minus having to work with Jordie, and enjoyed the staff. They were a family, everyone was. It was fun, and she looked forward to her future with the Assassins.

But she was really looking forward to the beer she had been thinking about all day.

Because she needed it.

Watching Jordie struggle through her exercises was downright disgusting. He was better than that; she had seen him at his best before his injury. He could squat the most of the team, but today, not so much. Even the new girl was squatting more than he was. Kacey knew she needed to remember his knee was still getting used to everything, but had he been sitting on his ass for the last eight months? She knew his PT guy was hard on him, so what the hell had been going on?

It killed her not knowing where he'd been and what he had been doing. She knew she could ask him, but she was sure it would lead into them "talking," something she was not ready for. She wasn't ready to hear about all the reasons why he couldn't love her but that he was sorry for all the pain he caused. She knew that was what he would tell her. It was the same story, yet she always fell into his tangled web of lies and deceit. And somehow, she still loved him!

She needed to go therapy or something because she was downright pathetic. No one should feel the way she did when she looked at him. She was like a sick little puppy, begging for a home and family, thinking Jordie was the answer to all her needs. She felt so many emotions that she found herself struggling to contain them. One minute, she was happy to see him, she missed him. But then she was instantly mad because he'd left her in his dust. Desire filled her belly because she wanted him more than her next breath, but then she felt stupid for feeling anything for him but a need to kick him in the balls. She just didn't understand any of it.

Most of all, why was she still with Liam when she continued to feel all of this for Jordie?

God, Liam was a whole other issue. After walking her out to the car that night because, of course, he had waited for her to get done with her meetings, he'd given her a kiss on the cheek and told her he'd see her the following day. She'd actually stood there, shocked. Jordie would have thrown her on top of the car and done her right there. No cares that anyone could find them, because his desire was so great. She missed that. The anytime, anywhere kind of longing that hit her straight in the core. She had no clue what she was going to do, but she needed to figure it out. It wasn't fair to anyone. Especially Liam. But still, her fear was that if she did break up with Liam, would she fall victim to the whirlwind that was Jordie Thomas?

She was clueless, but maybe he had changed his ways. Maybe he could love her because, hello, he cooked and did laundry. Two things Jordie had never done before…which again made her mad. Where had he been? What had he been doing? And why hadn't he wanted her there? It was so frustrating, but Kacey was quickly learning that her life was a big ball of maddening things.

Shaking her head, she parked her car beside Lacey's and headed in with her gym bag hanging loosely on her shoulder. Entering through the back like she always did, she found Lacey at the island, making a bottle.

"Hey," she said happily as she shook the bottle.

It was like night and day with Lacey. If anyone had said Lacey would be grinning while making a bottle a week ago, Kacey would have laughed in their face. The girl was screwed up and had been since about day three of Mena being home. But according to Karson, she was finally taking her meds. She had even texted Kacey that she went to her After Breast Cancer meeting that morning, which was huge. After Mena arrived, she claimed she didn't need the group, when really, she did. So the fact that she was going made Kacey's heart a lot happier and her nerves a bit calmer.

"Hey, you. You look great. Did you shower?" Kacey teased, throwing her gym bag down.

"Yeah, I told you I went to my meeting today," Lacey reminded her and Kacey nodded.

"Oh yeah, did you take Mena with ya?"

"I did, and they all just gushed over her. It was wonderful," she boasted before turning just as Karson entered with Mena in his arms. Taking the bottle from her, he kissed her cheek.

"You're superhot," he muttered against her lips. "Better be careful, I might try to make another baby."

Kacey gagged as Lacey giggled. "Um, we can practice, but we aren't having another one till Kacey has one," she said with a huge grin at Kacey. "So get busy, lady."

Kacey scoffed. "Gotta find a man first."

Karson rolled his eyes. "And I'm out. Mena Jane, boys are stupid, but please don't end up like your aunt with a billion cats watching a stupid movie about a hill," he said as he walked away.

"It's *Notting Hill*, asshole, and I don't have any cats 'cause I don't like them!" Kacey called at him, but he was too busy cooing to Mena Jane. "Your husband is a dick."

"Hey, he was your brother before he was my husband," Lacey pointed out with a grin before grabbing the sweet tea out of the fridge. She offered a glass to Kacey, but she shook her head.

"Hand me a beer, please," Kacey said, pulling out the chair and sitting down, letting out a long breath.

"We don't have any," Lacey informed her, and Kacey's head whipped up just as the tea was placed in front of her. "We have tea, water, and Gatorade."

Kacey made a face. "Where's the beer?"

"Gone. No beer or any kind of liquor in the house."

"Why?"

"Because there is a baby here," Lacey said simply.

"Okay? I promise I won't feed it to her!"

"No alcohol in my house," Lacey said sternly. "Now drink your tea, it's classier anyway. We are Nashvillians now. We have to be classy Southern bitches."

Kacey glared as she swigged her tea. "Classy girls don't say classy bitches."

"This one does," Lacey said and she took a sip of her tea with her pinky up just to show she meant what she said.

"Dork."

"Hag," she said with a wink. "So how was your first official day?"

Kacey leaned on her hand, letting out a long sigh. "Would be better if I could have a beer."

"Go to a bar then," Lacey suggested and Kacey shook her head.

"Rather not."

"Then suck it up, cupcake. Run a bath or something," she said and Kacey shrugged.

"Which would be ten times better with a glass of wine."

Lacey ignored her and asked, "What made it so bad?"

"Jordie," she answered simply and Lacey's brows rose in confusion.

"What did he do?"

"Nothing," she moaned. "Everything."

Lacey leaned on her hand, obviously confused. "I don't understand."

Kacey let out a breath and shook her head, her voice lowering as she leaned in closer to Lacey to make sure that Karson didn't hear them. "He's everywhere. In my home, in my gym, and in my head, twenty-four seven! I don't know what to do, because one second I want to slap him, but in the same second, I want to kiss him."

"Oh," Lacey said, leaning back some, her brows still raised to her hairline. "I thought you liked Liam?"

"I do," she moaned. "But I don't know. It's more curiosity where Jordie's concerned, I think. Like today, he couldn't do a simple dead lift without taking a lot of weight off. That's not Jordie. He could lift a house, he's so strong and burly. It made no sense. Like what the hell has he been doing? I know his PT guy was hard on him and worked him like a dog, so why isn't he in shape? It's driving me crazy and I want to know."

"Then ask," she suggested and Kacey shook her head.

"I don't want to know, but I do," she admitted, tracing the brim of her glass. "He told me last night that he wants to talk."

"Okay? So talk. It would be good for you to get the closure you want."

She nodded. "I know, but I think if I do, I'll fall for him all over again. He has my heart, Lacey."

Lacey reached out, lacing her fingers with Kacey's as she smiled. "Then why are you with Liam?"

"'Cause he's safe. He won't hurt me."

"And Jordie will?"

"Exactly."

"He's changed."

"So you've said," Kacey said, leaning back and untangling her hand from Lacey's. "If so though, how? Why? What was he doing? What woke him up?" When she met Lacey's knowing gaze, Kacey pointed at her. "You know why!"

"No, I don't," she tried to lie, but Lacey couldn't lie.

"Yes, you do! Tell me!"

"No way," Lacey said, folding like always. "I can't. Please don't try to make me. I love you, Kacey, I do, but I promised to keep it a secret. If you want to know, you ask him."

Kacey scrunched her nose up and glared. "But I don't want him to tell me, because he'll guilt me with those eyes, and I'll be head over heels all over again while he's just looking to screw."

"You don't know that. Maybe you should give him a chance."

"No, I know him. More than you. He doesn't do relationships, which is what I'm in the market for."

"Okay, if you know all that, then why are you worried about it? You are way too concerned with him for someone who is dating someone else," Lacey pointed out and Kacey's glare deepened.

"Shut up and you know why. He was really my first true love. It's hard to get over that. I'm trying, but it's hard."

"Because you believe in him."

Kacey didn't answer as her eyes clouded with tears. She didn't believe in him. She knew the real Jordie—he just piled all kinds of cocky-ass behavior and bad choices on top of himself.

"You know, that's how it was with Karson and me. I never stopped loving him," Lacey said, looking out into the living room where Karson was sitting with Mena Jane cuddled into his chest. Looking back at her dipwad brother, Kacey's heart skipped a beat. She'd always known he was going to be a good daddy. He took care of her like she was his. Sometimes it was annoying, but she still was thankful for everything he did for her. She respected him and looked up to him. He liked Liam, approved of them, so she knew what the best thing for her to do was. But for some reason, Jordie wouldn't get out of her head.

"I can't trust him," Kacey said then, bringing Lacey's attention back to her. "He hurt me so bad. Broke me."

"I know," Lacey said with a nod. "And, believe me, you don't owe him anything. I'll be the first to tell you that, but I would talk to him. I would see what he has to say and then make your decision after that."

Kacey eyed her, knowing that Lacey was up to something. Or maybe the meds were making her loopy. "You know what he wants to talk about."

"Maybe," Lacey said with a sly grin.

Why did that piss her off? "When did you two get so close?"

"When I saw the real Jordie, the good Jordie. I think if you gave him the chance to show him to you, you'd forgive him."

"I have forgiven him. A long time ago. But I can't let go of him. No matter how hard I try."

"So maybe that should tell you something," she said and shrugged. "Or keep dating Liam and see how that goes. Either way, I just want you to be happy, Kace. That's all."

"I know," she moaned, dropping her head to the island. "I just want to be happy."

"Then follow your heart," she said just as the back door opened. Kacey didn't have to turn to know it was Jordie. Plus, Lacey greeted him with a bright grin and said, "Hey, Jordie! Whoo-weee! Someone went and saw Billy Ray."

Sitting up, Kacey turned in her seat, and it really took everything out of her not to turn into a puddle of goo before sliding off the chair and just dying. It was downright wrong for someone to be as fucking hot as Jordie Thomas was. Standing before her in a thin gray shirt and athletic shorts was the man she fell in love with so long ago. His beard was trimmed up to perfection, not too long or short, just perfect and shiny. His hair was in a badass Mohawk and he was simply beautiful. She'd always thought he was the most gorgeous man she had ever seen—and she still thought that. But at that moment, she could see how much weight he had lost.

God, what happened to him?

Looking away to keep the tears at bay, she turned in her seat, biting her lip and wishing that things had played out so differently. That she was the one wearing a grin and running her fingers through his beard, holding their child while being indescribably happy. It was a dream, one that she had thought was within her grasp, but apparently, she hadn't wished on the right star. Fucking Disney really set her up for failure.

Getting off her stool, she went into the living room where Karson and Mena were. He was just getting up as she entered, and she held her hands out.

"I was gonna put her to bed," he informed her.

"I can," she offered and Karson shrugged.

"I do need to take a leak," he said before handing her Mena.

"Nice to know," she muttered as she gathered Mena close and then headed down the hall to her room. Taking her to the changing table, she got her ready for bed in her "I Love My Auntie" onesie before laying her in her crib. Mena was wide awake and didn't look like a kid who was ready for bed, but it was well past her bedtime.

Running her finger along the curve of the baby's cheek, Kacey whispered, "I hope when you get older, you don't have to deal with heartache. But I'm pretty sure you will, and let me tell you, it sucks. But you just come to Auntie Kacey, okay? We'll watch *Notting Hill* and eat lots of ice cream together. No matter what, I promise I'll always be there for you, Mena Jane. Always."

Mena flung her limbs in agreement and Kacey smiled. "Well, at least I have a partner in crime. Now, you go to sleep. I'm gonna go watch *Notting Hill* and eat ice cream for the both of us since your mother won't let me drink. You should talk that over with her. Auntie needs her booze." Leaning over the crib, she kissed Mena's forehead. "Love you, Mena Bena. You're my favorite niece in the whole world."

Mena just stared at her and Kacey felt a bit guilty for leaving her, but it wasn't like Mena was very social. Putting on her mobile and her nightlight, she walked out of the room and cracked the door before heading to the kitchen. As she walked through the living room, she noticed that Karson and Lacey were outside on the patio with the fire going. Popping her head out, she said, "Mena is down, and I'm about to go to bed too."

"Thanks, I'll turn the baby monitor on. Night," Lacey said, pulling it out of her pocket and doing as she said she was going to.

"Night," she said before shutting the door and heading to the kitchen. Grabbing her pint of cookie dough, she headed back to her room. After turning on her TV and setting her ice cream on the bedside table, she changed into her PJs and went to the bathroom. It was steamy when she entered, and she assumed Jordie had just taken a shower since his door was shut.

Sitting on the toilet, she thought for a second that she should lock the door. But there was a ledge, he wouldn't be able to see her using the bathroom. Plus, she would scream at him to leave before he would know what was going on. When she was done, she went to the sink to wash up, when from around the corner Jordie came out of the shower, rubbing his head with a towel and a razor in his hand.

With nothing around his waist.

Blinking dumbly, her jaw dropped as he threw his towel on the counter to clean out his razor. She hadn't seen him naked in months and, like before, she was positively breathless. His body was toned, not like it had been before, but the definition was there. Her mouth promptly went dry. As her eyes drank him in, she took in the body she had worshiped for those four amazing months. His arms were covered in tattoos just the way she loved, each one distinct and all him. He loved stylized skulls and had a few along his arm. They coexisted with a pin-up girl wearing a hockey jersey that hung off her shoulder. Roses took up most of the rest of the spaces on his arm. It was all black and gray and beautiful. Along his hip, he had a huge three with a hockey stick shooting a puck. He had gotten it when he was eighteen. His first tattoo. It was her favorite.

The hair on his chest was short from where he had shaved. She usually liked when he left it long, but that wasn't what she was looking at for long. His cock was hanging there, looking fucking delish, and she didn't know what to do. All kinds of images came to mind as her stomach clenched with want. The first time they'd had sex was against the very sink she was standing in front of, and it had all started when he came out of the shower naked.

But that would not happen again!

"Um?" she gasped, and he looked over at her blankly.

"Yeah?"

"You're naked."

He looked down, turning to her and nodding. "Yeah, I just got done showering and manscaping."

Of course, that caused her to look down at where he had, in fact, done a wonderful job manscaping around his huge cock. She gripped the sink, sucking in a breath as his grin grew.

"Looks good, right?" he said proudly, and she was speechless.

Utterly speechless.

"Okay, well, I'm beat. You kicked my ass today," he said, completely unaffected by her gawking. "I'll see you tomorrow. Good night."

He turned, heading for his room, his perfect, thick ass for all the world to see, and Kacey could not speak. She was stunned into silence. Was this really happening? Also, why was it taking everything out of her not to grab his ass?

When he reached the door, he turned and looked at her.

"By the way, Kelly is a big mountain of dildos. You could do a lot better."

She could only blink at him, but he waited for a response, which was very unlike him. Usually, he'd say something and then shut the door so he wouldn't have to hear her take. But this time, he waited, and that stunned her just as much as his huge monster of a cock did. Oh, and his statement.

Finally finding her voice, she spat out, "Why do you care?"

"Because I care about you."

He again waited for a response, but she had nothing. She knew this was the part when she should ask where he had been, why he had cut off contact. But instead, she just shook her head. She couldn't do this right now. She was exhausted, mentally and physically.

"Well, stop," she demanded, but Jordie was the one shaking his head.

"I can't," he said softly. "I won't."

Before she could say something, though, really, she wasn't even sure what that would be, he said, "Good night, Kacey."

And shut the door, ending the conversation.

Staring at the door, Kacey was unsure what had just happened. But she was sure she would never get the image of his cock out of her head. And if she were honest, she would admit that she hadn't ever since she'd last slept with him. But none of that mattered. What did matter was what he said: I can't. I won't. What did that even mean? He apparently didn't love her. Didn't want her. But what if he did?

Letting her head fall back, she swallowed hard and told herself to pull it together, that he didn't love her. But a small voice inside of her whispered,

Maybe he does.

Letting her head fall forward, she looked at her reflection, and she shook her head. As she took in her flushed face, her eyes that were full of bewilderment, she decided she had no clue who or what Jordie Thomas was. She had not the slightest idea, and that meant she really needed to go to bed and eat her ice cream. At least she understood Ben & Jerry's.

But before she could step away from the door, the strum of a guitar stopped her. It was faint, so of course, being the nosy one she was, she got closer. Her nose pressed to the door as the music fought to reach her, causing her heart to race. It was as if the music was getting louder and she worried that he would open the door, but he didn't.

When Jordie's low, rough voice started the lyrics to "Draw Me a Map" by Dierks Bentley, she closed her eyes, leaning her head against the door as his voice burst through the wood and washed over her. Each word of the song hit her square in the chest, and it gutted her. The words could be applied to them easily, but she wouldn't read into it. She loved this song, he knew she loved this song, and he was singing it to her. Hoping she heard it. But she couldn't tell him she had.

She had to let this go. Jordie wasn't the man she wanted. He didn't love her the way she loved him. She had to just walk away. But her feet wouldn't move. And as the tears streamed down her face, she had no clue what she was going to do.

Chapter TEN

Leaning against the wall outside of the massage room, Jordie played on his phone while he waited for his turn. He probably didn't need a rubdown, but if it meant Kacey touching him, he was there. She had been doing everything to avoid him; she wouldn't even look at him while they worked out each day. When they were at the house, she acted as if he wasn't there. He still picked at her every chance he got, just for her to acknowledge him, but it wasn't enough. He needed more. It had been three days since he'd walked out of the shower in his birthday suit, and she still hadn't looked him in the eye.

He didn't know if he should chalk that up as a good thing or bad.

She wasn't usually this quiet. She told him what she thought at all times and didn't hold back. He was unsure what that meant and didn't know how to proceed with her. Was she really happy with Liam? He honestly didn't believe so. Especially with Lacey chirping in his ear that Liam was no competition. A part of him wanted to leave her be, let her be happy with someone else, but the selfish part of him wanted her with only him. Forever. He could be the one to make her happy, he believed that now. He just needed the chance.

He had spoken of her at his AA meeting the night before, and everyone urged him to wait it out if he really believed she was the one. The problem he was having was that he never did share well with others. Kacey was his. He just needed her to remember that and leave Liam in her dust. He also didn't understand why she hadn't asked him what he wanted to talk about. Anytime he brought it up, she'd basically run. It was really weird and out of character for her. It was as if they both had changed from the shitty breakup, and he wanted nothing more than to know the girl he'd hurt. To mend the wounds he'd caused and love her more than she could ever imagine.

He just needed the chance.

Turning the Snickers in his hand that he had gotten for her, he waited for Shea to come out. It was a ballsy move to expect her to rub him down after the intense workout she'd inflicted on him, but Jordie was a lot of things, ballsy being one of them. He was craving her touch like a crackhead craved a hit. He needed it, and if this was the only way he could get it without crossing the lines of her relationship, he'd do it.

He knew she wouldn't cheat, nor would he ask her to. One of the many reasons he'd never gotten into a relationship was because he couldn't *not* cheat. It was in his blood; his mom was notorious for it. But now, after everything, he knew he would never do that to anyone.

Especially not Kacey.

He wanted her, his happily ever after. And after everything he had been through, changing himself completely, sobering up, he saw things in a different light. His mom issue was still loud and clear, but he was working on it. He wasn't done with himself. He still had a lot of work to do, but the great thing about Kacey was that she wouldn't hold him back—she'd lift him up. And he needed that lift from her. He was ready. At least he thought he was. Hoped he was. Prayed he was.

Letting out a long breath, his nerves getting the best of him, his phone vibrated with a text.

It was Natasha.

Natasha: What's up?

Tucking the Snickers bar in his pocket, he typed her back.

Jordie: Nothing much. About to get a massage.
Natasha: Mm. Sounds like fun.
Jordie: It will be. U?
Natasha: Nothing much, just saving people.
Jordie: You do it the best. Make sure not to get trapped in the shower with a hockey player with a busted leg. I hear they are trouble.
Natasha: haha. Trouble, indeed. But no worries, you're the only hockey player I'll blow in a shower.

Jordie grimaced a little. He'd kind of brought that on himself, but he was trying to be funny. Trying to keep it light with her. He liked his friendship with Natasha, but lately, ever since he'd told her about Kacey and the baby, she had been coming at him hard with sex. Basically serving herself up on a silver platter for him. Old Jordie would have jumped in dick first, but new Jordie had his dick and mind set on another.

> *Jordie: Good to know.*
> *Natasha: Want me to come and visit? Meet in a shower? At least the busted leg won't be a factor this time. We could do new things.*

Well, then.

> *Jordie: As great as that sounds, I told ya I'm trying to get Kacey back.*
> *Natasha: Yeah, but I thought she's ignoring you, dating someone else? Why wait for someone that doesn't want you?*

He hated when she did that. Turned hateful when things didn't go her way. She was a prideful woman, he knew that, but he'd never promised her anything. He hadn't promised anyone anything. Hence why he'd pushed the girl he loved away.

> *Jordie: So? That won't stop me. You know how much she means to me, I want her to be mine.*

When she didn't text him back right away, he shook his head, tucking his phone back in his pocket. He valued their friendship—she was a godsend through rehab—but he had to be honest. He wouldn't lie to her and lead her on. Pulling his phone back out, he checked it for a text, but nothing. Letting out a long breath, he texted her once more.

> *Jordie: Don't be mad. I'm trying to be honest.*
> *Natasha: Whatever. She wasn't there for you and I was.*
> *Jordie: Because I didn't allow her to be.*

He waited but nothing. Yup, she was officially pissed. Shaking his head, he tucked his phone into his pocket and figured that he wouldn't send her an invite to his and Kacey's wedding. He was pretty sure Natasha wouldn't come.

Hell, he wasn't even sure Kacey would come.

Ugh. The drama.

"Who you waiting on?" Karson said, bringing his attention up from his phone.

"Kacey," he answered and Karson nodded.

"Awesome. I don't have time to wait, so I'll get Dave, mainly since the thought of my sister touching my groin is gross."

Jordie snickered since he thought quite the opposite. "Maybe for you."

Karson gave him a sideways glance. "Don't be a douche. But on that note, what's going on with you two? She won't even look at you or anything. You two used to be two peas in a pod, messing with each other and flirting and shit. You piss her off?"

"You could say that," Jordie mumbled, and he knew that it was the time to come clean. Tell Karson that he loved Kacey, but this wasn't the time or place. He really needed to sit down with him and apologize for hurting his sister. He wanted to wait until she was on his side, but he may need to do it before. Because he felt like shit lying to his best friend. Shrugging his shoulders, Jordie said, "Probably. You know how she is."

Karson laughed just as Dave came out, beckoning him in. "She's as prickly as a cactus for sure, but don't be an asshole to her. She's emotional as shit lately. See ya at the house."

Jordie nodded as Karson disappeared inside before taking a deep breath in. Karson would flip his shit if he knew that Kacey was being emotional because of his stupid mistakes. Maybe he should have told him right there, just for the fact that there would be more witnesses.

Because he was going to need them.

Just as he went to pull out his phone, Shea came out, stretching his arms over his head. He looked over at Jordie and then pointed at him.

"We still good for Sunday?"

Jordie nodded. "Yup."

"Good, Shelli is begging to see you."

"Can't wait," he said with a grin.

"Okay, you're up. See ya tomorrow."

"Bye, Cap," Jordie called as he went in. Kacey's back was to him as she washed her hands. She was wearing some wind pants and a tight black tank, her hair in a mini little ponytail. He liked that she had grown her hair out—she looked gorgeous no matter what—but he liked to have something to pull when he was pounding into her. He always lost his grip with how short her hair was before.

"Lie down, I'll be with yo—" She stopped when she turned, seeing who was awkwardly standing in her doorway, and her eyes narrowed.

Jordie quickly held his hands up, showing the Snickers. "I come bearing gifts, and plus, I really need my leg rubbed down. And who better than the girl who helped rehab it a bit."

She wanted to say no, he could see it in her eyes, but then her eyes fell to his leg and the Snickers and he knew he was in. There was a commercial for the chocolaty goodness that said, "You're not yourself when you're hungry," and that was Kacey. He always said she got "hangry" all the time. You had to feed the beast or she would eat you. Plus, she couldn't say no to food.

Shaking her head, she said, "Fine, lie down and don't talk. Put the Snickers on my desk."

"Yes, ma'am," he said, doing as she said before removing his shorts. Lying bellydown on the table, he watched as she continued to wash her hands, working her lips. He hated how worried she looked, almost as if it were taking everything out of her to be there with him at that moment. He loved how easy it was before. They'd only had to look each other and they'd know. But back then, it was too much for him to handle. It was scary how easy it was to be with her.

He hadn't been ready.

But he was now.

He went to say something but then remembered she didn't want him to talk. Biting his lip, he watched as she grabbed a pair of gloves, which confused him.

"What's up with the gloves?" he asked and she sent him a look.

"I refuse to get slut on my hands," she snapped back. "And didn't I tell you not to talk to me? Because I don't have to do this."

"You don't have to be so bitchy about it," he grumbled and her head fell to the side.

"Oh, I don't? Maybe you should have thought about that before you took my heart, threw it on the ice, and then slap shot it against the boards. Blood, guts, and pride flying through the air."

Yup, she might as well have hit him. Her eyes said so much. Held so much pain. Nodding, he swallowed around the lump in his throat. "Great hockey analogy."

"I thought so," she agreed, coming to the table and then pressing her hands to his thigh. He was expecting her touch to bring back the greatest memories of his life. Instead, the gloves basically ripped out the hairs on his thigh as she started to move her talented fingers along his tired muscles. "Now, shut up."

"Before I shut up, can you lose the gloves? They are ripping the hair out of my legs." He grimaced, twitching side to side, trying to get away from her hands.

"Oh, does it hurt?" she asked condescendingly, twisting his leg hairs under her fingers.

"Yeah," he said flatly. "Lose them and the attitude. You're acting like a scorned teenager."

Her hands stopped and then he was hollering out in pain. "Dammit, Kacey!" he cried out, covering the spot where she'd just ripped out a chunk of his hair with her hand.

She looked at him innocently before dropping the chunk of hair. "Oh, my bad."

He only glared as she pulled the gloves off before throwing them in the trash. "You better hope I don't get slut on me."

"You won't," he promised as her fingers dug into his skin, and a certain kind of peace fell over him as a sigh left his lips.

"Don't make promises you can't keep," she reminded him, and he looked over his shoulder at her.

"I promise you won't get slut on you," he said sternly and she rolled her eyes.

"Whatever. Stop talking to me, please," she said with a sigh before getting to work on his leg.

Watching as she moved her hands along his thigh, down by his knee and then his hamstring, he admired her beauty and the little wrinkle her nose was in. She was frustrated with him, a normal occurrence. Her shoulders were taut, the veins in her skin visible as she moved her hands along his leg. She was so strong, so gorgeous and…not his.

"So tell me about your boyfriend," he said, using the word loosely. He could tell she was trying way too hard with the douche. He knew what she looked like when she was in love. He'd stared into those love-filled eyes for months, trying to ignore them, and then ultimately pushing them away.

She glanced up at him and glared. "No."

"What? Scared I'll get my feelings hurt?"

"You don't have feelings, Jordie. You're allergic to them," she said simply, her hand digging deeper into his skin.

He smiled, covering the grimace that was surfacing. She did her job great, but she had always been a little rough. "That's not true. I have feelings for you."

She paused and looked up at him. "Wanting to fuck me may be a feeling but not the feelings I want."

He held her gaze. "Oh, you want them all right, you just don't like that you do."

"You know nothing about me," she sneered, tearing her gaze from his. "And you know nothing about my relationship with Liam. He's a good guy, I like him."

"Maybe, but you don't feel an ounce of what you feel when you're with me."

She looked back up at him. "That's a bold, cocky statement."

"I'm nothing but bold and cocky."

"And a heartbreaker, a liar, and a deceitful pig," she informed him and he smiled, not letting any of that bother him. That was old Jordie. New Jordie was none of those things…. Well, maybe a pig because he sure did have a hard-on just from the feel of her hands.

"I always thought you loved the pig in me?" he teased and she glared.

"I did, but the other two, plus the rejection, are a little hard to forget," she said coldly. "Liam is none of those things. He is sweet."

"And a fucking pansy. He won't ever fuck you like I can."

She didn't even flinch, she only held his gaze. "Probably not, but at least he won't break my heart," she said quickly, her eyes diverting down to the leg she was working on. "And in case you didn't know this, I'm not looking for a fuck. That boat has sailed. I'm looking for forever."

So was he, but he wouldn't say that when she was with someone else. Instead, he laughed before saying, "And you think that asshole is forever?"

"He could be," she snapped back, and that only made Jordie laugh harder.

"Sugar thighs, if he is your forever, then I don't know you at all," he said and she looked back at him. Her eyes were full of so much sorrow and pain that it took his breath away.

"Yeah, you're right. Because if you knew me, you'd know I thought you were my forever. But you smashed that dream quick, huh?"

That hit him square in the chest, leaving him breathless as she held his gaze. Slowly he sat up, turning out of her hands, unable to keep it in any longer. He had to tell her that she was his forever. Yeah, he'd wanted to wait until doucheface was out of the picture, but she had to know that he felt the same. That he did know, he'd just tried to fight it.

He had to tell her now.

"Kace—"

"Hey, babe, you almost done?"

Jordie held her gaze despite the interruption of Liam. He begged her with his eyes to tell Liam to go somewhere, but when he saw the tears gather in her eyes, he had to look away. Call him a coward, but when that girl cried, Jordie felt smaller than a flea.

"Yeah, fine, Jordie was just leaving," she said, looking toward the wall. "Let me clean up and I'll be ready to go."

"All right, baby," he said, then looked to Jordie. "She has great hands, right?"

Jordie swallowed his explicit retort and glared as he hopped off the table, grabbing his shorts in the process.

Looking back up at him, he said, "Fuck off, Kelly."

Well, he tried to swallow it.

"Jordie!" Kacey scolded, but he ignored her as Liam sputtered, looking like a complete doofus.

Jordie then turned to Kacey, grasping her shoulder as her eyes met his, still full of tears. Holding her gaze, he said, "I do know you, and I'm sorry it took me so long to say that."

Her eyes widened as she shook off his hand, her eyes turning to slits, but the sadness in them still blinded him.

Instantly, he felt incomplete.

She was what he needed to feel complete, but she had a barrier the size of the Great Wall around her heart and he was the one who helped build it.

But what goes up, must come down.

And Jordie was going to bust right through that fucking wall and get his girl.

As Jordie walked out, his shorts in his hands and his shoulders back and taut, Kacey wanted nothing more than to curl up into a ball and cry. Alas, her boyfriend was standing in the doorway, hopelessly confused. She knew she needed to say something, anything. But not only could she not move for the simple fact she was worried she'd chase after Jordie, but she couldn't get his words out of her head.

I do know you, and I'm sorry it took me so long to say that.

But really, why did Jordie have to say things like that? It made her hope that he was being true. That he really meant it. But if he did, then why did he throw her to the side the way he did? Why was he messing with her? Fucking with her head!

But really, why did she fucking care!

She had Liam. And he was…

Ugh.

"Um, Kacey, what is going on?"

Drawing in a deep breath through her nose, she just wanted a moment. Just one. To breathe and figure out her next move. A part of her wanted to demand to know what Jordie was saying, the other part of her was scared to know. She knew Jordie, knew what he wanted from the opposite sex, so what the hell was he saying? She just wanted to know, but at the same time, she didn't. Letting Jordie in again would be a huge mistake. One she couldn't afford to make.

She needed to just ignore him. Completely shut him out the way he did her. She had a good man who wanted her. She needed to stick with that because Liam wasn't capable of what Jordie was. He also didn't make her feel what Jordie did, but that was beside the point. She needed to stay clear of Jordie and try hard to fall for Liam. Her mother would love him, so would her father, she just knew it. She just had to let him in. Stop holding him at arm's length and enjoy a man who actually wanted her and the things she did. It was so hard to find a man nowadays, and she was getting older. She couldn't let him go. Not yet. Love grew, it did. And it would for her.

Turning to do damage control, she could not only to see that his face was twisted in confusion but also that he had brought her a bouquet of wild flowers.

Ugh, she didn't want any more flowers.

Shit, that made her a bitch.

Fuck, she was trying to stop cussing.

Shit!

Shaking away her thoughts, she placed a smile on her face. "Oh! My fave," she said, coming toward him and taking the flowers. Smelling them, she grinned up at him and then kissed his lips softly. "Thank you."

She turned, taking them to her desk, where four other bouquets were there to brighten her day. But when her eyes fell to the Snickers that looked out of place, it was what brightened her day. Jordie knew that she loved food. That it was the way to her heart. She actually hated flowers, not that she had told Liam that.

Turning back, she threw him a grin and said, "So I think you've filled the quota for flowers this week."

His brows were together as he crossed his arms over his chest. "I asked you a question," he said sharply for the very first time.

Her brow rose. "And I'm choosing to ignore it."

"Why?" he demanded.

"Because I don't want to talk about it."

"But I do."

"Well, I'm sorry, but I don't."

He gave her a deadpan look and then asked, "So I'm just supposed to ignore the fact that my teammate told me to fuck off for no reason at all, while you stood there almost in tears?"

Kacey nodded. "Exactly. If you want to chase after him and ask him why he said that to you, be my guest, but my issues with Jordie are off-limits."

"Why?" he asked again. "Do you two have history?"

Letting her head fall back, she sucked in a deep breath and then let it out. "I don't want to talk about it."

"Well, I think you need to start talking because I'm upset. I feel like you're hiding something from me, and I don't like that," he said impatiently. But didn't he know that that sentence would have meant so much more if he'd added a few curse words?

She snapped her head back up and glared. "I don't have to talk about anything I don't want to talk about."

He held her gaze, his beautifully sharp, angled face in such twisted confusion. This was the first time she had seen him upset. He was kind of cute. Like a mad little puppy.

"That's unfair," he said, his voice calming a bit. "I just want to know the truth. I don't need details, but when I ask a question, I expect it to be answered. I'd do the same for you. Out of respect."

She shoved her hands in her pockets and looked away, annoyed. She didn't want to do this. She knew she was being a bitch because of what Jordie said. But also, if she didn't want to share about her and Jordie, why did she have to? Liam wasn't her daddy, but the way he was looking at her, like she did owe him a damn answer, made her realize that this was the way he operated. That if she wanted this to work, she'd have to bend a bit. He was the guy she was hoping would be her forever. The more she looked at him though, the more she knew Jordie was right.

But she wouldn't let him win. This would work. Liam was her forever.

Ugh, that didn't even sound right.

Rolling her eyes, she said, "Yes."

He held her gaze. "You and Jordie?"

She nodded. "Yeah."

"What happened?"

"That's details," she snapped. "And I'm not sharing."

His eyes went to slits, but then he looked away, sucking in a breath. "Why?"

"Because I'm not ready to."

"Is he the last guy? The one who broke your heart?"

Her lip trembled as she looked down at the floor, her breathing labored. She had forgotten she had told him that. "Yes."

When Liam closed the distance between them, she was surprised when he wrapped his arms around her, hugging her tightly. Tilting her head back with his forefinger, he looked deep into her eyes as he pressed his forehead to hers.

"I would never break your heart," he whispered, his breath hot against her lips.

Gazing into his eyes, she knew that he spoke the truth. There wasn't a heart-breaking bone in his body. He was a good guy. Sweet. Perfect. Everything she needed but nothing she wanted. But what she wanted would always break her heart, and she couldn't be his victim anymore. Not when Liam was begging for her love. She'd be an idiot to let him go.

"I know," she whispered back, her eyes falling shut, waiting for his wanton kiss, but it never came.

"I'm sorry I pressed for information. I just don't want you to be sad."

"It's fine, kiss me," she demanded, but instead of his lips, his thumb traced her bottom lip.

"Kacey, do you know how much you mean to me?"

She opened her eyes and said, "No, but kiss me and show me."

He smiled. "A lot, and I'm glad you trust me not to hurt you, because I won't."

She looked at him expectantly, but he just kept brushing his thumb along her lips, not kissing her, and it felt so forced. Jordie wouldn't even talk this much, he'd kiss her stupid, letting his body and hands do the talking. Instantly, she was disgusted with herself. She had this good man wanting to talk and be sweet, and she was thinking of a foulmouthed asshole who broke her heart.

What the hell was wrong with her?

"I'm excited to meet your parents. I'm sure I'll love them."

"Yeah, they'll love you," she said on a sigh. "I can't wait."

He sent her a sweet grin and then pressed his lips quickly to hers.

The kiss was over before it started.

No fireworks, bombs, or sparks.

Nothing.

Just a pressing of the lips, and as he pulled back, his eyes bright, he said, "Me neither."

And Kacey decided that she was unsure how long she could keep trying.

Because no matter how badly she wanted him to be, Liam Kelly was probably not for her.

Chapter ELEVEN

Kacey was doing everything in her power to avoid Jordie.

Everything.

But it was not working.

Coming out of the shower, she reached for her towel, wrapping it around herself, but when her eyes set on two round, bare butt cheeks, she groaned.

"Do you not know how to cover your ass up?" she sneered when she passed by a naked Jordie as he trimmed his beard. She tried so hard not to check out his buns, the perfect cut of his hips, and the muscles in his back, but she was having no luck at all. His body was a wonderland of muscle and skin—two things that really turned her on. She knew damn well he did this to drive her crazy; he knew she liked him naked.

A lot.

Turning, he leaned his hip against the counter and shrugged. "I never covered up before," he said it so matter-of-factly, it set her teeth on edge. "Not a peep came out of that mouth of yours in the past."

Glaring, she held her towel tighter to her body because he was, in fact, very right, and she'd also foregone anything to cover up her own body.

Easy access.

"That was back when we were doing it. Now, it's inappropriate."

His brows pulled together. "It is?"

Flabbergasted, she struck her hips with her hands. "Um, yes! I'm dating someone!"

"Someone you aren't happy with," he said mildly, his gaze not leaving hers.

"You don't know that," she snapped back.

"Don't worry, I won't tell anyone so that you can keep on acting like you do."

"I do!" she yelled, but he just laughed.

As he looked over at her, his lips turned up a bit as his eyes darkened. "Okay, answer me this: when you kiss him, do you think of me?"

"You're disgusting," she sneered. "And you're delusional. I don't think of you at all."

"Yeah, sure." He scoffed. "Y'know, the sooner you realize that he isn't for you, the better."

Her brows actually touched and she was almost speechless. Was he on something? Sputtering, she yelled, "Better for who?"

"Me," he said, and that time, she was speechless. But before she could even process what he was saying, he cocked his head toward her. "Also your tit is hanging out. Might want to tuck it back in before I touch it," he said, causing her to look down in horror to see that her tit was indeed hanging out.

"You pig!"

With a naughty grin, he looked over at her, sending chills down her back. "Oh, sugar thighs, remember, you love the pig-like qualities I have."

When he winked, her resolve almost cracked wide open. Crying out in frustration, she slammed her door and stomped to her dresser to get dressed. She swore that steam was coming out of her ears! He was positively evil and a royal pain in her ass. All week it had been like that, teasing and picking at her like they were buddies. And they definitely were not. He also kept saying little things like that. The kinds of little things that she practically had held her breath to hear before. But now, he was saying them left and right, and she didn't know what the hell was going on!

She didn't understand his game. But she was pretty damn sure she saw him naked more than dressed, and she worked with him for two hours a day. He was always prancing around with his cock out for her to gawk at, causing her, against her better judgment, to be hot and bothered. Thank God, Liam wasn't putting out because there was a good chance she would imagine Jordie instead of him.

Which was a whole other issue.

She really needed to let him go.

The more time she spent with Liam, the more she knew he wasn't it. Or maybe he was, but Jordie's cock was beckoning her to the dark side. She really wasn't sure, but it was all a fucking mess. Liam was doing nothing for her, and she felt as if she was doing what Lacey had said. She was grasping at straws. Trying to make something work with someone just to keep Jordie away. He knew she wouldn't cheat, unlike Jordie. She was insanely loyal, but it wasn't right what she was doing. It also would mean that Jordie would be right, and she hated to allow that. But she had to stop lying to everyone and herself. Because she didn't love Liam. Not even in the least.

But hell, he was coming to meet her parents that day.

They were coming in to visit since they were dying to see Mena Jane and they still hadn't sold their house. Apparently Karson and Kacey were chopped liver because all that mattered was their firstborn grandbaby. A part of Kacey was jealous that Karson had given them that precious gift. She knew good and well that her parents would be smitten with all their grandbabies, but she'd always thought she was going to be the one to give them their first.

But she was stripped of that chance.

Letting her head hang, she bit into her lip, trying so hard not to cry as her mind wandered past the closed door and straight to him. Like it always did. All week she had wondered what Jordie wanted to talk about. Would he speak of the baby more? Would he apologize more? She had already forgiven him, not that she had told him that. But it was driving her nuts not knowing what he had to say. She couldn't even focus on Liam because she sat there and thought up all kinds of different scenarios.

The girl she was before Jordie broke her would have pestered him for the info. But now, it scared her. She knew that she would crumble for him and allow him to wiggle his way back into her life. He would say everything she wanted to hear, get in her good graces, and when she finally thought they were good, marriage and happiness in sight, he'd remind her he only wanted a fuck buddy. That was Jordie. Great man, but allergic to the full spectrum of a human relationship with the opposite sex.

It was honestly so unfair, but that was him. He almost made her feel weak, and she knew that wasn't something she could allow to describe her. She was a strong-willed girl, but Jordie was her kryptonite. But maybe if she went in eyes wide open, she'd be fine. She would be able to keep her heart on lock. She had done so well working with him. Mainly, she ignored him and flirted with Liam to reiterate that she was happy without him. Which was all a lie, but he didn't know that. No one did; they all thought she was pleased as a peach, when really, she was a rotten, hole-filled apple, worms eating away at her soul because she didn't have Jordie.

Why did she want him so badly? What was this hold he had on her? And most of all, what would it take to get rid of her feelings for him? Was it because she hadn't really been with anyone but him? He had been only her third lover, and honestly, he blew the other two guys out of the water. When they were together, sparks just flew in the bedroom. They fit perfectly and that lingered in her heart. The feeling of his body against hers, the way he would look in her eyes… It was all-consuming and she missed it.

But his rejection still stung.

It stung so fucking badly.

She wasn't sure she could get past that.

She didn't know how to. Maybe she did need the closure that Lacey had spoken of. Maybe she did need to talk to him. But could she trust her heart to know his lies? She had no clue and that scared her more than seeing the blood in her panties only three days after finding out she was pregnant. And that not only scared her, it hurt, which was something Jordie continually inflicted on her. She'd be stupid to fall into his bed of lies, but her heart was slow to realize that.

One thing was for sure, he needed to stay clothed and stop playing with her head. He didn't want the things she wanted, so why say little things like that? He was obviously jealous of Liam. He wouldn't even talk to the guy and never had a kind look on his face when Liam was in the room. And that made no sense. Why would he be jealous when he'd had her and had thrown her away? It was all a clusterfuck of fucking crazy, and she knew what she had to do.

She had to talk to him.

Really talk to him. Not the snide, angry comments and the roll of her eyes. She needed to give him the chance to speak to her the way he'd been asking to. Then she could let him go. Move out and live her life. Maybe then they could live as civilized people. Or they'd rip each other's clothes off and she'd feel like shit afterward. Closing her eyes, she let her head fall forward as she shook it. She didn't know what; she just needed something to change. She felt like she was constantly drowning in the tension and that had to end. It had to. First things first, she needed to get through this visit with her parents. Maybe something would spark with Liam while she watched him interact with her parents?

One could hope.

After blow-drying her hair, she headed toward the kitchen to help Lacey with food preparations. Her parents should be getting there soon and so should Liam. Kacey wanted to make sure everything was almost done so that Lacey could enjoy time with her in-laws and she could force some feelings for Liam.

So pathetic.

As she entered the kitchen, she saw Jordie go out the back door and her brow rose.

"Where is he going?" she asked before she could stop herself. He wasn't her responsibility. It shouldn't matter where he was going.

But it did.

Lacey looked over at her from where she was cutting up apples, a little smile pulling at her lips. "He's going to church with the Adlers, and then they are gonna do lunch and stuff. Welcoming him home."

"Church?" she asked, her face scrunched up. "Like the holy house? Real church?"

Lacey nodded. "Yeah, he's been going for a while now."

What? Jordie hated church. "Really?"

Lacey smiled. "Really."

"That's weird."

"I think it's nice."

Kacey rolled her eyes; she hated how big a fan Lacey was of Jordie. Even after everything he did to Kacey. Yeah, Lacey didn't know about a lot of it, but still. It was kind of shitty. She was Kacey's sister-in-law, best friend, and shit. Shouldn't she hate him like Kacey tried to?

Pissy, she slammed down in her chair. "But Ma and Dad are coming in." She pouted because he always claimed her parents as his. Shouldn't he want to be here to see them? When Lacey raised a brow, Kacey shrugged. "What? I'm just saying."

"You're pouting. And why? I thought he didn't matter?"

"He doesn't," she muttered, rolling her eyes again and then looking to see what she could do. There were bags of food everywhere and a list of everything Lacey was making.

"Sure, he doesn't, but your parents are coming last minute, and he's had these plans with them for a while. Elli even invited all of us, but we already had company. He's gonna skip dinner to eat with us."

"Whatever," she muttered as she started to make a salad. "He isn't any concern of mine."

"Of course not," Lacey shot back, her knowing green eyes locking with Kacey's. That was until her phone went off. Glaring at her phone, she picked it up and shook her head, a disgruntled look on her face.

"Everything okay?"

"No, Rachel is pissing me the hell off!" she snapped, speaking of her sister-in-law who lived back in Chicago and ran her store there. She frowned as she typed back violently.

"Just fire her!" Karson called from the other room. Kacey looked back and hadn't even realized he was lying there with Mena Jane on his chest. She quickly worried that he'd heard her speaking of Jordie, but he would have said something if he had, so she smiled as his face filled with annoyance. "She's a bitch."

"I agree with him," Kacey said, hooking her thumb toward him. Rachel had done nothing good for Lacey since she married Karson. The chick was hard-set on ruining Lacey's marriage and even plotted with Lacey's estranged dad. Lacey needed to add Rachel to the list of people she didn't talk to anymore, because the chick was a huge bitch. Always so damn demanding and acting entitled to anything that Lacey had.

It was really annoying.

Lacey let out a long breath, letting her hands fall against the island. "She's pissed 'cause I won't bring Mena up to Chicago. But I just feel like that's such a big trip for a little bit like her. Also, I know she is setting me up so that my dad can see Mena. I don't want to see him, and I really don't want him in Mena's life. He doesn't even love Karson, so how is he going to love Mena?"

Kacey nodded. "True, but I mean, he is a grandpa, and we know my dad would kill anyone who tried to keep his grandbabies away from him. But you are her mommy and you know best," she added when Lacey glared.

"I haven't talked to him in over a year."

Knowing when something wasn't her business, Kacey nodded. "Then forget I said anything."

Her phone dinged again, causing Lacey to roll her eyes. "She's such a bitch! She is calling me selfish now."

"Why doesn't she come here?"

"Because I won't let my dad in the house. At least there, I'd go to her house and, oops, he'd just show up."

"What did Grady say?" Kacey asked, speaking of Lacey's older brother.

"He says he's staying out of it, but he'd like to see Mena too. I said, y'all are more than welcome to come here, and he said he'd see what he could swing, but Rachel is fixed on me going there."

Kacey didn't know what to say, but even before she could, Karson was saying, "Not only is she being a bitch to you, she's being a bitch to everyone at work and just shitty all around. Fire her and then stop talking to her."

"She's my sister-in-law, Karson!"

"So? She's insane."

"I won't get to see my nephews though," she said sadly, and Kacey bit the inside of her cheek, thankful that she and Karson didn't have these problems. They were solid.

"Sure, you will," he said, sitting up, cuddling Mena. "Grady will make sure of it, and just be nice to her when you need to."

"Yeah," she said softly, picking the knife back up to continue cutting the apples as Karson closed the distance between them.

"I mean, it's your decision. It's your family, and no matter what, I love you. But please do something. I don't want anything dulling your sunshine, especially since it just came back," he said before kissing her temple.

She smiled over at him, kissing his lips and then Mena's head. "I know, I'll work it out."

"Cool, I'm gonna go change this little lady and get her ready for Grandma," he said, bouncing her in his arms.

"Make sure to put her in the little Assassins dress Audrey made her."

"Will do. We need to get Mena Jane a little jersey. Yes, we do, with Daddy's number on the back," he cooed as he headed out of the kitchen, leaving Kacey to grin like a fool while Lacey giggled.

"He's a sucker for that little girl."

As Karson disappeared into Mena's room, Kacey couldn't help but think that Jordie would have been a sucker for their baby too.

Ugh, why was she thinking of him?

"Yeah," she agreed, her mind still wandering toward Jordie and how life would have been so great if he hadn't pushed her away. It was something she did often and she knew she needed to stop, but it was hard to break a habit.

What she needed was to get out of this house. The farther away from him, the better.

"I think I might start looking for a place," she said then, surprising not only herself but Lacey.

"Yeah?"

"Yeah, you're good now. You don't need me, not that I was much help since I really didn't understand what you were going through."

"You help me plenty, just being here," she said fondly, and Kacey smiled.

"Well, thanks, but, er… Would you hire me?" she asked when she realized she needed more money to move out.

"What? Really? Of course, but why?"

"'Cause while my job is awesome and amazing, it doesn't pay enough for me to live around here, and I want to be close to you guys. I saw some condos down the road, and maybe I could move there."

Lacey worked her lip as she threw the apples in the bowl before covering them with sugar. "You don't want to wait for your parents?"

Kacey shook her head. "They are taking too long. And also, I can't live with them forever."

"Yeah, true," she agreed, mixing with a spoon before popping an apple in her mouth. "Why the sudden change of mind? We aren't making you feel like you aren't welcome, are we?"

"No, not at all. There really isn't a reason," she said breezily, hoping that Lacey wouldn't catch on, but even she knew she was full of shit. "I just need a change."

"Or to get away from Jordie."

She shrugged. "That too."

Kacey peeked a look at her sister-in-law to find her shaking her head. "Why don't you just talk to him?"

"'Cause I don't want to."

"Then you'll never get over him."

"I am over—"

"Don't you dare lie to me, Kacey Marie King," she snapped and Kacey's eyes went wide. "And stop running. You want answers, get them."

She held her gaze for a moment and Kacey let out a long breath, wringing her fingers together. "I'm scared what those answers will accomplish."

Lacey shrugged. "I never pegged you as a scared girl, Kacey, or someone who hides. Get your head out of your ass and do what you want."

She bit her lip and shook her head. "What I want is unattainable. He doesn't want what I want, but Liam—"

Slamming her hands on the counter, Lacey shook her head. "Oh my God! Let him go. Like today. Please."

"Lacey!" she gasped, surprised by her outburst.

"What? I'm so tired of watching you try to make something work when it doesn't. I don't even see why you are bringing him over here. Your parents will not like him. Especially your dad."

"You don't know that!" Kacey argued, her heart picking up in speed. She wanted to believe what she said, but even she doubted that her parents would like Liam. Or that Liam would like them. Lord knows, her dad didn't know how to control his mouth.

"I do, because you don't even love him. So why would they? They loved me from the beginning because they knew how much Karson loved me. You know I'm right."

"You're wrong. You'll see," Kacey said as confidently as she could.

Lacey rolled her eyes just as the door opened and Karl King stepped inside.

Before Kacey or Lacey could welcome him, he hooked his thumb behind him and barked, "Who's the fucking dweeb in the Prius?"

Oh, sweet Jesus, Kacey groaned inwardly as Regina King stepped in behind him.

"Karl! He can hear you, plus, I told you about the cussing. The baby is here. Where is my baby?" her mother asked, pushing past Karl just as Karson entered the kitchen with Mena Jane looking adorable in purple.

"I don't fucking care. Who the hell is he?"

Lacey glanced over at Kacey and grinned as she said, "Oh, that's Kacey's boyfriend, Liam."

Karl's face twisted just as Kacey's stomach did and all she could think was this was going to be a great day.

Not.

"Gorgeous!" Shelli and Posey exclaimed before they held up the mirror for

Jordie. Looking at his reflection, his brow rose. They had braided his beard and put little flowers and barrettes in it too. Gorgeous really wasn't the word he'd use, but the grins on their little faces wouldn't allow him to use the word he was thinking.

"For sure," he agreed, moving a piece of hair out of his eyes, taking in their handiwork.

"I think you look handsome, Uncle Jordie. I did the flowers," Posey said proudly and Jordie leaned over, kissing her cheek.

"Great job. They really bring out my eyes."

"I did the braid, Uncle Jordie. I've been working on it all summer." Shelli pouted and he smiled before gathering them both up in his arms.

"You can tell. You're the best braider in the world!"

That had both little girls giggling as they cuddled into his arms, hugging him tightly. In no time at all, the twins, Evan and Owen, were climbing along his neck while Quinn watched from where he was playing with the new train set Jordie had brought over for the boys. Before he knew, which really, he should have expected, it was four against one in a fight to the death wrestling match. For girls, Shelli and Posey fought like men, and it was a bit scary. The twins were little ninjas, but Quinn honestly couldn't care less. He was too busy playing to worry about them. When Shelli twisted Jordie's finger back, he hollered out dramatically and all the kids giggled, which made him smile.

"Guys, don't hurt Jordie. I need him to play this fall," Elli called and all the kids paused, looking over at their mother, who stood in the doorway, Shea behind her.

"Yes, ma'am," they all called before crawling off him. That's when Quinn came over and kicked him in the good knee. But still, Jordie fell off the couch very dramatically, acting as if he was dead.

"Don't mess with us Adlers!" Quinn called then in his sweet little voice, and Jordie had to hold in his laughter as he hung his tongue out of his mouth.

"We won!" Shelli exclaimed and they all cheered.

But then he jumped up, taking all five of them in his arms and lifting them into the air over the couch in case one fell out. "You can't kill me! I'm a zombie!"

Their screams were delightful as they squirmed against him, each of them falling out of his arms and hitting the couch with a thud. He went to jump on them when Elli stopped him.

"Please don't kill my children, I need someone to care for me when I'm older," Elli said and he nodded.

"You five are lucky," he said and they all grinned up at him, giggling.

"Lunch is ready," she said and Jordie shrugged.

"This giant is hungry," he said, but he didn't get far before all of them were wrapped around his legs and his middle. As he dragged five little Adlers to the kitchen, he couldn't help but think of Kacey.

And the baby she lost.

They lost.

And how he really wanted another chance to not only have her as his, but to make another baby.

It was a dream that he felt in his soul. One he had to make a reality.

After lunch, they all gathered in the living room, the boys playing while the girls started on the hair on his head.

"You're gonna wear it all day, right, Uncle Jordie?" Shelli asked.

"Promise."

"Pinkie, I do?" she asked, holding out her hand, and he took it, cupping it before she took his pinkie and wrapped it around hers.

"Pinkie, I do," he said, and she grinned before going back to work.

"You don't have to," Elli called from where she was cuddled against Shea, looking blissfully happy. Shea looked like a man who had hit the lottery over and over again, and Jordie couldn't wait to feel that kind of bliss. To have his wife in the crook of his arm, their kids on the floor, and maybe a dog chasing his tail.

A life worth living for.

To stay sober for.

"I don't mind," he waved her off as he cringed from where one of the girls pulled his hair too hard.

"Better you than me," Shea commented and Jordie grinned. "I want to cry every time they get ahold of me."

"Daddy is tenderheaded," Posey informed him.

"But Momma calls him bullheaded," Shelli added. "And a crybaby."

Elli grinned as Shea kissed her temple. They had their problems, but no matter what, they had each other. Jordie was green with envy at that moment, but it was all his fault. He could have had all this, but he wouldn't take ahold of it when it was offered.

"Did you enjoy church, Jordie?"

He nodded. "Yeah, I think I'll keep going if you guys don't mind."

"Of course not, we'd love to have you." Elli beamed.

"Well, that is, unless you trade me," he added with a grin and she smiled.

"You aren't going anywhere," she said as a promise. But it was a business, so he didn't put too much stock in her words. "I'm actually in talks with your agent right now. I'm sending over my offer sheet Wednesday."

"Really?" he asked, his heart hammering against his ribs. He hadn't expected that, or asked for it. His contract wasn't up until October, but he was more than ready to sign on again with the Assassins. He didn't want to go anywhere else.

"I believe in you," she said softly, and then her eyes started to tear up. "I'm so damn proud of you."

"All of us are, keep it up. A year will be here before you know it," Shea added and Jordie smiled.

"Thanks, guys. And yeah, I'm excited to hit that. In the group—ow! Shelli, honey, that hurt," he said and Shelli dropped her head down.

"Sorry."

He chuckled as she went back to work and he continued, "In the group I'm in, I'm the only one not at a year."

"You'll get there," Elli said and Jordie nodded. "Are you going alone? Or is Karson still going?"

"He and Lacey have been going. I have one tomorrow, but they have company in town, so I'll go alone."

"If you want one of us to go, we will," Elli offered and Shea nodded.

"Yeah, just give us a ring."

Jordie nodded, the support they offered overwhelming him a bit. It wasn't that he couldn't go alone, he just didn't like to. Having someone there who knew him and believed in him helped. The group was nice, but like he said, they were well into their sobriety, and sometimes he felt like they thought he was going to fail. It may be his own insecurities, but he liked having his friends there. It made him feel stronger.

"All done!" Shelli cheered as she and Posey hopped down, assessing their work.

"We are awesome," Posey decided as Shelli held up the mirror so Jordie could take in his Cindy Lou hair.

"Oh wow," he gasped and they both beamed. "I'm beautiful," he said very slowly as Shea and Elli both snickered from the couch.

"Gorgeous!" Shelli agreed.

"You look silly, Uncle Jordie," Owen said and Evan nodded.

"Like a girl."

Quinn shook his head, and Jordie smiled at the girls who were unaffected by their brothers' comments. "I think I look great."

"You do," Posey agreed. "Way prettier than Daddy."

"Hey," Shea protested and they all dissolved into giggles as he picked them both up, tickling them. Looking away, Jordie grimaced at his reflection again. Karson was going to give him shit when he got home, but he didn't care. He loved making the girls happy.

When their laughter subsided, Shelli leaned her face against Shea and closed her eyes. As Jordie watched, his chest felt as if it were caving in. It was such a beautiful sight, a man with his daughter. He wondered what it was going to be like for him, and of course, he immediately thought of Kacey. That's all he did, think of her. He wished that she would give him a chance to explain himself. No, he didn't deserve her forgiveness, he needed to grovel, but she wouldn't even give him a chance. It was coming to the point where he was about to just force her to listen to him. But he really wanted her to want it. He wanted it to work out. He wanted her to want him again.

Staring at his reflection, he could honestly say he loved himself again. It had taken a long time. He used to hide from his reflection unless he was getting sexy for the world, but now, he was proud of who looked back at him. He was nowhere near done, but he was getting there. He was on the road to recovery, to happiness; all he needed was Kacey by his side.

"Daddy, can we sing?"

Looking up from the mirror, he watched as Shea nodded his head. "Sure, sweetheart, go get my guitar." Shelli was as fast as a rocket, off her daddy's lap and down the hall and back within seconds, handing Shea his guitar. Putting the mirror on the table, Jordie stood as Shea strummed his fingers along the strings.

"You got one I can use?"

Shea looked up and nodded. "Yeah, Shelli, take him to the music room."

Taking his hands, she took him down the hall and into a room that had a wall of guitars. A piano was in the corner, along with other instruments in the room. Elli used to be a Broadway star, and Shea had always loved music, so it only made sense that they would have a music room.

"I didn't know you played, Uncle Jordie."

"Yup, for a while now," he said, picking up each guitar until he found one he liked. Strumming it a few times, he nodded his head. "All right, let's go."

Together they went back into the living room where Shea was waiting. Quinn was lying on Elli's chest, while Posey lay along her legs. Both of them looked like they were fighting sleep. Sitting back in his chair, he ran his fingers along the strings and then glanced up at Shea.

"What are we playing?"

Shea shrugged. "Shelli?"

"'Jesus Take the Wheel.' I need to practice."

"For?" Jordie asked as she handed him the sheet music.

"My concert at church. You'll come?" she asked eagerly and he nodded. "You know it."

She clapped happily and he smiled before looking back down at the sheet music. He knew the song and figured he could pick it up pretty easily.

"Okay, let me try this real quick," he said more to himself, but as he started, Shea joined in and together they played while Shelli hummed along. He only messed up twice, but on the next go, he was surprised he could even keep up.

Because Shelli sang like an angel.

She was beautiful, every bit her daddy but with her mother's voice. As she hit the high notes, Shea joined in to support her vocals and then Elli joined in, and Jordie was in awe. They all blended beautifully, and soon, he stopped playing just to watch. It was downright unbelievable, and he wasn't the only one mesmerized. It was as if the whole room had gone still, the only thing mattering the sound coming from their mouths.

When Shelli finished, everyone clapped while Jordie was still speechless. She was going places, and he hoped he got a front row seat to see where.

When she grinned over at her daddy, Shea smiled as she shrugged nervously. "I messed up a little."

"You did?" Jordie asked, shocked, because he thought she was ready for *American Idol*. But to his surprise, Shea nodded as he smiled.

"You did, but we'll work on it. Still the greatest singer I know. Let's start from the chorus," he suggested, looking down to start, but instead, Shelli leaned over, kissing his cheek.

"I love you, Daddy," she whispered and he smiled.

"I love you, sweetie," he said back, his eyes full of hope and dreams for his firstborn. But above all, there was love. Undying and unadulterated love.

A love Jordie craved.

A love he'd never gotten.

But one he wanted to give his child.

And his wife.

"What in the Sam Hill happened to your hair?"

Jordie laughed as he shut the door behind him and Karl King looked at him as if he had stepped off a spaceship.

"Ya look like one of those cross-dressers," he called as he closed the distance between him and Jordie. Wrapping him up in a man-slapping hug, Jordie grinned. He had always had a special relationship with Karson's dad. Just like Karl was with his own children, he was hard on Jordie and hadn't held back when Jordie called to tell him he was in rehab. He was pretty sure Karl called him every name in the book, but in the end, he told Jordie he loved him and that he was proud of him. Two things that Karl didn't say very often.

"Shea Adler's daughters got ahold of me," Jordie said as they parted and Regina swooped in, hugging him tightly. He kissed her temple before she cupped his face.

"You look healthy," she said, kissing his cheek. "So damn healthy."

"Thanks, Ma," Jordie said, hugging her again.

"You do, but still like a sissy," Karl teased and Jordie scoffed. "But I'd take your sissy ass over this dumbass Kacey is passing off as her boyfriend."

"Karl!" Regina scolded before smacking him in the gut. He let out an oomph, and as much as Jordie wanted to laugh, he held his tongue as she glared up at Karl. "Be nice. She apparently likes him."

"No, she don't," Karl and Jordie said at the same time. Regina rolled her eyes and then looked back at Karl. "Be nice, you've already embarrassed her enough."

He shrugged as she turned her gaze to Jordie. "And I brought you some razors."

Jordie grinned, his eyes sparkling as they met her determined ones. "Ma, I still have the razors from the last four times I've seen you. I don't need them."

She made a face, poking at his beard and shaking her head. "You need to shave," she reminded him, and before he could say anything else, she walked away, leaving him with Karl, who was grumbling about not acting like he liked Liam. Jordie found it quite comical but held it in that he felt the same. He was sure that would bring attention to his feelings for Kacey.

"I swear, Karl King, I will hurt you," she warned once more before disappearing into the living room. But instead of following her, Karl rolled his eyes.

He said, "Let's go outside. I don't like that dork and refuse to act like I do."

Jordie chuckled as they started for the porch. When he saw the cooler he knew had drinks in it, he opened it. To his surprise, there was no beer, not that he was looking for it. He grabbed a pop before shutting the screen door and sitting across from his pseudofather.

Taking a cup off the table and pouring the drink into it, he took a swig and leaned back in his chair. Jordie grinned, his brow furrowed in confusion. "Where's your beer?"

Karl shrugged. "Not drinking when one of mine doesn't drink anymore."

Jordie looked down, his heartstrings tightening as he nodded. "Didn't know you cared that much."

Karl laughed. "Oh, shut up. How ya feeling?"

Jordie nodded, meeting his gaze. "Alive."

"Good, sobriety treating you good? I haven't heard from you in a while."

"It is," Jordie admitted. "And I'm sorry, I've been training hard, trying to get ready."

"You'll be ready."

"I damn well hope so."

Karl nodded. "You will be."

They shared a grin, toasting their drinks before both taking swigs. "Heard from your mom lately?"

Jordie swallowed hard. Karl knew his mother—they had gone to the same high school—but that didn't stop him from thinking she was an idiot ninety percent of the time. "Nope."

"Hear she's getting married again?"

"Yeah, surprised she hasn't invited me to another wedding."

"Don't go," Karl said and Jordie nodded.

"I won't."

"Good." He leaned down on his knees, looking across the fire at Jordie. "She'll drive you to drinking again for sure."

"Damn right," Jordie agreed. "She doesn't know about rehab."

"'Cause she's selfish, and even though it isn't my place to apologize for her, I am sorry."

"Thanks," Jordie said, running his finger along the rim of the cup. "I don't want it to bother me."

"But it does because she's your mom."

"Yeah." He nodded, his chest tightening as he looked up. "Sucks."

"I know," Karl said sadly. "But ya got me and Regina."

"Thank God," Jordie said, shooting him a grin.

Karl grinned back, but it dropped as he leaned his elbows against his knees again. "Now, explain to me what the hell this dweeb is doing with my daughter? I thought something was going on with you two."

He wasn't surprised by Karl's question. Karl had always suspected that something was happening between Jordie and Kacey, especially when he learned of her staying with Jordie in Colorado. Letting out a long breath, Jordie shrugged before looking over his shoulder, his eyes falling on Kacey as she sat on the edge of Liam's chair inside the house, forcing a smile. She was wearing jeans and a tee, looking undeniably sexy. Her hair brushed her shoulders, her lips were glossed, but her eyes didn't hold the spark they used to.

The spark that meant she loved him.

He hadn't seen it since she left his cabin almost nine months ago, and he yearned for it more than his next breath.

"I love her," he said more to himself than to the father of the girl he was in love with. It was the first time he had said that out loud. Even when he spoke of Kacey to Natasha or even in group, he never admitted to loving her. He just said he cared a lot about her and that she was meant to be his. He was only slightly worried that Karl might jump over the fire and tear his throat out when he admitted the next part. Karl may think of Jordie as his, but he was ten times worse that Karson when it came to Kacey. She was his baby, but Jordie wouldn't lie.

"But I messed up. Big-time. Broke her heart."

Karl held his gaze for a long time and then nodded as he laced his hands together. "You gonna fix it?"

Jordie's throat felt tight as he croaked out, "I'm trying."

"Try fucking harder. I don't like that douche, but I like you. She's happy when she's with you," Karl said and Jordie couldn't help but laugh. If there was one thing about Karl, he didn't hold back on his feelings.

"Will do."

"Don't make me kick your ass," Karl warned and Jordie grinned.

"I won't. If she gives me another chance, I'll love her the way I should have and more."

"All right," he said, nodding his head slowly. When the screen door slid open, they both looked up to see Karson appear as he shut it behind him, making a face.

"Jesus, they are killing me in there," he said, coming out and sitting beside Jordie. "Too much estrogen in there."

Jordie scoffed. "But Kelly is in there."

"Exactly," Karl and Karson said and they all started laughing.

Karl coughed a bit and then asked, "When's she gonna drop that guy? She obviously wears the pants in the relationship."

"Don't all women?" Jordie asked and both men just nodded.

"Shut up, you," he said, pointing to Jordie. "But really, that dude is not for my baby girl."

"I know, Dad. I thought it was a good idea," Karson said as he sighed. "Obviously an error on my part."

"You think? Dumbass," Karl said, shaking his head. "Oh well, hopefully, she drops him quick."

Jordie couldn't agree more, but thankfully, the subject changed to hockey, and soon the subject of Kacey and her lame-ass boyfriend was left alone. Which was good, because it was hard enough to see them together, hugging and cuddling, but hearing Karl talk about them made it realer than it was. It was supposed to be Jordie Karl was talking about.

Jordie and Kacey.

It had a sweet ring to it.

Liam and Kacey sounded stupid.

Kacey Kelly?

What the fuck? No way. Over his dead body.

"So you'll play with the new kid?"

Jordie looked up confused since he was too busy obsessing over Kacey. "What?"

Karl glared, clearing his throat. "That Sinclair kid. You'll play with him?"

Jordie nodded. "That's the line right now, but it could change."

"He's good. I've watched him play. Star player...but his wife, Baylor

Moore—"

"Wait, they're married?" Jordie asked, confused, and Karson laughed.

"Yeah, dumbass, where have you been?"

Jordie shook his head, he was obviously too obsessed with Kacey to pay attention.

Karl scoffed as he continued. "Like I was saying, she can play. It's gonna be awesome watching her on NHL ice. Kind of wish it was Kacey though."

Karson nodded along with Jordie before saying, "She didn't want it though. She wanted the medal and a family."

A family.

Looking away, his heart just hurt at the mere thought of Kacey being a mother. Growing the child in her belly and eating more food than the FDA would approve for a woman with child. But he wouldn't care, he'd feed it to her as long as she was happy.

He just needed to tell her that.

"Yeah, well, she got the medal, and please Lord, don't let that guy be my future son-in-law. I won't be able to do it. He flinches when I cuss! What the fuck!" Karl exclaimed and Karson laughed as Jordie smiled, even though he wasn't really paying attention.

"He told Kacey she cusses a lot."

"Fucking right, she does! People that cuss are honest, good people. We love Jesus, so I don't know what the problem is," Karl said and Jordie grinned.

"I think that's a sin maybe? Cussing?"

Karl glared. "Shh, you."

Jordie scoffed as the screen door opened, and when they all looked up, Jordie was surprised none of them groaned. Kelly shut the door and then waved awkwardly as he sat next to Karl. "Hey."

"Hey," Karson and Karl echoed, but Jordie looked in his cup, wishing like hell it was empty so he could leave. He was not a Liam Kelly fan.

For obvious reasons.

"Love the hair, Thomas. Shelli and Posey must have gotten ahold of you," he said, and Jordie looked up, a deadpan look on his face as he nodded.

"Must have," he muttered and then looked across at Karl. "You need a refill?"

"No, and neither do you," he snapped and Jordie groaned.

Silence fell over them and Jordie nearly choked on the tension. Pulling his phone out, he checked his Facebook and noticed that Karson was doing the same.

That was until Kelly said, "So…um. Sir, um…er, I mean, Mr. King, I'd like to speak with you. In private, please."

Both their heads popped up and Jordie looked at Karson, confused. What the hell did Liam want to talk to Karl about in private?

Karl's face scrunched up in annoyance. "Whatever ya gotta say to me, ya can say in front of these two. I'd tell them anyway."

"Oh," Kelly said, nervously moving his hands together, and Jordie's stomach dropped. What the hell was he doing? "Well, you see, I've been dating Kacey for a while now with the permission of Karson," he said, nodding his head to Karson, but Karson didn't acknowledge him. He only stared as Kelly swallowed hard, his nerves visible. "Um…and well, we are really happy, and there is really no one I'd rather spend the rest of my life with. So, um, I'd like to ask her to marry me. But first, I'd like your permission."

What. The. Fuck.

Kelly plastered a huge grin on his face, and Jordie wanted nothing more than to pound his fist into Kelly's face, but he was stunned to silence. His jaw actually dropped, and when he glanced at Karson, his had too. Karl though, he was stone-faced, his eyes picking Kelly apart before his head slowly started to shake.

"What? It's only been a month or two," Karson blurted out and Kelly looked over at Karson, nodding.

"When you know, you know," he said, his voice shaky.

"But she doesn't love you!" Jordie said, his heart picking up in speed. This douche was going to offer Kacey what she wanted. What if she said yes?

"You don't know that," Kelly said dryly, his eyes cutting Jordie's, which was surprising. The dude didn't have a mean bone in his body. The guys teased him all the time because he never got a penalty, never got into a fight because he was too busy saying sorry or excuse me than actually fighting for the puck. If he didn't have a sick-ass shot, Jordie would have questioned Elli on her decision to keep him on the team.

"I actually plan to love her and never hurt her," Kelly said then, and that made Jordie scoff.

So she'd told him about them.

He wasn't sure if that was a good thing or bad.

And before Jordie could tell Kelly exactly what he thought, Karl cleared his throat, bringing the attention to him.

"Liam, I can call you that, right?"

"Why, yes, sir," Liam said nodding, his grin directed to Karl.

"Liam," he started, but then he paused, sitting up and then back before leaning onto his knees, his eyes meeting Liam's. "Not even no, but hell, fuck no, you can't marry my daughter."

If Jordie were a man-kissing man, he'd kiss Karl King right at that moment.

Sputtering, Kelly went to say something, but Karl stood, holding his hand up as he shook his head. "Marry her. The fuck? Cold day in fucking hell."

He then walked to the door, slamming it open before hollering, "Kacey Marie King, it will be a cold day in fucking hell before I allow you to marry this idiot!"

"Oh shit," Karson said, hopping up to follow as Kelly ran in behind Karl.

Jordie slowly stood, a grin on his face as he headed toward the show.

He only wished he had time to make some popcorn.

Chapter TWELVE

Kacey saw the whole thing go down.

She wasn't too comfortable with Liam going out to hang with the guys but he was pretty persistent, and she had to say he'd been acting a little weird since he got there. He was holding her a little too much and kissing her and being really nice even though every other word out of her father's mouth was the f-bomb. Liam seemed to like him though, so when he got up to go out, she didn't stop him. Even though Jordie was out there, looking utterly delicious despite the done-up hair and beard job he had. Shelli and Posey must have gotten ahold of him and, of course, that made her want to aww.

But she didn't.

She couldn't pay much attention to him though. Because soon her father's face twisted up when Liam turned to talk to him. Then Karson's and Jordie's jaws dropped and they both said something that Liam just waved off. When her dad stood, throwing his hands up over his head as he yelled violently, she knew it wasn't good, but she didn't think it was what she thought her father just said.

Shaking her head, she jumped to her feet along with her mother and cried out, "What?"

He pointed at her, his brows touching as his face filled with anger. "You aren't marrying this guy! No! Over my dead fucking body!"

"Karl!" her mother yelled as Kacey stood there, shocked. Her eyes cut to Liam as he stepped in front of Karl, his back to Kacey

"I'm sorry, sir, but I'd like Kacey to—" Liam started, but Karl wasn't backing down.

Not that she'd expect him to.

"I said no! You hear me? Get out of my face," he said, pushing past Liam while Regina took ahold of his arm, trying to stop him. But he just dragged her along with him. "Let go of me, Regina. Do you hear what is going on? They've only known each other for a couple months! She don't even love him!"

"Karl, hush! You don't know that," Regina yelled back.

"I'd really like to talk to you privately, Kacey." Liam tried to be heard over all the yelling, but Kacey couldn't even move.

Was this really happening?

Was she dreaming?

She looked to Karson for help, but he was standing there, his mouth gaping open, no help at all. She looked to Lacey, but she was holding Mena, her eyes wide as she looked back and forth to each person who was yelling. When his eyes met hers, Jordie just grinned in a slow, very condescending way. Almost like he found this not only hilarious but downright stupid. She could read him like a book; it was easy for her, even with him holding back so much of himself. But sometimes, he opened up, and when he did, she absorbed everything he said and stored it in her heart for later. Now though, she wanted to smack him as his arms went over his chest, his eyes watching her so intently.

Waiting for her next move.

Asshole.

Not that she wanted his help, but Jesus! Could someone help out here?

"I won't allow it, Kacey Marie King! I refuse to!" her father yelled, bringing her attention to him.

"Allow it?" she muttered, her eyes narrowing angrily. "Daddy, I'll do whatever I please."

"The hell you will! You don't even like this guy! Better yet, love him!" he yelled at her, his nose flaring, and she really didn't understand why he was so mad. Yeah, he was right, but why did he feel the need to make a scene like this? Her daddy was overdramatic, but even this was a little crazy.

"Kacey, can we go outside?" Liam asked, but she held her hand up, stopping him.

"In a second," she said sharply, her eyes never leaving her dad's. "Why are you so mad?" she asked him then, trying to keep her cool even though she was beyond embarrassed.

"Because I don't like him."

"But what if I do? What if I want to marry him?" she asked and Karl basically shot steam out of his nose.

"What?!" he said, along with Karson and Jordie.

Jordie came off the wall, his aloofness gone as his eyes burned a hole in her head.

"You can't be serious," Karson said then. "You just met him."

"You sure as hell don't love him," Jordie added as Karson nodded.

"You don't know that," Liam shot at him and Jordie laughed.

"Dude, I know her and she don't love you," he snapped back and Liam glared as Karson nodded.

"Yeah, what he said," Karson agreed.

"Kacey, maybe you should think about this," Lacey said then.

"What the hell, Lacey!" Jordie yelled and she shrugged.

"Hey, don't yell at her," Karson shot at Jordie, but then he looked back her. "But really? What the hell?"

"I'm just saying! She needs to think this through."

"No, she don't," Karl said. "There is nothing to think about. This guy is not for you!"

"Kacey, can we please go outside and talk?" Liam asked again.

"We are trying to talk to her!" her mother yelled, but Kacey's eyes never left her father's as her face burned with embarrassment. This was her family and she knew if she looked at Liam, his face would be full of horror. Everyone was so loud, so opinionated, and that wasn't what Liam was about. She knew this and also knew that they were all right. He wasn't the man she was going to marry.

"Don't you think I can make my own decisions, Daddy?"

His eyes burned with fire, his body taut, and she was sure he was two seconds from slamming his fist into something. Preferably Liam's face, but she wouldn't allow him to. He was upset over nothing, and really, it made no sense to her. Yeah, he was overprotective, but he never flew off the handle like this. But this was the first time someone had asked to marry her, she guessed, and at least she knew what to prepare the future Mr. for.

If there ever was a future Mr. She had one proposal and, of course, she couldn't keep her eyes off the dude who broke her heart. Easy to say she was insane. Or stupid. Or both.

Karl's head fell to the side, his chest falling and rising. "Yeah, I do, but—"

"No *but* needed. Now, let me handle this," she said sternly, and he didn't say anything else as she turned to look at Liam. Like she knew he would be, his face was full of dismay, his cheeks bright red, his eyes wild, and his shoulders back and tight. "Let's go outside."

The room was silent as she went around the group that had gathered and out the front door with Liam on her heels. When she heard him say, "It was nice to meet you, Mr. and Mrs. King," she was surprised. After all that, she had fully expected him to run, and she'd be lying if she said she wasn't intrigued. When she reached his Prius, she turned just as he reached her.

"Well," he said, tucking his hands in his pockets. "That didn't go as planned."

She crossed her arms over her chest, looking up at him. "What the hell, Liam? You asked my dad to marry me?" she asked, her words coming out sharper than she'd intended. "We just met. It hasn't even been two months."

He nodded, looking down as he shrugged. "When you know, you know," he finally said, meeting her gaze. "I wanted you to come by tomorrow, and I had a dinner planned. And then I wanted to get intimate with you, and if it went as well as I'm sure it will, I wanted to ask you." He was rambling, but all she heard was that he wanted to get intimate.

Get. Intimate.

Not what she wanted to hear her future husband say. She wanted him to want her. To yearn, tear her apart, fuck her stupid, not plan to "get intimate." Ugh, why had she let this happen? Why did she think it would work? He was her polar and utter opposite. Man, she really fucked up here, and now she was going to hurt him because he was obviously in deeper than she was. Something she'd never intended but ultimately would do because she was too much of a coward to let him go when she knew he wasn't it.

Looking up at him, guilt slammed into her as she shook her head. "Liam, I'm sorry, but I don't love you."

"Yet," he said softly, reaching out and taking her hands with his. "But you will, I just know it."

"Liam—"

"No, listen," he said, interrupting her. "We don't have to get married tomorrow or even next month. It's just that I found out from my agent that my contract with the Assassins isn't being renewed, and I'm more than likely going to go to New York or Florida. I want you to go with me, Kacey." He paused, taking a deep breath as his eyes begged hers. Her heart pounded in her chest as he went on, "Maybe I jumped the gun, maybe marriage wasn't the way to go. But please, come with me. We can start a new journey together. You always say you want to travel. This is the best way."

"But I don't want to leave my family," she said softly.

"I know, but we can visit, all the time. I like them," he said with a grimace. "When they're not yelling at me," he added with a laugh.

"They don't like you," she admitted and he shrugged.

"They will."

"But I don't love you," she said again. "And that wouldn't be fair for you, Liam."

He was only derailed for a moment, his grin flattening for a split second before he squeezed her hands. "But you like me and that can turn to love. I feel something here, Kacey. I do, and I would never hurt you. I'd give you the world."

She knew this, but could she do it? Did she want to? She did want a change, but did she want it with him? Could she love him?

Looking deep into his eyes, she found herself wishing they were brown, and she knew the answer right then.

Before she could tell him that though, he was talking. "Listen, sleep on it and think it over. I'll know tomorrow where I am going, and we can discuss it over dinner. I really think this would be best for you, for us."

It wasn't. She needed change, she did, but he wasn't the one to give it to her. "Liam, I just—"

"Please, I love you, Kacey, and if you care about me at all, you'll at least think it over."

His eyes held so much hope, and soon she was drowning in the guilt as she looked away, shrugging her shoulders. She knew that she just needed to tell him no, but maybe… No, she didn't want to be with him. It was that simple, but she had brought this on herself and she did care for him as a friend. Only a friend. He didn't do anything for her. Nothing, but because she cared, she'd think it over, really weigh the options and then let him down easy. She owed him that.

"Okay," she said softly. "But—"

"No, no buts. I just want you to truly think it over. Really examine us. See how good I am to you, how I care about you and your needs. I think you'll see I'm a sure bet."

He was like a used car salesman and she wanted to laugh. She was never good at telling them no, always had to have her dad do it, but that wasn't an option right now. She had to do this herself. She made this mess; she had to clean it up.

Tomorrow.

She'd clean it up tomorrow.

Going up on her tiptoes, she gave him a quick kiss, but before she could pull away, he wrapped his arms around her waist, picking her up off the ground and deepening the kiss. Surprised, she opened her mouth in a gasp, which gave him full access, his tongue diving into her mouth. She wanted to say it was the greatest kiss of her life. She wanted to say that it wasn't awkward, feeling his tongue against hers. But she'd be struck dead by lightning if she didn't say it felt like kissing Karson.

Ew.

After he pulled away, his lips lingered against hers as his hands slid down her back to her ass, squeezing her lightly.

Which did nothing for her. Not even a little zing to the pussy. Nothing.

Looking deeply into her eyes, he whispered, "I love you. Call me tomorrow, and we'll meet up after you get done with the team."

She smiled. "Okay."

He kissed her again, this one just as long as the last, before kissing her nose and going around to get in his car. He waved sweetly at her and she smiled as he backed out of the driveway before disappearing down the road. Letting out a long breath, she looked up at the heavens and shook her head.

"Why? Why did I do this?"

She wasn't sure whom she was asking, but when the answer didn't come, she turned to head inside, seeing that her whole family was standing in the windows watching.

"Son of a bitch," she moaned, stomping toward the house, which caused all the curtains to fall. She fully expected everyone to be sitting, acting as if they hadn't seen anything, but Kacey didn't have a typical, subtle family.

She had the Kings.

So when she entered the house, they were all standing there expectantly.

Except Jordie. She didn't see Jordie anywhere. Not that she was looking.

"So?" Karl barked, his hands striking his hips. "It didn't look like you told him to fuck off!"

"Did you say yes?" Lacey asked, her eyes wide and full of shock, poor Mena in her arms, the only normal one of the bunch.

"I swear, you better not have," Karson grumbled. "When I told you to date him, it was to date. Not marry!"

"Oh, Kacey, please," Regina sniffed. "He really was dull, and you have too much…er, passion for him to handle."

Really? Passion? What did that even mean?

Shaking her head, she rolled her eyes; she did not have the patience for this. "I am not speaking to any of you for the rest of the night, maybe not even tomorrow," she spat before turning and heading down the hall to her room, slamming the door for good measure and to show she meant business. Leaning against the door, she let out a deep sigh, her heart still pounding from the last twenty minutes. It seemed like so much longer, like eons, especially when her eyes had met Jordie's. He'd looked so confident, like he knew she wouldn't marry Liam. It irritated her to no end, but it also intrigued her.

Why was he confident regarding something he knew nothing about?

Someone he left.

What was his game?

Looking at her bathroom door, she sucked in a breath and let it out through her nose. All she had to do was go through that door, then through his, and ask him. Demand to know what he was thinking. What he was doing? And where he had been.

But…

Maybe she should go with Liam—

No, she wasn't going with him, but she really did need to talk to Jordie. The sooner, the better, but not now. She couldn't do it now. Her family had stressed her out, embarrassed the hell out of her, and exhausted her. What she needed to do was take a shower, get some ice cream, and cuddle up to watch a movie.

Yes, that was a fabulous idea.

Standing up, she threw off her shirt and pants, reaching for a towel before heading inside to make sure Jordie wasn't there. His door was shut, thankfully. Walking to it, she locked it and turned to his sink to lay her towel on it. Reaching behind her to take her bra off, she looked up and cried out.

"Fucking hell!" she yelled, falling into the counter, her hands coming up to catch the cups of her bra as Jordie slowly rose off the closed toilet.

Holding his hands up quickly, he said, "Just me."

"I know! That's why I cried out in desperation, praying that someone would save me from your stalker-like actions," she gasped, her heart pounding against her chest. "Jesus, get out of here. I'm trying to take a shower."

But he wasn't moving. His eyes ran down her body, and if she were dressed, he'd be stripping her with those corrupt brown eyes.

Biting his lip, he met her gaze again and asked, "Did you tell him no?"

Her face scrunched up. "Why does that matter to you?"

He moved slowly, closing the distance between them as he twirled the end of his beard with his finger, his eyes still drinking her in. It was one of those things that brought her to her knees and had her wetter than she could think to be. He always looked so sinister, like he was about to tear her apart when he did that, those eyes trained on her. One look from Jordie turned her to goo; Liam grabbed her ass and raped her mouth and nothing.

Something was really wrong with her.

Gasping for breath, she watched as he stopped in front of her, his eyes boring into hers.

"Because it does," he said softly, his voice so rugged and full of dirty promises. "Did you?"

She didn't understand why her mouth started moving, but it did. "No, I didn't. I told him I'd tell him tomorrow. He's being traded and wants me to go with him."

His face didn't even move a muscle as he said, "Don't go."

She felt his words deep down in her soul. "Why?"

"Because you don't love him, for one. And two, because I want you to give me another chance."

She tried to scoff, not showing any signs of surprise. But instead, she sounded like she was choking as her heart came into her throat, because surely he was joking. "What? Another chance?"

He nodded, his eyes completely serious. The air around them was so thick with tension and lust as his eyes held hers. The hair on her arms stood at attention, her heart pounding as she waited for him to answer. When he didn't, she knew he was full of it. But then he reached out, his hand cupping her around the neck before dropping his mouth to hers and she was sure she was flying to the moon. His lips were butter against hers, moving and savoring her as if he had been starving for her taste.

Melting against him, she brought her hands up to his chest, but then she pulled away, gasping for breath. Her hand covered her lips as she turned to hold on to the counter, closing her eyes and begging her body to remember that she was still with Liam and also that Jordie had broken her heart in a thousand pieces.

And he could do it again.

Squeezing her eyes shut, she felt him behind her, his heat radiating off him in waves and burning her but also comforting her. His heat was always home to her. She was naturally cold all the damn time, but not when Jordie was around. He was her furnace.

Was.

Not anymore.

He didn't want you. She had to remember that.

But when she met his gaze in the mirror, his lips were red, parted as they slowly curved, sending heat straight between her thighs and remembering was the last thing she could do. She couldn't even think for that matter. She wanted him to take her against the counter and pull her hair.

Over. And over. And over again.

By the way he was looking at her, he wanted the same thing, but that's all he wanted. Sex. Nothing more, and Kacey just couldn't do it. She wanted more.

Clearing his throat, he said, "Yes. Another chance to love you. To be the man you want."

Whoa. What?

She could only blink as he slowly wrapped his arms around her body, his hands sliding down her waist, his thumbs brushing her mound. But his eyes never left hers as she gasped for breath, begging for the will to stop him, but stunned speechless instead. His lips trailed along her shoulder, his eyes burning into hers as he nibbled.

But wait, what did he just say?

Pressing a small kiss to the side of her neck, he whispered against her, "Meet me tomorrow. I have this thing after training, but come to our spot around three. Gives you time to blow off the dude and be with the man you want."

"Jordie—"

She wasn't sure what she was going to say, but before she could, he squeezed her mound. He might as well have electrocuted her because she cried out, her back pressing to his ever hard chest as his lips brushed along her ear. "Just say yes. Please. I have so much to say to you, promise me you'll come."

Swallowing hard, she opened her eyes, seeing in the mirror that his body was all but consuming her, and she knew she didn't want that. Well, she did, but she knew she shouldn't want it. She couldn't want it because it would only lead to him hurting her. She didn't know what he was saying or doing, but there was no way he meant it. He couldn't.

That was her fantasy.

And Jordie wasn't who he was in her fantasies.

He was relationship-impaired.

So as much as she wanted to become one with him, she pulled away, her body crying and begging for her to stop, but she knew she couldn't. Putting some distance between them, she closed her eyes and shrugged her shoulders.

"I don't know."

When his fingers came under her chin, lifting it slowly, she met his heated gaze and he smiled. Just a small smile. One that hit her straight in the gut.

"Yeah, you do," he said softly. "I know you are curious and want answers. I just want a chance to explain, Kacey. I want a chance to fix my mistakes, to love you the way you want to be loved."

She moved her face from his grip and shook her head in utter shock. Who was this guy? "You don't love anyone."

He shrugged. "Maybe before, but now is different. Meet me. Please."

Looking away, she bit the inside of her cheek as she thought it over. She did want to go. She did want to know what he was doing, but just hearing him say the words had her hoping for forever.

And Jordie didn't do forevers.

He really has changed.

Lacey's words rang in her head, but could she believe them?

Looking up, she met his expectant gaze, and while she wanted to press her lips to his, she also wanted to smack him. She hated that he'd put her in this position, that he had brought so much uncertainty in her heart. She didn't owe him anything and he knew that, but she wouldn't just submit to him. Wouldn't do as he asked just because. No, she'd keep him in the dark. The same way he did her.

Clearing her throat, she shrugged. "We'll see."

His smile grew as he crossed his arms over his chest. "We'll see?"

She nodded. "Yeah, maybe I can pencil you in. I might decide to go with Liam."

With his grin still there, he didn't say anything, and she knew she had to get out of there. It was obvious he wasn't going anywhere. Turning, she went through the doorway, but when she reached for the door to shut it, her eyes met his again. Before she could close it, he called out, "Then I'll drag you right on back home. Where you belong. With me. I'll see you tomorrow."

Breathless, she shut the door and leaned her head against it.

What the hell was going on?

First Liam was begging her to go with him and to love him, but the thing was, he didn't have her heart. Not even a piece of it. Then she had Jordie begging her to stay and supposedly let him love her, which was completely mind-blowing. But he had broken her heart. And still had it.

Letting her head hang, all she could do was think what a freaking mess she had gotten herself into.

And not even Ben & Jerry's could get her out of this.

Jordie was a confident man.

But even he was nervous that Kacey wouldn't show up.

There was something about the way she'd said, "We'll see" that kept him up most of the night. The following morning, all he could do was think over and over again about what he was going to do if she didn't show up. He tried not to think about it, but it wasn't working. As he spat his toothpaste out into the sink, he glanced over at her door. It was shut, and he wondered if she was taking a nap.

When he got home with Karson after training, she was on her way into her room and he hadn't seen or heard from her since. All through training she didn't even look at him. Not that that was a new occurrence, but he thought after the kiss they'd shared she would have been a little warmer to him.

No luck.

He was sure she made him work even harder just because she was mad or whatever she was. He wasn't sure, but he was ready to get his AA meeting over with so he could rush to their favorite Mexican restaurant and find out his fate. It was honestly killing him, not knowing what she was thinking. In the past, she'd be putty in his hands, and he knew he didn't deserve that now. But surely, after everything he'd said last night, she'd see that he meant business. That he wasn't playing around. But maybe not.

Maybe she hadn't seen the change, which meant he had to work a lot harder. He wasn't doing something right. Or maybe he had broken her heart so badly, she wanted nothing to do with him. He knew it was a possibility, but one he really hoped hadn't happened. Running his hands through his hair, he looked at his reflection and nodded.

"She'll be there. She loves you."

He felt stupid saying that out loud, but he thought maybe it would help him believe it.

It didn't.

Letting out a long breath, he shook his head and left the bathroom, despite the temptation to knock on her door and ask. He'd leave it to God, as Elli would tell him to do. He believed she was it, but maybe she wasn't. But then, that wasn't an option. He needed her to show up, or he was going to lose his shit. He had lived too long in a life that he did not love; he was ready to love his life and her.

Shutting his door, he looked toward Mena's door as he always did and saw that Karson was in there rocking her to sleep. He nodded his head at Jordie and Jordie nodded back before turning to head to the kitchen for a snack before he left. He really didn't like the stale cookies and coffee they served at AA. He wished he would have called Shea or Elli to go, but he figured he'd try to go alone. He'd have to do it sooner or later.

When he got into the living room, he noticed that Karl and Regina were outside, enjoying the sunshine and had a big bowl of something that look delicious. Deciding he'd spend some time with them and see if they'd share their food, he made his way toward the door, but he paused when he heard Kacey's voice.

"I just don't know what to do," she said, and then he heard the chair pull out. "I mean, I have to tell Liam no, I'm not going. I don't love him."

"Right," Lacey agreed. "There was no hope there."

"Exactly, but it's just so frustrating, you know? I mean, I tried so hard, but nothing."

"I know, but I think you did that to get someone else out of your mind," Lacey said and Kacey let out a long breath.

"With him, I never have to try," Kacey whispered and Jordie smiled.

"Which means something," Lacey sang and Kacey groaned.

"Ugh, Lacey, he kissed me last night."

"*What!?*" Lacey hollered and Kacey quickly shushed her. Leaning against the wall, Jordie knew he was wrong for listening, but he had to know what she was saying. What she was thinking? Scooting along the wall so he could hear better, he knocked into one of Mena's toys and closed his eyes in response.

"What was that?"

Shit! He was caught.

When neither of them started yelling at him, he opened his eyes as Lacey said, "Probably Karson playing with Mena. Now, focus! What do you mean he kissed you, and why are you just now telling me?"

"I didn't plan it, or even want it—okay, that's a lie—but he just did it and said all this stuff about wanting to love me. It was weird but perfect at the same time. I just don't know what to think."

"Maybe that he's telling the truth?" she asked. "I told you he changed."

He'd always loved Lacey. Since the moment he met her, he'd known she was a good gal, and after this, he was going to buy her whatever she wanted.

"Lacey, come on, people don't change."

"Yes, they do, if they really want to. I swear to you, Kacey, he isn't the same guy he was a year ago."

Wasn't that the damn truth?

"I don't know, he just hurt me so bad. Broke me in two. Yes, I know that's dramatic and very high school, but really. I'm haunted by it all. I mean, it took everything within me to pick myself up. Especially after the baby. That really gutted me."

"I know, Kacey, but everyone deserves a second chance, don't you think?"

"Yes, I do. But how can I trust him? I've forgiven him, but how do I forget?"

Jordie looked down, guilt drowning him as Lacey asked, "I don't know, but can you live with yourself if you don't give him the chance to at least explain himself? No one said anything about taking him back—though I vote yes. I know how you feel about him, but maybe just hear him out."

"I don't know," Kacey admitted. "Maybe I should say fuck it all and go with Liam?"

Lacey laughed. "I like the idea of giving Jordie the chance to explain why he did what he did better."

Some dishes crashed together and Jordie thought they were done, but then Kacey asked, "Would you give him a chance to explain if it was you and Karson and he did what Jordie did?"

Lacey didn't even hesitate. "Yes, because I've always loved him, and I know you love Jordie."

Jordie held his breath as he squeezed his eyes tightly, waiting for her to either confirm or deny.

He didn't have to wait long for her to whisper, "Yeah, you're right."

Thank God!

He knew she still loved him. There was no getting over what they had, but his mistake had broken her, and it was his job to fix what he had done. He knew that going in, but hearing how badly he'd hurt her when she wasn't aware he was listening was really heartbreaking. He'd never meant to cause so much pain. He was stupid and drunk.

God, he was so fucked up.

"I know, and I also know what it's like to have your heart broken. But remember this, if I hadn't given Karson a second chance, would I be sitting here looking at you right now?"

Kacey scoffed. "Lacey, he broke your heart because your dad made him.

Jordie broke mine because I wasn't enough."

Whoa, what?

Lifting his head, he opened his eyes, fully intending to go in there and set her straight. She was way more than enough for him, she was more than he deserved—he just had been too stupid to realize what he'd had in his arms. But before he could, his gaze met that of a very angry Karson and he froze. Karson didn't freeze though. He pulled his arm back, his face full of anger, and Jordie swore everything was moving in slo-mo.

Because right before Karson's fist connected with his mouth, he was able to say, "Well, shit."

Chapter THIRTEEN

"**Y**ou broke her heart!" Karson yelled, his fist connecting with Jordie's mouth again. Jordie's head whipped back, hitting the wall before he held his hand up, stopping Karson as he wiped his mouth with his other hand. "I should kill you! I trusted you! You told me it was one time and done, but obviously, it was more if you broke her heart. That means she loves your fucking ass!" Pushing Jordie's hand out of the way, Karson's fist connected, this time to his jaw, and Jordie swore he saw stars.

"Oh my God, Karson, stop," Lacey shrieked before stepping between them and holding her hands up. "Stop, they are adults. These things happen between adults!"

"Not between my best friend and my baby sister!"

"I am a grown-up and I do what I want, Karson! Shut up!" Kacey yelled. "I can't believe you actually hit him. I can care for myself, you big jerk!"

"I am defending your honor!" he spat back as Jordie tried to get his bearings. That last hook really did a number.

"What the hell is going on?" Karl yelled.

"Oh my goodness, Karson! Jordie, your mouth. Kacey, get a rag!" Regina yelled, coming to his aid. "What is going on?!"

"He broke Kacey's heart!" Karson yelled, trying to come at him again, but Karl stopped him.

"And like your wife said, they are adults. It's none of your fucking business, now stop!" Karl yelled, his booming voice shaking even Jordie's bones.

146

Regina looked at Jordie and then to Kacey. "Kacey Marie, what in the world? You two were together?"

"Yes, Ma! Obviously!" Kacey yelled. "What is wrong with all of you? Why is everything such an ordeal all the damn time? And why is my love life always on blast?"

Ignoring her outburst, Regina looked to Jordie and glared. "You broke my baby's heart?"

"I did, but—"

Before he could finish, Regina slapped him across the face, causing Kacey to cry out, "Ma! Jesus!"

"He broke your heart," she said simply, throwing the rag she had at him and walking away.

Looking at Kacey, Jordie scoffed. "Very violent family you have," he said and she shot him a deadpan look.

"Shut up," she snapped. "And can everyone just calm the hell down?"

"No, not until I beat the shit out of him," Karson yelled, his chest puffed up, his eyes wild. Jordie had always known it wasn't going to go over well when Karson found out, he'd even expected it to come to blows, but the anger in Karson's eyes was scary.

He could actually lose his best friend.

Holding his hands up, he said, "Karson, buddy, listen to me. I deserve everything you've done, and more. I do. But you can't beat me up any more than I already have. I fucked up."

"What else is new? You always fuck up!" Karson yelled, and that hurt. Looking away, Jordie nodded.

"You're right. I'm sorry."

"Sorry isn't good enough! She should never feel like she isn't enough!"

"Absolutely," Jordie said. Turning to Kacey, he reached out, taking her elbow in his hand, running his thumb along it. "You were always too good for me. Always more than enough. I was too fucked up to see it. I'm pretty sure I told you I was gonna regret hurting you that day, and I have. Ever since you walked out the door."

When she looked away, moving her elbow out of his grasp, he looked to Karson. "Bro, I'm sorry."

Karson went to say something, but Lacey stopped him. "We forgave him. Everything he did all those months ago. Together we did, and you told me we can't go back on it. That was old Jordie," she reiterated, and to Jordie's surprise, when Karson looked down at her, his expression softened. "We said that nothing mattered except his actions from the moment he apologized."

"But he never told me about this."

"Because he was embarrassed and also a little fucked up from it. They have their own issues, and who are you to get mad about it? What will that fix? He made the mistake. He's the one who has to live with it."

"Yes, but hitting him makes me feel better," Karson said before glancing up at Jordie. "And I'm not sorry."

"Don't blame you," Jordie agreed. "It hurt."

"Good," Karson said as he shook his head.

A silence fell over the room and Jordie didn't know what to do. Kacey was looking twenty shades of pissed, Karson was shaking, and Regina wouldn't look at him. Karl and Lacey were the only ones who looked approachable, but still he didn't move. That was until he noticed the clock that said he needed to go.

As he smacked his hands together, Karson's gaze cut to his and Jordie nodded. "I fucked up, I'm sorry. But I gotta go, gotta work on me a bit."

He knew his feelings shouldn't have been hurt when Karson didn't offer to go with him, but they kind of were. Karson had been going with him all the time, except when Lacey wanted to go. Those were the times he spoke of Kacey, because Lacey supported them. The pain he was feeling at that moment was brought on solely by himself. He'd had every opportunity to talk to Karson. Instead, he'd hid what happened.

He was a coward.

When Karl's hand came crashing down on Jordie's shoulder, he looked back as Karl said, "I'll go with you."

Nodding his head, he said, "Cool, let me go wash my mouth out and we'll leave."

As he headed to the bathroom, he heard Regina say, "Kacey, where are you going?"

"No way am I staying here with you so you can press me for info. I have nothing to say, and I have somewhere to be."

He wanted to believe she was leaving to meet him, but it was too early, and then he remembered that she had to go see Liam. He hoped that she would break up with him, but after everything that had just happened, he was unsure if she would be meeting him later.

And that scared him more than losing his relationship with Karson did.

"Jordie, how are you doing?" Bethany, the AA group leader, asked.

Falling deeper into his seat, he nodded. "I'm good."

"Any cravings?"

Jordie scoffed. "All the time, but I'm managing them. No slipups."

Karl squeezed his shoulder and Jordie smiled over at him.

"That's good. Have you noticed anything in particular that is triggering them? Or is it just a constant craving?"

Jordie sat up, leaning on his thighs, and he shrugged. "I've been stressing more than usual, and before I would have a drink to calm me and forget the things I didn't want to think about. Now, all I do is think. I drive myself crazy overthinking things."

"Why is that?"

"Because I hate the mistakes I made."

"They are in the past though, right? When you were drinking?"

"Yeah," he said, sitting up and letting out a breath. "But my mistakes keep haunting me. They stare back at me every day, they sleep in the room next door to me, and I'm worried there is no way to fix them. To make her see that I'm not that man anymore."

"She? Um…what was her name? Kacey?"

Dropping his head, he closed his eyes as her words played over and over again in his head.

I wasn't enough.

He nodded slowly before saying, "How do I get her to trust me? To forget everything I did?"

"You know, Jordie, it isn't very smart to get into a relationship when you are in recovery," she said, but Jordie shook his head.

"I don't care," he said simply, and when Bethany didn't say anything to that, he looked up to see everyone looking at him. "I don't want to be who I was. I want to be someone better, I want to be sober, I want to play hockey, I want to be happy, and I want to love and be loved by her. I know she'll make me a better person, the person I want to be. That person wants to sit here a year from now, looking at the new guy the way you guys do, like they won't make it but hoping that they'll prove me wrong. And, believe me, I'm gonna prove all of you wrong."

Everyone smiled as Bethany nodded. "And we hope you do. I'm just saying I don't want you to do something that could trigger a setback."

"Anything could trigger a setback. And I'm sorry, but I'm gonna live my life and I'm gonna keep fighting this addiction I have," he said and she nodded.

"And I want you to, but I also want you to be realistic about this. Know going in that you are doing it because you love her and want to be with her. Not because you are looking for a distraction from your addiction."

Jordie glared. "I have loved this girl a long time; I just fought it because I didn't think I could be the man she needs. In the last couple months, I've changed and I actually love me."

"That's what we want, Jordie. But just keep in mind, don't replace one addiction with another."

OVERTIME

He understood where she was coming from, but he didn't think of Kacey that way. He was addicted to her, but in a good way. In a healthy way. He wouldn't use her and then throw her away. He wanted to love her for the rest of her life.

"Back to the comment you made, let me ask you something though. Did you know that everyone in this room had a slipup during their first year?"

"No, I didn't know that."

"All of us, even me, but you know what? We got right back up, and we tried again. So yes, live your life, but I am here to coach you, to warn you of what could happen. I was you. I thought after coming out of rehab, I'd be great for my husband and all would be good. I'd get pregnant and we'd be happy. I had a miscarriage, got drunk, hid it from him, got drunk again, and he found out and divorced me. So just remember, you have to fix you, she can't."

Jordie nodded.

"But always remember, you can't change the past, Jordie. You can only make your future what you want. You have to make the decisions that will better your life."

"And Kacey is one of them because I won't have the future I want if I don't have her."

He'd never spoken truer words.

But he wanted to speak them to her.

He just hoped she gave him the chance to.

When they were done with the meeting, Jordie was heading toward the door when Phil, one of the other members, stopped him. He was a tall man, a pro football player who Jordie had known for a while. "Hey, man, what you said tonight, it really touched me. I've just been existing, scared I'm gonna relapse at every second. I keep forgetting to live."

"Yeah, it's a hard balance," Jordie agreed, shaking his hand. "But these groups are here for a reason."

"For sure, but man, I just wanted to let you know that I don't look at you like you are gonna fail. I look at you like you're gonna make it. If anyone could do it, it's you."

He then pulled Jordie into a manly hug, slapping his back. "Stay strong, bro," he said and he waved at Karl before walking away.

"He's right," Karl said and Jordie looked back at him.

"I know, I just have to fight for it," Jordie said before pushing the door open and heading out with Karl on his tail.

"Yeah, and you will. You have a great support system."

"I do. Hoping to add your daughter to the top of the list," he said with a grin before going outside. Once in the sunlight, Jordie took in a long breath.

It was the moment of truth. It only took six minutes to get to El Bracero from the church where the meeting was held. He had planned to walk but then remembered that he had Karl with him.

"You okay?" Karl asked and Jordie nodded, glancing at his watch. He wasn't supposed to meet Kacey for another twenty minutes. "Karson will get over it. I know you're worried about that."

He was, but he was more worried that Kacey wouldn't show up. Then all the trouble he'd caused in his friendship with Karson would just be extra shit on top of the shit sandwich he'd have once he accepted she didn't want him. But deep down in his soul, he knew she'd show up. She had to. If anything, just out of curiosity. For answers. For closure. But he wouldn't let her go without a fight.

"How long you think he'll stay mad?" Jordie asked with a sullen look. "I fucked up pretty bad. Kacey is his baby sister and your baby… I'm surprised you aren't trying to swing at me."

Karl chuckled. "Between Karson and Regina, I think you got a beating. Plus, I know Kacey, she can handle her own. If she wanted to hurt you, she'd hurt you. She don't like me picking up the pieces of her heart. It embarrasses her. She's a prideful woman, that daughter of mine."

"That's the damn truth," Jordie agreed. "That's why I'm worried she won't give me another chance."

Karl nodded. "She probably won't," he said, which had Jordie gawking at him. "So you work for her love. You show her who you are and pray that she'll give you another chance."

Jordie nodded as he looked to the left, fishing his keys out of his pocket. "I gotta go meet said prideful woman at the Mexican restaurant down the road, hand her my balls on a silver platter, and own up to my mistakes. Here are my keys. If she doesn't show, I'll take a cab home. Or if she tells me to kiss it, I'll take one home."

Karl laughed, slapping his shoulder. "I'll go with you. If she shows, I'll leave. If she doesn't, we'll eat and… Shit, I was about to say drink margaritas."

Jordie laughed along with him. "Yeah, that can't happen."

"How depressing. Way to go, ruining the fun for everyone," he said with a wink and Jordie grinned.

"You didn't know? I'm a fuckup," Jordie joked but Karl paused, shaking his head.

"No, Jordie, you're not. Not anymore," he said, squeezing his shoulder. "You're a damn good man with a past that you're working on. Now, come on."

As he walked away, Jordie stood there and let his words sink in. He was right. He wasn't a fuckup anymore. His past was full of all his mistakes, but he was fixing each one. But this one… The one that he made with Kacey was the biggest and the one he most regretted.

But he would fix it.

Why was she the only normal one in her family?

The whole way to Liam's house, she replayed everything that happened and really didn't understand how it had even occurred. She and Lacey were usually careful when they talked about Jordie, but apparently they weren't careful enough. She still couldn't believe that Karson hit Jordie repeatedly like that. He was a big doofus, but a sweet doofus, and, God, she loved him. But she still couldn't believe it. Did Jordie deserve that? Oh, yeah. But did she like seeing him bleeding? No. Each drop of blood might as well have been hers. It was horrifying to see and all just so stupid.

But even with everything that had happened, all she could do was think about what Lacey had said to Karson as she tried to stop him. About forgiving Jordie and only caring about what he did after. After what? What was going on, and why did she seem to be the only one who was lost? Even her parents seemed to know what was going on. They were all nodding in agreement, and Jordie, he just looked stricken. She could tell that he hadn't intended to hurt her or Karson. Before, he would have laughed it off. But when he said sorry, he meant it.

More so when he said she was enough.

Ugh, she could still feel his words absorbing into her skin. She had waited so long to hear him say it, to give some kind of explanation, and she was almost there.

But first, she had to break it off with Liam.

Parking her car near his, she shut it off and headed toward his door, trying to think of a nice and easy way to turn him down. She couldn't think of anything but the truth. Before she could think harder, he opened the door.

"Hey!" he called out before glancing at his watch. "I expected you earlier."

"Yeah, sorry, some family shit went down," she said, waving him off. He leaned over, kissing her hard on the lips, but she pulled away just as quickly as he started, her hands coming to his chest as she looked up at his beautiful, chiseled face. He really was a handsome man and someone would really love him, but she just wasn't the one.

"That's not a good sign," he said, standing up straight.

"Yeah, not really," she agreed and then she stood awkwardly, crossing her ankles and leaning her arm on her hip.

"Well, come on in," he said, but she shook her head.

"I don't really see the point," she said simply, and she decided the truth was the only way to go. "I thought I owed it to you to do this in person, but I'm sorry, I can't go with you."

He looked down and then nodded. "Can I ask why?"

"Because as much as I want to love you, I can't. Not when my heart is still with someone else."

"Jordie?"

She didn't want to admit it out loud, especially to him, but soon her mouth was moving. "Yeah."

"You know he won't ever love you or treat you the way I can," he said, and Kacey bit the inside of her lip.

"No? Do you even know him?" she asked, and she was unsure why she was defending him. But she didn't like the way he talked about Jordie. Even if he was right, she didn't like it.

"He isn't that kind of guy. He's too busy screwing around."

Kacey nodded, her throat tightening before looking up at him. "I know that, but I'd rather be alone than be with someone I don't love."

Liam tucked his hands in his pockets and shrugged. "Then we have nothing else to say."

She nodded. "You're right. We don't."

Going up on her toes, she kissed his cheek, but he flinched away, his anger apparent. But really, what did he expect? She'd never loved him. "I wish you the best. Good luck."

Turning, she'd made it down the stairs when he called out, "You too, but believe me when I say you won't have that with Jordie. He won't ever do right by you. You're crazy to let me go for a dude like him."

Stopping and turning back around, she looked up at him. "I'm not leaving you for him. I'm leaving you for me," she said, and she could tell that he didn't like that one bit. But she had to stay true to herself. Their relationship had been a dead end since the beginning, but she'd kept driving down that road, praying something would open up. She refused to live a life that wasn't what she wanted. She really did regret hurting Liam—he was a good guy, but she wasn't living for him. She was living for her.

Waving, she said, "Bye, Liam."

"Bye, Kacey," he called, and when she turned, she heard the door shut and she shook her head.

That was hard, but not as hard as talking to Jordie was about to be.

When she pulled into the parking lot of El Bracero, the first person she saw was Jordie. She figured he'd get a table and wait for her like he had before, so it was easy to say she was surprised. When she got out of the car, he came off the stone pillar he was leaning against, his smile taking up his whole face, which was a hard feat with the beard he was sporting.

She hadn't gotten to drink him in when her brother was using him as a punching bag, but now, as she closed the distance between them, she took in the fitted jeans and thin blue Henley he wore. His hair was back in a black ball cap, but his eyes weren't covered by it. No, she could see the depths of those dark brown eyes a mile away. Also the fat lip and bruise on his jaw. Stupid Karson.

What she didn't expect was to see her daddy come off the second stone pillar. Making a face as her brows touched, she said, "Daddy? What are you doing here?"

"I was the backup plan in case you didn't show up," he teased, sending a wink at Jordie as he laughed. They had always been close, always. Almost as close as Karson and her father were, but it was obvious that Jordie was definitely a part of the family. That was one of the reasons she'd fallen so hard for him. Her daddy loved him. When he slapped Jordie on the back, something just clicked in Kacey's head.

"You knew about me and him?" she asked, and her dad looked back at her.

"Yeah, why?"

"How?"

He pointed to Jordie. "He told me."

"And you're okay with that?"

"Yeah," he said with a shrug.

"Is that why you threw a damn fit yesterday with Liam?" she asked and Karl laughed. She glared and she wasn't sure why she even asked because she knew the truth before he answered.

"Yeah, I don't like that guy. But I love this one," he said like it was common knowledge, and she guessed it was. But still, he'd acted like a damn two-year-old!

"Daddy, you embarrassed the shit out of me!" she complained, but he only shrugged.

"Don't date dudes that drive Priuses then," he said with a grin and leaned over to kiss her cheek. "Really listen, Kace, don't jump to conclusions," he whispered before pulling away and pinching her nose. Taking a set of keys from Jordie, he looked back at Kacey. "Be good, kids."

And then he walked away.

Shaking her head, she said, "I can't believe him."

Jordie nodded. "I hadn't even put two and two together. I just thought he really didn't like the guy."

She shrugged, her heart kicking up in speed when she realized she was alone.

With Jordie.

Sucking in a breath, she looked over at him to find that he was watching her. "Well, come on. I need a drink to get through this."

He only nodded before going to the door and pulling it open for her. Going past him, she tried to ignore the thick coconut smell that came off him in waves, but that was like ignoring a wide-open net.

She couldn't.

Standing as still as she could, she waited as he told the host how many people and then followed as he led them to their table. It was a booth in the back, only one table nearby, but it was empty, much like the rest of the place. As she slid into the booth, Jordie did the same across from her, picking up the menu as she threw her purse beside her.

"What can I get you to drink?" the waitress asked and Kacey couldn't order a mango margarita quick enough.

She looked to Jordie and he smiled as he said, "A water, please."

Her brows drew together as her lips curved. Looking across the table at him, she scoffed. "A water."

He nodded as he laid the menu down, dunking a chip in the salsa before looking back at her. "Yup."

"Weird. I thought you'd get a Corona like you always do. Maybe you have changed," she said offhandedly. She meant it as a joke to break the tension, but his eyes didn't leave hers as he nodded.

"Yeah, I have. I don't drink anymore."

That was huge, and very surprising since Jordie was a big drinker. So to be sure she hadn't heard him wrong, she asked, "Really?"

"Yeah, I'm an alcoholic, Kacey. But I am a hundred and fifteen days sober now."

Her jaw dropped.

Wait, no, that couldn't be.

But he wasn't smiling. No, it wasn't a joke.

He was serious.

Holy. Shit.

Chapter FOURTEEN

"You're serious?"

Kacey watched him as he slowly nodded, lacing his fingers together as he leaned back in the booth. Stunned to silence, she could only stare at him wide-eyed as the waitress came back, setting their drinks down for them and asking if they were ready.

"Can we have another few minutes, please?" Jordie asked, and she nodded before walking away.

"Like, really? You know for sure?" she asked, but really, she'd always known he was. He really didn't know how to stop when he started, and sometimes he drank for no reason. She was always too scared to say something because she knew it would give him a reason to blow up and break it off with her.

"Yeah," he nodded, his eyes cutting to her drink and then to her.

"Does this bother you?" she asked, pointing to the drink.

"Kinda, if I'm honest. But I'll have to get used to people drinking around me sooner, rather than later. Sort of pisses me off that I want it, y'know? Thought I would be cured by now."

"It's not an overnight thing," she said softly, sympathy filling her chest.

"Yeah, but I want it to be."

She could see the truth in his eyes, not to mention the way he was eyeing her drink. He was salivating for it, but he only glanced at it a few times. Who could blame him? It looked like a great margarita. One she wanted, but refused to drink with him across from her.

"I really don't know what to say," she said before stopping the waitress. "I decided not to drink, I have to drive."

She nodded, but Kacey didn't miss the annoyed look as she picked up her drink. "Water?"

"Yes, please," she answered before looking down at the table, sucking in a breath. "That was the last thing I thought you'd say. I'm a little shocked. But I'm glad; it was a problem."

"It was," he agreed. "But I didn't realize it until halfway through rehab."

She sat up straighter, her eyes widening. "So you actually went to rehab?"

He nodded. "Yeah, for ninety days. Elli made me."

Kacey looked away, hating that he didn't go for her. She knew he wouldn't; she didn't mean anything to him, apparently. But still, it hurt that he went because of Elli. "Yeah?"

"Yeah, since I already threw away everything that mattered because I was fucked in the head, all I had was hockey, and she threatened to take it from me."

Oh. Well, didn't she feel like a jerk. She assumed Elli had talked him into it, not threatened him. "Oh, wow."

"She wasn't playing. She had me in a group until a spot could open at the rehab ranch, but I was still drinking while going through the group, though."

"Why?"

"Because I didn't think I had a problem, because I thought it was stupid."

Just then the waitress came back and they gave their orders, but Kacey instantly forgot what she ordered. Looking at him, she waited for him to continue. She knew there was more, and she wasn't sure if she could handle it. Those first days back, he'd looked so defeated, and while she'd assumed he was still fucking around and being him, he was actually fighting to be healthy. But that didn't mean he wasn't fucking around, that he had changed. She had to keep her wits about her. She couldn't just jump across the table and cuddle him like she wanted.

Not only for him, but for her.

He looked across the table at her, catching her attention with those sullen brown eyes and shrugged. "I was wrong, obviously. Something I'm not proud to admit, but when you walked out that door back in Colorado, everything went to shit. Everything. I was drinking heavily, showing up to PT drunk, and then I went on this weekend in Louisiana that was a downright disaster. You'd think I'd learn from that, but I didn't. I just drank and drank and drank."

"Louisiana? When you got hurt?" she asked, her heart in her throat. She hadn't realized he had gotten so bad. And why the hell hadn't he called or returned her phone calls? She would have helped him, been there for him, but he'd pushed her away.

"Yeah," he said, letting out a long breath and then slowly looking back up at her. "I went down there, met up with one of my old buddies. He had a party and I got shit-faced, high on some Molly that he had put in my drink without me knowing. And that was what Elli found out and used to send me to rehab."

"Oh my God," she gasped, her jaw dropping. "But you don't do drugs."

"You know that, I know that, even Elli knew that, but I put myself in a position to let it happen. Add in the fact that I was high, drunk, and fucking anyone who would have me, and the trip was not a success."

She looked away and shook her head. She shouldn't have been surprised, but it still hurt to know he'd been fucking around when she couldn't even dream of sleeping with anyone. She knew he had. It was Jordie; his sex drive was like a sixteen-year-old's, but still, why wasn't he as broken as she was?

Because he didn't love you! So what was he doing here?

"I know—disgusting. But I want to be honest."

She looked up. "Well, it hurts 'cause while you were off fucking everything, I was borderline depressed, losing a child, and fighting for an Olympic medal— all while still loving you so much it hurt," she said sharply, her throat thick. "So yeah, it sucks hearing you be honest."

He looked away first, pulling in a breath and letting it out. "Want me to lie and tell you that I left you because I didn't want you?"

She bit into her lip as she shook her head. "No, I want the truth."

"Good, 'cause I was gonna give it to you anyway," he said, looking up at her. "I know it hurts—it hurts me rehashing it, but we can't move forward without me fixing what I did."

Her brow raised. "You can fix it?"

He shrugged. "I have no clue, but I want to try."

She looked away then, swallowing hard around the lump that was her heart in her throat. He wanted to try to fix what he had done, and Lord knew she wanted him to do it, but what would happen afterward? Before he could go on, their food came, but neither one touched it.

Clearing his throat, he said, "I fell trying to get between two girls and hurt my knee, then I went to the hospital, where they shot me up with pain-killers. I hooked up with my doctor, who took me home, and I spent the rest of my time with her."

"Wow," she muttered. "So while I was trying to get ahold of you, you moved on?" she snapped and he shook his head. She knew she was being difficult, but it was a hard pill to swallow. How could he have moved on? Why wasn't she enough?

"No, I used her."

Her eyes met his pleading ones. "Did it work?"

He shook his head. "Not at all."

She should have been happy that it didn't, but the pain in his eyes was gut-wrenching.

"I went home, got drunk, popped pills, and drank some more. I'd go to sleep with a bottle in my hand, wake up the next morning, and kill it before brushing my teeth. It was a vicious cycle. I lied over and over again to Karson and Lacey, telling them I was fine, when really, I was two seconds from drinking myself to death. I think at one point I even prayed for death."

Everything just hurt for him; that wasn't her Jordie. He loved life, or at least she thought he did. "Jordie," she mumbled and he shrugged.

"I had nothing to live for."

She shook her head. "You did. Yourself."

He nodded. "You're right, but I forgot that along the way. The only thing I cared about was forgetting you because I was too stupid to hold on to what was good in my life."

Shocked, she leaned back in the booth and shook her head. Why hadn't she seen how much he was hurting when she was with him? He was obviously using the drinking as a crutch, but she was having too much fun. When she realized she loved him, she freaked because she knew he wouldn't love her. He couldn't love her, and because of that, she didn't look back. Then when he wouldn't talk to her, she chalked it up to him being a dick, when really, he was hurting. Drowning in his own issues. But he wouldn't let her in!

"Why did you shut me out?" she asked, looking up at him. "Why didn't you reach out for me? I would have been there for you."

"Because at the time, I thought I couldn't give you what you wanted."

"Fine, but I would have been there as a friend."

"I can't be your friend, Kacey. I just can't."

"What? Why?"

"Because I feel too much for you, and it hurts to not have you be mine."

"That's stupid," she snapped, her heart pounding in her chest. "So instead, you just shut me out? Break my heart in the process and drink yourself stupid?"

He nodded. "At the time, it seemed like a good idea. I mean, Kacey," he paused, looking down and biting his lip. She watched him, this big, beautiful, burly man sitting across from her, and she could tell that he felt two feet tall. That it was taking everything out of him to sit there and admit all this to her. It was something she had never seen before because Jordie was a confident man. He was exuberant and full of life. Yeah, he drank—a lot—but it didn't seem to have a hold on him. But when he'd snapped his leg in two, she could see that he was slowly submitting to the darkness. She should have said something, but the fear of his rejection had been too great.

"I mean, you know my past. You know what happened with one of my mom's husbands. You know that I didn't know my dad, that I watched my mom beg for love from all these men, and that she never loved me the way she should have. It's not an excuse, I promise you that's not what I'm saying, but love seemed very unattainable to me. I didn't know how to love."

"But you do now?" she asked skeptically, and she felt like a bitch. But this dude could honestly manipulate a cow into buying milk. He was smooth with his words. When he wanted something, he got it, and she refused to fall victim to his brand of heartache again. "You go to rehab and somehow decide you can love me?

Holding her gaze, he licked his lips and leaned onto the table, coming a little closer to her. "Wanna know what made me realize I had a problem and that I wanted to change?"

Feeling like he was giving her whiplash since that wasn't what she'd expected him to say, she could only nod as his eyes bored into hers, the coconut scent from his beard intoxicating her.

"Mena Jane," he said fondly, his mouth turning up a bit. "Karson called and told me, and then Lacey sent me a picture of Mena and you. I just sat there staring at the picture, and I may have teared up a little bit because I had never seen such beauty in my life. One girl who stole my heart, and the other who owned it."

Her brows furrowed as she looked deep into his eyes. He smiled, his white teeth so bright against the dark hair on his face, but it didn't reach his eyes. "I decided right then that I wanted to be the godfather and man that you two deserved. I wanted to come home healthy, and I wanted to change."

She was speechless, her heart pounding in her chest as he held her gaze.

"I fucked up majorly with you, Kacey. I really did."

She nodded as she looked away, tears filling her eyes.

"And I won't make an excuse—it was me and my issues. But to answer your question, I found out who I was in rehab. I know him, I want to be him. And no, I don't know how to love someone, but then sometimes I think maybe I do. Because when I look at Mena, I love her. So fucking much. I know I love your family, and I also know that I have thought of you every second of every day for the last nine months. I yearn for your touch, I wonder what you are doing, what you are thinking, and if you'll ever have me again. So while I may not fully know how to love someone, I don't want to try with anyone but you."

She looked up, a tear slowly sliding down her face as their eyes locked. Her mind tried to wrap itself around everything he was saying, and she still found herself trying to find little clues that he was trying to deceive her. But when he looked up, his eyes reiterated his honesty. That he was sorry. That he was telling the truth. He meant every word.

But that still couldn't make her forget.

Wiping her hand across her face, she shook her head. "I would have been there for you. I would have held your hand. I would have loved you through it all, but you didn't let me."

He nodded. "I know. I'm sorry, Kacey. Really, I am."

"So instead, I was left in the dark. And now you want me to just forget it all and trust you again? To allow you to love me and be the man I want? When before you didn't want love and you pushed me away?"

He leaned back, sucking in a breath. "That would be great, but I know it won't happen. I know I have to prove it to you. That I have changed."

She shook her head. "No, I see that you've changed, Jordie, I do. And I see the remorse. I know you're sorry, but I don't know how to get over the fact that you didn't want me or trust me to help you. Instead, you've fucked your way through the phone book and drunk yourself into a stupor."

"Kacey—"

"No, let me finish," she insisted and he snapped his mouth shut. "I am so proud of you for changing, for getting sober, and being honest," she said, the tears falling quicker. "No one is as proud of you as I am, and no one loves you the way I do. I can promise you that. I've wanted this for you, I've begged for this for you. But Jordie, you didn't want me to help you, and that hurts. You couldn't even text me back and just let me know you were okay. You shut me out, and that pains me more now that I know the truth than it did thinking you were fucking around and I was just one of your many sluts."

"I didn't tell anyone, Kacey. I held it all in and drowned myself until I got caught. And even then, I still tried to say I didn't have a problem. I can't change what I did. All I can do is say it won't happen again and that I'm sorry. I'm so fucking sorry," he said, and she could hear the desperation in his voice.

Holding his gaze, she could barely see him through her tear-flooded eyes. She knew he was sorry—that wasn't the problem. The problem was that she not only felt rejected, she felt used. Closing her eyes, her tears leaked out as she said in a shaking voice, "What do you want from me, Jordie?"

She opened her eyes, the tears streaming down her face, and all she could do was think what she was going to say when he said what she expected.

"You. I want you," he said sternly, like she knew he would, though what surprised her was that his eyes clouded with tears. But she had to stay strong.

"That's the thing you've always had—me. But you used me for sex and someone to keep you warm instead of loving me back the way I loved you."

"No, I didn't, and I never intended for you to feel that way. I was fucked up, Kacey. I wasn't someone even I could love. How could I expect you to love me? I'm—"

"You're sorry," she said for him, and he nodded. "I know, and I've forgiven you, Jordie, I have. But it hurts and I need to process all this before I even try to decide to give you another chance. Because, with you, I don't think, I act, and that's how I get in trouble. That's what leaves me heartbroken. I just don't understand why you couldn't trust me enough to help you."

"Because I was spinning out of control and I refused to take you with me, so I pushed you away. I didn't know how to admit to you how fucked up I was. I was already a gimp, if I admitted that I was thinking of killing myself, how would you have handled it? I couldn't expect—"

"I would have loved you. I would have helped you, but you wouldn't allow me to."

"Because I was too prideful, too scared of how you made me feel. And, instead of doing the right thing, I always do the wrong. I know that. What I'm asking for is another chance to do all the right things for you."

Shaking her head, she looked down, her tears staining her shirt as his words played over and over in her head. He was saying everything she wanted. Everything she had been praying for, but something told her to step back. She couldn't just jump in and trust that he wouldn't hurt her again. Too much had happened for her to be so careless. But how would she ever know? A relationship hardly ever played out the way someone hoped. Love wasn't a Cinderella tale, it was hard and it hurt.

Looking up at him, she blinked away her tears before reaching for her purse. "Jordie, I want to lean across the table and kiss you, I do. I want to ride off into the sunset and know that we'll live happily ever after. Believe me, that's something I truly want. But you want me right now. Because of how it was when you had me before, you know I'm good for you. But what's gonna happen when you meet someone else? When you decide you're done with me? Then what? Or if you hit another dark spot and you don't want to share it with me, pushing me away in the end. Jordie, I'll be right back where you left me. I'll be heartbroken and alone."

He was shaking his head before she even finished. "No, that won't happen," he said. She looked up as a tear slowly rolled down his face, and it honestly murdered her to see it. He never cried. Never. But with his heart in his eyes, he admitted, "I've learned from my mistakes, I have. And, baby, you're it."

But could she believe him?

Kacey's tears were falling in sheets down her face and it was killing him to see. He hated when she cried. It didn't happen often, but when it did, it hurt. It was like little daggers were falling from her eyes and stabbing him over and over again in the chest. He wanted to comfort her, take her in his arms and tell her how sorry he was, but he didn't know what else to say. He'd said everything he had in his heart, and all he could do was pray it was enough.

The way she was looking at him though, it didn't seem like it was.

It took everything for him to do that. He didn't care to share his secrets, his issues, but he would do it for her. He would do anything for her but, for some reason, she wasn't seeing that. She was caught up on one detail that, yes, was shitty, but he saw no other way. If he hadn't pushed her away, then she would have been subjected to all the shit he was feeling, and he couldn't do that to her. It wouldn't have been fair. He loved her more than that.

Clutching her purse to her chest like a shield against him, she nodded. "I need to go."

His heart sank. "But you haven't eaten," he said, grasping at anything to keep her there. He wasn't done talking. There had to be something to reach her, to make her realize how shitty a place he'd been in and how he could never have been the man she needed.

She made a face. "I'm not hungry."

Oh yeah, he was in deep shit. Those words never left her lips. She was always hungry.

"Kace, please don't leave."

But she was already getting out of the booth. He took her hand, stopping her, and she looked down at him, adjusting her purse as he held her hand, his thumb slowly covering each bump of her knuckles on her hand.

"Please," he asked, but she shook her head.

"I need space, Jordie. Please." She slid her hand from his, but instead of walking away, she leaned over, pressing her lips to his cheek. He closed his eyes, his hand coming up to cup her face, holding there, breathing in her scent. He didn't want to let her go, but he knew he had to. He had to trust that she'd see that he meant everything he said. He had to.

"I'll wait," he said. "I'll wait forever," he whispered, his lips ever so close to hers.

She pulled away, tears rushing from her eyes, and then she was gone.

Slowly, he let his head fall before letting out a long breath. That didn't go like he'd hoped it would. He'd been convinced that just getting her there was the key. Once he said his peace, she'd take him back in a heartbeat. But oh, how wrong he was.

"Um, you still eating?"

He looked up at the waitress, sniffing back his own tears. He felt like a failure, something he hated feeling. "No."

Their waitress made a face before gathering their plates. "Do you want anything else?"

A Corona and, hell, even a margarita.

But despite his craving, or better yet his crutch for getting rid of the feelings he was feeling, he shook his head. "No, thank you. Just the check."

She grumbled something in Spanish before laying the check on the table. Retrieving his phone out of his pocket, he called for a taxi and laid two twenties on the table for the food they didn't eat. Getting up, he headed outside for some fresh air and sat on the bench to wait for the taxi, replaying the whole interaction. But everything went the way he feared it would. He knew she wouldn't want to hear about him with other women, but he had to be honest. He told her everything he was feeling. Everything, and yet she still walked away.

Kicking at the cement, he let out a long breath He should have just ridden home with her, tried some more. But what else could he say? Plus, she needed time. She needed to think, and he would give her the space she wanted.

No matter how much he didn't want to.

She'd come back to him.

She would.

He hoped.

The whole ride back to the house, Jordie watched the world speed by and wondered what he was going to do if she didn't give him another chance. He wondered if she'd cried the whole way home, like he wanted to. Wondered if she thought he was weak, pathetic, like he felt. He hadn't done right by her, and maybe he didn't deserve another chance. Maybe this was his punishment for all the wrong he'd done.

Not having the one person he wanted.

When the cab stopped in front of the house, he paid and glanced out at it. It was everything that Karson and Lacey wanted, full of love and happiness. He wanted this. He wanted it so damn bad, he could taste it. Getting out, he noticed that Karson was sitting on the porch, Mena Jane in his lap. Groaning inwardly, he wasn't sure he could do another drag-out with Karson. His heart was still pounding in his chest. The look of such pain in Kacey's eyes haunted him. He couldn't deal with his best friend breaking up with him too.

He wanted to go to the side door, but he felt that would make him a coward. Before he could make the decision though, Karson hollered out at him.

"How's your face?" Karson's lip curved up as he slowly danced in the chair with Mena.

Jordie didn't feel like laughing, but he did as he headed toward Karson, brushing his fingers along his swollen lip. It hurt, but it was nothing compared to what he was feeling inside. "Sore."

"Good," Karson decided as Jordie sat next to him. He reached over, taking Mena from Karson and kissing her head.

"For protection," he teased and Karson scoffed.

"I'm not gonna hit you again," he said but then paused. "But I'm not saying sorry either, like Lacey told me to."

"Wouldn't expect you to. I deserved it."

Karson nodded. "Why didn't you just tell me? Why did you hide the truth like that? I asked you if it was serious and you laughed me off."

"Because I didn't want it to be serious. If it was serious, then that meant I could hurt her."

"But you still hurt her," Karson said, wringing his fingers together. "And I really don't understand why you'd do that. I thought you cared about her."

"I do. I love her, man," he said, and Karson's eyes widened. "I do, but I wasn't thinking right. I didn't want to feel what she made me feel because I didn't think what she wanted was in my cards." He leaned down, kissing the top of Mena's little head. "It still may not be in my cards, but I've decided I want it to be. I want your life, bro. I want the wife, the kids, the happiness. I'm done being lonely and drunk and living because I have to. I want to live for something. For someone and for myself."

Leaning on his knees, Karson shook his head as he looked over at Jordie. "Man, bro, I want to be mad at you, I want to slam my fist in your face, but I just feel for you. For so long you held all this in. I mean, I knew you were a jackass and drank too much, but man, you've been living with all this shit just suffocating you. Why couldn't you reach out? We would have helped."

Jordie shrugged. "Seems to be the question of the day."

"Huh?"

"Kacey and I talked today. I told her everything, asked for another chance."

"And she said?"

"That she needed time to think," he said softly, his lips dusting the top of Mena's head.

"Are you gonna be okay if she doesn't give it to you?"

Jordie nodded. "Not at first, but I won't go back to the way I was. I almost didn't make it back then, and I refuse to allow myself to go back to that," he admitted, thinking of the many times he'd thought about just ending it all. It went all the way back to his teen years. He'd always hit those low points and had never had anyone to lift him back up. That was why he'd never taken what Kacey was offering, because he'd never had it before and didn't know how to ask for help. "But, I honestly need you in my life, so if you need to swing on me to feel better, please do."

Karson scoffed then, grasping Jordie's shoulder. "I'm good, bro, just don't lie to me ever again."

"No problem," he promised.

"And about Kacey, Lacey told me she really loves you. If you continue being the man you are now, then I'm good with you being with her."

Jordie smiled. "I won't just be with her, Karson. I'll want to marry her."

Karson nodded, biting his lip as his fingers locked together before he turned to look at Jordie. "And I'll stand beside you at the wedding. Like I always have."

There was no one else like Karson, and Jordie sure as hell had done nothing to warrant a friend like him. Karson was a good man, one that Jordie strived to be. Clearing his throat free of the emotion that was clogging it, he nodded.

"Thanks, bro."

"Anytime. Just be honest and stay healthy."

"That's my plan," he said as the door opened. They both turned to see Lacey in the doorway. Her eyes widened as her gaze cut back and forth between them. Seeing that there was no new blood, she nodded.

"You two good?"

They both nodded and she smiled. "Good. Come on in, it's getting chilly for her, or give her here."

Karson stood and shook his head. "No, we're coming," he said, taking Mena back and then heading in before Jordie.

Shutting the door, Lacey stopped him and asked, "How did it go?"

Jordie shrugged. "She said she needed space."

She made a face. "Hm. Okay. Well, keep your chin up."

"Will do," he said before kissing her cheek. "I'm heading to bed. Goodnight."

"You don't want to eat dinner with us?" she asked, and he saw her look. He knew it was only five, but he was done with this day.

"I'm not hungry."

"That's what Kacey said too," she said, her eyes full of worry as he walked away, and his heart sank a little more. She wouldn't eat with her family? Pausing at her door, he wondered if he should check on her, but he wasn't sure how that would go.

Letting out a long breath, he went to his room, shutting the door and then glancing into the bathroom. She wasn't there and her door was shut. Probably locked. Throwing his wallet on his dresser, he toed out of his shoes and threw off his shirt. Falling back on the bed, he looked over and stared at her door.

God, he wondered what she was doing.

What she was thinking.

Was she crying?

Looking up at the ceiling, he sighed heavily.

The waiting was going to kill him.

It wouldn't be an excessive amount of drinking or an STD or even his own doing. No, it would be waiting that would kill him.

But he'd wait.

Because he loved her.

When his phone vibrated in his pocket, he pulled it out to see that it was a Facebook notification. Lucas had posted a video to his timeline, but instead of clicking on it, he clicked on his messages. He didn't have to scroll far to find his and Kacey's thread. He always deleted his threads, but not hers. Her messages kept him warm and toasty at night, along with the many naked pictures he had of her, but that wasn't what he went to. No, he opened it to the last message:

> *Kacey: You know what, I bet you're already off fucking someone else, huh?*

God, he hated that that had been the last thing she said to him, and for some reason, as he read it over and over again, his thumbs started moving across the keys.

> *Jordie: I was because I wanted to forget you. I wanted to stop thinking about how stupid I was, about how I wasn't the guy for you, about how I would never be the guy you deserve. I wanted to be that guy, but I wasn't. You were smart to walk away, but I was dumb to let you go and I'm so sorry. I can promise you, Kacey, I'll never let you go again. Never.*

He hit send and waited, but he didn't have to wait long for the little chat bubble to pop up. Holding his breath, he waited and then finally her message came through.

> *Kacey: I wish you would have let me in. Trusted me.*

Sitting up, he typed back quickly.

> *Jordie: I did, I do, I just didn't trust myself. I knew I was gonna hurt you, so I kept you at arm's length, but that didn't work. You consumed me, Kacey. Completely, you took my heart and I don't want it back. Please keep it, just allow me to reap the benefits, give me another chance. You won't regret it, I promise.*
> *Kacey: I just don't know.*

Shaking his head, he knew he couldn't do this on the phone. He needed to do this face-to-face.

> *Jordie: Just let me in.*
> *Kacey: I've always let you in. I've never lied or held anything*

back from you. You did.

He shook his head, standing up and going toward her bathroom door.

Jordie: No, I know that. What I mean is open your door. Let me in.

He waited for her to do it, but it didn't open.

Kacey: Why?
Jordie: 'Cause I don't want to do this over the phone. I want to talk to you.
Kacey: We've talked Jordie. There can't be anything else left to say.
Jordie: I'm sure I can think of something. I can't do this. The unknowing. I know I hurt you. I'm fucking sorry and I'll never do it again. Just take one last chance on me. Just one.

Her text bubble didn't pop up and the door didn't open either. Seconds turned into minutes as he stood like an idiot in the middle of the bathroom, staring at his phone and then the door. A sullen feeling came over him as he began to think she wasn't going to open the door.

Looking down at his phone, he was about to text her when he heard the door unlock and then slowly open. Meeting her tearstained face, he sucked in a breath.

Clearing her throat, she said, "Don't make me regret this."

Her breathing was labored, her breasts rising and falling as if she had run to the door while contemplating if she was going to open it. Her eyes wandered down his chest, stopping at his crotch before running back up his body and meeting his eyes. Something in her eyes, lust maybe, caught him off guard, hitting him straight in the chest. He fully expected to come in there and talk, work it out because he wanted to be with her, but...but...he fucking needed her.

Pushing the door open, he pulled her into his arms and, thank the Lord, she came willingly. He wrapped his arms tightly around her, lifting her off the ground, his mouth so close to hers as his eyes searched hers.

Against those naughty lips, he whispered, "Never."

Chapter FIFTEEN

*P*lease, Lord, don't let this backfire, Kacey thought as Jordie pushed her into the door, pressing his body against hers, his mouth ever so close to hers. Ugh, she wanted him. She wanted him so badly she couldn't stand it, but maybe she shouldn't… Then his hand tangled in her hair and she was a goner.

Call her a hussy, but hell in a handbasket, he was irresistible. And, man, she wanted him.

His chest was hot against her thin tank, and in just seconds under his intensely wanton gaze, she was dripping with arousal. She wasn't sure she was doing the right thing, but all she'd kept thinking since she walked out of the Mexican restaurant was, *There was your chance. Your forever. And you're walking away?* If she didn't give it another go, she knew she'd regret it for the rest of her life. She wasn't sure what would happen, and she wasn't sure if her heart was safe. But she figured, if she couldn't get over him in the nine months since she'd walked away, and as he'd come to her wanting another chance, claiming to be a changed man, she might as well take what he was giving.

That either made her an idiot…or she was holding her forever in her arms at that very second.

She was praying for the latter.

Holding her breath, she waited for him to kiss her. The kiss in the bathroom the night before had been too short. She had been thinking of his mouth, still feeling it on hers since then, and she was ready for a repeat. Practically begging for it. Moving her fingers through the hair on his chest, she nuzzled his beard with her nose before running her nose along his lips, and then against his own nose. She just wanted to feel him. Rediscover him after so many months without him. She needed him. She was all but shaking for him because that was what they did. They made love, and they did it damn well.

But why wasn't he kissing her?

"If my mouth touches you, Kacey, I won't stop."

"Okay," she gasped against his lips. "Not sure this is smart, but okay."

He smiled. "Eh, maybe not, but I can't stop once I start."

"And I don't want you to," she admitted, her center pulsing for him.

"Good. Is Liam out of the picture?"

Her brows came together, surprised by his question, but also she found it very sweet. "Yeah. I broke it off with him this afternoon. Wait, does that make me a whore since I'm about to be with you?"

He chuckled, his lips ever so close to hers, his hands sliding down over her ass and holding her thighs. "When did you sleep with him last?"

His eyes were intent on hers, waiting for her answer, and she shrugged. "I didn't. He wanted to wait till I loved him."

He scoffed. "Which would never happen. Okay, good," he said, his arms tightening around her. "And it doesn't make you a whore. It makes you mine," he growled against her lips. "Now, tell me he meant nothing to you."

His eyes were full of desire, his breath coming hot against her mouth, his poor, busted lip begging for her attention. "He didn't mean anything to me."

"That's right," he snarled before finally dropping his mouth to hers. Wrapping her legs tightly around his waist, she hung on as his mouth devoured hers. His tongue was hot against her lips and felt oh so good. As she opened her mouth to his, their tongues played like old friends, and she almost came at the feeling. She had been craving him for months, and finally, she had him. His beard tickled her chin, but she felt it deep within her gut too. That fluttering, first-time kind of feeling. He always did that. Every damn time. Squeezing her arms around his neck, she never wanted to leave this spot. Never wanted to leave his arms. They'd figure everything out later. Right now, she needed him.

Carrying her to the bed, he laid her down so slowly and with so much care, she was breathless. Jordie wasn't careful, he wasn't sweet all the time, but when he was, she felt it in her soul. Hovering over her, he trailed kisses along her neck, her jaw, and her bottom lip as he held her breast in his hand. When he squeezed her nipple with his thumb and forefinger, she hissed against his cheek, his mouth nibbling at her neck. Kissing up her jaw, he whispered against her mouth, "Please tell me the door is locked."

She nodded, threading her fingers through his hair.

"Good," he moaned against her lips before falling between her legs, pressing his hard cock against her hidden, dripping wet pussy. Even with his jeans and her shorts, she could feel every inch of him and the heat he put off, and she shook at the mere thought of him being inside her again. Sitting up, he pulled her shorts off as she threw off her tank. Then his mouth was on her breast, his hand between her legs, his finger sliding up her wet lips as he feasted on her breast.

Arching her back, she bit her lip to keep from screaming out like she wanted. Man, she needed her own place, or maybe they… *Whoa, hold your horses*, she thought. This could only be about sex, and if it was, she was going to kick him in the balls and swear off all men. But it couldn't be. He was cherishing her body, tasting it. As his fingers trailed down the middle of her chest to her belly button, she whimpered, her pussy clenching with need. His eyes were so intense, so beautiful and, damn it, they were full of love.

She remembered that look. It only came out sometimes, but when it did, Kacey felt like the most gorgeous girl in the world. She never felt like that except when she was under his gaze.

"So beautiful," he whispered, his finger tracing the outline of the abs she had worked her ass off to get. "So strong."

She gasped as his tongue followed his fingers, the tickling sensation from his beard along her pubic area driving her utterly mad. Thrashing beneath him, she arched against his mouth as he nibbled on her belly button. He grinned against her skin. To her dismay though, he pulled away, his eyes drinking her in before he looked up and met her gaze.

"You are, by far, the most magnificent woman I've ever seen," he said huskily, and she swore she felt the words he said.

It was one thing to hear them, but with Jordie, she felt them. Deep in her heart and soul. Man, she hoped this wasn't just about sex. But before she could overthink it and start to consider stopping him, his mouth dropped to hers as his hands unbuttoned his jeans. He rolled them over, her legs falling on either side of his hips as her fingers threaded through his hair on his chest, her nails digging into his skin. He gasped against her mouth, biting at her bottom lip as she slid her wet center along his hard stomach. Squeezing her ass, he kept kissing her before wiggling out of his pants and freeing his cock. It smacked against her ass, and she grinned as his tongue moved along her bottom lip.

Rolling them over again, he pulled back her leg and entered her with one thrust, taking her breath from her. Her soul. Her heart. Everything. He took it. But then, he'd always had it.

His fingers bit into her thigh as her eyes rolled back in her head, his cock filling her to the hilt and eliminating the void that had been taunting her since she'd left all those months ago. She thought it would feel the same, him being in her, but it was completely different. They were different.

While he thrust into her, his mouth stayed on hers, and he pulled all the way out and then slammed back into her. Each time, she squeezed him, her breath whooshing out of her as he took what he wanted. Needed. His eyes were so dark, so intense, and only on her. Sliding his hand from her thigh to between her legs, he found her nub of nerves and pressed it hard, causing her to cry out against his mouth. Covering her mouth with his to mask her cries, he slowly moved his thumb along the sensitive bud. She felt herself about to come, felt it all over and with each thrust. And the flick of his thumb had her inching closer and closer to her release. Taking her mouth with his, he slid his tongue along hers and soon it was too much. She came and she couldn't help herself as she uttered his name against his lips. He smiled against her mouth as her eyes squeezed shut, her chest seizing as she arched up, his name falling again and again from her lips.

"That's right, sugar thighs," he whispered, kissing down her jaw. "Come all over me. I love the way you feel."

She couldn't answer him, her breathing was labored, her heart felt as if it were going to come out of her chest, and it very well could. He went up on his knees and she opened her eyes as he pushed her knees farther apart, his thumbs digging into the backs of her thighs as he filled her to the hilt, his cock throbbing inside her. Looking down at her, he smiled, and she smiled back. Just that simple little smile hit her straight in the gut, and she knew this wasn't just sex.

This was way more.

Pulling out of her, he drove into her again and again and again until he squeezed her so hard she was sure she was going to have bruises all over her, and he came with a guttural yell. He fell onto her, his heart slamming into her chest, shaking her own as his cock throbbed inside of her. He was heavy, so damn heavy, but she wrapped her arms around his middle, her legs around his, nuzzling her nose under his beard, taking in the addictive smell. When he gasped against her temple, she felt him smile as he rolled them to their sides, holding her tightly, his cock still inside her as they grabbed at each other. Soon their breathing returned to normal, but she couldn't let him go.

Not yet.

His fingers came along her jaw before he tilted her face up, his eyes meeting hers. Running his thumbs along her cheeks, he whispered, "I love you, Kacey."

Her heart melted, and she felt like she was flying through the fucking clouds. They'd had sex a lot, a whole lot, but never had he looked at her and said those words. The words she wanted so desperately. It almost seemed like a dream, but she could feel him against her. Her body absorbing his and not letting go.

"I love you."

His face lit up and she swore she saw his eyes glaze over a little bit. But before she could really see if they did, he nuzzled his nose along hers, kissing her lips as his eyes fell shut. Closing her eyes, she held on to him and wouldn't let go due to the fear of him disappearing. Surely, this was a dream. But it wasn't. His heat was burning her, his heart still thumping against her chest, his breath in her hair, and his scent…it took over every one of her senses. They didn't move for a very long time, and as she watched as the sun slowly lower, she knew she didn't want to be anywhere else. And felt maybe she had made the right choice.

She prayed she did, at least.

"I would have ruined you," he whispered against her temple and her breath caught at his affirmation. "If I would have tried in the state I was in, we wouldn't have made it. I didn't tell you how bad it was because I didn't think I had a problem. I made excuse after excuse for everything I did, when, really, it was because I didn't love myself. How could I love you when I didn't even love myself?"

Moving her face out from underneath his, she looked up at him. "I tried to love you enough for both of us."

"I know," he said, his voice raspy and full of emotion. "And that's not fair. I knew I wasn't the man for you. I knew I would hurt you, cheat on you, or do something equally stupid. I couldn't risk it. Hell, I'm nervous now that something could happen, that I could relapse and let you down, but I gotta live, Kacey. I have to be who I want to be, and that person is yours."

Her eyes slowly filled with tears, his face blurring out until she blinked them away. "I'd really like that, Jordie, and you won't relapse because I'm gonna be there for you. I'm going to help."

"I might need it," he admitted shyly, and she reached up, brushing her thumb along his lip.

"I'm here. I was always here," she reminded him and he nodded.

"I'm not letting go this time."

"Neither am I. In it to win it," she said, her lips curving into a small smile. Soon his face broke into one too, his fingers catching her tears. His eyes searched hers, and his arms wrapped around her and she swore they were about to become one as he squeezed her so tightly. Honestly, she was okay with that. She had yearned for him for so long and now having him was almost a fantasy.

"I'm sorry, so fucking sorry for everything, baby," he whispered against her lips and she nodded slowly.

"I forgave you a long time ago," she admitted, her nose moving along his, her lips grazing his. "I knew what I was getting into."

"It shouldn't have ever been like that. I should have loved you the way I wanted to."

"But you do now," she declared.

"And I won't stop."

He said it as a promise.

One she prayed he'd keep.

Because she couldn't do the heartache again.

She just couldn't.

Jordie hadn't expected after the way Kacey ran out of the restaurant that he would be lying in her bed with her in his arms, but he was pretty sure he was grinning from ear to ear with no plans of ever wiping it off his face. Cuddling her closer, he kissed her nose as she looked deep into his eyes. She was so beautiful, so delicate but strong as an ox. He had done her so dirty but, yet, here she was, trusting him again. He didn't deserve her, but he'd be damned if he'd let her go. This was it. She was his.

"We should probably get a shower," he murmured against her lips. "I bet you're hungry."

On cue, her stomach growled and she giggled. "Yeah, I am. But just a few more minutes," she said, nuzzling her nose against his beard.

She'd always had a thing for his beard and it pleased him to no end. She was the reason he didn't shave it off, despite Regina's request every time she saw him. He didn't care one way or another; he liked it but didn't need it. But Kacey, she loved it. There were plenty of times in the last year where he'd wanted to just chop it all off, but then she'd nuzzle her nose in it and ask him not to.

So he didn't.

He now knew he'd always loved her, had since he first saw her. But he'd fought it so hard and, as he held her, he wondered why he'd been so clueless. This woman loved with everything inside her. Her eyes made him feel worshiped, her body made him feel good, and her love made him feel complete. He'd had this in his grasp and, instead of taking ahold of her, he'd pushed her away. He wanted to hate himself for it, but really, it was all meant to be. He had to be sober to actually appreciate her. To be what she needed. And now he was more than ready. He just hoped she was too.

Kissing her nose again, he asked, "So you're giving me another chance?"

"Yeah. I think I am."

"We are together, right?"

He saw her cheeks rise like she was smiling as she said, "Oh, I thought we were gonna keep it light. Like before."

He heard the teasing in her voice and he smiled against her. "Nope, I want more."

She looked up at him, her eyes bright and her grin unstoppable. "Good, 'cause that was the only thing I would accept."

"Me too," he said, rolling over and bringing her with him. Her legs came to the sides of his hips while her elbows came down on his chest, bracing her head as she looked down at him. When her brows came together, his matched hers as he asked, "What?"

"Something is running down my leg."

He grinned. "Probably my love juices."

"You didn't use a condom?" she asked, shocked, but when the hell had he had time to put one on?

"No," he admitted. "I didn't even think about it."

She gave him a panicked look. "You better be clean."

He scoffed. "Very much so. I haven't even had sex in eight months, so I'm sure if I had something, I'd know by now, what with all the testing in rehab."

Her mouth fell open. "Really?"

He nodded, smiling shyly. "Sex meant nothing to me if it wasn't you. So I replaced my need with porn and alcohol."

She smiled, but it didn't reach her eyes. "What every girl wants to hear."

"Um, I thought it was very romantic. Even my therapist was surprised by it."

Her eyes met his. "You talked about me in rehab?"

He nodded. "All the time. You're a piece of me."

"See, that's romantic," she commented, her lips curving as her fingers twirled in his chest hair. She didn't say anything for a while, and he watched as she moved her fingers along his body. "Is it hard?" she asked then, her eyes meeting his. "Are you suffering at all?

He shook his head. "No, I feel great, especially now." His hand cupped her ass and her laughter was music to his ears. "But yeah, some days it's hard. And others, I'm good. I've been playing the guitar again and that helps a lot."

"You play way better than I ever imagined. When you spoke of it before, I didn't think you were that good."

Pride filled his chest as he shrugged, trying to play off how good she'd just made him feel. He took great pride in his playing; it honestly calmed him, and to know she enjoyed it was really special. "Thanks. Maybe I'll play for you and you'll actually acknowledge my playing." He knew she had heard him all those weeks ago, despite her attempts to ignore him.

She smiled sheepishly and shrugged. "I'd like that," she whispered, her fingers crawling up his chest to his face.

Cupping her face, he moved his thumb along her jaw and asked, "What happened with Liam?"

She shrugged. "There wasn't anything to really end. I mean, we kissed a bit, but it wasn't anything more. He was pissed, obviously. Told me you would hurt me again if I was leaving him for you, but I told him I was leaving him for me. Because I deserve more than to settle for the safe guy."

"You deserve the world."

She nodded. "Yeah, so make sure you give it to me, unsafe guy," she teased and he smiled.

"Maybe I could be the safe guy?"

She shook her head. "I don't want the safe guy. I want the guy who's gonna keep me on my toes, make me live, and love me with so much intensity, I feel it everywhere. I want him to fuck me, to make love to me, not plan to 'get intimate.' I want him covered in tattoos, with a crazy beard, and to play hockey. I want you," she said, her eyes meeting his. "I've always wanted you."

"You've got me," he said breathlessly, his eyes burning into hers.

"Good," she decided, leaning back down and running her fingers through his beard. As he watched her, he couldn't believe how lucky he was. How beautiful she was. He loved her hair, and soon he was reaching out, tucking her hair back behind her ear. "I really like your hair like this."

She smiled, scrunching her face up. "It's getting there."

"I don't think I can handle you with long hair, you'll be too hot," he decided and she rolled her eyes.

"Oh, hush," she said, sitting up and smacking his chest. "Come on, let's get in the shower."

She didn't have to ask him twice. As she climbed off him, he smacked her ass playfully and she grinned back at him as she sauntered into the bathroom.

"See, that turns me on. Safe guys don't do that," she called back at him as he got out of bed.

Grinning, he took her by her hips and stopped her, kissing her shoulder and then her neck. "Then I'm as unsafe as they come, because this ass needs slapping."

She giggled, her body hot and irresistible against his. He wanted to lean her against the counter, take her, and tell her how much she meant to him. Deciding that was a fucking great idea, he started nibbling on her, his hands grazing along her stomach, but then he paused.

"Are you on the pill or something?" he asked and she nodded.

"IUD," she said. "Like before."

He thought that over as she broke out of his arms, starting the shower, and his moment to take her on the counter was gone.

"But you got pregnant on it?" he asked and she paused.

She looked over at him and nodded. "Yeah, I did," she said, but she didn't seem very concerned. If he was honest, neither was he. "So maybe I should be worried, huh?"

"Or not?" he suggested and she eyed him.

"Or not."

She studied him and he grinned. "Maybe we should put this conversation on hold, 'cause the way you are looking at me is like you want to have a baby right now."

He shrugged, feeling sheepish as he ran his hand through his hair. Did he want a baby? Yeah, he did, but the look in her eyes said if he confessed that, he would be rushing this. He didn't want to rush it. He wanted to build a life with her, a foundation, a love that could withstand any storm. Since his life was one hell of a hurricane, they would need it.

But still, he admitted, "I wish you hadn't miscarried the first one. I wish I had been there."

Her head fell back as she nodded, wrapping her arms around her middle in such a defeated way. "Me too."

Closing the distance between them, he enveloped her in his arms, kissing her pursed mouth. "But everything happens for a reason. We are starting over."

"Yeah," she agreed. "If it happens again, then we will address it at that point."

"Together," he promised, but he'd never tell her he was hoping and praying that she would get knocked up again. He knew he needed to take this slow, to show her that he meant business. But he wanted it all. He wanted her, marriage, a kid, and a dog. Everything. It could be very naïve of him, but he felt good about them. Knew they would succeed, because he wasn't giving up.

On him.

Or her.

Or their future.

Kissing her again, he slowly backed her under the hot water, and as her arms wrapped around him, his eyes drifted shut. Both the feel of her and the hot stream of water were almost too much to handle. He finally had everything he wanted.

He had Kacey.

"It's very overwhelming," she whispered against his throat. "I've dreamed and prayed that this would happen. That you'd come back for me."

"Did I live up to the dreams?"

"You surpassed them," she said as she looked up at him. "I never thought you'd be this guy."

He smiled, cupping her face. "I never thought I would be either, but there is no going back."

She grinned back at him. "You got that right. Because this is it, Jordie, your one and only last chance."

He already knew that, and while it did scare him since he was prone to fuck up, he knew he was ready. He had been thinking about this moment since he watched her walk away. It was time to stand up and be the man he wanted to be. It was time to take what he wanted in his grip and never let go. It was time to love Kacey King the way she deserved.

And he wasn't going to fail.

Chapter SIXTEEN

Meeting Jordie's eyes in the mirror, Kacey gave him a satisfied smile. He was naked, as was she, but it wasn't his muscular body or his thick cock that had her attention. All she could see was the grin he was wearing. His eyes were bright and full of love as he held her gaze. They'd spent more time groping each other than actually cleaning off the sweat they had worked up, but Kacey wasn't complaining. She loved showering with him. It felt right. It felt like them. They had a long history of sex in the shower, and out of it, but this time was different. They'd talked while he washed her hair. They'd laughed when he almost fell on his face trying to get the shampoo and it was just perfect.

So perfect that it almost felt unreal.

And that scared her.

Was it so perfect that it would end? It would be so easy for it to. He could start drinking again, decide he didn't want what she did, and that would be it. But she prayed it wouldn't, because they just worked. Though she kept thinking that maybe she should have waited a bit longer. Thought it through a little more than she had.

But when she'd opened that door and saw his brown eyes trained on her, all she wanted was him. She'd always wanted him. She'd be lying if she said it was easy to live and breathe without him. Because it wasn't. Watching each other, sending little grins, it all just felt so right. Like they were meant to do this. But was she in over her head? Was it too early to look at him and just know that this was forever?

"Did we rush this?" she asked suddenly as he brushed out his beard.

He shrugged, the comb stopping as his eyes held hers. "Do you love me?" She nodded. "I do."

"Then, no, we didn't. There is no reason for two people who love each other not to be together."

"But I didn't even make you work for it. I just jumped you like a cat in heat."

His grin grew. "Thank God," he said with a wink, and she smacked him playfully on the arm.

"I'm serious!"

He chuckled, the sound swirling the desire in her belly as he laid his comb down before turning to reach for her. He pulled her into his arms, his deliciously naked body hard against hers as he nipped at her bottom lip. "You didn't have to make me work for it, Kace. Don't you know that I've been working to be with you for a while? I've been working on me, and I'm far from done. I still have growing to do, but I want to grow with you."

All her previous fears always dissolved away when he held her gaze. Her heart thudded in her chest as she laced her fingers at the back of his head, and she couldn't help but think that this could be it. "I loved the old you, and I'll love the new you. I think it's just the *you* part that has my heart."

He grinned, dropping his mouth toward hers. She held her breath as his lips grazed along hers. "I'm not giving it back either."

"I didn't think you would. You don't share well."

"Got that right," he said roughly before taking her mouth with his. Wrapping her arms around his neck, she melted into him as their mouths danced. Maybe she didn't make him wait, maybe she didn't make him work or grovel like some other woman would have but, in a way, she couldn't. She had waited and wanted this for far too long. To be with the man she loved. To have her fairy-tale ending.

Jordie was her frog turned prince, and she wasn't letting him go.

Pulling away, he kissed her nose. "I promise I'm gonna do right by you this time around."

She smiled, her nose pressing into his, unable to say anything. Meeting her gaze, he squeezed his arms around her, pressing his lips to her nose.

"What's wrong?"

"I'm scared," she admitted, her eyes holding his. "Scared this is too good to be true."

He nodded. "Yeah, I was just thinking the same thing."

"Is that normal?"

His lips curved as he lifted her off the ground. "It's our normal, and I'm good with it."

Wrapping her arms tightly around his neck, she whispered, "Me too."

He smiled against her lips before she closed her eyes and kissed him. As their mouths moved together, she clung to him as he carried her into his room, laying her down and covering her body with his. When she ran her fingers up his back, he looked down at her, his eyes drinking her in, and she couldn't help but smile.

"I had no chance," she whispered, her fingers moving along his jaw. "I should have known I had no chance when I first saw you standing in the kitchen."

"What do you mean?" he asked, leaning into her hand, his hand coming up to cup her breast.

"I mean, that once you had your mind set on getting me back, I had no chance."

He nodded. "Basically," he joked, biting her jaw. "I knew from the beginning you'd be mine again."

He flashed her a huge grin, waggling his eyebrows, and she laughed. Dropping his face to hers, he grinned against her jaw, both of them knowing that wasn't the truth.

"You're full of shit," she accused and he scoffed, pulling back to look at her.

"What are you saying? That I didn't think I'd be lying on top of you naked, declaring I loved you, when we were at dinner earlier?"

"Exactly."

"Well, you'd be right, but those are just details. Shut up and kiss me," he demanded and she laughed before his mouth took hers in a heated assault. Closing her eyes tightly, she prayed that it wasn't too good to be true. That, from then on, it was going to be easy for them. It was so easy to love him, to be completely engrossed in him, and she really didn't want any hiccups. But as quickly as she thought that, she knew that they'd have hiccups.

One big one being Karson.

Pulling back, she looked up at him and said, "Karson is gonna kill you."

Jordie laughed, shaking his head. "No, we're good."

"Um, not when we tell him we are together."

"I promise, sugar thighs, we're good. I talked to him earlier and told him that we talked, and he's good with it."

Her brows came together. "Really?"

Jordie grinned. "Don't sound so surprised."

She laughed. "I'm just saying, Karson isn't good with anyone being with me, especially you. Did you forget where you got that busted lip?"

He smiled, rolling his eyes. "No, I didn't forget, but I promise, he's good with it."

"Okay," she said skeptically. "I'll take your word for it, but if he swings at you, don't say I didn't tell you so."

"So what, you want to hide us?" he asked, and she could tell he was testing her.

"No, dork, I'm just worried he's gonna flip. And ugh, my dad would join in. You know how he is. He loves drama just as much as an old lady does."

He gave her a look before hopping up and pointing to her. "Get dressed. We'll go tell him now."

She looked at him like he was crazy, scoffing. "Shut up and come here. Don't be silly."

"No, really," he said, glancing at the clock. "They're all up, we can tell everyone."

"Are you serious?" she laughed, looking at the clock herself and seeing that it was only seven. Her family was up, but still, he was crazy! "You don't want to get used to the idea of us before we tell my family about it?"

His face scrunched up. "Kacey, I've been used to the idea of us. What, you're not?"

She sat up, holding her hands out. "Whoa, now, that's not what I'm saying."

"Then what are you saying?"

She grinned. "I'm saying I'd rather stay in here and have sex all night than go talk to them and be questioned. At least, if we wait till tomorrow, I can be good and relaxed."

He shook his head. "You are like a cat in heat."

She kicked his thigh and he cried out before jumping on top of her as she laughed. She tried to get away from him, but she didn't get far before he started kissing her, his arms holding her hostage.

Pulling away, he kissed the side of her mouth before saying, "I want to tell everyone and anyone that will listen. I'm ten seconds from changing my relationship status on Facebook."

She feigned shock, but her heart did skip a beat. "No way. The horror all your little hussies will suffer."

"No one matters but you, baby. But will you approve my friend request? I mean, you did delete me."

She laughed. "Because you broke my heart and wouldn't talk to me. I was mad."

"Touché, but do you know how hard it is to Facebook-stalk someone that blocks you?"

Her face hurt from smiling. "I imagine pretty hard. That's the point of the block."

"Yeah, you imagine right. I had to log in to Karson's account and do it."

She almost choked on her laughter, smacking him in the chest. "Creeper."

"Whatever. You know you like it," he said, nibbling on her chest, and she did. She loved it to no end.

"Maybe, but whatever, it's all in the past."

"Yeah," he agreed. "So you'll approve my friend request?"

She giggled as she turned her face to look at him. "I guess."

He grinned before biting her tit. She cried out, arching her back as he laughed. "Get dressed."

"Seriously!" she cried as he crawled off her and went to his dresser.

"Yes," he said without turning to look at her. As he reached for a pair of shorts, she couldn't believe he wanted to go right now.

"But I'm naked."

He looked over his shoulder and nodded. "And you'll get that way later too."

"You're impossible!" she complained, sitting up and climbing off the bed. Heading toward her room, she was almost to the bathroom when his arms came around her waist, stopping her.

She looked back at him and he dropped his mouth to hers. "I changed my mind."

Turning her in his arms, he lifted her up, her legs and arms wrapping around him as he carried her to what she assumed was the bed. But she was wrong. When her ass landed on the cool surface of his dresser, she hissed out a breath against his lips. But then she gasped for one when he smacked her thighs open, dropping to his knees.

With his eyes full of lust, he said, "Just sit back and relax."

And then his mouth was between her legs.

Arching against the mirror on his dresser, she grasped it with her fingers as his mouth moved along her wet lips. After scooting her to the edge, his mouth dove into her and she brought her legs up onto his shoulders as he devoured her. Letting her head fall back against the mirror, she gasped as he took her wet lips between his own. When he tongued her entrance, she opened her legs wider, holding her ankles to give him full access.

Leaning back, he shook his head as he drank her in. "So hot, so fucking hot," he muttered before dropping his mouth onto her. Squeezing her eyes closed tightly, she dug her nails into her ankles as he swirled his tongue around her clit, his other hand holding her open while his fingers slid in and out of her. As he sucked her clit between his lips, she cried out, her body seizing as he fucked her with his fingers and assaulted her with his mouth. Her belly clenched, her heart slammed into her chest, and soon it was too much to handle as she came hard against his mouth, coming completely undone beneath his talented lips.

Gasping for breath, she looked up at the ceiling, filling her lungs and letting the air out in a whoosh. Her heart was pounding in her ears, but before she could even regain any kind of composure, he slid his hands between the opening her arms and legs made, taking her by the waist and lifting her off the dresser, suspending her in the air.

She cried out in shock, but he said, "I got you. Put my cock in that fucking hot pussy of yours."

Breathless, she almost came again at his demand. She loved when he talked to her like that. It was very primal of him and made her shake with need. Letting go of her ankle, her hand shook as she took his cock and directed it inside of her, both of them groaning as he disappeared into her. As her head fell back, she grabbed hold of her ankles again as he pulled out of her, only to thrust back into her and then pull out again, her breasts bouncing with each thrust. He was going slow, drawing out of her in such a delicate but perfect way.

But he was driving her crazy.

"Harder."

When he slammed into her, she cried out as he lifted her and she raised her head up to look at him. "Harder?"

She could only nod, speaking not an option as his mouth turned up in the most sinful way. Taking her mouth with his, he pulled out of her, almost all the way before slamming back into her and repeating each thrust harder, leaving her breathless. She cried out against his mouth, her orgasm rattling her soul, her body clenching his as his nails bit into her hips. Soon he was fucking her so hard, her whole body was shaking from his thunder-like thrusts. The smacking sound from her ass hitting his thighs was almost as loud as her heartbeat, but the best sound was the three words he growled in her ear.

"I love you," he said roughly in her ear as he thrust one last time, a harsh moan leaving his lips. "So fucking much."

Letting her ankles go, she wrapped her arms and legs around him as his cock pulsated inside her, filling her. He took a few steps back and then sat down, her ass hot against his thighs as he took hold of her face and kissed her swollen lips. Threading his fingers in her hair, he squeezed a fistful of her hair as he deepened the kiss and her belly fluttered with desire for him.

With love.

Pulling away only a breath, he kissed her lips once more before she opened her eyes to look at him. His eyes were full of such tenderness, such need, it left her fighting for her next breath. Reaching up, her fingers traced his lips and she couldn't feel anything but utter completion. Before, when he'd been gone, waves of missing him and yearning for him would drown her. But now, she was drowning in her love for him.

He was really there.

He was really hers.

And nothing could take him away from her.

Not even him.

She is finally mine, Jordie thought as he watched Kacey dress. His body was still shaking with the aftershocks of their amazing lovemaking but also with the deep-down, life-altering connection he had with her. Sitting on his bed, he couldn't believe it. When she said it was too good to be true, she wasn't lying. They just fit. It was like they went right back to how they were. Except now, he wasn't denying his feelings. No, he wanted to scream them, not only at her but also to the world. He was with the girl of his dreams. His everything.

He still worried though. What if he relapsed and hurt her all over again?

No. He couldn't think that way.

This would work. They were meant to be.

"You're thinking too hard," she called from the bathroom. "This was your idea, mind you."

He smiled. "Just thinking."

"About?"

"You. Us."

"Good things?" she asked, putting her hair up in a little ponytail before turning the water on.

"I just want this to work."

She looked over at him and asked, "Is there a reason it wouldn't?"

He shrugged. "I could fuck up again."

She nodded. "But you could not."

He smiled, hopeful. "True. Hoping I don't."

"Me too. I'm invested, remember?" she said with a grin, but her eyes were serious.

"Me too, Kace," he promised before standing up and grabbing his phone off the dresser.

As he opened his Facebook app, she said, "Then we are good."

He grinned as he sat back down, praying to sweet baby Jesus she was right while he typed her name in. But before he could ask for her to be friends, she was there, pushing his hands apart and climbing into his lap, her legs wrapping around his waist. Threading her fingers through the hair on his jaw, she smiled as she met his gaze.

"Do you know what I love about you?" she asked, her thumbs grazing his bottom lip.

"Everything?" he teased and her grin grew.

"Well, duh," she laughed. "But I love your drive, your tenacity. You won't give up on anything."

He gave her a deadpan look. "I gave up on myself though."

She nodded. "Everyone does at some point in their life. It's about getting back up, and you have. Am I worried you'll hurt me? Yeah, but that's only because I want this to work so damn bad. I've wanted you to be mine for the rest of my life for a very long time. But for so long, you were unattainable. But still I loved you because I know you, and I know what you are capable of. When you want something, you go for it. Hence why you are sober now and also why you are with me."

She was right. Even with everything he had been through, the molestation, the death of his friend, and even fighting to get into the NHL—because it wasn't as easy as everyone thought it was to be as good as he was—he never gave up. He fought to be normal, to not hurt, to win. And when it became too much and he failed, he picked himself back up. That's why for so long he didn't believe he had a problem. When he needed to stop, he did, but this last time, he was in far too deep. Everything was drowning him, his career was hanging in the balance, Kacey was gone, and he had no one because he'd pushed them all away.

But again, he did it. He picked himself back up.

"So whenever that fear creeps back into your mind, just remember that you don't back down, that you fight for what you want," she said, leaning her head against his. "I believe in you, Jordie, or I wouldn't be sitting in your lap right now, feeling so damn perfect. Only you can make me feel like this, so please don't ever stop."

"I won't," he promised, his eyes meeting hers.

"Good," she said with a wink. "Now come on, I'm hungry. I'm gonna eat while you get interrogated by the family."

She pressed her mouth to his, and his eyes drifted shut as her lips warmed his. Pulling away, she kissed his cheek before climbing off his lap. Smiling, he stood up and followed after her, his phone held loosely in his hand. He hadn't forgotten what he was doing before their little talk, but before he could do what he wanted, she stopped at the door and turned to him.

"Should I go out my door and you go out yours?"

He gave her a perplexed look. "What for?"

"I don't know, doesn't it say we've been doing it if we go out the same door?"

"We have been doing it."

"I know that, and you know that, but I don't want my daddy knowing it!" she complained.

"He's probably outside by the fire eating something, and I'd like to join him. Now go," he said, reaching around her to open the door. She shot him an exasperated look but went out with only a sigh. Smiling, he followed behind her, opening his Facebook app again to ask her to be friends. Before he could complete the request though, Karl's booming voice stopped him right as Kacey halted in front of him, causing him to run into her.

"So I guess you two are together. And if not, I need you to explain why you've spent the last two hours moaning each other's names."

"Oh my God," Kacey gasped, letting her head fall back. "Please tell me my father did not just say that to me."

"No, he did. But were we that loud?" Jordie asked innocently, and Lacey laughed as Kacey glared.

"You guys gave me and Karson a run for our money, that's for sure," she decided, rocking Mena back and forth.

"At one point we had to go outside," Regina said, shaking her head. "I mean, goodness me, Kacey."

"This is my life," Kacey said with her eyes shut, and it took everything for Jordie not to laugh.

"I should kick your ass for defiling my sister...again," Karson said, meeting Jordie's gaze, his eyes dancing with laughter.

"And I should kick your ass for making me look like I'm lacking in the bedroom," Karl said, and on cue, everyone except for Regina heaved.

"Gross!" Kacey cried.

"Come on, Dad! Really?" Karson complained as Lacey just laughed.

"Wow, I'm not sure if I should be proud or disgusted," Jordie said, his face scrunched up.

"Maybe you should give him some pointers," Regina sang, trying not to laugh.

"Yup, I'm disgusted," Jordie said to Kacey. "I think your mom just asked me to tell your dad how to screw her."

Kacey gagged. "Please, don't repeat it," she said, holding her stomach.

"Sorry, I can't get the vision out of my head," he said, trying to shake the image away.

It wasn't working though.

"Hey, I know how to do you just fine!" Karl yelled and Regina waved him off.

"Please make them stop," Karson cried out, leaning his head against Lacey's, but she was no help, she couldn't stop laughing.

"Lord knows I've never screamed the way she did," Regina said, pointing to Kacey.

"I think I just died of embarrassment," Kacey mumbled to Jordie and he nodded.

"I'm right there with ya," he agreed just as Karl scoffed.

"Because obviously you don't know how to enjoy good sex!"

"Oh God, Karson, make them stop," Lacey said, covering Mena's ears.

But Karson shook his head, his hands over his ears. "Sorry, can't hear you."

"You guys are ridiculous," Regina said, shaking her head as Karl wrapped his arms around her waist. "Everyone does it. We all know they do."

Jordie's head hung as he shook it. Chancing a look at Kacey, he saw that her whole face was red, and soon he couldn't help it, he started laughing. She looked over at him in horror, but even she couldn't hold it in. Then they were all laughing. Holding his stomach, he decided he had never laughed that hard in his life. Kacey leaned against him, her perfume clouding his senses as she dissolved into giggles. This could only happen to them. Only the King family would do this. Anyone else would have been embarrassed and tried to hide their uncomfortable feelings, but not the Kings. No, they let their crazy flags fly.

He wasn't sure how, but soon he recovered, wiping the tears away from his face. "This is great," he chuckled, laughter still bubbling in his chest.

"That's one word for it." Kacey scoffed, shaking her head.

"So," Karl said, squeezing Regina in his arms. "You two together now?"

Jordie looked over at Kacey just as she looked at him. Smiling, he laced his fingers with hers and nodded. "Yeah, she's giving me a second chance."

Regina aww'd while Lacey cried out in delight, almost bouncing on her heels. "I knew it!"

Karson nodded. "Cool."

"Cool?" Kacey gasped. "You hit him this morning for being with me before."

Karson pointed at her. "No, I hit him before because he broke your heart and lied to me. He told me earlier that he was gonna get you back. I'm cool with it. You two are good for each other."

Kacey looked up at Jordie, shocked, and he shrugged. "Told ya."

She shook her head then as Karl yelled, "Now, boy, I gave you a pass before 'cause you were messed up. But you hurt my baby again, I'll hang you by your toes on a clothes hanger and skin you alive."

"How very country of you," Lacey commented. "I think I've heard Elli say that before."

"You have," Karson agreed. "That's where he heard it."

"What can I say, I am adapting to the South," Karl said, but then his gaze cut to Jordie. "I'm not kidding either."

"10-4, won't happen," Jordie said, holding up his hands. "Promise."

"Holding you to that," Karl warned.

"I think we all are," Regina commented and soon everyone was nodding as Kacey looked up at him. Wrapping his arm around her, he kissed her forehead and she smiled. He'd lay down and die before he hurt her. He just couldn't. It would be catastrophic if he did. He would not only lose Kacey, he'd lose them all. They all believed in him, supported him, and he couldn't let them down.

He couldn't let himself down.

"There is dinner in the kitchen. Might need to feed the appetite you built up," Lacey teased.

"Might want to drink some hot tea after all that screaming, sweetheart," Regina added, and Kacey's face burned once more, while Jordie sputtered with laughter. She shot him a dirty look and he shrugged.

"Well, we are hungry," he said and she shook her head. "And you do scream really loud."

"We are never gonna live this down," she groaned as the rest of the family laughed.

"Probably not, but I'm okay with it," he said, pulling her to the kitchen.

"Why? It's embarrassing!"

He looked back at her, his lips curved. "But it was fun."

Her lips pursed as she shrugged. "Very true."

"Hey, keep it down tonight though. Mena needs her sleep," Karson called at them and Kacey let her head fall back.

"I need a place of my own," she groaned as she plopped down on a stool. Jordie glanced over at her as he grabbed the two plates that had been left out and put them in the microwave. Turning, he leaned against the counter, eyeing her. "What?" she asked and he shrugged, not sure how she was gonna take his next suggestion. Figuring that it was now or never, he smiled.

"We could get a place," he offered and her eyes widened.

"I mean, shit, Jordie, can you take me on a date first?" she joked and he chuckled.

"Just saying," he said and she grinned. "But what are you doing tomorrow night?"

"Whatever you are," she decided and he grinned back.

"Dinner and movie? Maybe some surfing on the realty site before I make you scream all night. Which, in return, would lead to more teasing by your family, which would lead to you wanting your own place."

"You're insufferable!" she said, throwing an empty cup at him. He caught it, laughing as she said, "I don't know. That seems a little crazy."

"No, crazy is getting married."

She gave him a deadpan look. "Well, duh."

"But I'm down for that too."

"Oh my God, please tell me that's not how you are proposing to me," she groaned, shaking her head.

"Nah, but just saying."

"I can't handle you right now, you're giving me whiplash," she said, shaking her head. "But yes to the date, and maybe to the screaming sex if it goes well."

"Oh, it will, and I don't think we'll make it home," he said, his eyes dancing with desire.

"I like the way you think," she said, licking her lips. "But we'll have to take your truck, my car won't give us enough room."

"Good thinking," he agreed before getting their plates out of the microwave just as a knock came at the back door.

Setting them down, he looked at the door as she got up, a bewildered look on her face. "I wonder who that is," she said as she went to the door. She opened it and he watched as her face twisted in confusion as she said, "Liam?"

Chapter
SEVENTEEN

"**W**hat the fuck is he doing here?" Jordie called out, and Kacey waved him off as Liam rolled his eyes. He looked a mess, not his usual, put together self. Though what surprised her most was not that he was there, but that he was holding flowers. What could he possibly want?

"I know it's late and I'm sorry I came by unannounced, but I need to see you," he said, holding out the flowers. She took them, confused, as he said, "I wanted to talk to you. I feel like earlier I didn't really get to express how much it would mean to me for you to go with me. You didn't give me much of a chance to talk."

"I thought it was pretty cut-and-dried, Liam. I'm sorry, but I don't know what to say right now."

He nodded. "I know. Can I come in?"

She knew she should say no, but before she could say anything, Jordie yelled out, "No."

Turning to glare at him, she said, "Hush, you."

"What?" he asked innocently. "Why does he need to come in?"

To her surprise, Liam barreled in, glaring at Jordie. "Why does it matter to you?"

Letting out a sigh, she knew this was going to get ugly if she didn't control the situation, but unfortunately—and, of course—Karson and her dad had come into the kitchen.

"What's going on?" Karl asked. "What the hell is he doing here?"

Karson looked at Kacey. "No, really, what's going on?"

"Nothing, it's fine. Everyone just chill out," Kacey said, holding her hands up before placing a hand on Liam, but he shook it off. "He's leaving."

"I'm talking to you, Thomas!" Liam yelled.

"Or not," she groaned as Jordie came out from behind the counter, but thankfully Karson stopped him.

"Oh, you're talking to me?" Jordie scoffed, looking down at where Karson's hand lay. "What?"

"Just precautions. This looks like it could get violent," Karson said before looking over at Liam. "I suggest you leave."

"No, I want to know why it's any of his business why Kacey and I talk. We had something special. She should be going with me to New York—"

"See, that would make sense. But she doesn't love you, she loves me," Jordie said, cutting him off, and Kacey covered her face.

Why was this happening?

"Oh, so you did break up with me for him," Liam accused and she shook her head.

"No," she said, but Jordie thought differently.

"Of course, she did. You can't make her feel an ounce of what I make her feel."

"Jordie, stop," Kacey warned. "That's enough. And Liam, I didn't break up with you for him. It just kinda happened that I got back with him the same day I broke up with you. I never planned it, and I know that sounds bad, but really, that's how it happened."

"Sure, it did," he seethed and she shook her head.

"I'm telling you the truth," she stressed, but she could tell he didn't believe her.

"I put time into you, I love you, and I thought I was doing right by you. But you're gonna pick some drunk asshole who's more than likely gonna cheat on you left and right? Why? Explain that to me?"

"Liam—"

"It's pretty simple. I can make her come, you can't," Jordie said and Liam glared.

"Really, Jordie?" she yelled and he shrugged.

"Yeah, because you practice on every woman in the world. Shut up, I'm not speaking to you anymore," he snapped back.

"Yeah, maybe you should try it because you obviously can't keep a girl."

"You're a disgusting drunk, and you won't keep her either."

Jordie pushed past Karson, and Kacey decided he wasn't trying very hard to keep Jordie contained as he went toe-to-toe with Liam. But Liam was looking at Kacey, his eyes intent on her as Jordie stared him down.

"You're halfway right. I am a drunk, recovering though, but I am not disgusting, nor will I lose her. She is mine. Not yours."

"Oh my God, stop it. I'm not something to own, for one, and for two, this is insane," she said to Liam and he gave her a look.

"Tell this dude to leave—before I remove him," he demanded, and Kacey rolled her eyes.

"Why are you acting like this? You got me, we're good. Let me explain this to him because I do care about his feelings. He is a nice guy."

"He's a pussy," Jordie sneered.

"Screw you," Liam said, glaring at him, and Jordie laughed.

"See!"

"Karson!" she yelled and he shrugged.

"I'm trying," he said, pulling Jordie by his shirt, but of course, he wasn't moving.

"What did I do wrong?" Liam asked. "Why don't you want me?"

"Dude, do you know how pathetic you sound right now?" Jordie asked, but they both ignored him while Liam's eyes searched hers.

"We have history, Liam. I love him," she said, but Liam shook his head. "When he's not being a jealous, pigheaded jerk, he's a good guy."

"He won't treat you like I do."

"Yeah, I'll do better and I'll make her come," Jordie reminded him and she was going to kill him.

Smacking him, she asked, "Will you go eat or something? Let me handle this."

"No," he said simply, not moving at all.

"Daddy?"

"What?" Karl asked, crossing his arms.

"Remove him!" she yelled, but he shook his head.

"I'm on his side."

Looking at Jordie, Liam bit out, "You're just mad that I had her because you couldn't keep her. She wanted to have sex with me, she wanted me so damn bad, just to get over your punk ass."

"Is that right?" Jordie asked, his chest puffing out. "Did you know I know every detail about your relationship with her? Wanna know why? Because she loved me enough to tell me. What do you know about us? That I hurt her, right? That's it, because you meant nothing to her."

"But I was with her and that kills you inside," he yelled back. "I can see it all over your face. You hate me because I was good enough for her to try."

"You know nothing, fuckface," Jordie bellowed and that was enough.

"Okay, that's it," she said as Liam looked back at her. "Look, there is really nothing else to say. I'm sorry for how this went down and how this may look.

But I promise, I never meant to hurt you."

"No, you just strung me along, made me think you could love me—"

"Nope, never did that," she reminded him. "I always told you that I wasn't there yet."

"But you never were going to be there 'cause you were obsessed with this asshole!"

She hadn't realized how upset he was until that moment. He never cussed, and the fact that his hands were in fists worried her. She really didn't want this to come to blows, but both of them were just itching for it.

Stupid male egos.

Making a face, she said, "I mean, 'obsessed' is a little over the top. I did love him and I wasn't over him."

"You told me you were!" he yelled and Jordie stepped between them.

"Don't yell at her," he warned, and with all her might, she pushed him to the side before staring at him

"I can take care of myself!" she yelled at him, but Jordie wasn't listening. His eyes were trained on Liam, just waiting for a reason to hit him. She really needed to get him out of there. "I wanted to be over him and figured if I said I was, it would be true. But I never was and I'm sorry, but you—"

"So you used me?"

She had asked herself that many times and she knew the answer. She just didn't want to own up to it. She wasn't that kind of person, but in her quest to lose her feelings for Jordie, she lost a bit of her humility. Something she was not proud of. And if she could, she'd make it up to Liam. But she was unsure how to do that or if he even wanted her to. But she didn't owe him the whole truth. "I guess so. I didn't mean to though, if that makes it any better. And I am very, very sorry."

"It doesn't," he snapped and she nodded. "And I don't think you are. You just needed someone to keep you warm till he came back."

"Um, no. We broke up like nine months ago and we'd only been together two months, so please don't think that of me."

"You made the bed, now lie in it," he snapped back and Kacey took a cleansing breath in. She wouldn't let this dude make her feel like shit. She was guilty and hated what she did to him, but she never lied. She never told him she loved him when she didn't. He was upset and trying to keep his pride. She understood that, but it was time for him to go.

"I'm really sorry, Liam. I am. And like I said, I wish you the best. Some woman will be really happy to be with you."

"Yeah, and let's pray she isn't a heartbreaking whore like you," he sneered, and she'd never expected him to actually say the words he'd been insinuating. That shocked her, but what didn't shock her was the speed of Jordie's fist as it smashed into Liam's pretty face.

"Jordie!" she yelled as Karson wrapped his arms around him.

"Say what you want about me, dickface, but you will not talk to her like that," Jordie yelled as Liam covered his mouth, in obvious pain.

"Really? You had to hit him?" she yelled as Karl pushed Liam out the door, slamming it.

"Yes! He won't talk to you like that," he yelled, trying to get past Karson, but this time he actually held him back.

"You are acting like a child!"

"I'm protecting you!"

"Oh please, you're just jealous."

"You're fucking right, I am!" he yelled back and, for some reason, she was surprised by that. Breaking out of Karson's hold, Jordie spoke quickly and with conviction, holding her gaze. "That asshole touched you, kissed you, and was a part of your life when that's all I wanted. So yeah, I'm jealous, and yeah, I'm acting like a child because I don't fucking like sharing! You know this."

"I think it's safe for me to leave," Karson said, but Kacey wasn't listening to him, her eyes locked with Jordie's. His chest was rising quickly, up and down, probably matching hers. She thought she heard her dad say something, but she couldn't get over the pain in Jordie's eyes.

"Jordie, I'm with you."

"But he mattered enough for you to be with and to try to forget me. Do you know what it was like to watch the woman I love with someone else?"

"Doubt it was easy, but do you know how hard it was to be left behind like a piece of trash with no explanation at all? While you were off trying to forget me? Both of us are guilty of it. Just let it go and move on."

His shoulders dropped as he shook his head. Looking up at her, he asked, "Do you forgive what I did, Kacey? Honestly? You say you have, but when you say shit like that, it's hard to believe."

She eyed him, and she couldn't believe he was asking that. If she hadn't forgiven him, then why was she with him? "Yes, Jordie, but I haven't forgotten."

He nodded, his eyes not leaving hers. "I get that, and I completely understand, but you are throwing it in my face. I know what I did was wrong, and I've apologized. You don't have to remind me."

Her heart was pounding in her chest, and she couldn't believe this was happening. Because she was pretty sure they were fighting. "I am sorry for doing that. You're right, that was wrong. But you just punched my ex and then tried to make me feel bad for being with him!"

"I wasn't trying to make you feel bad, Kacey. I am upset that he meant something to you."

"Oh my God, he didn't! You do!"

He shook his head. "No, you don't get what I'm trying to say," he stressed, his eyes wild as he held her gaze. "I know I fucked up, and I hate that. It hurts me, maybe not as much as it does you since you were the one that I did it to. But it does, and I don't want to think about it anymore. I want to look at our future, not our past. But we gotta let go of all of it if we are gonna succeed."

"Exactly, so don't go postal and punch exes."

"Don't bring said exes in the house and allow them to call you a whore."

"'Cause I could control that," she snapped, complete fed up with their argument. "Why are we arguing about this? We've been together maybe four hours now, and in that time, we've gotten back together, screwed each other's brains out, and now fought. If this is a peek of what's to come, Jesus help us!"

"I'm not fighting. I'm telling you how it is."

Glaring, she took a step toward him, taking ahold of his shirt and yanking him down to her level. "Fine. Then let me tell you how it is, Jordie Scott Thomas. I love you. You only. Yes, I haven't forgotten everything that happened, and I probably never will. But I promise I won't ever bring it back up as long as you promise never to throw Liam in my face. He meant nothing. He was more a friend than anything. So let it go, and I'll work on letting go of what happened."

Cupping the back of her neck, he snaked his arm around her waist, his mouth only inches away from hers. His chest was rising and falling quickly against hers, his eyes searching hers before he slowly nodded. "Deal."

"Deal," she said just as his mouth dropped to hers. Wrapping her arms around his chest, she deepened the kiss as his heart pounded against her. She loved how strong and loud it felt against her body. It was her home and she knew that the whole thing with Liam upset him, but it would never measure up to the pain she felt being without him. He was a man though, and he was proud too. She knew it dented his ego to see her with Liam, but it didn't matter anymore.

They had each other.

As she pulled away, his eyes bored into hers. They were full of so much remorse, so much pain, and she hated that. Cupping his face, she shook her head and asked, "This won't be easy, will it? You and me, it's gonna be work."

He scoffed. "It wasn't before; I doubt it will be now. So are you sure? Because you can try to get out, but I don't think I'll let you," he said, his arms tightening around her to reiterate what he was saying.

She didn't even have to think about it as her face broke into a grin. With all the love in the world for this broken, beautiful man, she whispered, "I don't even want to try to live life without you again."

"Good, I wasn't gonna let you anyway," he said, kissing her top lip. "Now, let's eat."

"Please," she almost begged before he led her to the counter where they sat down and started to eat the food that had already begun to get cold again. Neither of them cared though; they were both famished. They ate in comfortable silence, but he finished first, like always. He ate as if someone was going to steal his plate. She found it quite comical and annoying because usually he tried to steal her food.

As if on cue, he reached for one of her green beans and she stabbed him with her fork, shaking her head at him as she brought her plate closer to her. "You know I don't share food."

"Stingy," he threw back and she stuck her tongue out at him. As she devoured the moistest chicken on earth, her phone dinged with a notification. Looking down at it, she saw it was a Facebook friend request from one Jordie Thomas. She felt him staring at her, and she grinned as she clicked a few times, accepting his friendship.

And more.

"Aw, cool, we're friends now," he teased, but she rolled her eyes before continuing to eat and fighting her grin.

"Yeah, you won't have to stalk me through Karson's account."

"Thank God," he muttered as she went back to eating.

When her phone dinged again, she glanced down to see that Jordie Thomas had said he was in a relationship with her. It asked if she accepted his relationship and she smiled before pressing Confirm.

Glancing over at him, her fork pressed against her bottom lip, she said, "We are for real now, Mr. Thomas. It's Facebook official. The world knows."

He grinned back at her, sliding his hand up her thigh. "Yup, no going back now," he teased and she grinned.

Leaning in, his lips pressed to hers and she couldn't agree more. But really, there was never really any going back when you loved a person like Jordie Thomas.

He consumed you.

And she was completely okay with that.

"You're supposed to watch the movie," Kacey complained as Jordie scrolled through the realty site, looking at apartments.

Looking over at her, he shrugged. "Baby, I've seen this movie a billion times. You know I don't like it."

She grinned. "It's a great movie," she countered, but he didn't agree. Not even a little bit. He didn't even understand why she loved *Notting Hill*. Yeah, Julia Roberts was a classic beauty, but come on, the movie sucked.

"It really isn't," he said and she gave him a flat look.

"And why not?"

"She's a bitch. And he's a schmuck."

"It's sweet! She's damaged from the spotlight and he's clueless. It's adorable," she complained, but he just shook his head.

"Watch your movie, Kace, I'll just lie here and look at stuff on my phone."

"If you don't want to watch it, then why are you in here?"

He looked from his phone to her. "For the ice cream. Give me another bite."

She pursed her lips at him, and he shot her a grin before she directed the spoon in his mouth. "Plus, you'll be all hot and bothered and feeling all romantic after it's over, so I'm bound to get laid."

"Pig."

Leaning closer, he snorted in her ear, nuzzling her and causing her to giggle before pushing him away. Grinning, he fell back against the pillows as she cuddled in closer to him.

"What are you looking at?" she asked after a moment.

"Apartments."

"Really?"

"Yeah, as soon as I sign my new contract, I'm gonna move out. I told Karson that when I came back. I'm sure they want their house back."

She paused her movie and leaned on his shoulder, looking down at his phone as he went through each apartment. "Are you gonna stay close to Karson?"

He shrugged. "Not sure yet."

"Do you want an apartment or a house? I mean, you don't plan on leaving, do you?"

"Not really. I wanna retire here," he admitted and she nodded.

"I know, so why don't you just buy a house?"

"A house might be too big for just me," he suggested, curious to see what she would say to that.

"You could get a dog," she said and he smiled.

"I could," he agreed.

"And I might come visit."

"Just a visit?" he asked and she looked up at him.

"Um, yeah, you still haven't taken me on a date," she said and he laughed.

"I got you tomorrow," he decided and she grinned before looking back down at his phone. Taking it from him, she clicked a few things and then gave it back.

"If I were to come visit, I'd want to visit a house in this neighborhood."

Fighting his grin, he said, "Good idea."

Clicking through each house, they found something in each that neither of them cared for. He realized they essentially wanted the same thing. A huge kitchen, a huge yard, and a master bedroom with at least four other bedrooms. When one that was down the road came up, she looked up at him. "That's a nice house."

"It is," he agreed, clicking through each picture. It was almost the same layout as Karson and Lacey's, and the price wasn't too frightening. "It's huge just for me and a dog."

"Yeah, but maybe you'll get married and have some kids?"

Scoffing, he looked down at her as she looked up at him. "I'll buy it tomorrow if you'll move in with me."

She eyed him and then looked away. "We are going on six hours, Jordie. You can't get me back, have mind-blowing sex, punch my ex, fight with me, and then ask me to move in."

"I think I asked before the punching of the ex happened," he corrected her and she shot him a salty look.

"Don't be so literal. Give us a little time before we jump into something like that."

"Okay, answer me this—will we be sleeping alone from this point forward?"

Her eyes narrowed. "That's not fair. I like sleeping with you."

"Oh, I do too, which is why I won't be sleeping without you unless I'm on the road. But at least this way, we can do it as loud as we want and anywhere we want."

She shook her head. "Let me sleep on that," she decided and he nodded.

"Fine, I don't sign my contract till Friday."

"I'll have an answer by then," she agreed.

"Good," he said just as a text message came through, surprising him. It was late, who was texting him? The sound caught Kacey's attention, her eyes moving to the screen as he clicked on his message.

> Mom: Jordie, honey! I haven't heard from you. Remember I am your mother and you have to call me every once in a while. But anyway, call me tomorrow when you wake up! I have great news.

His stomach twisted in anguish as he deleted the text, shutting off his phone. Silence stretched as Kacey's fingers tapped against his chest.

"Have you talked to her lately?"

He shook his head, feeling her gaze on him. "No."

"Does she know about you going to rehab?"

"Nope, I only told your family."

"Ma and Dad knew?"

"Yeah, your mom even came and brought me cookies a time or two," he said, hating that his own mother didn't even think to do something like that or even ask if he was okay. She didn't care about him. The only time she cared was when it was beneficial to her.

"Are you going to call her?"

"No," he decided, tossing his phone on the nightstand. "Push play, let's watch this stupid movie."

But she didn't move. Pushing the blankets off them, she climbed on top of him, and instantly his hands came to her ass. "Or we can do this."

Cupping his face, she let her gaze bore into his. There wasn't any lust in her eyes, only determination. "Are you okay?"

"No," he admitted. "She fucks with my head."

"I know and I'm sorry. Don't call her, okay? Please?"

"I won't."

"Okay, and don't let it bother you. You have my mom and dad and Karson."

"And you," he said, his hands sliding up her back, underneath her shirt, to bring her down to him. "And that's all I need."

"I know it hurts though. I know how much you want her love."

He shrugged. "Can't miss what you never had though."

Her eyes turned sad as she dropped her forehead to hers. "I'm gonna make up for the love she doesn't give you."

"You already do, Kacey," he whispered as her nose moved along his. "You love enough for the world."

She gave him a faint smile before shaking her head. "I'm sorry she sucks."

"Not everyone has perfect parents like you, Kacey. It's not your fault, don't worry about it," he said, but as soon as he said it, he regretted it. It was something he would have said before, when he'd brush off the hurt his mother caused and pick up the bottle. Kacey knew that though; she knew him and his antics, and soon her eyes narrowed as she held his gaze.

"Don't push me away."

"I'm not trying to," he said sternly. "I just don't want to talk about someone who doesn't even love me."

"Talking about it might make the pain stop," she suggested and he shook his head.

"It won't. It just reminds me of the craptastic family life I have," he said and her mouth turned down. "The fact that my mother doesn't love me, I have no clue who my dad is, and hey, I have nine stepdads, but still no siblings to be just as fucked up as me."

As she threaded her fingers into his hair, he closed his eyes, hating that he'd unloaded like that. She didn't need to hear all that; it showed his weakness. He hated how much pain his mother brought to him with only one text. All his progress felt like nothing. She could honestly drive him to drinking all over again, but as soon as the thought came, Kacey pressed her lips to his. Just as quickly as he'd wanted a drink, he wanted her more. Rolling her over so that he was on top, he pulled away, looking down into her beautiful face.

Her eyes were on him, her chest rising and falling as her eyes searched his. "You're not trying to have sex with me to replace your cravings are you?"

He could lie. It would be so easy, but he knew he couldn't. "Yes."

"Okay," she said with a nod. "At least you know what you're doing."

"But it isn't okay, is it?" he asked and she shrugged.

"I don't know," she admitted. "That's something you need to ask your therapist. But for now, use me, Jordie, though also know I'm here to talk. That I'll listen till you can't talk anymore. I'll always be here. For whatever you need."

"I have nothing to say about her," he said, his eyes closing as he pressed his nose to hers. "I'm just so mad at her, but I can't hate her."

"I know," she whispered.

"She constantly hurts me."

"I know," she said once more. "Want me to kick her ass?"

He smiled against her lips and shook his head. "Wouldn't be worth it. She wouldn't understand why. In her mind, she does right by me."

"But she doesn't. I know that, and so do you."

"Yeah," he agreed. "But why does her rejection still hurt?"

"It hurts because it matters. Unfortunately, she doesn't realize what she is doing to you, and until you tell her, it won't ever get better."

"Is she worth it, though?" he asked and she shrugged.

"That's up to you to decide. Either way, I support you, love you, and will stand beside you," she whispered against his lips. "And when you're ready, I'll Spartan kick her in the face."

Grinning, he shook his head. "That's intense."

"For you, I'd do an intense Spartan kick," she promised. "Just to see that smile, I'd do anything."

Closing his eyes, he gathered her in his arms and kissed her lips softly. "I love you, Kacey."

"I love you too, Jordie," she whispered, her fingers grazing over his neck. "Do you feel better?"

He nodded. "I do."

More so than she could even fathom. Months of rehab and therapy and still the pain of his mother burned from one text. But all he needed was to hear Kacey say she loved him and that she'd Spartan kick his mom and the pain didn't burn as bad. It still stung, but then he looked into her eyes, and he wondered why he even cared. That woman didn't want him, but this woman— this beautiful, gorgeous angel—did.

And her love was way more than enough.

It was everything.

It was his saving grace.

"Is it okay to have sex now?" he whispered playfully against her mouth and she grinned.

"It was okay before, but I'm glad we talked."

"Me too," he admitted. "I honestly need you, Kacey. Really."

"I'm here and I'm not going anywhere," she promised as the room went dark from her turning the TV off. "I'm yours."

And he was hers. But instead, he said, "All mine?"

"Every single piece of me," she said roughly against his mouth.

"Even this piece?" he said, cupping her pussy, and she gasped against his mouth, arching up in his hand.

"Especially that piece," she murmured against his lips and he nipped at her bottom lip, feeling utterly perfect. The text from his mom was forgotten, and all that mattered was this woman who lay beneath him. And nothing could change that.

Not a text from his mom.

Not another woman.

Not the bottle.

Nothing, because Kacey was it.

And as her mouth moved along his, her hand covering over his heart, he knew just as he owned every single piece of her, she owned every piece of him.

Especially his heart.

Chapter
EIGHTEEN

"**H**ey, JT," Erik Titov called from the blue line, catching Jordie's attention from where he stood by the bench. He sent the puck to him and Jordie stopped it with the front of his stick, his brows coming together. Titov wasn't on his line, nor was it Jordie's turn to go. He was supposed to be waiting for a play from Coach. Glancing at Coach Baxter, he saw that he was going over different plays with the offense coach, Brady, while Tommy, the defense coach, talked with Adler and Sinclair. That left Karson and Jordie to shoot the shit while they waited since Fontaine and Paxton were passing the puck back and forth, waiting for some direction too.

They were still working out the kinks with the new additions to the team.

The final lines had been announced the day before, and Jordie would be lying if he said he wasn't surprised that the girl made the team and wasn't sent down. Elli really liked her and believed in her. Coach was a little leery, and even some of the guys were too but, man, she could hold her own. Also, with a few trades, they had two new forwards and two new defense guys. They seemed okay, but Jordie hadn't really gotten to know them much. He wasn't one for change, and the team dynamic was certainly changing. Elli was building a team for the Cup, he could see that, and he was ready, no matter how much he didn't like change. The team was full of some heavy hitters, and Jordie was excited.

But he still had no clue why Erik was passing him the puck. Looking back at him, he said, "Yeah?"

He smacked his stick to the ice, and Jordie shot it to him as he asked, "You and Kacey together?"

Jordie grinned as he nodded. "Yeah, why?"

"'Cause she's been sitting there for the last week watching us practice, and she never did that before," he said with a grin, moving the puck back and forth with his stick. "I wasn't sure you knew."

Jordie laughed as he looked up at where Kacey sat, her arms wrapped around her legs as she watched. When she saw that he was watching her, she smiled, which made him smile. She had been coming to practice all week, and he really liked that she was there. After killing him in the training room, she'd sometimes hit the ice with him before the rest of the guys did. It was fun, and soon, they had fallen into a routine. Morning sex, work, and then he would go to AA meetings or therapy, come home for dinner, playtime with Mena, chilling with Karson and Lacey, and more sex. It was great and easy, but today he was signing his contract before his AA meeting, and Kacey hadn't said a word about getting a place together. He was a little worried, not that he'd let her know that.

"It's weird seeing you two googly-eye each other," Karson mentioned as he leaned against the boards, making a face, and Jordie laughed.

"It's not like we are thinking about having sex as we stare into each other's eyes, if that makes it any better."

His troubled face deepened and he reached out, smacking Jordie's arm. "Dude, no."

Jordie laughed. "I like that she's here."

"So things are good? Seems that way," he said and Jordie agreed.

"Things are great, really excited for our future."

"Which is?"

"Marriage and kids and shit," Jordie said, looking back at him, and Karson laughed.

"Never thought I'd hear you utter those words," he said, shaking his head. "Well, not the word shit, you say that all the time, but those other two. Mind-blowing, especially with my kid sister. And what's really surprising is the fact that I don't want to kill you for it."

Jordie grinned. "'Cause you know I'd die before I'd hurt her."

"For sure," he said with a nod. "So, you're good? AA has been pretty uneventful. You haven't been sharing much."

Karson had gone with him all week since his mom and dad had left. Karl and Regina finally got an offer on their house, one that they couldn't turn down, which meant they'd be moving to Nashville soon. Everyone was ecstatic about that too. It just felt right having the whole family in one state. But, other than that, Karson was right, AA had been uneventful. He wasn't sharing much because he was trying to figure out how to approach the issue of not only his mom calling but also the fact that he wanted Kacey to move in with him. She'd asked him to ask his leader or therapist, and he figured he needed to do that today.

"Yeah, I'm good," he said with a nod. "My mom did text me the other day."

Karson's head whipped around. "What the hell for?"

"She wants me to call her."

"Did you tell her to fuck off?"

"I ignored her. She's called twice since."

"Keep ignoring her. She wasn't there the whole time you went through your shit; she doesn't deserve you now."

Jordie couldn't agree more, but before he could say that, Coach blew the whistle and practice was back on. As he rushed the net with Karson, he decided that he loved playing with Karson. They did it well and could really read each other. It sucked last year when Karson went up with Shea because Shea's linemate Jakob retired, but Jordie was happy for him. Shea made you a better player when you played with him, which was why Sinclair was on his line. Rumor was that Sinclair was being molded into the next captain, and Jordie believed it. The kid was one hell of a team player, and Jordie had liked him the moment they met.

But being on the ice again, playing with his boy, really had Jordie flying high. It just seemed like everything was falling into place. He was about to sign a new contract for six years, over three million dollars a year. He was with the girl of his dreams, hoping to build a future with her, and he was healthy. He couldn't ask for more. He had it all. He just hoped he could keep it.

Because the calls from his mom worried him.

It gave him anxiety and made him want to throw his phone against the wall just so she couldn't get ahold of him. Kacey suggested changing his number, but that wouldn't stop her. She'd start hitting him up on Facebook and then, knowing her, she'd just pop in. He was going to have to answer her call, and he needed to be honest that he wanted nothing to do with her. But his mom was one hell of a manipulative bitch, and he had a hard time saying no to her.

He just didn't want to relapse. He didn't want to go back to how it was, and she had the power to throw him back into bad habits. He had been doing so well—he wasn't even craving anything to drink because he was so fucking happy. It scared him to think that his cravings, his need for the bottle, could come back as soon as the darkness started to creep back. That was why he had to cut all ties. Not matter how hard it was going to be, he had to let her go.

She was the darkness.

When the whistle blew, calling his line, he let his issues with his mom go and focused on what made him happy. The sound of his skates against the ice, the feel of the force of the puck as it hit his blade, and the unbelievable feeling when he scored on Tate. But the greatest feeling was when he looked up and Kacey was waving her arms in the air, cheering for him.

He had it all.

Rubbing his hands together, Jordie leaned on the edge of his seat as he waited for Elli to call him in. He wasn't sure why he was nervous. This was cut-and-dried and already in the books. He knew his salary, he knew she was keeping him, so why was his heart pounding in his chest? Letting out a long breath, he leaned back in his chair and stretched out his legs. It had been a long, hard practice, which was why he was kind of late, not that Elli would mind. His agent wasn't even there yet.

But why was he nervous?

When his phone dinged with a message, he pulled it out of his pocket to see that it was from Kacey.

> *Kacey: What are you doing after the meeting with Elli?*
> *Jordie: AA.*
> *Kacey: With Karson?*
> *Jordie: Going alone today.*

He waited for her to text him back, but to his surprise, it took longer than he thought.

> *Kacey: Are you coming back to the house afterward?*
> *Jordie: Yeah, you'll be there, right?*
> *Kacey: Yeah, waiting on you.*

Jordie smiled.

> *Jordie: Naked?*
> *Kacey: Maybe, this is what I look like right now.*

He grinned as a picture of her in only a thong came up in his thread.

> *Jordie: You really do have the best ass I've ever seen.*
> *Kacey: Thanks ☺ I bought these from Lacey's shop for you to tear off. I might start there.*

His brow raised in confusion.

> *Jordie: Start there?*
> *Kacey: Yeah, I don't make that much with the Assassins and I only work in the mornings now. I'm kind of bored come the afternoon.*
> *Jordie: You really don't need that much money. I'm about to sign a huge contract.*
> *Kacey: I know, but I can't depend on you to support me.*

His face scrunched up more.

> *Jordie: Why the hell not? You're my woman.*
> *Kacey: This is very true, but you know, what if it doesn't work out? And then I've been depending on you and I have nothing.*

He glared.

> *Jordie: Won't happen. You aren't going anywhere.*
> *Kacey: lol. Okay, so this is a convo for later, I guess.*
> *Jordie: I guess so. Have you thought about moving in with me?*
> *Kacey: You're killing me.*
> *Jordie: I'll take that as a no. Stop being a relationship staller and get it together, Kacey King. Be my woman, move in with me, and have lots of loud sex.*
> *Kacey: Dork, I'll see you when you get back.*
> *Jordie: Fine, love your stubborn ass.*
> *Kacey: Love your dorky ass more.*

He smiled as he clicked off his messages and went to his Facebook. Hitting the status update section, he wrote:

> *My girlfriend is the most stubborn-ass woman in the world, but I wouldn't be head over heels in love with anyone but her.*
> *Love you, Kacey King.*

He posted it and then grinned. He wasn't that big a Facebooker, but when he updated his status, it usually meant something. The world needed to know what he thought of his girlfriend, and he was sure to get some kind of response. Hopefully out of her. He also wanted to remind her that he cared. He may not have had to woo her like Lacey had suggested in the beginning, but he still thought that little things like Facebook posts and Snickers would keep her happy. She didn't like flowers like a normal chick, so he fed her. It usually worked.

As he expected, his Facebook started to blow up, his phone dinging left and right, stealing his attention.

Hitting the comments, he laughed as he read through each one.

> *Lucas Brooks: I'm surprised she even dates a guy from Duck Dynasty. You should be happy she's staying. BTW it's not playoff season, do something about your face.*
> *Erik Titov: Pansy ass.*
> *Karson King: Loser, stop posting shit about my sister. But really, she is the biggest pain in the ass I know.*
> *Kacey King: Shut up, Karson King. And don't you mean you're the biggest pain in the ass? And you hush too, Jordie, but I do love you too.*
> *Shea Adler: Aren't you in a meeting? Show some respect for my wife and stop Facebooking about your high school romance. Big dweeb.*
> *Tate Odder: Cap, people don't say dweeb anymore.*
> *Shea Adler: Says the kid that doesn't speak English.*
> *Tate Odder: Yes, I'm a little delayed in your language, but at least I'm a kid and not an old ass.*
> *Karson King: BUUUUUURRRNNNNNNNN!!!! But he said it. Not me. Don't hate me and get me traded.*
> *Lucas Brooks: Good one, Tate Odder.*
> *Shea Adler: I will kill you all, no trades needed.*
> *Phillip Anderson: All of you are losers, especially you, pussy ass Jordie Thomas! No one Facebooks this girlie shit.*
> *Reese Anderson: Yes, they do, he did it yesterday. Don't listen to him, Jordie. I can't wait to meet her.*

Jordie was cracking up as the comments kept coming, but then Elli interrupted him as she said, "You can come in now."

Looking up at her, he smiled. "Check out Facebook later."

She returned the smile and nodded. "Shenanigans, I'm guessing?"

"Our team is full of crazies," he commented as he walked past her.

"Ain't that the damn truth," she agreed as she shut the door. "Charles is running late, so we'll go over the contract while we wait. But I wanted to talk to you about something," she said and he paused before lowering down into the chair.

"Am I in trouble?"

She laughed. "No, actually, you've been doing very well. Everyone is extremely pleased. Coach is boasting about you every time I see him."

He relaxed in the chair, nodding his head. "I'm working hard."

"We can tell and we are thrilled," she said, flashing him a winning grin. "Especially me since I kind of stuck my neck out for you."

He laughed as he nodded. "Couldn't let you down."

"Yeah, that means a lot," she said, letting out a contented sigh. "So while it's on my mind, you're welcome to skip the team party this weekend. It isn't really a dry event, and I wouldn't want to tempt you."

Jordie shook his head. He had been preparing for the team party. He knew that there would be drinking and partying, and he had to get used to that stuff sooner rather than later. There was alcohol everywhere; it was his duty to resist it. "No, I'll be there. No biggie."

"You sure?" she asked skeptically. "I would make an excuse for why you can't come."

"Thanks, Elli, but I want to be there. I got a date," he said with a wink and she laughed.

"I see that you and my trainer have worked it out?"

"Yup."

"Good, I hope it lasts a lifetime."

"It will," he said with a grin. "Was that what you needed to talk to me about? The party?"

She shook her head. "No, actually, I wanted to talk to you about Benji Paxton."

His brows came together. What did the new defensive guy have anything to do with him? "Cool dude, what about him?"

"He's a recovering alcoholic, eleven years sober."

"Really?" he asked, surprised by that. "He seems so straitlaced."

"Now he is, but he has one hell of a past. Though that's not my place to tell you. And I would like to suggest that you and him room on road trips. He would be a good friend for you."

Jordie shrugged. He could see why she would think that, but that wouldn't work. "But I room with Karson, always have."

"I know, but Fontaine is known to be a partier, and Karson won't stand for Fontaine's antics, you know? Can you try it out? For me?"

She batted her lashes at him and he laughed. He'd do just about anything for Elli and she knew that. "Sure. No problem."

"You are awesome. Thank you," she said, clapping her hands together. "Now, let's get to signing some paperwork."

Excited, Jordie leaned forward toward the contract, ready to add some more brick to the foundation he was building. Signing this contract ensured his future with the Assassins, and that meant it was time to move out of Karson's house and get a place of his own. Now all he had to do was hope that Kacey would be on board to go with him.

Because he couldn't leave her behind.

"You and your friends act worse than children," Kacey accused as Karson laughed, looking down at his phone. As another notification from the "roast," as the guys were calling it, came across her phone, she rolled her eyes. She almost wanted to tell Jordie to delete it, but if she was honest, it was sweet. Even if he did think she was stubborn. Which she was. But that wasn't the point. He'd told the world that he loved her and that made her breathless.

Pointing at her, he said, "Shut up, this is awesome. Lucas just said that you are holding Jordie's balls in your purse."

She shot him a wry look as he laughed from the gut, Lacey only snickering as she shook her head. Putting the nipple on Mena's bottle, she handed it to him. "Try to keep the laughing to a minimum. I don't want my baby to have shaken baby syndrome."

He scoffed, taking the bottle and kissing her cheek. "Are you reading this stuff? It's classic."

Walking away, he let out another gut-busting laugh and Kacey rolled her eyes. "He's a dork."

"That is very true," Lacey agreed, cleaning the counter before leaning against it. "But the status is cute. It's weird seeing you two so lovey-dovey after you almost murdered him in the living room however many weeks ago."

Kacey shrugged her shoulders. "Yeah, but it's good, right? Like, you don't think we are rushing it?"

Lacey shrugged her shoulders. "Don't ask me about rushing. I married your brother after seeing him for the first time in like nine years. Not sure I'm the right person for advice on that. I mean, some people said I was crazy," she said with a grin. "But if it helps, I wouldn't change a thing."

Kacey smiled as she nodded. "It's just been so perfect. Like we laugh constantly, and when we aren't laughing, we are doing it, and when we aren't doing it, he's telling me he loves me. And God, Lacey, I waited so long to hear those words leave his mouth that I find myself absorbing them, just in case he stops telling me. It's like I'm just waiting for the other shoe to drop, for all this good to just evaporate."

Holding her gaze, Lacey said, "It will."

Kacey's mouth dropped open, shocked. "What the hell do you mean? Do you think we won't last?"

Lacey shook her head. "No, Kace, I think y'all are solid, there is so much love between you two. But you have to remember, he is recovering. He is finding his footing in this thing called sobriety. His go-to was to drink when he was mad, hurt, or sad. Now he is having to find new outlets. But the thing is, he chose you to make this journey with him."

"I know that," Kacey agreed. "And I won't let him do it alone."

"Right, but with the good comes the bad. And while, yeah, it's too good to be true right now, and you are living the life you want, it won't last. He's gonna hit a bad spell, and that's when you need to worry. Because will you be able to be the rock he needs? Don't look at me like that!" she shrieked then, and Kacey held her hands out.

"You're freaking me out!" she accused, but Lacey shook her head. "I know all this, but you are making it seem like I can't handle it, which is making me second-guess myself."

"I'm just saying that when it's sunny, it's great. But it's how you weather the storm. So enjoy the good now, because there's no telling when the storm will come thundering through your life, and you'll be left holding on with everything inside of you," she said with more conviction. "You are so strong, Kacey, and Jordie knows this; he feeds off you and loves you something insane. And I know you love him, but my thing is, don't overthink this. Enjoy it, love him, and when it gets bad, then you'll be ready. But why wait for the possible impending doom? It won't do anything but stress you out."

Deadpan, she asked, "Impending doom?"

Lacey shrugged, not even smiling. "He is hard-set on not relapsing, Kacey, but do you know the statistics on that? Hardly a single alcoholic makes it through the first year without failing at least once."

Panicking a little bit, Kacey looked wide-eyed at her. "So you think he will? Do you think I'm crazy for being with him?" she asked and, really, she wasn't sure why she asked. It didn't matter what Lacey thought. She wasn't going to leave Jordie. She believed in him, loved him, and would stand beside him no matter what.

"I don't know, and no, I don't think you're crazy. I know how much you care for him, how long you've been in love with him. I just hope and pray that he doesn't let you down. Let all of us down. But alcoholism, it's really a disease, such a scary sickness."

Kacey couldn't agree more. "He's got this though, I know he does."

"I hope so," Lacey agreed. "It worries me because, if he does fail, I know what that will do to you if he doesn't pick himself right back up. And that scares me. You're invested to the extreme. No matter how much you try to hold that back and control it, you are, Kacey. And I really don't want to see y'all crash and burn."

Letting out a long breath, Kacey leaned on her hand. "This is a really reassuring talk. Thanks."

Sensing her sarcasm, Lacey smiled. "I told him the same thing, but he promised me he wouldn't hurt you, and I want to believe him. I do believe him. It's just the statistics are against him."

"But Jordie isn't a statistic," Kacey decided. "He's above that, you'll see."

"I really do hope so, and I hope that you guys get married and have babies and move out of here," she said with a teasing grin, and Kacey smiled despite not really wanting to.

All week she had been living in a little fantasy world, but then Lacey came along and didn't scare her, per se, but she did worry her. Everything she said was everything Kacey had thought, but hearing it from Lacey validated her fears. So many things could go wrong, but Kacey didn't really care. She'd be there—it was that simple. Like before, she knew going in what Jordie was about, and she loved him anyway. He wasn't an easy man to love, but his love was worth it and she wasn't going to let go of that.

"He hasn't invited me to AA groups or even therapy, but he takes Karson. My feelings shouldn't be hurt, should they?"

"Do you want to go?" Lacey asked, looking up from her phone, smiling. "They are crazy," she said, pointing down to it and Kacey rolled her eyes.

"Focus, Lacey," she snapped and Lacey laid her phone down.

"Right. Now, do you want to go?"

"Yes."

"Tell him that," she said simply. "Jordie isn't shy when it comes to that kind of stuff, plus I'm sure he wants you to go."

"Yeah," she agreed, leaning to the side to stretch her back as Lacey picked her phone back up and then laughed.

"Jordie just said that they're all just mad 'cause he's hung like a horse and they traded their dicks for strollers," she snorted and slapped her hand against the counter. "Such dorks."

"Right? I'm dying," Karson said as he entered the kitchen, Mena tucked in his arms. Lately, you didn't see Karson without Mena. It was adorable, but when Lacey told Kacey he was sad he was going to have to leave Mena when they went on road trips, it kind of broke her heart. He was such a good daddy.

Leaning against each other, Karson and Lacey looked on their phones, both of them laughing and looking like the poster couple for *Better Homes and Gardens* magazine. She was tempted to look too, but glancing at the clock, she saw that Jordie would be home soon and he'd want an answer. It wasn't that she didn't want to live with him—she pretty much already did—she just felt like it was too soon. But then, looking up, she saw the pillar of the love she wanted. They seriously got married like two or three days after seeing each other in however many years. They did rush into it, and Lacey even left him at one point, but Karson would be damned if she was going to leave him without a fight. He went up and got his woman, and Kacey knew in her heart that Jordie would do the same thing. So what was holding her back?

"Jordie asked me to move in with him."

They looked up at her, both with quizzical expressions on their faces. Shrugging, Karson said, "Okay?"

"What did you say?" Lacey asked.

"I told him I didn't know. It just seems fast."

"Fast?" Karson scoffed. "We got married right away, and when I came back here, I was living with Jordie. Kind of forgot to tell you that, too," he laughed, but Lacey shot him a dark look.

"Those damn tissues," she said, shaking her head. "But yeah, and we're good, Kacey."

"You know people do this every day. They meet, they know, and, boom! Married."

"I just thought it would take longer than this," she said with a shrug. "It all seems like it's happening and it's great, but then it will all disappear and I'll be heartbroken again."

Lacey made a face as Karson shrugged. "And if it does, at least you tried."

"Kacey, have you talked to Jordie about this? I mean, you don't sound very sure about you two. Maybe you need him to, I don't know, reassure you?"

She shrugged, leaning against her hand. "No, he has. It's me. I'm just scared."

"Stop being a pussy," Karson barked at her. "It's not cute and also not you. You wanted to be with him, right?"

"Right," she agreed.

"Then stop worrying or you're gonna be the one to mess it up, not him and his issues. You, with your worrying," he explained. "The thing is, I know Jordie. I know what he wants, and that's you. If you don't feel the same, then you need to let him know."

"I do want him," she snapped back. "God, shut up!"

"Then you shut up," he yelled and she glared.

"Asshole."

"Crybaby," he shot back, kissing Mena's head. "Stop being a baby and go for what you want. You two have been sleeping in the same room all week, so why not get a place of your own so us normal-sex folks can enjoy some peace."

Kacey scoffed. "Please, I know you two are freaks," she accused, and Karson shrugged as Lacey feigned shock.

"We are not," she said, and Kacey laughed.

"Whatever, and please spare me the details," she said, holding up her hand and letting her shoulders drop. "But I think here is a safety net. If it goes bad, I have you two."

"Well, sweetheart, there comes a time in everyone's life when they grow up and leave Mom and Dad. We love you, and we've—"

"Fuck off, Karson!" she yelled, throwing the cap to her water bottle. "I'm just nervous is all."

"Like I said, it's called growing up. You know, that thing you wanted to do? And, oh shit, it's with someone you actually like, so put your big-girl panties on and be happy. I don't see why you are bitching, it makes no sense. You've always wanted this."

Biting her lip, she shrugged. "I just never thought I'd get it with him," she said, looking up at them.

"But you are, so live, Kacey. 'Cause some people don't get this, and Jordie has worked hard to be the guy you want, so don't hold back on him, y'know?" Karson asked. "'Cause I'll kick your ass if you hurt him."

Kacey's face scrunched at him as Lacey giggled. "That's so not what a dude says about another dude."

"Um, excuse me, but Jordie is my BFF, like foreva," he said, sounding like a Valley girl and Lacey and Kacey snickered.

"It's true though, he's my ride-or-die dude," Jordie said, surprising everyone. Kacey's heart jumped up into her throat at the thought of him hearing about her uncertainty, and when his gaze met hers, she knew he had.

Shit.

"What's going on?" he asked. "Family meeting?"

Before she could say anything, Karson said, "No, she's a scared little brat, thinking that you two are going to fail."

Well, if he didn't know before, he knew now.

Rolling her eyes, she let out a long breath. "Wow, thanks, Karson," she said, her face burning, but Karson just shrugged.

"No problem. Come on, baby, let's give them some privacy," he said, pulling Lacey out of the kitchen despite her protests.

"Do you want me to leave?" Lacey asked, but Kacey shrugged as Karson pulled her.

"Do I have a choice?" she asked and Lacey shook her head.

"Don't think so," she called back as he directed her down the hall.

"Jerk," she called at Karson, but he ignored her, shutting Mena's door.

"So you don't want to be around me alone?" Jordie asked, tucking his hands in his pockets. "That's weird."

She shook her head. "No, come here. I missed you," she said, closing the distance between them before snaking her arms around his waist and kissing his lips. But he didn't kiss her back. "You're mad."

"Nope, just wondering what's going on," he said simply. "You breaking up with me?"

"No," she said automatically. "Not even thinking that."

"Then what's wrong?"

"Just nervous," she admitted. "It's all so scary because it's everything I want."

A mystified look came over his face as he shook his head. "Yeah, I have no clue what to say to that."

"*I* don't even know what to say," she admitted, leaning her forehead to his. "But don't worry about it."

"No, I will worry about it," he said, lifting her chin with his finger. "What do I have to do to ease your concerns?"

She shrugged. "I have no clue," she said and she was being honest. She didn't know what he could do to fix her worries. It was all on her. She either believed in them or she didn't.

"I can't fix it if you don't tell me what it is."

Looking up at him, she bit her lip. She needed to get a grip. This man was here, he was hers, and what else did she want? How much more reassurance did she need? He had become the man he felt she deserved. He woke up every morning with a grin on his face and I *love you* falling off his lips. He looked at her like she was the Stanley Cup and he couldn't keep his hands off her. He loved her and that's what she wanted. She needed to stop creating problems in her head. They had the potential to have loads of them, so she needed to enjoy right now, like Lacey said.

"Don't do anything," she said, looking up at him. "Except get the computer so we can look at houses."

His face didn't change like she thought it would. His eyes were still trained on hers, his breathing hard. "Really?"

"Yeah, I just never thought I'd have you, and I'm still waiting to wake up," she admitted, and his lips curved up at the side before his arms wrapped around her.

"You're not dreaming, baby," he whispered against her lips. "This is real. This is our life."

Our life.

He was so invested, so sure, and she knew she was too, but still, she worried.

And she wasn't sure if it was a survival tactic to prepare for the worst.

Or if it was really her subconscious telling her they weren't going to last.

Either way, she wrapped her arms tighter around his waist and decided that she wouldn't make him worry. Her fears would buff out and everything would be fine.

She hoped.

Chapter
NINETEEN

Squaring off in front of Jordie, Kacey set her stick to the ice and grinned.
"The name of the game is I win, you lose," he teased and she laughed.
"Other way around, buddy," she called out around her mouthguard as she stretched out her neck. "You're going down."

He gave her a dismissive look and shook his head. "Don't hurt yourself, sweetie," he called, moving the puck back and forth. "Now, when I win, we go to the three houses I like first. You win, we go to yours."

They had spent the last couple of nights looking at different houses and talking to a Realtor. Kacey was excited to see what they had picked out in person but really excited to know that they'd be staying in Karson and Lacey's neighborhood. Especially since her parents had just bought the house next door to them, despite Karson's protests. She was glad that they bought before she and Jordie did. Knowing her dad, he'd pick her to move next door to, and there was no way in hell she could deal with her father on a daily basis. She loved her daddy, very much so, but he was loud and liked to tell her what she should be doing.

First, it would be the lawn, then what color the shutters should be, then he'd be redecorating their house. And the next thing you knew, he'd be naming their children. Then, Lord, her mother would be over every day cleaning and teaching her how to cook, while making them both fat with all the food she prepared. Nope, Karl and Regina King could stay right next to her big brother and his wife. Then again, physical distance couldn't keep them out of her way

216

before, so she doubted a few streets over would keep them at bay. Might as well get used to the idea of them poking their noses into their business. Thankfully, Jordie loved them as much as she did.

But that didn't matter today. No, this morning, Jordie was going down.

When he shot her a grin, she glared, placing her hand on her hip as she held her stick loosely in her hand. "Stop talking so much and let's do this. Post shots?"

He nodded. "Take it back to the line if you get possession," he reminded her and she nodded. "First to three, wins."

"Fine, drop it," she said, moving her mouthguard back in her mouth. He looked deep into her eyes and when he puckered a kiss at her, she was seconds from smacking him with her stick. Finally, he dropped the puck. Taking it off the draw, she sailed past him, hitting the brakes when she heard him behind her. Like she wanted, he hit her hip, going headfirst into the ice. Not letting that faze her, she took the shot, hitting it off the crossbar.

"One for me!" she cheered before getting the puck to pass to him. But he was still lying on the ice.

"That was cheap," he said, getting up, and she shrugged.

"I don't play fair. I play to win."

He nodded. "I see how this is going to go," he said before taking the puck from her and then to the line. Toeing the ice, he took off, but she knew what he was going to do before he did and cut left as he did, spinning the puck away and going back to the line. Glaring at her, he shook his head.

"Bullshit, I'm still healing," he tried and she laughed, moving the puck between her legs and back out.

"Bullshit, don't get all pissy 'cause I'm gonna beat you," she teased and his glare deepened. When she went left, he followed and she sent the puck through his legs, going around him to pick it up. She didn't have the shot, so she went wide of the net, and when he barreled after her, she watched as it hit off the boards before coming to the slot. Lifting the puck, she hit the side of the post and grinned back at him.

"First to three right?"

He set her with a serious look, breathing hard. "I said five."

She giggled. "Sure ya did."

"It isn't fair. You're fast as shit, and it isn't like I can slam you against the boards to stop you," he complained, and she looked over her shoulder at him as she got in place before he took the puck out.

"Are you crying like a little bitch, Thomas?"

"Did you just call me a bitch?" he asked, shocked, and she nodded.

"I did. Now hush, girlie girl, and let's do this."

"Oh no, you didn't," he said in the same Valley girl voice that Karson liked to use. Taking off, she thought he was going to go left, so she deked, ready to cut him off. But he threw the puck over her, and then to her surprise, batted the puck into the net. Throwing his hands up, he said, "Boom!"

"Boom, what?" she screeched. "You didn't even hit the post."

He looked at the net and then to her. "Yes, I did."

"You liar! You did not!" she yelled, and she was about to go on when he shot her a big grin.

"Fine, I didn't. But I should get a point for the awesome batting I did," he suggested and she shook her head, taking the puck out.

"I don't give charity goals," she shot at him and he laughed.

"Such a badass," he teased and she grinned as she went to the line.

"I score, I win," she reminded him and he shrugged.

"Won't happen. I'm gonna stop you and then score three in a row," he proclaimed and it took everything out of her not to laugh, but he just looked so adorably hot. His brow was furrowed, his breathing hard, and he had sweat dripping from his beard. But the best part was his intense gaze. He wanted to win, and she was so sad to disappoint him, but he was going down. She knew it wasn't fair. He'd had practice before they hit the ice, but it wasn't her fault he'd challenged her. She doubted he would ever make that mistake again.

Grinning, she slap shot the puck, whizzing it past him and knocking into the boards.

"What the hell?" he called. And as she knew it would, it caught him off guard, so she rushed, catching the rebound and then lifting it off the ice to hit the crossbar. "Now, that's not fair! You distracted me!"

Giggling, she shrugged as she pulled off her helmet, shaking out her hair and then taking her mouthguard out. "Told ya I'd win."

He shook his head. "You already did that move though!"

"There are no rules for repeat moves. It worked the first time, and I figured it'd work the second."

He glared. "You know I'm worn out from practice too. You wouldn't have beat me if I was at full strength."

"Of course not," she said, trying not to smile.

"Plus, my core hurts. You made me do a billion crunches and seven billion burpees," he accused and she shrugged.

"Helped with your slap shot though. So in the long run, you'll be thanking me and you'll forget about your little bruised ego."

"You're being condescending, aren't you?" he asked, coming toe-to-toe with her, his eyes locked on hers.

"Just a little. I won fair and square."

His face twisted in shock. "The hell you did! You did some cutesy shit that no one does and caught me off guard."

"You're full of it! I've seen plenty of people do that in the NHL. You're just mad that you got beat by Khaotic Kacey!"

Looking up at the roof, he laughed from his gut. "Are you really busting out that wack-ass nickname? You aren't Khaotic Kacey, you're crazy!"

She scoffed. "Hater."

"Brat," he said, taking her by her jersey and pulling her to him.

"Sore loser."

"Show-off," he shot back before his mouth came down to hers.

"I don't kiss losers," she muttered right as his lips came to hers.

"Well, you're in luck, 'cause I love kissing chaotic, crazy winners who make up stupid nicknames for themselves," he said with a grin before capturing her mouth with his. She wanted to laugh, but there was no laughing when Jordie Thomas's mouth was on hers. Dropping her gloves, she wrapped her arms around his neck, deepening the kiss. He nibbled on her bottom lip and she felt his gloves hit the ground before his hands snaked into her girdle, grabbing her bottom. "I also love sex with said person I just described."

"Well, you're gonna have to wait, because I am not having sex here."

"No one is here though," he said, thrusting into her.

"Whatever, this place isn't empty, for one. And two, who wants to have sex in an ice rink? That's so unbelievably dumb. What if your ass sticks to the ice? Or, by God, your dick! I would die…and so take pictures to post on Facebook," she said, dissolving into laughter as his face filled with horror.

Removing his hands from her body, he shook his head. "And the moment is dead."

"Good, make sure it stays that way. You don't disrespect the ice by fucking on it." She scoffed and he laughed.

"But it's combining two of my favorite things: hockey and you."

"We'll play," she shot at him as they picked up their gear. "And I'll keep winning."

"What the hell ever," he barked as they skated toward the bench. "But on a serious note, why didn't you keep playing? You're good, baby," he said, smacking her shin with his stick.

She smiled. "Thanks, but you know I reached the end goal for me. I wanted to win the gold. I did, and that's it."

"You know I'm sorry for not being there. I watched on the TV though, drank a lot for you."

She rolled her eyes. "You should have stopped at the you watched part."

He shrugged. "Maybe, but really, you should have done more with it. Like, go into the NHL."

"I never thought about going into the NHL 'cause I didn't think it was possible, but Baylor Moore proved that wrong."

And boy, did she. She was all over the media, and she was a little rough around the edges, so of course, Kacey liked her. She was nice enough, but driven. She played her heart out and had truly embarrassed all the naysayers. With a daddy like star Bruins forward River Moore, it only made sense. But still, it was so cool to see a woman in the NHL. Kacey was probably more excited than Baylor was about the first game. She just hoped it opened the door for other little girls who wanted that as their end goal.

"You could still do it, y'know," he suggested, but she shook her head.

"I don't want to. I want to be a wife and a mom one day. Can't do that while I'm working to further my hockey career. And plus, I think I always knew I would end up with a hockey player. I kinda think they're hot—"

"You mean, I'm hot," he corrected. "Singular. One hockey player. Me."

She rolled her eyes. "Yes, I kinda think you're hot, and I don't think it'd be fair to the kids when they are being raised by a nanny," she said and he nodded.

"Yeah, you're right. I just wish you'd use your talent on something. Maybe coaching some girlies?"

She shrugged. It was an idea, but one she really hadn't thought about. "Maybe."

He leaned over, kissing the side of her mouth. "You'd be good," he said, kissing her again. "Plus, you'd be hot blowing a whistle. Which, by the way, wanna blow mine?"

He waggled his eyebrows at her and she smacked him as she laughed. "You're a horndog."

"Yes, ma'am. Only for you though," he said with a wink. She grinned, going over the boards and onto the bench to untie her laces. "What are you doing after this?"

She looked up and shrugged. "You have AA, right?"

He threw off his jersey and lifted his leg, stretching it. "Yeah, in about forty. I'm gonna grab a shower and head out."

"Cool, can I go?"

He looked over at her. "You want to?"

"Yeah," she said slowly. "If that's okay."

"Yeah, I guess. I'm...um, actually, I don't go today on normal weeks, but since tonight is the team party, I figured it'd be a good idea to go."

"Sure, absolutely," she agreed, and she'd be lying if she said she wasn't nervous about him being around all the alcohol. He seemed confident and brushed off her concerns, but still, it made her nervous. It was like putting a kid in a candy store and saying they couldn't have any. It scared her.

"I'm...um—"

"What's up with all the pausing and the ums?" she asked, chuckling, and he shot her a grin.

"I just got nervous for some reason that you're going," he admitted and her grin dropped.

"Do you not want me to go?" she asked, giving him an out. "I'd understand."

"No, I do. It's just…I'm singing today."

Her head spun to the side. "Singing?"

"Yeah," he answered sheepishly.

"Well, then, hell yeah, I'm there," she said earnestly.

And thank God she went.

Because as Jordie's beautiful, smoky voice filled the church, his fingers moving ever so effortlessly across the strings, Kacey was completely entranced by him. He sang the song like it was his and not Love and Theft's "Whiskey on My Breath." She was totally blown away, and she knew it wasn't the first time she had seen or heard him sing, but it felt like it. As his eyes drifted shut, his voice so raspy and full of conviction, the words left his lips like they were made just for him, and Kacey's eyes quickly filled with tears.

She hadn't really listened to the song before, but she was convinced that the duo had written it with Jordie, and anyone else who was fighting the battle of addiction, in mind. It was such a moving thing to see and she wanted to make sure everyone else felt the same, but she couldn't take her eyes off him. She would admit that she didn't understand what he had gone through—the struggle, the pain, and the need—but she was proud, so freaking proud of him for overcoming it all.

That was her man and he was so fucking beautiful.

As he sang the chorus once more, people started to sing with him. When the person beside her slid his hand into hers, she looked at him and he was crying. Big, huge tears, rushing down his face and staining his shirt, and he slowly nodded, feeling every single one of the words like she was. Her heart just hurt as she gave him the best smile she could before turning her gaze back to Jordie. The room was full of so much promise, so much need to succeed, and Kacey was proud to be witnessing it.

She just prayed the others were as moved as she was.

When he finished, everyone clapped as Jordie smiled proudly, leaning into his guitar, his gaze meeting hers. Wiping away her tears, she smiled back and nodded, hoping that he knew she was saying that he was downright amazing.

I'm so proud of you, she mouthed and his grin grew.

Thanks, he mouthed back. *For everything.*

Anytime.

And always.

"So hold on," Jordie said as Kacey took his hand, getting out of the car. "I not only have to let you out, looking so fucking hot that I'm pretty sure my friends will want to gangbang you—"

"What every girl wants to hear," she laughed, pulling her skirt down a bit. But it didn't help. The skirt was short, showing off those toned thighs, and tight, hugging the ass that drove him nuts. The dress was also low-cut, cupping her breasts with the sole mission to give him blue balls. That was the only thing he could come up with. Her hair was in curls, framing her face, and her makeup was dark and dramatic, making the red of her dress pop even more against her bronze skin. Add in the fact that she was wearing strappy fuck-me-stupid heels, and Jordie was having a hard time just forming a coherent thought, let alone coming up with a reason why they should just go back home.

"Anyway, you're so hot my friends are gonna be checking you out. And I'm not supposed to kick anyone's ass? But also, I'm unable to grope you? Or even sneak you off into the bathroom for a quickie? That's just rude," he said, feigning hurt, and like he wanted, she grinned, her dark red, glossed-up mouth puckering out at him before she shook her head.

"It took me, no joke, three hours to look this good. And that was while smacking away your hands from grabbing my kitty. So please, let me bask in my hotness for the party, and then you can have your way with me once we get home."

He thought that over for a moment. "So I can put it in your butt?"

Lucas and his wife Fallon looked back at him, wide-eyed, and started to laugh. It didn't faze him. He wasn't shy around his friends, but apparently, it mortified the hell out of Kacey. Smacking him with her purse, she mock yelled, "Really? I'm gonna kill you."

"What? Baby, that's a tight ass," he teased, kissing her bare shoulder as they walked into the arena. It was decorated in the team's colors, purple and black, but still had a very elegant feel to it. Everyone was dressed to the nines, but Jordie couldn't look at anyone but Kacey.

"You'll be lucky if I let you touch it," she sneered, smacking his hand away as he took ahold of her butt. "Jesus, man, behave yourself!"

"Come on. A quickie. It'll take two seconds maybe, and I swear, I'll put you back together," he begged playfully and she rolled her eyes.

"One, I don't know if I can get this dress back on, and two, I work here, Jordie. No!" She was trying to be mad, she was, but she wasn't committed to it yet. He may be annoying her, but she loved every second of it. He knew because her nipples were hard and, man, how he wanted to put one or both in his mouth.

Jesus, he wasn't gonna make it.

"I work here too, it's okay. I'll bring the Cup home for Elli to make up for all the sex I'm gonna have all over this arena," he said. And when Phillip Anderson looked over at him laughing, Kacey groaned.

"Will you hush!" she demanded.

Taking ahold of her waist, he brought her back hard against his chest. His cock rested against her ass as he chuckled into her neck. "Your fault, it should be illegal for you to be this hot."

Closing her eyes, she grinned as she shook out of his arms. "You're making me blush. Stop."

"You're making me hard," he whispered against her neck. "Please don't ever stop."

Looking over at him, she shook her head, but she wasn't mad. She was loving it. Moving her hair behind her ear, he nibbled on her lobe, feeling her grin against his cheek. "Since you're making it hard for me to walk right now, just know, you won't be walking tomorrow." Pulling away, he chuckled at her shocked face as he asked, "Want something to drink?"

Looking at him incredulously, she nodded her head. "Water. Ice water, please," she muttered before turning and heading toward where Lacey and Karson were. As he watched her ass move side to side, he bit his knuckle to keep from groaning.

God, she was hot.

And all his.

"Damn, please tell me that's not your girlfriend," Benji Paxton said from his left. Looking over at him, Jordie grinned like a fool, nodding his head.

"That is, and also our trainer."

"No way!" he gasped, his head falling to the side. "When did she get that hot? And also, way to go, bro. She's killer."

Jordie nodded, shaking his hand. "Some would object to our appreciative talk of my girlfriend."

"Are you part of that *some*?" he asked and Jordie thought for a moment.

"Nope, she's fucking hot and all mine."

Benji laughed as he nodded. "Lucky bastard."

"I am," he said, taking two cups of water from the waiter. "Whatcha drinking?"

"Pop with no alcohol whatsoever," Benji said with a grin. "Eleven years sober."

Jordie nodded. "Hundred twenty-seven days sober for me."

"Ah, my sobriety brother, great job and way to go. The first hundred days are tough, but the year will fly by," he said excitedly and Jordie's heart sped up.

"Really? Did you relapse?"

"Nope, never, but those first hundred take a toll. How long was rehab for you?"

"Ninety."

"Oh, awesome. Did you do, like, a stay-in one or just meetings?"

"Both," Jordie said, taking a sip. "Sucked ass."

"I know. I did the same, but only for thirty. That's why the hundred was tough for me, but you can do it, dude. Don't lose faith."

"Thanks, bro," Jordie said, grinning. "I'm only a little bit nervous. If I fail, I let down a lot of people."

"Good motivation. I had no one to let down but myself and the memory of my wife, daughter, and brother. But that story is one for the road. I'll let you get back to your hot-ass girlfriend," he said, tipping his head to her. "But I look forward to getting to know each other."

"You too, bro. Have a good night," he said and Benji shrugged.

"Dude, let's be honest. I'll leave here and go home to watch *Game of Thrones*," he said and Jordie laughed because he assumed he was joking. The dude wasn't ugly by any means, sorta looked like an underwear model with his chiseled cheekbones and puffy lips. But when he just turned around and walked away, defeat in his eyes, it left Jordie with the assumption that he would really go home and watch *Game of Thrones* instead of finding a lady to go home with.

Poor sap.

That wouldn't be Jordie though. Oh no, he had himself a firecracker of a hottie that he would be all over as soon as he found her.

Walking toward where he thought she was, he ran right into Audrey Odder, Tate's wife. Smacking him, she hugged him tightly. "JT! I haven't seen you in eons! I always make your favorite cupcake every Friday, hoping you'll come in."

His mouth watered at the thought of the snickerdoodle cupcakes she made. She owned a little cupcakery that he used to pass every day on his way home. He was pretty sure he had been sporting not only a whiskey belly but an Audrey Jane's cupcake belly. He used to joke that he had a body by Audrey Jane's. With everything that had been going on, he sort of forgot about Audrey and her shop. He should take Kacey there.

She'd love it.

"I'll be there this Friday. I promise."

"You better be! Penny and Philly would love to see you!"

He nodded. "I do need to see the little man. I'm so happy for you guys."

"Thanks," she said cheerfully. "We are so blessed. But I have to say, Tate told me where ya been, and I'm really proud of ya. I think everyone is. You seem so much happier."

He shrugged, bashful as he met her caring gaze. "I am."

"Good, now it's time for you to settle down," she said with a wink and he chuckled.

"Working on it. Which reminds me, I gotta bring my woman some water. Excuse me, okay?"

Leaning over, she kissed his cheek, and he smiled as she said, "Of course, see you Friday. Bring her with you."

"Promise," he said, going around her to find Kacey. He didn't have to go far; she was standing with Baylor and Jayden, watching him like a hawk.

"That's Tate's wife, right?" she asked once he handed her her drink.

"It is," he said, taking a long pull of his water. His mouth was dry.

"Good, because she has one hell of an ass, and I was about to get superjealous," she admitted and Jordie laughed, rolling his eyes.

"While you could be right, my eyes are glued to this beauty," he said, taking ahold of one of her cheeks.

"Please don't sue the team for sexual harassment."

He looked over and saw Elli grinning at him as Kacey smacked his hand away.

"Can't sue if it's my boyfriend," Kacey laughed, but then she cut him a look. "Or can I?"

Jordie scoffed as Elli laughed, her eyes bright as Shea towered over her, looking ever the doting husband. But even with how large Shea was compared to Elli, Jordie couldn't help but appreciate how gorgeous she looked in a floor-length purple dress that sparkled at the top. In the dress, he could tell that Elli had lost even more weight.

"I'm convinced you aren't feeding this woman," Jordie accused Shea, and he scoffed.

"Please, I'm trying to get her to eat more. She's on some diet, wanting to be thinner for our trip to Disney," he said, rolling his eyes. That was, until Elli smacked him.

"Do you know how embarrassing it is when you go to hug Mickey and he can't get his arms around you? Shea ruined my body with all our blessings, and I'm getting my body back."

"If you need help, let me know," Kacey suggested but Elli shook her head.

"No, you'd kill me."

Kacey laughed as Shea and Jordie said, "Yeah, she would."

"No, I'd take it easy. We can do one of my workouts," she suggested, but as Elli's eyes traveled down Kacey's beautiful, fit body, he could see the apprehension in her eyes.

"I can't fire you if you hurt me, can I?"

"No, I'd make you sign a waiver," Kacey said with a wink and Elli laughed.

"Fine, I'll come down after the boys train on Monday."

Kacey bounced on her heels. "Can't wait!"

Shea snorted with laughter. "Do I need to hire a sitter? Or call Grace?"

"Shut up, Shea," she snapped, smacking his stomach. "I'll be able to walk...I hope."

But Kacey shook her head. "Nope."

"Jesus, what did I just sign up for?" she whined and Jordie laughed.

"Hell," was his opinion and that didn't seem to please Elli.

Rolling her eyes, she said, "Okay, I'm gonna go eat my feelings and prepare myself for Monday. Y'all have fun."

"Thanks for making sure I wasn't drinking," he called to her, and she shot him a grin over her shoulder as her fingers tangled with Shea's.

"I almost licked your cup to make sure, but instead I sniffed it when you were watching Kacey talk," Elli teased and he laughed as she leaned into her husband.

"Good people," he declared and Kacey grinned up at him.

"They love you," she said, resting her head against his shoulder. "I do too."

"Good," he said, kissing her nose.

Smiling up at him, she cocked her head to Baylor. "We were talking about her dad, you know, River Moore."

"Everyone knows River Moore. Great player, scored two minutes into overtime, game seven."

Kacey nodded as Baylor grinned. "Yes, him. He's looking for an assistant coach for the Bullies."

"Oh, really?" he asked with a grin.

"Yeah, Baylor said she can get me an in."

"We like ins," he noted.

"I told her she should go for the head coach position for the girls' team," Baylor suggested and Jayden nodded, his arm snaked around Baylor's waist. Jordie sometimes forgot they were together until they were near each other. They reminded him of two magnets, attracted through any barrier.

"I think you should too. Those girls could learn a lot from you," Jayden added and Jordie nodded.

"Either is good, I feel," he decided and Kacey shrugged.

"We'll see," she said just as Lacey turned to them, her eyes wild with anger.

Jordie made a face, his brows touching. "What the hell is wrong with you?"

Blistering with anger, she burst out, "I'm gonna kill her. She closed my store! Closed it! For a fucking week! No pay for my employees or anything."

"Who?" Jordie asked, confused, while Karson shook his head.

"Rachel did? Oh my goodness, what are you going to do?" Kacey asked.

"Fire her ass!" she snapped, typing violently on her phone. "Karson, call your mom to see if she can keep Mena. I can't take her, I might go to jail, and knowing them, this is a big ploy to get me home!"

"Or we can keep her," Jordie suggested, and everyone stopped and turned their attention to him. "What? It isn't like we are doing anything. No reason to call Ma and Dad down. We can do it."

"Watch Mena? You two?" Lacey asked, pointing to the both of them, and he gave her a look.

"I hope you aren't implying that I can't care for my goddaughter?" he asked sternly and she shrugged.

"No, but…can you?" she asked and Kacey nodded.

"Sure, no big deal. We'd love to. You two go, fire some folks, and maybe have a little night out, just the two of you. She'll be great."

Lacey looked to Karson and he shrugged. "I mean, they are her godparents. If we die, they get her. Might as well give them practice while we're alive."

"Way to think, bro," Jordie laughed, smacking his arm, and Karson grinned.

"I mean, just saying," he said innocently as Lacey glared, but then she chewed her lip, deep in thought.

Finally, she said, "Fine, thank you. I'll plan everything tomorrow."

"Sounds good. In the meantime, I'm taking my woman to dance," he said, taking Kacey's water from her and handing it to a guy who was walking around with a platter. When he reached for her, she went willingly, smiling as they headed to the floor to dance. A few couples were dancing, and as he spun her out and back in, he wrapped his arms around her, holding her close as they swayed to some slow song he hadn't heard before. Leaning his cheek to hers, he closed his eyes, dizzy from her perfume. It was a mix between fruity and floral, and it drove him crazy with need.

"We've never danced before," she whispered against his cheek. "Never."

"Yes, we have," he said, pulling back to look at her.

"When?"

"Back in college, right before Karson locked you in the room, we danced to 'Slow Dancing in a Burning Room' by John Mayer."

She paused for a moment and then smiled. "We did. You remember that?"

He nodded. "I do, and I remember the Team USA shirt you wore, because your tits looked so good in it. And also the tight jeans, because of your ass—it was so juicy back then, unlike now, when it's so strong. Oh, and how long your hair was. All the way to your butt."

Her grin didn't stop. "I didn't think you remembered me from back then."

"How could I forget?" he asked, moving with her as the music played. "I kind of had a crush on ya, but Karson was quick to shut that down."

Her face reddened as she nodded. "Because I liked you too."

He smiled, running his nose along hers. "Funny thing, this story of us."

"And it isn't even over," she reminded him.

"Because it won't ever end," he promised, and she smiled against his lips before he kissed her long and hard. Every single ounce of his feelings were in that kiss. As much as he wished that they had hooked up back then, he knew it would have been pointless. He was a baby looking for a good time to forget his friend's death. He had always been looking for something to make him forget. It was the story of his old life.

But now, his story was different.

When the music changed to "Marvin Gaye" by Charlie Puth, Kacey pulled back, her eyes widening as she cried, "Oh, no."

"Oh, yes!" he said, pulling back and starting to dance, pelvis thrusting to the beat. Anytime this song came on and they were together, he'd serenade her and she hated it. He wasn't sure why though. Every girl loved when a man sang to them, but Kacey did not. Maybe it was the way he humped her as he did it. Nonetheless, he yelled out, "This is my jam!"

"Please stop," she begged as he pulled her to him, moving like they did in *Dirty Dancing*. "Please, tell me you didn't plan this!"

He sang very loudly, ignoring her. "Of course not, it's fate."

"Jesus help me," she said as he jerked her around playfully, rubbing himself all over her. "Oh my God! Jordie!" she screeched as he started singing at the top of his lungs. Everyone around them was laughing and cheering him on, while Kacey's cheeks burned the same color of her dress. She was going to kill him, but he didn't care. If he couldn't drink to have fun, he'd find another way to do it.

And singing to her was the ticket.

"Come on, baby, dance with me. Sing the chick part," he urged and she shook her head, her face twisting in horror.

"This is not *High School Musical*!" she complained as he slowly humped her leg, getting catcalls from the guys while she tried to shake him off.

"You're right, because the things I'm gonna do to you as soon as we leave are definitely NC-17," he said and her eyes widened, but her mouth curved before she started laughing.

Then finally, she stopped fighting it and moved with him to the music. As she smiled, her eyes twinkling while their bodies became one, he knew that their story was just beginning.

And he couldn't wait to fill the pages with their adventures.

Especially the NC-17 parts.

Chapter TWENTY

"**B**abe, come on, this is it."

Kacey looked around the living room. The high ceilings were appealing, and she did like the floor-to-ceiling windows, but it didn't have a fenced-in backyard, and the driveway was on a slant because the house was on a hill. The winters in Tennessee were so unpredictable, so no telling if she'd be able to leave the house. Also, it just felt so large.

"I don't know. It's big," she said to him, looking through the kitchen once more. It was huge like she wanted, almost like Karson's, and an open floor plan like theirs, but it seemed so much bigger and not theirs. She always imagined when she walked into a house, it would be hers, and this did not seem like hers.

"It's empty, Kace. Once we get some furniture in here, a dog or two, it'll be perfect," he said, coming to stand by her, looking out the windows she was staring out of.

"There is no fence," she said, pointing outside.

"I'll make sure they put one in. It's a new build, so that won't be a problem," their Realtor Jamie said in her thick, happy, country accent. She was always so chipper and ready to sell. It should have made Kacey happy, but she was a bit annoyed. She wanted to do this with only Jordie so they could talk and discuss it without someone trying to sell to them.

"I don't know. It just doesn't seem like us," she admitted, looking up at him.

"Really? I think it does. I like it," he said simply as he looked down at her.

"You like anything to get out of Karson's," she accused and he shrugged.

"I mean, an apartment would be fine too, baby. Whatever, as long as I'm waking up beside you."

She sent him a smile because she did feel the same, but still. This wasn't it. "But I think a house would be a better idea. And also we can be close to Lacey and Karson so I'm not lonely while you're gone," she protested and he nodded.

"I got you. That's why we've spent the last two weeks looking at houses, and I really like this one."

"It's nice and, yeah, it would give us everything we need. But it's really far out from where my family is. For the longest time, we've always had hundreds, almost thousands of miles, between us. Now that we live in the same city, I'd like to be close."

"Yeah, I get that. But it's only a twenty-minute drive to them, and also the price is killer good. They are selling it twenty thousand under the value for a quick sale. It's move-in ready, babe."

She shrugged. "I know, but I don't want to move in to a house that isn't us."

"But what doesn't make it us? I think it's us," he said, getting annoyed. He had a short attention span when it came to things other than sex and hockey. She knew this, but she wouldn't rush into something as big as buying a house.

"I mean, it's nice, yes, but I don't like that it's on a hill or that the backyard looks so shitty."

He looked out and shrugged. "Okay, then what do you want to do?" he snapped, and she glared.

"It doesn't matter what I want, and it's your money. Do what you want," she said dismissively, and when she glanced over at him, she could tell she'd just pissed him off.

"Don't be like that."

"Don't be all pissy with me because I don't want to rush into this."

Letting his head fall back, he let out a long breath. "Sugar thighs, it's a house. It's not choosing a name for a kid."

"I understand that, but if I am going to live here, make a life here, it better be what I want."

He pulled in a long breath through his nose and she glanced over at him. The annoyance was very apparent on his face, but his eyes had humor in them. As much as they picked and argued about stuff, he still loved her difficult ass.

"Do you want this house?" he asked. "Because it will be our house, both our names, and you will live in it with me. Probably forever."

Her heart skipped a beat at his words. She hadn't expected that. She thought it would be his house; she didn't think he'd want her to be on the paperwork. She knew moving in meant she wasn't going anywhere, but it would have her name too? "Really?"

"Yes, we are making a life together. So everything will be fifty-fifty."

She glanced over at him. "Are you trying to tell me I don't need a prenup so you can steal all my money?"

He laughed, wrapping his arms around her waist and pulling her to his chest. "No prenup. Do you want this house?"

She shook her head, smiling against his jaw. "No."

"Okay, have you seen one that you think is *us*?"

This was a pick of both of theirs, and they had already seen all the others they liked. But only one stood out in her mind. It was smaller than they wanted by a bedroom, but it was perfect for them. The backyard was huge and fenced. The kitchen was gourmet and had an awesome double stove she wanted. The master bedroom was huge, essentially two rooms with a bathroom to die for and enough closet space for all her gym clothes. There was even a little nursery that made Kacey breathless when she stepped into it. The basement was finished as a man cave that would be perfect as a gym and playroom for Jordie. It screamed them, and he had loved it but wanted to see more houses. She had gone along with him, but now it was time to speak up for what she wanted.

"The one behind Karson's."

He scoffed. "I knew it. I knew when we left that you didn't want to leave it."

"I didn't. I loved it, Jordie."

"You know that means we can't have sex on the deck, 'cause more than likely Karson will see us," he told her and she giggled.

"Is that a negative factor for us?"

"Well, yes, it's a huge factor for us. We do love sex."

She smiled, her body breaking out in gooseflesh. "You are correct, but I don't think that's an issue. Karson is getting older, his eyesight is going," she teased and he laughed.

"Okay, if that's the house you want, it's the one we'll get."

"You sure?" she asked, biting her lip.

"If it makes you happy, yes. I told you, I don't care as long as we are together."

Her face broke into a grin. "Okay, well, I can throw in maybe a grand on the price."

He smiled, cupping her chin. "Do you want it then, or do we need to go back and look?"

"No, I could tell you everything about it. I want it."

"Then give me your thousand bucks, and let's go buy it."

He kissed her nose and she smacked his chest before hugging him close as her heart went wild. The last two weeks while they had looked, she almost didn't believe it was happening. But as he talked to Jamie about the house and what they needed to do, she dug her nails into her arms, waiting to wake up.

But she didn't.

They were really doing this.

Her happily ever after was happening.

"What is one of your biggest regrets, Jordie?"

Kacey crossed her legs and glanced over at Jordie as he leaned on his thighs, looking over at his therapist, Julie, and chewing on his lip. Folding her hands in her lap, she watched as his gaze flickered to her and then back to Julie. This was the second therapy session she had sat in on, and she was still as nervous as the first time she came. In the AA group, he was more laid-back and chill as he shared his daily struggles. But in therapy, it was different. He was closed off, he moved his hands continually, and he couldn't sit still. It made her stomach hurt watching him so uncomfortable.

She wanted to ease his concerns and fix him, but this was his time. She was there for support and that was all.

"I have two," he said roughly, looking over at Julie. "One is losing Robbie and the other is pushing Kacey away."

She nodded as Kacey held her breath, tucking her hands between his thighs. She knew she was one of them, but the way he said it was like a knife in her belly.

"Why is that?"

He leaned back, his chest rising and falling as he shrugged. "I hate knowing that someone was killed trying to protect me," he said softly. "It's been years, almost thirteen, but I can still see the blood, still see his eyes go blank, and still hear my screams as I tried to shake him back to life."

"Can you talk about what happened?"

Kacey looked down, sucking in a breath. She knew this story, knew it well because Jordie still held so much guilt from the whole thing. He had only talked twice about it, but both those times had ended with him wrapped in a ball, her body covering his.

"I was dating a girl that I really thought I was in love with, but Robbie never liked her. He said she was too rich. And since we were poor, he thought it was a little weird. But I was hot and, of course, she'd like me," he said and Kacey shook her head. He tried so hard to hide his pain with humor, but when she glanced up, Julie wasn't smiling. She was watching him intensely as he looked back down, sensing that his joke hadn't gone over well. "Um, well, one night, after we got done having sex, we were talking, and I told her what happened to me from one of my stepdads."

"Why?"

Kacey looked up then because she had always wondered that. Why did he tell her?

"'Cause I wanted someone to care, to be sad with me." Kacey's heart sank as she reached out, lacing her fingers with his. "I just hated myself, thought it was my fault, and I wanted someone to make me feel differently."

"Did it work?" Julie asked.

"No, she looked freaked out by it all, but I joked it off and that was it," he said, sitting up again and holding Kacey's hand. "The next day, she went to school and told everyone that I had sex with one of my stepdads. Left out a lot of what I'd said and turned it into me being gay instead of me being a victim."

Kacey had never met the girl, didn't even know her name, but if she ever came across her, she'd kill her. It was that simple. As hard as it was for Jordie, Lord knows he didn't need what that girl did on top of it. No one deserved that.

"Apparently, I'd taken her boyfriend's spot on the hockey team and she wanted to get back at me. Well, her boyfriend and some of his buddies were calling me names and fucking with me outside as we stood next to Robbie's car." He paused and it was like a wave of pain just washed over him. She could see the light slowly leaving his eyes. "I told the dude to fuck off. If I wasn't hurt—I had dislocated my shoulder in gym the day before—I would have just kicked his ass. But he kept coming at me, and then Robbie stepped in. They called him names, saying that he was my boyfriend and stupid childish stuff like that. Robbie, being the hothead he was, didn't hold back. He whaled on the dude, and then it all happened so fast. Someone pulled out a knife, and then they were stabbing him in the back of the neck."

She hadn't realized she had started crying until a tear fell on her arm. Wiping it away, she kept her eyes trained on him as he sucked in a deep breath.

"He died right there, and I felt like the world should have stopped, they should have mourned with me, but they didn't. It was like he was nothing to no one, and when his mom turned on me, blaming me, it only made it worse."

"And the drinking started?"

He nodded. "Yup, I didn't have to think of the blood or his lifeless eyes when I was drunk."

Julie nodded. "You know it's not your fault, right?" she asked and he shrugged.

"Yeah, I know, but it doesn't make the pain stop, or make me forget."

"Because you haven't fully forgiven yourself," she said slowly and Kacey's hand squeezed his. "Same with Kacey. You've spoken many times about what you did to her, and I know you still hold so much guilt. Especially with the miscarriage."

Kacey looked up at him, seeing the tears welling up in his eyes, and she broke. It hurt her because she had gone through it, but they had never really spoken about it. She hadn't realized that he was hurting because of it as well.

Closing her eyes, she leaned her head against his shoulder as he slowly nodded.

"I should have been there. I should have been a man and done right by her."

"Yes, but everyone makes mistakes."

"I know that, and I own up to mine. But because of my mistakes, my betrayal, and my rejection, she questions us. She believes that this life I am working so hard to give her will be taken from her in an instant, and it kills me."

Biting into her lip, she looked up at him as the tears slowly rolled down his face, disappearing into his beard.

"We are buying a house, and I see it in her eyes. She wants to say, 'But what if we break up?' And I just hate it. I'm not leaving her. And she isn't leaving me. I will fight tooth and nail to keep her, to be healthy for her, and to be the man she wants. I just want to ease her concerns, but I don't know how, and it all goes back to my biggest regret. I wish I wouldn't have pushed her away. I did this, and I'm worried that her fears, her apprehension with me, will never go away."

Kacey was fully crying, snot and tears rushing down her face as she watched him come undone and be completely and utterly honest. She hadn't meant to make him feel this way. It was her issues, her fears that were mentally fucking her. She never meant for them to come out and affect him. He was supposed to be getting healthy, not worrying about what she felt. Closing her eyes, she squeezed his hands as her heart jackhammered in her chest.

"Have you told her this?"

He shook his head and then shrugged. "I guess I just did," he said, looking over at Kacey, his own heart in his eyes.

"Have you forgiven him, Kacey?" Julie asked her then, but Kacey couldn't tear her gaze from him.

Sucking in a breath, she nodded. "I have, and I'm sorry, Jordie. I didn't mean to make you feel this way."

"No, it's fine, I caused those feelings."

"But I need to let them go. I need to do what I said, and that is that I've forgiven you and we are moving forward."

"Exactly," Julie agreed, handing Kacey a tissue. "If you two are going to make it, you have to communicate what you are feeling. Jordie, you're so used to keeping everything inside and you can't do that. It won't help your recovery if you hold everything in."

He nodded. "I've been better," he pointed out and Kacey nodded.

"He has," she said, leaning into him. "We communicate."

"But Kacey, I feel like you are so nervous to hurt him, to drive him to drinking that you won't share what you're feeling and your anxiety. He can't advance in his recovery if he is continually trying to make you feel good about you two and not succeeding."

She was right, and Kacey hated that she hadn't seen that she was doing that.

"This is hard," she admitted, her eyes flooding with tears and Jordie nodded.

"It is hard, but I want this to work."

"I do too, I really do," she whispered, pressing her nose to his. "I don't want any other hard but you, Jordie."

"And it will work," Julie agreed. "As long as you two communicate. I like that you are coming with him, Kacey. Please continue to do so."

She nodded, getting lost in his eyes. "I'm not going anywhere. I'll always be here."

"Damn right," he said, his mouth curving up before he pressed his lips to her nose. As his lips warmed the tip of her nose, she felt as if a billion-pound weight had been lifted off her chest. She'd thought a couple weeks ago that she had let go of her nervousness, but she hadn't. Seeing Jordie come undone, how she was causing him pain with her worries over losing him, really opened her eyes. She was stressing about nothing. Jordie was there, Jordie loved her, and together, they would conquer whatever storm came their way.

There was no other option.

Because she wasn't going anywhere without him.

"We can move in in two weeks," Jordie said, leaning back in the chair with Mena on his chest as he hung up the phone. "That's the earliest."

Kacey looked over from her phone and smiled. "Cool school. We need furniture."

"Yeah, we'll go shopping tomorrow if you want."

"I don't know, I'm pretty sure Lacey would flip if we took Mena anywhere," she muttered as her phone went off. "Speaking of the devil, she asked if Mena was okay."

Jordie laughed, looking down at the little bundle of cuteness. "You okay, Mena?" She cooed softly, her little brown eyes wide and aware, locked on him, and he nodded. "She said she's good."

Kacey giggled as she shook her head, typing Lacey back. "I'm so blessed to be with a man who speaks baby."

He smiled. "It's one of my many talents."

"Yes, so many, yet you can't beat me on the ice."

He glared. "Now, we have yet to play before I have practice. Which will happen soon, 'cause your bragging is killing me."

"Four and oh, baby," she said, shrugging her shoulders in a pathetic dance as she grinned.

He rolled his eyes, annoyed. So what if she kept beating him? He was tired and she was fast with her long legs and stealthy ways. Again, it wasn't like he could plaster her against the wall. Also, she was doing little tricks that no one could pull off in the NHL. She was a pain, but his pain, and he wouldn't trade her in for anyone.

Ever since last week when he took her to therapy with him, things had been different. He felt like she was more confident in them, and that took one hell of a load off his shoulders. He already had so much up there, and he was thankful to have her anxiety gone. He understood he'd caused it, it was his fault, but it had been tearing him down slowly. He wanted her to look at him and only see love, not nervousness about them ending. Since his session, it had been just like he wanted, and because of that, they were now enjoying the house-buying process.

Moaning as her phone went off again, Kacey rolled her eyes. "She's gonna drive us batty."

He couldn't agree more. Lacey had only left four hours ago and had texted them or called at least nine times since. He understood that she was freaking out a bit as it was her first time without her baby, but they were more than capable of caring for Mena Jane. They were her godparents; they had this.

Grinning, he looked over at her. "Hey, we should mess with her."

She looked up. "Why do I feel like that's a bad idea?"

He scoffed. "What's the worst she could do?"

"Kill us if we hurt Mena Jane," she reminded him and he laughed.

"I don't want to hurt her, weirdo," he said, getting up and holding Mena close. "I'm saying we should send her pictures of Mena doing things she shouldn't be doing."

"See that's tiptoeing on the line between getting killed and making her laugh. She's not in her right mind right now. I'm pretty sure Karson went just to make sure she didn't kill that chick."

Jordie shrugged. "Right, so we should send her some comic relief."

Kacey eyed him and then slowly shrugged. "Okay, I'm intrigued."

"Good, come on."

And for the next hour, between laughing so hard and then laughing some more, they set Mena up in different scenarios. Mena was eating it up, having a blast, all smiles as they went all over the house doing things that Lacey wouldn't even think to do. At one point they were in the car, Mena holding on to the steering wheel with a huge toothless grin on her face, while Jordie and Kacey acted as if they were screaming out in horror of her crashing the car. The caption read, "Who let the baby drive?" Then they had her with bras on her head, lace in her mouth, and the caption on the picture was, "Following in her mom's footsteps." After stuffing her in a helmet, they sent a picture to Karson that said, "Or maybe daddy's footsteps?" When they handed her Kacey's gold medal, she looked at it like it was the Holy Grail—which to Kacey it was—and Jordie quickly snapped the picture since Kacey had started twitching from the medal being out of the box. Sending it to Lacey, he said, "Or maybe her auntie's?"

It went on like this for quite a while…that was, until Lacey called just as he was stuffing Mena in the fridge.

"Okay, it was all cute until you stuffed her in a pot and said, 'Baby. It's what's for dinner,'" she complained and Jordie laughed as Kacey snickered, holding Mena close, kissing her head.

"It's supposed to make you laugh," he said. "No baby was hurt in the process of making Mommy laugh."

She did laugh then and Jordie's grin grew. "There's what we wanted. You okay?"

She let out a long breath. "No, I fired her and we aren't speaking. My dad came up to the shop, but I called the cops on him. I'm now in the process of hiring a new manager. So we probably won't be home till Monday since Karson won't leave me," she said, saying the last bit louder for him.

"I don't trust these people. I'd say close the shop, but I know you won't," Karson yelled and Jordie grimaced. They both sounded stressed. "Not that I think you should."

"Yeah, I'm not, and it will be fine, no worries," she said, but she sounded very worried. "Please don't stuff my baby anywhere else."

"Will do, boss lady. She's actually about to get a bottle and go to bed."

"Oh good," she said, sounding relieved.

"Hey, you're taking your meds, right?"

"Yeah, I am," she said, and he could tell she was telling the truth.

"You sound frazzled," he commented and she scoffed.

"I am, but no worries. Promise. Let me let you go though. I need to get some paperwork done. Give Mena kisses for me, and don't roll your eyes and make fun of me when I text every thirty minutes."

Jordie smiled as Kacey laughed. "We will try not to."

They said bye and Jordie laid his phone down, grinning at Mena. "Well, my little rock star model, we are done for today."

"Yup, bedtime," Kacey sang, bouncing her around, which had Mena giggling before they headed out of the kitchen. "Bring the bottle, I'm gonna go change her."

"Be there in a second," he called to her before turning to make the bottle. As he filled the bottle with water, he couldn't help but think how easy this was for them. They were going to be good parents. They fed off each other while laughing and having a good time. He still thought of the child they had lost though. Would it have been a boy, born with pads and a stick? Or a little girl, also born with pads and a stick? He didn't know, but he wanted to have another chance. Soon.

Shaking the bottle, he went down the hall into Mena's room, just as Kacey lifted her off the changing table and settled into the rocking chair. "Mm, nighttime snack is here," she cooed before taking it from Jordie and putting it in Mena's mouth. She sucked happily, her eyes trained on Kacey, and he couldn't blame her. Kacey was beautiful.

She was only wearing sweats and a tank, her hair in a short little ponytail, but Jordie was completely taken by her. To him, she was wearing the red dress from the team party, her heels teasing him—she was always that gorgeous. Emotion choked him as he watched her, wishing like hell that it was their baby instead of Karson and Lacey's.

"You look good, baby," he said, clearing his throat. "Holding a baby."

She smiled up at him. "Yeah, one day."

"Soon?" he asked and she shrugged, looking back down at Mena. Smiling, she glanced back up at him.

"Maybe after we get married?"

"So tomorrow we get married and, boom, baby time?" he asked and she laughed.

"Or, maybe after your first year of sobriety, we get married, and then we enjoy time just the two us, and then we try?" she asked slowly.

"That sounds like a much smarter plan instead of just doing it tomorrow, huh?"

She winked. "Just a bit smarter."

"You aren't hesitant, are you?"

She shrugged. "I just want you to get to a year and then see if it's still all that you want."

His face remained blank. She was being honest and he wanted that. "It will be."

"Good, I hope so," she said, a grin pulling at her mouth. "It would be awkward living with someone who doesn't want me. I'm not leaving my new house."

"Me either," he said, his grin matching hers.

She shook her head and then her grin dropped. "I'm actually nervous that I'll miscarry again once we do decide to go down that road."

"Don't be, please," he urged and she nodded, biting her lip.

"If I can't have babies, will you still want to be with me?" she asked hopefully, and his heart lurched in his chest.

He didn't even pause. "Why would you ask that? Of course, I will."

She smiled, her eyes locking with his as she whispered, "Just making sure."

He shot her a dubious look as Mena's eyes slowly fell shut. Waiting a few more minutes, Kacey handed the bottle to him before getting up and carrying

Mena to her crib. Laying her down slowly, she smiled as the baby sprawled out in the crib.

"She's perfect," she whispered, tracing Mena's palm with her finger. "So pretty."

"She really is," Jordie agreed, kissing her shoulder. "So are you."

She leaned into his face, and his eyes drifted shut before he wrapped his arms around her waist. Holding her, a part of him knew it was smart to wait because they still were young in the relationship. But the other part of him said, fuck it, let's do it now. They hadn't been together long, he understood that, but there wasn't a moment he didn't think she was the one. Even when he was pushing her away, he'd always loved her. They had spent so much time apart, and he didn't want to waste any more time. He was in love with being in love with her. It was so fulfilling, but it was probably smart to wait it out. Enjoy them, enjoy her, and get settled. It was just easy to rush in, though. They had the love, the money, and now the house; nothing could hold them back.

Except his alcoholism.

That was the one thing that could make them crash and burn, but he was doing everything to ensure that wouldn't happen. He was winning, he felt it, and he wouldn't back down. But he would do as she said, wait until his year, and then he'd marry her and get her pregnant quicker than she could say yes.

He would have his happiness. His forever.

Nothing would keep him from that.

When his phone rang, he glanced down, and everything stopped. It was his mom. His stomach twisted as he declined the call, but she called back almost immediately. Glaring at it, he rejected the call again and tucked it into his pocket before saying, "Come on."

He then pulled her toward the door, his pocket still vibrating as she checked everything to make sure that Mena was okay before following him out of the room. Once outside, he shut the door slowly before turning to reach for her, pulling her back to his chest, kissing her neck.

"I want you," he whispered and she let out a breathy laugh.

"Do you?" she asked, turning on the baby monitor.

"Always," he said, nibbling up her neck and then her ear as his hands explored the abs on her stomach. Slowly dropping his hands into her pants, he cupped her, his breath coming out in a whoosh and making him hard as a rock.

"Why's my ass vibrating?" she asked as his hand stopped.

"My mom is calling," he said, continuing to ignore it, but she turned in his arms, looking up at him.

"How many times has she called?"

He paused. "That's the seventh time," he said as his phone went off again.

"Should you answer?"

He shrugged, pulling his phone out of his pocket. "I don't know."

"She could be dying or something," she suggested and he nodded.

"So I should answer?"

She gave him a troubled look. "I have no clue, that's up to you."

His phone started going off again, and he glanced up at her before hitting accept and saying, "Hey, Mom."

But Stacey Thomas was anything but a mother and every bit the darkness that shadowed his soul.

Chapter
TWENTY-ONE

"Jordie Scott Thomas, I have been calling you for weeks," his mother complained. Disappointment and anger laced her words, and for some reason, he felt like he was six again.

Glancing at Kacey, he looked away just as quickly. Sucking in a breath, he went into his room and sat on the bed, leaning on his thighs. "Yeah, sorry, I've been busy. Are you okay?"

"Oh, I'm fine! But you wouldn't know that since you don't call me at all. How sad. I'm your mother and you can't even call me."

Kacey sat beside him and shook her head as he said, "I haven't heard from you either."

"Well, that's 'cause I've been so busy! Roger died, God rest his soul. But thankfully, he left me a nice little amount of money to get me by. But then, by the grace of God, I met Phil. Oh Jordie, you're gonna love him. He is a doll baby and loves me so much! We are getting married on Christmas! You'll have to come, of course. But he wants to meet you before that, and we are coming to Nashville in about a month. I made sure you weren't on a trip with the team, and we are even coming to a game. Glass seats! Only the best for me, as Phil says. So I'll get to watch my baby, up close and personal!"

She didn't even take a breath and, like always, it was only about her. Feeling like he was in a spinning car, he said, "So you're okay?"

She paused. "Yes, I'm in love and happy. Have you not been listening?"

"No, I heard you," he said sullenly. "Figured since you called nine times in

241

a row, you had cancer or something."

"Well, that is a rude and unthinkable thing to say. Jesus, how did I raise such an asshole for a son?" she snapped and Kacey glared, but he shook his head.

"Okay, Mom, I guess I'll—"

"Like I was saying, you should be very happy for me. Phil is my age, so pray God he don't die. And he is loaded, son, so rich and so sweet. I think he might be the winner, the one that lasts. Isn't that great?" she asked and Jordie let his head hang.

"Yeah, great," he said, and why couldn't he just tell her to fuck off? Why was he sitting there, listening to how they went all over the country the last couple months? How he helped her get over whatever-his-name-was's death? By the look Kacey was giving him, he was sure she thought the same. But he said nothing as she rambled on and on about her life. He sat there. Hoping, praying, she'd ask how he was doing. But the question never came.

"Okay, so we will plan to get together in about a month, I think it's the twenty-seventh of October. I'll have Phil make reservations and send you an email. He's so excited to meet you. He's a big hockey fan."

"Um, Mom, I don't know," he started, but she cut him off.

"Now, you'll meet me, Jordie Scott. I haven't seen you in almost a year because you're off gallivanting across the country, playing with a stick and puck and whatever else you do. You don't call, you don't Facebook me, and you sure as hell don't act like you care one bit for me. So you'll be there," she snapped and he closed his eyes.

Tell her to fuck off.

"Tell her no," Kacey whispered but he shook his head. He knew he needed to say it. To stay away from her. But the need for approval was still there.

He wanted her to love him.

To be proud of him.

To care about him.

"Is someone there?"

Kacey snapped her mouth shut and he nodded, his throat thick. "Yeah."

"One of your many sluts, I'm sure. What did she say? I thought I heard her say no. Tell her I'm not another of your sluts, I'm your mother."

Kacey's mouth dropped and Jordie shook his head. "It's my girlfriend."

She paused. "Like a real girlfriend? You haven't had one of those since what's her name, the one whose boyfriend killed that kid you were friends with."

"Angie, and his name was Robbie," he said, looking up, a wave of guilt slamming into him.

"Yes, him. I saw his momma about two weeks ago. She still hates you."

"Yeah, well, her son was killed acting in my defense. I wouldn't care for me much either," he said dryly and his mom made a noncommittal sound.

"Eh, yeah, I guess you're right," she said and he let out a breath as Kacey shook her head quickly, her anger radiating off her. "Oh, well, bring her too, I guess. If you think it will last, I guess I should meet her. I really don't want to though. I'd like it to be just you, me, and Phil," she said, and he didn't miss the way she spoke louder.

"Fucking bitch," Kacey muttered, standing up and folding her arms, looking down at him as he held the phone to his ear. He couldn't look at her, not in the eyes. He knew she was mad, he knew she was probably disappointed in him, but he couldn't just hang up.

"I don't know, Mom. I'll text you."

"No, tell me now you'll go," she snapped, and he knew when he looked to Kacey, she'd be shaking her head no, so he looked at the floor.

"I told you, I don't know. We will see," he said as sternly as he could. "I have a lot going on," he said slowly, hoping she'd ask what he had going on. But that would mean she was a good parent.

And she wasn't. Not even a little bit.

"Well, cancel it. I'm your mother; you will be there to meet your new soon-to-be stepdad. I'll send you the address and info as soon as I get it. Oh, Phil just walked in. Yeah, baby, it's him. He says hi too! Okay, gotta run, bye, honey!"

And then she hung up.

No, "Can't wait to see you!" No, "I love you!" No, "Fuck off." No, nothing.

Closing his eyes, he let his head hang as he shook it. Why had he even answered the phone? He could feel Kacey's hostility pouring off her, and when he looked up at her, her face was flushed and she was working her lip.

"Not right now, okay? I know she sucks, I know she's a bitch, and I know I should have said no," he said quickly, feeling like the weakest piece of shit in the world.

"You're right, on all accounts," she said before coming onto the bed and wrapping her body around his like a koala bear. "But I know it hurts."

"It does," he whispered, holding her arm as she held him. "I don't want to go."

"We won't."

"But she'll find a way to me," he said and she nodded.

"You need to tell her in person that she can't do this to you anymore. That she needs to just stay away."

"I know," he said roughly. "But the shitty thing is, I still want to hear her tell me she loves me, that she's proud of me, and that she cares. Not once did she ask about me."

"Because she's a poor excuse for a human, and if she hadn't have had you, she would be on this earth for no reason," Kacey proclaimed, hugging him tighter. "You are better than her, Jordie. So much fucking better. You'd never treat anyone like she does."

He paused, closing his eyes as more guilt washed over him. "I did, though. I used to do it to you," he said softly, looking over at her. "What if I am like her?"

Taking his face between her hands, she shook him hard. "No, Jordie! You are not fucking her! You get that out of your head right now. You hear me?" She was screaming, her eyes filling with tears. "No, no fucking way. You are good. You are the most beautiful man in the world, and I fucking love you. All of you. Even this shitty part of you that is basically a wound that she keeps stabbing at! You hear me?"

His eyes glazed over as he turned, wrapping his arms tightly around her waist. Burying his face in her chest, he sucked in a deep breath, telling himself that he would never give his mom any more of his time. Kacey was right; he was nothing like her. He knew how to love someone, because he did it every moment Kacey was on his mind. But as much as he wanted to be strong, he wanted to brush her off, he wanted to let the pain she was causing him go, he couldn't. His feelings and his pain were there, oozing and throbbing like a wound. A big, gaping wound that his mother stood above and poured salt into.

A wound he wasn't sure how to close.

As soon as the thought came, he wished he could make it go away. But he could drown the wound and himself with whiskey in a second.

Everything would go away. He would be free of everything.

"It isn't worth it," she whispered, kissing his temple, and he looked up at her. "I can feel it, I can see it on your face. You want a drink but, Jordie, it isn't worth it. The pain right now, yeah, it fucking sucks. But afterward, when you disappoint everyone and possibly start losing people, you'll look back on this pain and say, I'd rather have suffered that a bit, because this will go away," she reminded him as her eyes burned into his. "Please, don't think that is the answer."

"I don't want to," he admitted. "But it's so easy."

"But usually what's easy isn't worth it, remember?" she whispered, pressing her nose to his. "Hockey isn't easy, but worth it. Life isn't easy, but it's worth it too. Hell, we aren't easy, Jordie, no matter how much we think we are. The truth is, we aren't. But, yet, we are still worth it. You're worth more than anything to me, Jordie. Please, let this go." Her eyes held his as she shook him gently. "Tell me what to do. Anything. Let me get your guitar," she suggested, releasing him, but he wouldn't let her go.

"No, just hold me?" he asked, but he was too embarrassed to look her in the eyes. Slowly, she laid them back, holding him tightly to her and kissing the top of his head. Wrapping his legs and arms around her, he held on, his chest clenching, his heart pounding, and he didn't understand why this had happened.

Why couldn't he be stronger?

And what would he have done if Kacey hadn't been there?

He thought he had come so far, but maybe he was wrong.

Maybe he hadn't come far at all.

"You've been quiet lately."

Jordie looked up from where he was breaking down boxes, his brows coming together. Karson stood at the counter, unloading a box of silverware, his gaze on him as he lined the silverware up in its drawer.

"What?" he asked, unsure of what Karson meant. They were unloading boxes in Jordie and Kacey's new kitchen; why would they be talking? She had been psycho about the placement of stuff. He had to make sure he did it all right and to her liking because he really wanted to have sex, and they hadn't done that in a couple days. With her family and Lacey basically moving in to get everything done before the first game of the season, it was easy to say that their sex life had been lacking. Mostly because they were both dog-tired come the end of the day.

"You've been kind of standoffish. I know that I've been busy and shit, but you haven't really been talking to me."

Jordie shrugged. "Nothing to say, I guess. Just been playing and getting ready for the move. Do you know how hard it is to go shopping with your sister? I swear, she was a gypsy in another life. She likes the weirdest shit," he said with a chuckle, shaking his head, trying had to cover up the fact that he was battling something dark inside of him. Karson had been dealing with a lot the last couple weeks. With Lacey stressed about her store in Chicago, firing her sister-in-law, and apparently causing a war with her family, he had his hands full. Add in the fact that they had a baby who was rolling now and wanted attention all the time, and he was sure that Karson couldn't deal with Jordie's issues. It wasn't fair to him.

Or to Jordie.

He wanted to say that the last two weeks had been fun, the best two weeks, picking out furniture for his new house and getting ready to spend the rest of his life with Kacey, but it had been hell.

He wanted to drink.

All he could hear was his mom's voice, demanding his attention and not caring one bit about him. Their conversation played over and over in his head, and he didn't know why she didn't care. She hadn't asked anything about him.

She degraded Kacey and she was just mean. Only caring about her new fiancé. It hurt him to the bone, and for the last twelve days, he'd had to keep telling himself why he shouldn't drink. Why it would ruin everything and how Kacey was right when she said that the regret that he would feel would be worse than the pain. He just wanted to forget, though.

And that made him feel weak.

Like he didn't deserve any of this.

Especially not Kacey.

Looking over at Karson, he flashed him a grin and shrugged. "I'm good, though."

Karson nodded, his eyes narrowing. "Do you know I see right through you, and the only reason you got away with a lot of shit before was because we weren't face-to-face?"

Jordie looked away and shrugged again. "I'm fine."

"You're full of shit. Tell me what happened. If it's my sister, I'll put away the fact that she's my sister and not want to kill you if you hurt her. But only for like twenty minutes," he said before shaking out his arms and then striking his hips. "So yeah, hit me, I'm ready."

Jordie laughed, kicking a box with more force than was necessary. He didn't want to feel like this, he wanted to be strong, to beat this. But fuck, his mom fucked with his head. When Kacey talked of the darkness that filled him, it was his mother. She always overlooked his problems...or ignored them because they didn't affect her. Or they did, and she wouldn't fix them because it would be too much work. He was always a second thought, someone who didn't matter to her unless she needed something.

He knew this. So why did it hurt?

And why was it so hard to talk about? The last two weeks, he'd only said his cravings were bad, but never why. He blamed it on the stress of the move, and he didn't understand why he did that. Was he actually covering for his mother? Trying to cover up the fact that she was a shitty person? Why? Why was he doing that?

"My mom called," is all he said, and Karson's hands fell from his hips, his shoulders drooping.

"And you answered?"

"Yeah," he said, nodding. "She wants me to come to dinner with her and her new husband-to-be."

"You said no," Karson said, and it wasn't a question.

"She didn't let me," he admitted, chancing a glaze at him, and what he found was what he expected. Pure hatred on Karson's face.

"Don't go."

"She'll come to my house, or yours, if I don't," he protested, but Karson shook his head.

"Let her come; I'll let Lacey loose."

"Lacey couldn't hurt a fly." Jordie scoffed.

"Fine, I'll let my mom loose," he provided and Jordie smiled.

"Now that's a thought. Even though Kacey wants to Spartan kick her in the face."

Karson grinned, pointing at Jordie. "That's a great idea. I favor that one 'cause my mom's hips are getting bad," he said and Jordie smiled.

As much as he wanted to laugh and joke with Karson, he couldn't. Her rejection weighed heavy on his chest, and he didn't know what to do. He knew he couldn't depend on anyone to make the pain go away. He had to handle it and get rid of it, but he didn't know how. He didn't know how to look at the person he loved and whose love he so desperately wanted and to tell her to fuck off.

"My cravings have been worse lately," he admitted. "I want to forget, and whiskey makes me forget."

Karson nodded. "I know, but once it's gone, you'll remember, and then you'll be back to where you were," he reminded. "Also, you've tried that on my sister and it never worked."

"I know," Jordie agreed, his heart clenching in his chest. "But I'll also lose everything I've fought so hard to have."

"Yeah, you will, and you'll bring Kacey down 'cause she won't leave you. She'll stay in hopes of fixing you," he said sternly, and Jordie knew this. "Have you been talking about it in AA or even therapy?"

Jordie shook his head, feeling like Karson was the dad, scolding him for not being the man he needed to be. "No."

"Why? Bro, why are you so fucked up about this woman? She doesn't even act like your mom, you know this. Let her go."

"I'm trying."

"No, you're not. You're holding it in. I'm going to therapy with you next week," he proclaimed.

"Kacey's been going," he said slowly, but Karson shook his head.

"I'm going. Hell, she can too. But, Jordie, you need to look at me right now and tell me you won't bring my sister down."

Jordie didn't answer right away, which he knew didn't look good, but he was seriously thinking it over. He had to make sure before he made a promise to Karson that he could keep it. One of the main things he'd learned through his journey was that when he made a promise, he had to hold it instead of just blowing it off. Karson meant a lot to him, they had been through a lot, and Jordie wouldn't betray him. But he also knew that he wouldn't do that to Kacey. He couldn't let her go because he loved her so much, but he wouldn't fail her. He wouldn't bring her down.

"I'm gonna up my therapy sessions," he suggested and Karson nodded.

"Me and Kace can take turns, then."

"Thanks," he said, sucking in a breath. "But I won't bring her down. She can't fix me, but I can."

Walking around the island, Karson stopped in front of him and reached out, squeezing his shoulder. "You're already doing it, bro. Don't give up. Stay strong."

Jordie nodded, his heart pounding in his chest. Glancing over at his best friend, he nodded before sucking in another breath. "Would it be gay if I asked for a hug?"

Karson smiled, and without answering, he wrapped his arms tightly around Jordie, hugging him tightly. "I think it's in the rules that our bromance allows hugs," he muttered as he squeezed Jordie tightly to him.

Closing his eyes, he hugged Karson back, needing the support and strength that Karson was giving him. Karson was the closest thing to a brother he had, and he thanked God for him every chance he got.

"You've got this," Karson whispered roughly. "I believe in you and know you can do this. Don't hold in anything. Tell me, tell Kacey."

"I just feel like a failure," he whispered as Karson pulled back, gripping his shoulders.

"But you're not. You are beating this. You are winning. Just look how far you've come." Jordie nodded, pulling in a breath through his nose. He had come so far, but he still had so much further to go. Karson squeezed him tightly. "Don't let her get in your head. You don't need her. I know you want her, and hell, I wish she could be the person you need. But you have me, Lacey, Kacey, Ma and Dad, and a team full of dudes that love you like a brother. So many people love you. Why fight for the love of one who doesn't deserve you?"

Nodding his head, he knew that Karson was right, but still he craved her love.

More than he craved the bottle.

And the problem was, he wasn't sure which would kill him faster if he gave in to his cravings.

As he met Karson's gaze, he knew there was really only one thing to do and that was to continue his road to sobriety and completely cut off all communication with his mom.

But how do you tell the person who gave you life that you don't want them in it?

"Hey, sugar thighs."

Kacey turned from the stove and grinned as Jordie came into the kitchen, his hockey bag hanging from his shoulder. He was wearing a suit, the shade of blue that really popped against his skin. His hair was brushed to the side and his beard was perfectly trimmed and shiny with oil. And those eyes, they were downright sinful.

In other words, he was fucking gorgeous.

Placing her hand over her heart, she shook her head, biting her lip. "Jesus, I don't know if I can handle seeing you on game days."

Her grinned, throwing down his bag and coming to her. "Did you know that this is the first time we are alone in our house and not dead asleep?"

She grinned, he was right. Between Karson, Lacey, and her parents, the last three days had been full of moving, decorating, and then sleeping. She had been ungodly tired with working, playing hockey with Jordie, and then moving. But all it took was that look in his eyes and she was feeling all sorts of naughty things.

And man, she felt good. Happy. Really happy.

They had only been in the new house for three days, and yeah, they hadn't even had sex in it yet, but just knowing it was theirs filled her heart with so much love. It was so them and waking up next to him was perfect…until her dad came into the room screaming at them to get up. But those two seconds, looking into his eyes, were magic. He was hers, but she still worried so much about him.

She wasn't sure if his mom's goal was to fuck with his head, but Kacey was pretty sure she had succeeded. He didn't talk about it though, not even in AA or therapy. He never brought her up, and that worried her. She wasn't sure if he was okay, and she was worried to ask, which pissed her off because they were supposed to be communicating. But they hadn't. The move was a lot of work, and they were still finding their footing. But looking at him now, he looked happy, he looked good. Maybe he was okay?

"This is true, but you look so snazzy, ready to go," she pointed out, her breath catching as he stroked his beard. "Maybe we could make it a date to meet in the bedroom tonight?"

He shook his head though, slowly removing his jacket and then unbuttoning his shirt as he started for her, desire burning in his eyes. He wanted her and he was going to take what he wanted, no matter what she said.

That pleased her to no end.

"No, see, my plan was to tease you, since dudes in suits are basically for girls like girls in lingerie are for dudes, and then I was gonna do you. Against the counter. But first, I want to eat you like you're my breakfast."

Before she utter a word or even form a thought, he had her by her waist, lifting her up and plopping her down on her counter. Grinning, she wrapped her arms around his neck as he went between her legs, his eyes dark with desire.

"It worked," she muttered as she pulled the belt out of his pants, letting it hit the floor hard. "But I'm cooking you breakfast," she said as his mouth trailed up her neck while she pushed his slacks down to his ankles, stroking his cock with one finger. He gasped against her mouth before smiling against her lips. He was so hard, so thick and, ugh, she wanted him.

"But I'm hungry for this," he demanded, cupping her pussy as he lifted her shirt with his other hand. Taking it off, he threw it over his shoulder before kissing down her breasts, pulling the cups of her bra down to take her nipple in between his teeth. As he feasted on her breast, he pulled her shorts down as she lifted up, helping him take them off. The counter was cold against her naked butt, but the desire burning inside of her counteracted the cold. Quickly she forgot that he looked spectacular, that he had to leave for his first game of the season, and that they were about to eat on this counter, because she wanted him to make love to her right here.

As his mouth trailed down her stomach, biting and licking her abs, his beard burning her belly in the most delicious way, she leaned back as he pushed her leg to the side, taking her whole in his mouth. "Oh my God," she gasped, arching up into his mouth. "I have to say," she gasped as his tongue flicked along her clit, "your choice of food is pretty fucking great."

"I think so," he said roughly against her pussy, making her quiver. The hair on his mouth tickled her lips and made her wetter, if that was possible, making her cry out in need. As he drove his tongue inside her, she bit down hard on her lip, moving herself against his mouth, and it felt so fucking good. Not just what he was doing but because with no one to hear them, no one to tell them to keep it down, she was free to scream as loud as she wanted.

As he slid a finger inside of her, she gasped, moaning his name as he started to move his finger in and out of her, the tip of his tongue quickly flicking against her clit. Letting her head fall back, she gripped the counter, her thighs squeezing his head as she arched up into his mouth.

But when she sucked in a deep breath of smoke, her head snapped back up. "What is that smell?"

He glanced up at her. "All I smell is this delicious pussy," he said, dropping his mouth back to her, but she lifted his head to stop him.

"It smells like smoke," she said just as she looked over his shoulder and saw a blaze of flames. She screamed out, smacking his shoulders in distress as she yelled, "Jordie! The stove is on fire!"

Turning around quickly, he said, "Oh shit!"

Going to the left, he tripped over his pants, falling onto the floor with a huge thump. "Oh fuck, my dick."

Crying out, Kacey jumped off the counter as he writhed on the floor, moaning like a man who could possibly have broken his dick. She went for the extinguisher by the washer. Running back to the stove, she pulled the clip and sprayed all the flames until they were out. Her heart was pounding, she was choking on fumes, and Jordie was still hollering out. When the final flame was out, she let her arms fall, the extinguisher by her legs as she took in what was left of her shirt on the skillet. As the fire alarm blared and Jordie groaned, she couldn't help it, she started laughing.

"Guess our sex is so hot, we start fires," she said as Jordie rolled over and looked up at her, holding his dick.

"I think I broke my dick," he said, and she tried not to laugh as she came down on her knees to check on him.

"I doubt it. Want me to check it?"

Raising his brows, he asked, "With your mouth?"

She sputtered with laughter as he sat up, cupping the back of her neck. He pulled her to him, kissing her lips hard, swallowing her laughter. Leaning back, he kissed her nose. "I hate to say this, but I'm not in the mood anymore, and I think I'm dying from smoke inhalation."

She giggled as she nodded. "I know, me too. Come on, let's open the windows."

Together, they stood, getting dressed before opening the windows and letting the smoke out, laughing. This could only happen to them. Everything was getting in the way of them doing it in their house, and it was becoming not only frustrating but also very comical.

When she lifted her Assassins tee that was burned to a crisp, she turned to him. He had already gotten dressed and washed his face. He wasn't as clean as he had been when he first came out, but he still looked as gorgeous as ever. Smiling, she held up the burned black shirt and said, "I need a new Assassins tee."

"I need to work on my aim," he said with a chuckle.

"Yeah, no big deal. Story for the ages, I guess," she said as his arms wrapped around her waist.

"Yeah, we'll tell the grandkids about how I was eating breakfast and the stove caught fire," he said roughly against her neck, nibbling on her jaw as she squirmed against him, his beard tickling her neck. Kissing her jaw, he said, "But I will get you a nice #3 T-shirt, with my name on the back."

"Good, I'll wear it proudly."

"That's right, and also, Ms. King, I will have sex with you in this house."

She nodded. "Damn right, you will. Tonight."

He grinned, his hands drifting down her belly. "Oh yeah?"

"Yup, no matter how tired and worn out you are, and even if your dick is kinda crooked, it's happening."

He buried his face in her neck and squeezed her. "I can't wait."

"Me either, so hurry home. I'll be naked and ready."

"Just the way I like you," he teased as he went to grab his bag. "See ya in a bit."

"I'll be the one screaming your name," she said as he reached the door.

"As you should be," he said with a wink. "Love you."

"Love you," she called as the door shut. Looking around, the room was still pretty hazy, and very quickly she was getting light-headed. Before she could leave though, her face twisted in agony as she held her stomach and gagged. The smell was horrendous and soon too much to bear. Going into the living room, she sucked in a deep breath as the wave of nausea hit her hard. Bracing her hands on her thighs, she swallowed past the need to vomit and stood back up just as the door opened.

"Kace? You okay?" Jordie asked, coming in and placing his hand on her back.

She nodded, her stomach clenching as the vomit rushed up her throat, but she swallowed hard again. She hated puking and she wasn't puking today. Today was game day. "Yeah, the smoke got to me. I feel like I might spew everywhere."

"You're green, baby. Come here, sit down," he said, trying to move her, but she shook her head.

"No, I'm fine," she said, sucking in another breath. "Do you not feel icky?"

He shrugged. "My head hurts, but I don't want to puke."

"I guess that's a good thing, huh?" she said as another wave hit her hard. "Guess our sex is dangerous."

He laughed, stroking her head. "You sure you're okay? I forgot my keys, but I can stay if you need me."

She shot him a deadpan look. "You know you can't. Go, I'm fine."

"Okay," he said, and she knew he was in a rush. "Are you sure?"

"Yeah, fine," she said quickly, clearing her throat.

He kissed her forehead and set her with a serious look. "Text me later. Let me know you're okay."

"I will," she said, standing up and sucking in a breath as the feeling of puking everywhere subsided. He looked at her skeptically and she waved him off. "I'm fine, Jordie. Promise."

"Okay, going. Text me, okay?"

"Okay," she said and nodded as he went out the door hesitantly, but she waved him off and he shut the door. Pulling in another breath, she felt a bit better and decided that they would not be having sex in the kitchen.

Things got too hot.

Chuckling to herself, she decided she was hilarious and went to get ready for Jordie's first game.

"How's the house coming?" Lacey asked as they settled into their seats. Mena sat in her lap, her little Assassins jersey dress on and tiny headphones covering her ears from the noise of the crowd. It was electrifying, the first game of the season, and everyone, including Kacey, was excited. She had been waiting since Jordie had gotten hurt for him to get back on the ice in full beast mode. He did well in the preseason games he played in, but tonight—tonight, he was going to rock it. He was ready, she was ready, and she just hoped the fans were ready.

Because Jordie Thomas was back.

"It's coming," she said, leaning back in her seat, thankful her nausea was practically gone by the time she got to the arena. "Although, Jordie and I tried to have sex in the kitchen and almost caught it on fire. I was cleaning smoke and burned shit off my brand-new stove all afternoon."

Lacey's face twisted in confusion and she sputtered with laughter. "Do I even want to know how this happened?"

Kacey grinned. "He threw my shirt on the stove, and I had forgotten to shut it off. Boom! Flames, fire, poor guy fell and almost broke his dick."

She tried to hold it in, bless Lacey's heart, she did, but soon, she was laughing so hard she was crying. Kacey was right there with her, holding her own stomach as she laughed until she couldn't breathe. Still gasping, she said, "I'm sitting there, spraying the fire with the extinguisher as he's moaning on the ground. It was by far the funniest thing that has ever happened to me during sex."

"Oh my God, I'm dying," Lacey proclaimed as Karl and Regina sat down beside her.

"Give me my baby then," Karl said, taking Mena and cuddling her into his chest. "You watch hockey with Pawpaw."

Wiping her face, Lacey shook her head. "Oh my, to be a fly on the wall. I'd pay, I'd seriously pay to see that."

"It was humorous," Kacey decided, crossing her legs. "I think I almost died from smoke inhalation though. I almost puked everywhere."

"That happened to me when I caught the chicken on fire a couple weeks before I had Mena. Remember that?"

Kacey nodded. "I do! We were both so sick."

"Yeah, I hate that. Thank God y'all didn't burn the house down."

"Right!" Kacey agreed as the lights went dark. "Give us a few weeks though. We are so hot when we do it."

Lacey scoffed. "Jeez, get over yourself."

OVERTIME

Kacey grinned as the light show started before the guys hit the ice. Cheering along with the rest of the crowd that was there, Kacey got the little flutters in her stomach that she always got at the start of the game. It used to be for Karson, or even herself, but now it was for Jordie. She loved watching him play, but this was his first real game since being hurt. She was excited to see him hit the ice, to see him back to full Jordie mode. *Hopefully, this will help,* she thought to herself. He craved the smell of the ice, the feel of the ice beneath his skates, and the feel of his stick in his hands. So surely, those cravings would cancel out the ones of drinking. He hadn't told her lately that he wanted to drink, but he had mentioned it in AA, and it honestly scared her. She felt like she should follow him around, make sure he wasn't doing it, but she told herself she wouldn't do that. She'd trust and believe in him until he proved her wrong, and he hadn't done it yet.

He wouldn't.

"Number Three! Jordie Thomas!" the announcer said and the crowd lost it. Smiling, she watched as he held up his stick, his grin unstoppable. He looked like her Jordie.

He looked happy.

Leaning over, Lacey said, "He looks good."

Kacey nodded. "He's home."

"Yeah, Karson said they had a talk the other day and that his momma messed him up pretty bad."

Looking over at her, she nodded. "Yeah. She's a bitch."

"Agreed, but Karson's worried."

Kacey's heart stopped. "He is?"

"Yeah, he's been okay though, right?"

She shook her head. "I can tell he's hurting, but everything seems okay..."

"Yeah, that's what Karson said. We just need to be there for him."

"I'm not going anywhere," Kacey said and Lacey nodded.

"I know, but he really needs to cut that woman out of his life."

"You're right."

As the puck dropped, Lacey looked away, her attention on the ice as Kacey looked on too. The Assassins were hosting the Panthers, and within seconds, Kacey knew it was going to be a good game. They both wanted that first win of the season, that was easy to see, and soon Kacey was on the edge of her seat. As Phillip Anderson sent the puck back to Jordie, she watched as he skated around the net, watching at his forwards got into position. Sending the puck to Karson, he skated up as Karson whizzed it up to Anderson, who passed it quickly to Erik Titov. He shot, hitting the goalie's leg pad, which gave off one hell of a rebound. Anderson got it, sending it to the goal again, but again it was rebounded back to the corner. Brooks rushed the boards, getting the puck and sending it out to Karson, but he didn't put his stick down in time and it went out of the zone. They changed up, and the game continued as Shea and the new kid, Sinclair, sent puck after puck at the net. The goalie was giving up huge rebounds, and when one came back, right onto the stick of Baylor Moore, Kacey held her breath as she shot top shelf, scoring the first goal. She had forgotten all about Baylor because of Jordie, and her stomach fluttered as Baylor held her arms up, everyone hugging her, and the crowd losing their shit.

"That should be you!" her father yelled, but Kacey didn't agree. She was where she was supposed to be. In love and happy with Jordie. She sent her dad a smile as everyone cheered but then it dropped when Mena started crying. Taking her from Karl, Lacey cuddled her as they lined up for the next puck drop. Winning the puck back, Jordie was the first to pick it up, sending it quickly up to Anderson, who was rushing the net. He was stopped though, and the puck was swiped from him. But Jordie got it, shooting it hard to the net. The goalie blocked it though, sending it back to Erik, who sent it fast to Jordie, who acted as if he was going to shoot, but instead, sent it to Karson, who went five-hole, getting another goal.

Kacey was the first one to say that she loved hockey. Lived and breathed it. And when her brother scored, with the help of her boyfriend, she was so proud. But when she saw the grin on Jordie's face, it wasn't the goal Karson scored that brought her to tears, it was the happiness in Jordie's eyes. The guys were wrapped up in a huge bromance hug and Lacey was hollering beside her as she just stood there, tears rushing down her face. Wiping them away, she shook her head and knew that this was what Jordie had needed. He'd needed to be on the ice to help push him along the road to recovery.

And now he was.

Chapter
TWENTY-TWO

Moving her nose along Jordie's jaw, Kacey let out a long breath.

She didn't want to let him go.

"I want to go play, but I don't want to leave you," he said, reading her thoughts as his lips skimmed along the middle of her brow. Closing her eyes, she held on to him tighter, nodding her head. She knew that he had to go, it was his job, but it didn't suck any less.

"I don't want to let you go," she agreed, taking a huge sniff of his beard, memorizing the smell, though she couldn't forget it if she tried. "I sent you an email with AA groups in every city."

He smiled against her forehead, kissing it before nodding. "Thank you."

"You're welcome," she said softly, and her heart just hurt. This was the first time he'd be leaving since their reunion. They had been inseparable for the last two months. Just them, well, her family included, but mainly just them. He was going to be gone for a week, a whole damn week. She wouldn't have anything to do because the team would be gone, so she didn't have to do any workouts for them. It sucked. The only good thing was she still got to work out with Elli. Even Lacey had started too, and from what Elli said the other day, a couple of other girls might be joining in too. Which was cool—she needed the distraction.

She needed something to help her not worry about Jordie relapsing.

"I'm gonna be fine, sugar thighs," he said roughly against her face. "Don't worry."

"Oh I know," she said, playing it off. "But it does make me nervous."

"I know," he whispered. "Me too, but I'm rooming with Benji."

"Yeah, that's good too," she said, because it was. With Benji winning against the disease of alcoholism, Kacey was excited that he would be with Jordie. Maybe he'd even be a little motivational. He seemed like a good guy, and Jordie needed that. Too many hockey players were dicks, but Elli's team only had a few. Kacey hoped Jordie stayed away from them. She prayed so at least. "I know you'll be fine," she said, more for herself than for him.

"I will be," he agreed, kissing the side of her mouth. "Will you miss me, sugar thighs?" he whispered huskily against her lips, and she smiled as she nodded.

"Just a little bit," she teased and he smiled. "I'll be lonely, and who is going to cook? Also, who will keep me warm at night and make love to me?"

With desire burning in his eyes, he gathered her in his arms. "Only me, so you'll have to wait for me to get home."

She nodded, her nose moving along his, her lips grazing his. "Not at all a problem."

"Good." He rolled her over, his body covering hers. "Now let me between these sweet sugary thighs before I have to go shower."

She could only nod as he took her mouth with his, his hand running up her ribs and taking ahold of her breast. Deepening the kiss, she closed her eyes, his body settling between her legs, his thick cock hard against her wanton pussy. Gasping against his mouth, she arched into him as he moaned.

"How do you do this to me?" he whispered, pulling her leg back, her pussy opening for him, his cock laying against her wet center. "Make me so fucking crazy with need?" he asked, his eyes trained on hers, making her hot all over. "Just a kiss, baby, and I'm harder than ever."

She smiled as she moved her pussy up the length of his cock and back down, her eyes never leaving his. "It's a talent," she teased, and his lips curved as he took ahold of his cock and directed it inside of her, each inch of him disappearing ever so slowly. When he was in to the hilt, he pushed both her legs back to her shoulders, groaning loudly. Her heart slammed into her chest as his eyes moved along her body, stopping at where they were connected. As he thrust into her, she cried out and he slowly pulled out and then pushed back into her in a perfect and utterly breathless sequence. Sweat dripped down his arms onto her legs as he continued to move in and out of her, his eyes never leaving the spot where they were joined.

"So hot," he muttered, his fingers biting into her thighs. "So fucking hot," he grunted out, his strokes of total pleasure moving a little faster. Letting go of her leg, he reached out, putting his fingers into her mouth. She bit down playfully, a hiss of breath leaving his mouth before she swirled her tongue around his fingers, sucking them into her mouth. Pulling them out, he reached between them, moving them along her extended clit, her body rocketing up against his as he went deeper inside of her. Squeezing her thigh, he moved his fingers faster along her, quickly, wanting her to come. She was almost there. Closing her eyes, she took ahold of her breast, arching her back as he flicked his fingers along her bundle of nerves.

Crying out, she squirmed underneath him, but then he stopped. Opening her eyes, she went to say something but then he pulled out, his mouth dropping between her legs and sucking her clit between his lips. Screaming his name, her legs went limp beside his head as her fingers drove into his hair, gripping and hanging on for dear life. As he swirled his tongue along her clit quickly, she writhed, trying to get away from the assault of pleasure his mouth was giving her. But he brought his hands up, holding her ass, and she wasn't going anywhere out from under that talented mouth of his.

It didn't take long before she cried out, her body shaking with her orgasm, her pussy pulsating as he slowly moved his tongue up her lips, licking up her wetness. Kissing her pussy, he then kissed her hip bones and her stomach before sitting back on his haunches, looking down at her flushed, shaking body. Reaching out, he flipped her over in one swift motion as she cried out in surprise. Lifting her ass up, he entered her from behind, his body slamming into hers, her ass smacking against his hips and stomach. Holding on to the sheets, she felt herself still shaking under him, her breathing labored and her body squeezing his. It was amazing, perfect even, and she had never felt so loved in her life as he wrapped his arms around her waist, kissing her back.

He lifted her up, his cock going deeper into her as he turned her face so that his mouth could take hers. Thrusting into her, he drove his tongue into her mouth, searching and playing as his cock went deeper and deeper inside of her. Squeezing her face with his hand, he thrust once more inside of her as a loud, harsh sound left his mouth, his body jerking inside of hers. Stilling, her body went limp against his as he held her close, trailing kisses down her throat and jaw.

Falling to his side, he brought her with him, wrapping his arms around her as she turned to face him, her leg hooking over his hip. He kissed her nose, then her mouth, and she closed her eyes as the kiss deepened, her leg sliding along his since both of their bodies were covered in sweat.

"I can't get enough of you," he whispered, his breath coming out in a whoosh. "Seriously. I want you again. Right now."

She scoffed, her body still shaking from her life-shattering orgasm. "You're gonna have to give me a minute. I can't breathe."

"Fine, five minutes," he teased and she laughed.

"I'm gonna miss you."

He chuckled against her mouth, his hand cupping her face. Looking deep into her eyes, he kissed the side of her mouth and whispered, "I'll miss you more."

Kissing her lips softly, he pulled away way too soon before muttering, "I love you."

Smiling, she held on to him, her head pounding against his. She didn't know how she'd gotten so lucky to live her fairy tale, but she was and she wouldn't let it go. Closing her eyes, she pressed her head against his as she whispered, "I love you too."

And she knew she always would.

"I didn't think the airfield would be that bad," Kacey said as she cuddled Mena into her side, kissing her temple. "I cried just seeing everyone else crying. You would think the guys were going off to war or some shit."

Lacey laughed as Elli nodded. "It can be a little tough. Owen didn't do well this time. He and Shea are superclose, so yeah, it was hell. He's currently sleeping with me."

They both smiled as Lacey said, "Thankfully, this trip is a short one. I hate when they leave."

"Amen to that," Elli agreed. "Between working out and killing my body and raising the Adler clan, I need some extra help. But then, we all knew what we were getting into when we married those hunky men."

Lacey nodded as Kacey smiled. "I'm not even married to him and it sucks."

Both of them made sounds of agreement as the door opened and more women spilled in. It had only been two days since Jordie had left and they'd both sucked. Kacey had nothing to do, so she found herself at Lacey's house, begging for human interaction and something to keep her busy. Since Lacey had been spending a lot of time designing for a new line she was thinking of doing for her shop, it was Kacey's job to entertain Mena and cut lace. It wasn't a bad job and Lacey paid her in cookies. So really, she was winning, but still missing Jordie more than a lot.

As Lacey and Elli hugged the six women, Kacey held back, holding Mena since she hadn't met any of them yet. She knew who they were—the wives of some of the guys Jordie played with but, for some reason, she felt out of place. They were all supposed to do dinner a few nights ago, but life got in the way and a lot of people canceled, leaving Kacey and Lacey at the dinner table. She was excited to meet the women but also very intimidated, which was insane. Like her, they were all very successful and very much in love with their hockey-playing husbands. So really, they had something in common—sex with hockey players—so why was she nervous?

When Elli turned, she sent a grin to Kacey as she came to her, everyone following. "Guys, this is our torture-giver, Kacey King."

"Ah, the trainer with the hands," one of them said. She was very pretty, thick dark hair and even darker eyes. She had a nice body, but it was easy to see she had been having babies. "Lucas talks about you fondly."

Kacey smiled. "Yeah, his shoulder's been giving him shit lately," she said, figuring this must be Fallon, Lucas's wife.

"Yeah, and if you didn't him keep from bitching about it, I might have to try to kick your ass. But seeing that he is happy, and you are also a good six inches taller than me and have abs and arms that could squash small children, I'm gonna just say, hey! It's nice to meet you!" she said and everyone laughed as they shook hands.

"So that's Fallon," Elli said with a smile. "Her sister, Audrey, my best friend, Harper, her sisters, Piper and Reese. We are all good friends, and for the first time in, like, ever, none of us are pregnant."

That had everyone snickering as Kacey grinned, cuddling Mena. "It's great to meet you. Your husbands are great to work with, and I'm excited to get to work on you guys too."

"Why am I scared?" Audrey asked, wrapping her arms around her middle as she took Kacey in.

"Because she's gonna kill us," Piper muttered, eyeing her too, and Kacey smiled.

"Just a little, and you won't be able to walk tomorrow. But in six months, I bet all of you will be down at least twenty pounds," she said happily before laying Mena in her playpen. "Now let's get started."

Kacey had been playing and working out with women her whole life, but working out with the Assassins' wives was a whole other thing. Unlike the Assassins' men, who were focused and ready to work, the women were everything but. They were chatty, talking about everything and anything. And while it was good that they all got along, she did have a job to do, and that was to make them work.

"Shea does the same thing. It drives me crazy. What is your obsession with my ass?" Elli complained.

"Right!? Erik is all about it, and I'm like whoa, dude, it's an exit," Piper agreed as a few of them snickered.

"I like it every once in a while. Especially when I'm drunk, makes me feel like a sexy porn star," Reese commented as she lay on her belly, when she was supposed to be planking.

"Ew, you're such a closet slut," Piper blanched and Reese glared.

"Hey now, just cause she likes it in the ass doesn't make her a slut," Lacey called. "I like it a lot, and I don't have to be drunk."

"And I just threw up," Kacey said, Audrey laughing beside her. "Okay, guys, come on, this is your workout. So if you don't do it to the full extreme, don't be bitching later when you aren't losing weight or toning up."

They all groaned and finally got to work, while Kacey watched. Eventually, each of them was working her ass off and Kacey was extremely pleased. She liked this and she was good at it. When she decided to go to school for nutrition and personal training, she never thought she could use it except for training and massage therapy for a sports team. But maybe she could make it into a little business.

She actually had an interview with the board of directors for the coaching position over at Bellevue, but did she really want it? She would have to travel, and that would mean that her and Jordie's schedules could conflict. But if she had her own little business for training, she wouldn't have to go anywhere.

Hm. That was an idea.

As they finished up, all the women were dripping with sweat and Audrey had thrown up twice. She was the least fit one of the group, but she still worked her ass off and killed it. "You did great, Audrey."

She waved her off, gagging, which in return had Kacey's stomach lurching. It had been doing that a lot lately. Little things making her super pukey. It was weird and annoying.

"So while I have all of us here," Lacey said, stealing Kacey's attention from where she was grasping her belly. "I am working on a sports bra and work-out pants line for the shop. It's gonna be really hip and flirty, and I was thinking that we could do another Assassins' wives photo shoot. The last one went so wonderfully."

And it had. Lacey had been featured in all kinds of sports magazines and even fashion magazines. She was convinced that the spread about the Assassins' wives was what made her successful. Truthfully, it was because Lacey had the biggest heart imaginable and loved helping breast cancer survivors.

"If I lose some weight, yes," Audrey agreed, and that was everyone else's opinion too.

"I got all of you. As long as you stick to the food plans and my workouts, you'll all get there."

They didn't seem very enthused, but they said bye while hugging her tightly, which she guessed meant she was in the in-crowd with the Assassins' power ladies. As Elli left to go upstairs, letting them know she'd lock up, Kacey helped Lacey get Mena ready to go. As Kacey lifted her out of the pack 'n play, Mena coughed and then white gunk came flying out of her mouth, landing on Kacey's chest. Heaving, she held Mena out, looking the other way to keep from gagging. The gunk she threw up was hot and ran down her chest into her cleavage, and soon, Kacey couldn't hold it. Handing Mena to Lacey, she rushed to the trash can and threw up her life.

"It's spit-up, you baby," Lacey teased as Kacey's sides heaved as she puked.

"It smells," she gasped, her stomach lurching, and then she was puking again.

"You're ridiculous," Lacey decided, putting Mena into her car seat.

"Shut up, I've been really icky lately," she said, wiping her mouth with the back of her hand.

"You pregnant?" Lacey joked and Kacey paused.

Oh, shit. Was she?

"No, I can't be. I have an IUD in."

"Didn't you have that when you got pregnant before?"

She had. Shit.

"I did," she said, pausing. Reaching up, she grabbed her boobs, but they didn't ache like they had before.

"My boobs don't hurt," she said and Lacey shrugged.

"No breast tissue, so that didn't happen to me. But the simplest of smells got me bad and I was puking everywhere."

"Me too, but I remember with my miscarriage, it was horrible pain with just a simple brush of my hand to my tits."

Lacey made a face. "Have you skipped a period?"

"I always skip, I'm never regular."

Lacey's mouth dropped a bit before she asked, "Are y'all not using condoms or something? Could this really be happening?"

Kacey shrugged. "I don't know, seems kind of crazy if it is. I mean, shit, that dude's got some supersperm."

"So you want a baby?"

"Of course I do," Kacey said as she eyed Lacey. "I've always wanted a kid, but I really don't think I'm pregnant."

Lacey shrugged. "Okay, well, let's hope not. And maybe start using some condoms since that IUD of yours is a little iffy."

Kacey's eyes narrowed. "Why? What's wrong with us having a kid?"

Lacey gave her a dry look. "Jordie doesn't need that right now. He's already under so much stress, the stress of a child would screw with him."

Kacey's face scrunched up in disagreement. "I don't think that's true," Kacey shot back, her hands coming to her hips. "He loves kids."

"Of course he does, and he'll be a great dad, but so much is going on with his mom, he really needs to get over that before he does the dad thing."

"He wants a child though, with me."

"I don't doubt that, but you've only been together for two months, Kacey."

"And you and Karson were only together like six when you guys got pregnant with Mena," she snapped back. She couldn't believe her! She was supposed to be her best friend, her supporter. Plus, Kacey wasn't even pregnant! They were arguing over nothing. "Plus, I'm not pregnant."

"I'm just saying, if you aren't, then make sure you start taking precautions." Lacey shook her head, sucking in a breath, her eyes locked on Kacey's. "Are we fighting?"

Kacey nodded. "I think so."

"Why? This is stupid."

"Exactly," Kacey agreed. "I was just telling you I didn't feel good."

"Yeah, it's probably nothing," she said with a shrug. "But still, be careful. Jordie is fragile right now."

Kacey shook her head. "I know, but if it did happen, he'd be happy."

"Yeah, but it would stress him out not to mess up. He doesn't need that. It already stresses him out knowing he could fail you."

"Lacey, I promise you, he's a much stronger man than you're giving him credit for."

"Yeah, but you forget that he tells your brother a lot more than he tells you, and Karson tells me everything. He's tiptoeing the line at just the thought of his mom. No need to push him over."

While she knew that Jordie and Karson were close, it bothered her that Lacey had said that. "So are you saying you know my boyfriend better than me?"

Lacey looked back at her from putting Mena's car seat on her arm. "No, I'm only telling you what Karson has told me."

"And I know all that. Jordie is okay, he is fighting it."

"But the dinner is creeping up on him, and he'll go. You know he will."

She did, but still. "Whatever. He is doing great."

"I don't doubt him. I'm just saying be careful."

"Heard you," she said, reaching for her bag and walking away.

But Lacey called out, "Wait, are you mad?"

Kacey looked back at her and shrugged. "Kinda."

Lacey shook her head, catching up to her, and said, "Why? Because I'm telling you what you already know? That I'm trying to be the voice of reason before you come back to me, asking for advice on everything I've already said?"

"No, because you think you know Jordie better than me, and plus, you doubt him."

"I'm not doubting him," she snapped, her voice rising. "I want him to succeed, I want you guys to succeed. But I am worried that if you do get pregnant and he relapses or whatever, can you imagine the strain it would put on not only him but you? It will break you, and you'll be sitting there with a baby and a drunk boyfriend."

"That won't happen," Kacey said, her voice laced with anger. "He's fine, we are good."

"I hope so, Kacey, I do," she said, her eyes pleading with hers. "But please don't be mad at me. I'm just trying to look out for you. I love you. You know this."

Looking away, Kacey pulled in a breath through her nose, letting it out slowly before looking back at Lacey. "I love you too."

"Good," she said, squeezing her hand. "Now go home and get a test so that later we can sit here and laugh over how overdramatic we are."

"Yeah, I will."

"Come here," Lacey said, pulling her into a hug. "I'm sorry I upset you."

She shook her head. "You didn't. I'm just emotional. I miss Jordie."

"I know," she agreed, and Kacey knew she missed Karson too.

Pulling away, she looked over at Lacey and asked, "If I am, will you be there for me if I need you?"

"Of course," Lacey said, not even pausing or thinking. "Please don't think I wouldn't. It's just I worry about it being more of a stressor than a blessing. You don't want to end up like me, on drugs just to get through the day."

Kacey gave her a deadpan look. "You're doing great and you've cut down on your meds, drastically."

"I know. But, y'know, I just hate that I'm weak."

"You're not," Kacey promised. "But thanks for thinking of me."

"I always do. You're the sister I never had but always wanted."

Kacey smiled, leaning into her and hugging her tightly. "Same here."

But as they parted, Lacey's words ran over and over in her head. The whole way to CVS, they kept playing on repeat and she wondered if she was right.

Could Jordie not handle them having a child along with everything else that was going on?

Was she even pregnant?

And what was she gonna do if she was and he couldn't handle it?

Leaning back against his headboard, Jordie played on FarmVille as he waited for Kacey to call. She'd needed a shower and wouldn't just set up the FaceTime so he could watch her shower. He thought it was rude, but she told him he was a pig and hung up. Typical conversation between them. With a grin on his face, he finished watering his crops and then opened his Facebook to update his status, just to mess with her.

I think it's unfair my girlfriend won't let me watch her take a shower on FaceTime. I highly doubt the government is watching, as she claims. Please tell me someone agrees with me. #RoadTripsSuck #MissMyBaby #ImNotAPig – with Kacey King.

As soon as he hit post, he scrolled through his feed, liking and commenting on stuff as he waited for her to call him back. It sucked being away from her, and he could tell she was bored without him. She apparently was assisting Lacey, which he thought was funny. She didn't have a designing bone in her body. She was more of a throw everything in one spot and hope for the best type. Plus, she hardly wore anything but gym clothes or sweats. But at least she had something to do. He had Facebook, FarmVille, and Netflix. To some that sounded like paradise, but he missed Kacey. A lot.

When a comment came through, he grinned when he saw it was Karson.

> *Karson King: Really, dude? Come on.*
> *Lacey King: Don't act like you don't ask for that all the time.*
> *Karson King: She's my sister!*
> *Lacey King: Who is doing your best friend. So really, what did you expect?*
> *Karson King: Shh, woman.*
> *Lacey King: Don't shh me. I'll kick your butt.*
> *Jordie Thomas: Lacey King, say Kick your ass, makes you sound more badass.*
> *Lacey King: Fine, kick your ass, and yes, I did that with a head roll.*
> *Jordie Thomas: That's my girl.*
> *Karson King: Still not scared.*

Laughing, Jordie looked up as the door opened and Benji came in with takeout for them. To his surprise, sharing with Benji hadn't been bad. The dude was funny, obsessed with *Game of Thrones* and other nerdy shit, but still a cool dude.

"Hey, here ya go. Sorry it took me so long," he said, out of breath as he set the bag of sushi down. "This chick was gorgeous, legs for days, but instead of talking to her like I should have, I spilled soy sauce on her."

He was always very bad with the ladies.

Chuckling, Jordie shook his head. "You need a class in game, man."

Benji scoffed as he shrugged. "You know, I used to have game, but I lost that when I stopped drinking."

"Happens. Thankfully mine is intertwined with my DNA," Jordie teased and Benji laughed.

"Well, please, share some, 'cause I haven't been with a woman in months. I think I'm rubbing my dick raw."

"Overshare, dude," Jordie said, grimacing. He was sympathetic though, since he had been there at one point.

"I heard you begging your girl to let you watch her shower. So really, is there such a thing as oversharing when you room with someone?"

Jordie thought that over for a moment. "Maybe you're right. But still, go out and get laid. You aren't ugly," he said as he opened his tray of sushi.

"Well, thanks," Benji said, waving him off and acting shy, which made Jordie laugh. "No, really. I just don't think I'm ready."

He opened his own tray and Jordie watched him. He was pretty sure it had to do with his wife, daughter, and brother that had Benji not wanting to be with someone. He thought maybe it was a touchy subject, but he asked anyway. "Because…?"

Benji looked up from his sushi and shook his head. "Sometimes I don't think I'm meant to be with anyone. Ava was my soul mate. I met her when I was a kid, and we stayed together all through middle and high school."

Sadness washed over Benji's face as he threw a piece of sushi in his mouth, chewing while Jordie waited for him to go on. When he didn't and just kept eating, Jordie asked, "And? What happened?"

Benji looked up at him and shrugged. "She died."

"I'm sorry, dude."

"Yeah, blows. We got pregnant when we were seventeen. Leary was my everything and so cute. She looked just like Ava. And though we were young and scared out of our minds, we got married and I promised to make our life good. I worked hard, got drafted, and things were great."

He paused, leaning his elbow on his leg as he bit his lip, clicking the chopsticks he held in his hand over and over again. "We went home to Chicago for a family reunion and I got shit-faced, doing shots with my uncle and my dad. Since I was so shitty, my brother Silas offered to drive us back to the hotel. Leary needed sleep, and it was so loud because everyone was still partying."

Jordie's stomach dropped from the look of pure pain on Benji's face as he went on. "I don't remember any of it. I was passed out in the back, leaned up against the door, my hand in Leary's. But when I woke up, I wasn't holding her hand because she was gone, along with Ava and Silas. Apparently a semi T-boned them, killing Silas and Leary instantly, while a piece of glass slit Ava's neck and she bled out before they could get her cut out of the car. Meanwhile, I was so drunk that I didn't even know anything had happened."

Jordie was stunned to silence. He had suffered some shitty stuff but nothing like what Benji had been through. Losing his baby, his wife, and his brother?

Jesus.

"It was bad, obviously. I was depressed, let go from the Rangers because I wasn't playing and performing. No one wanted me because I had become a drunk, and my family and hers turned on me. Blaming me for all of it. It was bad, dude, so damn bad."

"Why did they turn on you?" he asked incredulously.

"Because I should have been dead," Benji asked. "Why did I get to stay alive when I was a worthless drunk and they didn't?"

"Dude, that's wrong," Jordie gasped and Benji nodded.

"Yeah, and for a long time, I just floated through life. Then one day, I woke up in the alley of the bar I had gone to, and along the wall was a mirror. When I saw my reflection, it was as if Ava was looking back at me, disgusted," he muttered, and Jordie could sense he was about to start crying. Who could blame him? It might have been eleven years ago, but the pain was obviously still raw. "I went straight to the closest church and I prayed. I prayed for forgiveness, for strength, and I apologized not only to God, but to Ava, Leary, and Silas. Then I went to rehab and checked myself in. Never looked back either. Not one relapse in eleven years, and while some days I wouldn't mind having a drink, others I'm glad that I gave it up."

"How though? Did you have support?"

Benji shook his head. "Just my sponsor, Richie. I still, to this day, don't talk to my family."

"Really?"

"Yeah, I live by the motto, if you don't add to my life, you're out of my life. And because of that, anyone who didn't contribute to making me better, I left behind. I work every day to make a better me. I'm nowhere near perfect, believe me, but I want to be the man I was before the accident. I want to move on, I want to try again. Even though it really does give me anxiety," he said with a laugh, but there was no humor in the sound. "I have my faith, and that's helped me a lot too."

Jordie nodded. "I've depended a lot on mine, even though I just found it."

"Which is okay. For a long time, I was mad at God for taking them from me, but then I thank God for helping me get up and find help."

"For sure, bro," Jordie agreed, nodding his head. "Not sure it will mean anything, but I'm proud of you."

Benji grinned. "Thanks, you too, bro. You're doing great."

Jordie grimaced a little as he shrugged. "I thought I was, but lately things have been tough."

"Anything you want to share?"

Not really, but maybe he'd know how to handle it. "My mom is a bitch to the tenth power who doesn't give two shits about me except for when she needs me."

"Cut her out," he said simply. "Tell her you want nothing from her."

Jordie nodded. "See, I know this. But how do I do that to the person who gave me life?"

"Because if you don't, she'll take the life she gave," he said matter-of-factly. "My mom looked me in the eyes and told me she hated me for taking her baby from her. I can still hear those words, feel them rattle my soul. And you know what? I gave her one chance to apologize afterward, when I'd been sober for two years. When she didn't take that chance, called the police to escort me off her property, I told her she was dead to me and walked away. Was it hard? Yes. Do I miss her? Every day. But she gave up on me, she didn't care about me the way she should have. My dad too. And, yeah, it hurts, but I had to think of me. We are in survival mode, Jordie, and some people may call us selfish, but I call it making us better."

Jordie looked down, picking up a piece of sushi before throwing it in his mouth. "My mom is getting married for the tenth time. She's loved the men she's married more than me every time."

"And she will never love you. If by now, after however many years you've been alive, she still hasn't come around, she won't. Stop letting her hurt you and cut her out."

Jordie nodded, his heart pounding in his chest as Benji held his gaze. "And when you do it, don't think of it as a loss, think of it as a win. Something you have to do to make *you* better. Because in the end, only the people who have helped lift you up through your recovery will be the people who matter."

Jordie knew very well who those people were, and his mother was not on that list. When his phone sounded with an email, he looked down to see that it was from her. It was the reservation information for dinner. With no "I love yous," "can't wait to see you," or "see you soon." Nothing, just the restaurant and the time. Soon his heart picked up in speed and his throat started to close. He knew what he had to do. He felt it, knew the words he needed to say, but still, like a child, he wanted her love.

"She won't ever love you though," Benji said, and Jordie hadn't realized he had said what he was thinking out loud. "She'll continue to hurt you, until you start hurting other people and you're all alone. Then I'll read about you in the news, offing yourself. So really, you need to decide what's more important: her love, or the love of all the people that help lift you up?"

Before he could answer, Benji nodded. "The love of the people that lift you up: Kacey, Karson, just to name a few."

"Exactly," Jordie agreed just as his phone rang. Looking down, he saw Kacey's smiling face and he smiled back before saying, "My girl is calling. Give me a few."

2222

222222

As he answered, Benji nodded before reaching for the remote and Jordie said, "Hey, there."

Kacey looked back at him, her hair wet and her face red like she had been crying. "Hey, you crying?"

She shook her head. "No, new face cream, my face is on fire. What are you doing?"

"Talking with Benji. Oh, and my mom emailed me the reservations for dinner."

She made a face as her lip went between her teeth. "Are we going?"

He smiled; he loved that she automatically assumed she was going. He wanted her to go, to be there for him, but maybe he should do it alone. "Maybe I should go alone?"

She shook her head. "I really want to go. So if she says something stupid I can kick her."

"I like her," Benji said and Jordie grinned.

"She's a violent little thing," he joked and Kacey rolled her eyes. "I want you there, baby."

"Then I'm there. Are you sure though? Can't you just call her and tell her to fuck off?"

He shook his head. "No, I need to go and do it in person."

She slowly nodded her head. "Okay, we'll go."

"Thanks, babe."

"Always," she said slowly, looking down and sucking in a deep breath.

He eyed her, and he knew something seemed off. "You sure you are okay?"

She nodded, looking back up at him. "Just really tired and I miss you."

"I miss you more," he promised, holding the phone closer. "Show me some boob."

"Jordie!" she scolded and he laughed as she fought her grin. When she pulled her shirt up suddenly, both her tits on the screen, he slowly nodded his head.

"Mm, can't wait to get home."

"Me either," she said, her eyes watering up, and that surprised him.

"You're being weird."

"I don't like being away from you," she said as a tear slowly fell. "Are you okay?"

He nodded. "I'm fine."

"Going to your AA meetings?"

"I went to one yesterday, and I'll go again tomorrow. Might make Benji go with me. Roommate bonding and shit," he said and Benji nodded as Kacey smiled.

"Good, the email didn't bother you too much, did it?"

He shrugged. "Kinda, but nothing I can't handle."

She worked her lip, letting out a long breath. "Okay, well, call me if you need me. I'm dead on my feet."

He nodded. "Okay, baby, I'll call you in the morning. I'm gonna finish my dinner and start *Game of Thrones* with Benji."

She grinned. "Sounds like fun, talk to you tomorrow then."

"Love you."

"Love you more," she said, and she waved before the screen went black and she was gone. Something really did seem off, but he wasn't sure what it was. It was hard to push for info when they were so far apart. He was ready to get home, but he still had five days before he would be able to.

"You're lucky to have her," Benji said from his bed, pausing the TV.

"I know," Jordie agreed.

"And she obviously loves you," he said slowly and Jordie nodded.

"Yeah, she does, as do I."

"Then don't let your mom fuck it up," he said sternly. "Let her go because she will ruin you, dude."

"It's harder than it sounds," he said slowly, but Benji shook his head.

"It's not. Look deep inside of you, and if you can write down three reasons why you need to keep her, then do it. But if you can't, then let her go," he said before opening the drawer in the side table and grabbing a pen and paper. Throwing them to Jordie, he said, "And if you can find three reasons to keep her, make a list of the things that need to change, and then give them to her. If she can't change them, let her go."

Jordie looked down at the piece of paper and then back at Benji. "Seriously?"

He nodded. "I have so many lists that I make for every person I form a relationship with. It's something Richie taught me, and it's worked for me."

"So I have a list on me?"

Benji grinned as he shrugged. "Yeah, and you made the cut."

Jordie shot him back a grin as he reached for the pen. Looking up to see if Benji was watching him, he found that he wasn't. He was watching TV, and when Jordie looked back down, he sucked in a breath.

He could do this. His pencil shook as he wrote, but even he didn't believe what he wrote. Or at least he thought the reasons meant enough to go through the pain she put him through.

I love her.

She gave me life.

Staring at the piece of the paper, he smacked his pen to it and shook his head. He couldn't come up with a three. Staring at the paper, he read one and two again, and then slowly crossed out one. He didn't love her. He couldn't. She gave him no reason to love her. Before, he'd told himself it was love. But really, that was because he was a kid and she was all he knew. He didn't have a dad, didn't have someone who could show him love. But then he met Karson, his family, and ultimately, Kacey.

Because of them, he knew real love—true, undeniable love.

The kind of love that people die for.

And Stacey Thomas did not deserve that love.

Especially not from him.

Chapter
TWENTY-THREE

Holding the puck behind the Stars' net, Jordie looked to Karson, who was watching with him, waiting for the puck. An offenseman was waiting for him to go but, acting as if he was going to pass it, he deked it to the other side, going around the net, sending it hard up to Erik who was waiting at the line. As he carried it into the zone, Jordie skated hard to catch up, crossing the blue line with Karson. As Karson shot, it was knocked away. Anderson and Titov fought for it in the corner as Baylor waited in the slot. Finally getting it out, Erik shot it over to Karson, who took the shot. But it was quickly rebounded right to Baylor. She had no shot, but Jordie would. She sent it back to Jordie, he deked around two offensemen, but just as he was about to shoot, a defenseman tripped him, the puck hitting the goalie's shoulder as Jordie went face first into the goal, the post smacking him right between his neck and shoulder. Looking up, he groaned.

Fuck. It didn't go in.

Pain shot down his shoulder, his neck throbbing as he got up slowly, and Karson came to make sure he was okay. He could hear Coach screaming, even Erik, and when he realized the whistle was blown for a penalty against him for high-sticking the dick that tripped him, he was screaming too.

"Are you serious?"

"High stick," the ref yelled as he went for center ice, but Jordie followed.

"My stick went up because the douche tripped me!"

"Fucking pussy," the guy called, but Jordie ignored him.

"No, you high-sticked him before you fell."

"No! Fucking horseshit fucking call!" Jordie screamed, throwing his hands up. "Man, if I'd known you needed your dick sucked before the game for a decent call, I would have hired someone!"

The ref glared as he called the penalty, and Jordie headed into the box. Sitting down, Jordie glowered, watching as his team fought to keep the Stars from scoring. Tate was doing ninja goalie moves, smacking everything away, the boys clearing the zone every chance they got. They killed off the penalty, and when the time ran down, Jordie broke out of the box just as Erik sent it along the boards. Getting control of the puck, Jordie rushed the goal, the goalie coming out to stop him. But, taking a page out of Kacey's book, Jordie deked to the left, then the right, confusing the hell out of the goalie, and then shot top shelf, getting the goal.

Hell. YES.

It was his first goal of the year.

And it felt damn good.

"Baby, you see my goal? That was for you," Jordie boasted as Kacey grinned back at him.

"You mean, you stole my move and knew you had to dedicate the goal to me?" she teased and he nodded.

"Exactly."

"Great goal, nonetheless. I'm proud of you," she said with a bright grin, her eyes locked on his. He hated that this was the only way he could see her. He wanted to hold her, kiss her, but thankfully, only two more days.

"Thanks, sugar thighs."

She sent him a grin. "How's your shoulder?"

He pulled his shirt down, showing her that he had one hell of a nasty bruise along his neck and shoulder. It hurt, but the scans said nothing was broken, and when they offered him pain meds, he declined. He actually felt sort of badass and extremely proud of himself.

Looking at the screen, she grimaced and said, "Ouch."

"Yeah, wish you were here to kiss it better."

"Me too," she agreed, moving her hand through her hair. He loved how long it was getting. It'd be to the middle of her back in no time.

"I said no to the pain meds," he said and her face lit up.

"'Cause you're badass."

"Very true," he agreed, the pride bursting inside of him. Meeting her gaze, he asked, "Hey, you still miss me?"

She nodded as she looked down. "A lot."

"Good." She grinned up at him and he shot her one back. "You look tired. You all right?"

She laughed. "Is that the way you tell me I look like shit?"

"No, brat, you just look beat. Wanna call me back?"

She shook her head. "No, I miss you and haven't spoken to you much today."

"Yeah, sorry. I had AA and then Elli found me a therapist to go talk to today."

That sparked her interest as she sat up, taking the phone with her. "Are you okay?"

"Yeah," he said confidently. "Few nights ago, Benji told me to make a list of three reasons why I needed my mom in my life. I could only come up with one, and it's been weighing heavy on my heart. So Elli called this morning, asking how I was doing, and I told her about it and she found me someone to go talk to."

She nodded slowly, her eyes looking down as she picked at her sweatpants. "And it went well?"

"Yeah, I think I'm ready to face her."

"Awesome," she said, but Jordie felt like there was more she wanted to say. "And?"

She shrugged, looking up at him. "You could have talked to me… No, wait, never mind. That makes me an asshole to say that, and I don't mean it. I'm glad you went. I just miss you, and I feel like we aren't that close when you are gone."

When her eyes filled with tears and she looked away, his heart lurched in his chest. "Baby," he said softly and she shook her head.

"Ignore me. I'm on a whole other level right now."

"Sugar thighs, we are still very close and I miss you so much," he said to reassure her. "I know I could have talked to you, but you are one-sided, y'know? You hate my mom with good reason, and I know what you would say. I wanted the opinion of someone who doesn't know her."

"Yeah, I know," she said slowly, wiping her face. She waved him off. "I'm just tired, I'm sorry."

"Don't be," he said quickly, his eyes searching hers. He wanted nothing more than to reach through the phone and pull her into his arms. He could tell she was struggling, which he was too. For the last couple of months, it had been just the two of them, and now it was only her. In a huge house, by herself, when she never had lived alone before.

"So the therapist did help?" she asked, wiping her face, and he nodded.

"Yeah, baby, she did. She was nice," he said and she smiled.

"I'm glad."

"Are you okay?" he asked and she shrugged.

"Yeah, I am. Like I said, just tired."

But he felt like it was something more. "Talk to me, baby."

She leaned on her hand, wiping her face and then sucking in a deep breath. "I'm lonely."

He figured, and as his lips curled, he said, "I'll be home in two days, and I promise I'll do you in the car."

She giggled, which was what he wanted, her face breaking into a grin as she let her head fall back, laughing. "There's my smile," he said and she glanced back at the phone and smiled wider.

"It sucks you being gone, like really."

"I know," he agreed and she looked away.

"I've actually been thinking a lot, and what do you think of me opening a gym?"

He made a face, surprised by her statement. "Don't you have those interviews with Bellevue?"

She nodded. "And I'm gonna go. But I've been training the Assassins' wives and it's so much fun. I love it."

"Then do it," he said quickly. "Anything that makes you happy, I'm down for."

She smiled. "Yeah, I'm still considering it."

"You should do it. Talk to Lacey, she's good with that stuff. Business and all."

She chewed on her lip, thinking for a moment. "Yeah, maybe I will. I'm gonna see her tomorrow."

"Good, let me know what happens."

"Of course, I will," she promised and then she looked up. "So we are still going to dinner with your mom?"

"Yeah, I'm gonna give her a chance to be in my life, and if she doesn't want it, then I'm gone."

She nodded and he could tell she didn't think his mom deserved even that much, which she didn't. "Well, you know how I feel about it."

He grinned. "Yeah, I do."

"Well, then I guess I'll prepare myself not to punch her in the throat, no matter how much I want to."

"Yeah, hold that in," he laughed. "I don't want to bail you out of jail when I need to be investing in Gym Khaos, with K, of course," he said with a wink and she grinned big.

"You do love me, huh?" she said sweetly, batting her lashes, and he nodded.

"More than you know," he admitted. "So much more."

As her eyes lit up and a grin spread across her whole face, he knew he could never love her enough.

There wouldn't be enough time.

He'd need at least seven lifetimes, but since he only had one, he wouldn't stop until that smile never left her lips.

"I forgot my darn flip-flops," Lacey complained as she met Kacey in front of the nail shop. "Did you bring yours?"

Kacey shook her head, her fingers wringing together as her heart pounded in her chest. Ever since she'd sat on the toilet in her bathroom and watched as the word PREGNANT came up on the pregnancy test, her heart hadn't slowed. To say she was elated and surprised was an understatement, but she was already scared out of her mind. She sort of felt bipolar, because one minute she was ecstatic, couldn't wait to tell Jordie and get ready for a new baby. Then the next, she was curled up in a ball, worried that not only was Jordie not going to be able to handle a new baby, based on what Lacey said, but also that this was the second time she had gotten pregnant on her IUD. That couldn't be good for the baby, and what if she lost this one too?

What if she couldn't have children?

"It's okay, we aren't even going to the salon," Kacey said before walking toward her OB-GYN, which happened to be right next door to the nail salon.

Lacey's face warped in confusion as she looked at Kacey expectantly. "What the hell? You said girls' day, Elli is watching Mena, I need my feet done, and why are we going to the OB-GYN... *Oh my God*, you're pregnant?" she asked and Kacey rolled her eyes as she went through the door.

"Apparently. Come on," she said, still not a hundred percent sure the nine home pregnancy tests she took were right. It seemed a little unreal, but yet she was still puking her brains out and now finally, her boobs were hurting. She knew that she was, but a part of her was in denial.

"Seriously? You took a test?"

She nodded as she went up to the desk, signing in. "Yup, nine positives and my tits started hurting."

"Oh, shit."

That was one thought Kacey had.

"Jesus, Jordie's sperm is strong as hell," Lacey commented as they went to sit down after Kacey had checked in.

"Agreed," she said, her knee bouncing. "I don't think I am though."

"Liar," Lacey laughed. "You know you are. I can see it on your face."

"Okay, yeah," she said with a nod, and then a smile crept up on her face.

"I'm really excited but scared out of my mind."

Lacey threaded her fingers with Kacey's. "It's gonna be fine."

Kacey shot her a look. "A couple days ago you were singing a different tune."

She shrugged. "A couple days ago we weren't sure. Now we are, and now we will be fine."

The way she said that, it almost seemed as if she meant her and Kacey, which was confusing. Was she already counting Jordie out? Holding Lacey's gaze, she asked, "You still don't think he'll be able to handle this?"

Lacey looked away, sucking in a deep breath. "I don't know," she admitted. "But if he can't, I got you," she promised before squeezing Kacey's hand.

Leaning back in the chair, Kacey bit her lip as she waited. The news of her pregnancy came as a shock, it really did. And while this was both something she and Jordie wanted, it felt almost too good to be true. As most of their whirlwind romance had been. Biting hard on her lip, she couldn't imagine losing this baby. It would devastate both of them, and what if it made him relapse? Closing her eyes, she prayed that wouldn't happen, and then she scolded herself for thinking it at all. This was her second chance. She had a man who loved her, and they wanted this.

It would be fine.

"Kacey King?"

Hearing her name, she shot up, her hand hitting her thigh from where Lacey was still holding it as she sat waiting. Standing up, Lacey shot her a grin and squeezed her hand.

"It's okay."

No, it wasn't.

But not even ten minutes later, her new doctor, Dr. Richards, said, "Yay, we're having a baby!"

It took her a minute to get over how hot her doctor was before she realized that he had confirmed what she already knew. Lacey looked over at her and smiled happily as Kacey slowly nodded her head.

"But I have an IUD in."

His brow quirked as he looked down at her records, and then he shook his head. "In my paperwork, you don't."

"Excuse me?"

He smiled. "Yeah, they said they removed it after your miscarriage, and you would come in at a later time to have it put back in."

Holy shit. She hadn't had an IUD in for this long and didn't even know it? Wait, oh shit, she didn't. She had started practicing for the Olympics with the rest of Team USA and forgot to go back. Crap on a cracker! Thank God, she never had sex with anyone! As she stared into Dr. Richards's sky blue eyes, she almost couldn't believe it. Was this a sign from God? Did she not have sex with anyone because she was supposed to be with Jordie? He was supposed to get her pregnant, and then they'd live happily ever after?

Why was that all too hard to believe?

"But I'll check to make sure," he said, sitting on his stool before sliding between her legs. "Lie back and be calm."

"I'm pregnant," she said slowly as his hands moved between her legs. She always felt dirty during her visit with the OB-GYN, but today, she wasn't even worried about him. "Really pregnant?

"Yup! That means that Mena and the new baby will only be a year apart. They'll be best friends! Hopefully, you'll have a girl," Lacey cheered and Kacey's head fell to the side to look at her. Tears welled up in her eyes as the doctor stood back up, taking his gloves off.

"No IUD and everything looks good," he said, flashing her his pearly whites.

"But I had a miscarriage before," she said softly as she sat up, her eyes holding his.

He nodded. "And we'll monitor you through the first trimester. I want you to come in every four weeks for ultrasounds, and if you start bleeding, please go to the ER. Yeah, it could happen again, but let's be positive and hope not, okay?"

She bit down on her lip and nodded, her tears spilling over onto her cheeks. "There is no way to tell one way or another, right?"

He shook his head, his grin gone, a sullen look on his face. "I'm sorry. No."

She nodded again, wiping her face. "Okay, so we'll stay positive."

Patting her knee, he smiled. "Exactly. See you in four weeks. Call if you have any questions."

She hadn't realized she said bye until the door shut and Lacey came to her side. "It's gonna be great, no worries," she said, smiling at Kacey extra hard. But not even Kacey could be that optimistic.

"Yeah. I hope."

"So I saw all these supercute ideas for telling a spouse you are pregnant. We should so do one of them for Jordie. He'd love that. Are you gonna wait to tell the family until you reach the second trimester? Just in case, not saying that you should, but just in case. But I doubt you'll have to worry about it," she said, waving her off as she handed her her jeans.

Kacey's heart started pounding, her chest seizing up and everything began to spin. The thought of telling everyone and them getting excited, only for her to lose it, was a heart-shattering thought. Her mother would cry for days, not only because it would be a sad situation of what-ifs but because she knew how much Kacey wanted a family. Her dad would act weird around her and act as if he couldn't pick on her, which was very unacceptable. She'd want everyone to act the same, but she knew they wouldn't. Not even Lacey and Karson. They wouldn't know how to handle it. That was the light at the end of the tunnel from her first miscarriage. No one knew. Only she did, and while it wasn't okay and she'd wanted Jordie to be there for her, she was glad that no one had had to share her pain.

And she knew she had to do it that way again.

"I'm not telling anyone," she said, her jeans loose in her hands, her thong laying on top of them. "You can't say anything," she demanded, and Lacey nodded quickly.

"Not a soul."

"Not even Mena."

She made a face. "That's not fair. She can't talk."

"I know that, but everyone is always at your house. I don't need anyone overhearing you."

She shrugged, and Kacey could tell she didn't like it, but she'd do it. "Fine, put your jeans on and let me show you these things on Pinterest. I'm sure Jordie will get a kick out of it. *Oh!* You should go order his favorite cupcakes and have Audrey spell out on them, 'You're gonna be a daddy!' He'd totally eat that up. Literally."

But Kacey shook her head. "I'm not gonna tell him."

Lacey's head whipped back to her, and Kacey was surprised she didn't give herself whiplash. "What?!" she shrieked. "Are you insane?"

"No, listen," she said, holding her hands out. "We are already worried he can't handle it—"

"But Kacey, if he found out you hid it from him and then lost the baby, he'd lose it. That alone would have him looking for the bottle because you didn't include him in something life-altering. You can't do that," she stressed, her head shaking and her eyes wide. "Seriously. You can't. You have to tell him. I get not telling the family, but you have to tell Jordie."

"But what if I lose it?"

She shrugged. "I guess it's the true test of your relationship, huh? His sobriety and everything. Yeah, it's a lot, and I agree that maybe you should have made sure you had an IUD in or, hell, used some condoms, but there is no changing that now. You're in it to win it, and soon he will be too."

Kacey's tears came faster down her face as she slowly shook her head. "I don't want to hurt him by not telling him, but I also don't want him to have the anxiety I have."

But Lacey shook her head. "You have to tell him, Kacey. Seriously."

She bit the inside of her cheek and didn't say anything else as she got dressed. She walked in silence to make her next appointment and still said nothing when Lacey talked her into getting her feet done. As the lady painted her toes and massaged her feet, Kacey sat there, hating that she couldn't tell the future. She wanted to know what would happen. If she'd keep the baby and if they'd be happy. She wanted the reassurance, but life never gave it. It was a constantly changing traffic light, and you never knew what you were gonna get when you came up on it. Sometimes it was good, sometimes it was all right, and sometimes it was downright bad.

Placing her hand on her stomach, she looked down as her eyes welled up with tears. She wanted to be excited, happy, but the thought of what losing this baby would mean was too great, and soon the tears were rolling down her cheeks again. So much was going on. Jordie was finally on the ice, enjoying it. His sobriety was going great and he was doing well. But his mother's visit loomed over them and she wasn't sure what would happen. That woman had the power to knock him back a hundred odd days, and he'd be right back where he was.

And so would she.

Loving a man who couldn't be the man she wanted.

But this time she'd be stuck, because there was no way Jordie wouldn't be there for his child and she knew she wouldn't leave him. She'd stay, trying to fix him and raise their child, all while being so fucking unhappy that her life wouldn't matter.

No. That wouldn't happen.

Taking Kacey's hand in hers, Lacey squeezed it, demanding her attention. As she met Kacey's brown-eyed gaze, Lacey smiled. "Don't cry, it's gonna be great."

"Maybe I should wait till after his mom comes?"

But she was already shaking her head. "No, you tell him as soon as he gets home. Don't do it on the phone. He's gonna wanna kiss and love on you."

Bringing her lip between her teeth, she shrugged. "But all this at once? His mom is gonna be here in a week's time."

"So? He's got this; you've said that yourself."

She had.

And she had to believe that, or like the therapist, Karson, and everyone else said, she'd be the one to ruin them.

"Does he want this, Kacey?" she asked, and Kacey looked up. "I mean, obviously, since you guys weren't using protection, he had to know this could happen."

She nodded. "Yeah, it was mentioned a while back after the first time we hooked up again. But I brushed it off because I trusted the IUD that I don't have in me."

She smiled. "That's kinda funny."

"To who?" she asked and Lacey smiled.

"I guess just me," she said offhandedly, but then she shrugged. "Do you want this?"

"You know I do."

"Then what's the problem? If it all comes crashing down and Jordie relapses, at least you'll have the baby you wanted. And it will be with the man you love."

"But can't even have," she said, and Lacey looked away. "I'd stay because I love him so much and he'd ruin me. I really didn't fucking think this through."

Her tears came faster as she slowly shook her head. "I rushed into this, jumped in bed with him, and just fucking loved him. I didn't think through what would happen if he failed because I wanted to believe he wouldn't. I wanted to think he'd beat this and be the man I want."

"Then believe it!" Lacey yelled, getting the attention of most of the clients in the salon. "Stop doubting him."

"I don't doubt him!" Kacey yelled back and Lacey glared.

"Obviously, you do or you wouldn't be saying all this," she pointed out. And this time, Kacey was glaring.

"I'm scared out of my mind, Lacey. I want to trust my gut and know that I made the right decision. But what if I was thinking with my heart and not my brain?"

"You did!" she yelled, her eyes wide. "With all your heart, and that's okay. Because if it ends, at least you know you've tried and you'll regret nothing."

"I'm sorry, but y'all are distracting the customers," the salon owner said and Kacey turned, her breathing labored as she glared.

"I have salt and sugar at home, but I'm paying eighty bucks to have y'all rub it on my feet. If I want to yell at my sister-in-law about that fact that I just found out I am pregnant, and how my boyfriend, the recovering alcoholic, is still fragile and I don't know if he'll make it, whether I'm going to miscarry like I did before, and a whole other list of shit, like, hell, I don't know, what I'm gonna be when I grow up, then I will! And maybe, just maybe, for the eighty bucks you're charging me, I can yell a bit."

The woman only blinked as Lacey snickered beside her. "Keep it down and congratulations."

"Thanks, and I'll try," Kacey said as the woman walked away. She then turned to Lacey, who was fully laughing at this point. "Really? This is not funny."

"Oh, I'm cracking up because if you're already this emotional and bitchy, God help us all once you reach the third trimester."

"If I get to that," she muttered and Lacey smacked her hard in the arm. "Ow!"

"Stop talking like that. You're gonna keep this baby. Our children will grow up a year apart, and Jordie is gonna be fine. I just know it."

But Kacey shook her head. "Doesn't it seem unreal though?"

OVERTIME

"No," Lacey answered automatically. "It sounds right. It sounds like what is going to happen."

"I hope you're right."

"I am," she said confidently. "It's going to be fine."

But as much as Kacey wanted to believe her, she couldn't find it in her to do that.

It all just seemed so impossible.

And unreal.

But man, how badly she wanted it all to be true.

Chapter
TWENTY-FOUR

"**A**re you sure about this?"

Jordie looked over his shoulder at Karson and nodded. "Yeah."

"Don't you think you should ask Kacey first?"

"I'm getting it for her."

"I understand that, but that's a big commitment."

"I know that," he said, giving him an annoyed look. "I'm not a dumbass."

"That's debatable," Karson muttered while Jordie glared. "I don't know, maybe she'd want to be here?"

"No, I want her to be surprised. She's gonna flip."

Karson nodded. "She sure is."

They both looked down at where the little beagle puppy was looking up at them, his tail wagging with a little happy dog smile. Jordie knew that Kacey would have liked to be there, but like he had told Karson, he really wanted to surprise her. She had been so lonely lately, and he had plenty of road trips coming up, so it was the perfect idea to get her a little furry companion. He remembered way back when, before Christmas, when she lay in bed with him and told him that she wanted a white picket fence that would hold in a bunch of kids and a couple of beagle dogs. He may have acted like he wasn't listening, but he'd heard her loud and clear.

She wanted to settle down.

At the time, he wasn't there yet, but now was a different story. Reaching out, he petted the dog's head as the lady got the paperwork together. When his phone sounded, he pulled it out to see that it was the woman who was always on his mind.

"Hey, baby."

"Hey, where are you? I thought you'd be home now," she asked, and she sounded a bit frustrated.

"Karson had some stops to make. I'm on my way in a bit. What's wrong?"

"Nothing, just want you home. You promised me sex."

"Ew, Jesus," Karson groaned and Jordie laughed.

"Your brother heard that."

She scoffed. "Don't care, hurry up. I want you."

Turning from Karson, he held the phone closer as he whispered, "Oh, baby, believe me, I want you more."

"I can still hear you." Karson's tone was salty and Jordie grinned.

"So bad," he said, his voice rough. "But I'll be home soon."

"Fine, hurry."

Letting out a long breath, he hung up the phone and said, "Sorry, but are we almost ready?"

The shelter lady looked over at him and nodded. "Yes, but you know it's not a full beagle. They think it's mixed with pug. We called it a puggle."

Karson scoffed. "Puggle?"

Jordie shrugged. "She won't care. She'll like that I came here for a dog."

"Well, we like it, that's for sure," she said, handing Jordie some paperwork to sign.

When she turned, Karson said, "I'm still not cool knowing you are doing my sister."

Jordie scoffed, his lips curving. "Well, know it, bro, that's my hot little—"

"Stop," he demanded and Jordie grinned.

"Just saying."

"No, please stop," Karson said, shaking his head. "It still doesn't sit well."

Jordie only rolled his eyes, and after getting everything filled out and paying her, Jordie walked out of the shelter with a beagle-pug mixed puppy, also known as a puggle, that was still unnamed.

"I think you should name him Ugly," Karson said as he looked sideways at the dog that sat between them. They were on their way to the pet store for Kacey's new little friend.

"I can't name him after you," Jordie said and Karson scoffed.

"Please, ugly isn't even in my vocab. I'm a hot piece of ass," he said confidently and Jordie's brow rose.

"Um, I don't know what mirror you're looking in, but, dude, you ugly."

"Please, at least I don't look like Paul Bunyan."

"I rather look like Paul Bunyan than Neville from *Harry Potter* before he hit puberty."

"Damn, really? That's ugly," Karson asked, feigning hurt as he grasped his chest. "I thought I meant more to you than that."

Jordie shrugged. "I mean, you have hope if that kid did."

Karson laughed. "Whatever, you know I'm hot."

"No, I don't know that," he said as Karson parked and they got out. "But I do know that this little man is not ugly," he said to the dog and he licked his face happily.

Karson made a noise of contempt, but Jordie ignored him as they shopped for everything they needed. With a brand-new green collar and all the things a puppy would need, they were on their way home when Jordie looked over at Karson.

"You know I'm gonna marry her, right? And we'll have sex then, to make children?"

Karson's face went blank as he shook his head. "See, you had me at marrying her. But after that, you lost me. In my mind, my sister is the Virgin Mary, because I know what you do to girls. I've seen it," he said before shuddering. "I mean, I like to fuck as much as the next dude, but you don't hold back. And thinking you're doing that to my sister is just wrong."

Jordie laughed as he shrugged. "If it makes you feel better, I only give her what she wants."

Karson gagged as Jordie continued to laugh. "That didn't make me feel better. Worse actually," he said as he pulled into Jordie's driveway. "But whatever, get out of my car."

Grinning, Jordie grabbed his bags and was about to get out when Karson asked, "When is that dinner with your mom?"

His stomach dropped at the reminder, and he let out a long breath as the puppy licked his throat. He was a friendly little thing. "Next week."

"Do you want me to go?"

He shook his head. "I do, but it wouldn't go over well. You know she's never liked you; she doesn't even want Kacey to go."

"Are you taking her?"

"I am," he said with a nod. "Do you think that's a good idea?"

Karson nodded. "Yeah, she'll keep you calm, and someone needs to be there with you," he said, but then he set him with a look. "But remember, Kacey has a temper and she's crazy protective of you, so if you need bail money, let me know."

Jordie laughed because little did Karson know, he was completely right. While he would be down for Kacey to take care of his mother, he wouldn't let her. He had to do this himself. This was his problem and he had to fix it. As he got out, the puppy and pet store bags in one arm and his hockey bag in the other, he glanced over at Karson and nodded. "Will do, boss."

OVERTIME

Karson looked him over and then laughed. "I'd help you, but the thought of seeing my sister naked makes me cringe, so you're on your own."

"Appreciate it," Jordie said, sending him a smirk before kicking the car door shut and heading to the front door. While he wanted Kacey to be good and naked, he kinda hoped she wasn't so she could enjoy the dog. It would be hard to take her on the couch when the puppy was dead set on licking everything in sight. He shuddered at the thought of the dog getting ahold of his balls or something. He'd already almost broken his dick during sex, no reason to flop his balls in front of a new puppy's eyes.

On that note, yeah, he hoped she wasn't naked.

When the door opened before he could even reach it, he saw that Kacey was dressed, thank God, before she took off out the door, running to him. He dropped the bags, keeping the puppy though, as she jumped up into his arms, kissing him hard against the lips.

God, he had missed her.

As her mouth moved against his, he squeezed her tightly as the puppy got more excited and started kissing him too. Laughing, he pulled away as Kacey shrieked, taking the dog from him.

"Surprise!" he cheered while doing jazz hands.

She beamed up at him as he put her on her feet. "Oh my goodness, he is perfect," she cooed, kissing his head. "Is he ours?"

"Yup," he said happily, petting its head. "I thought since you seemed so lonely that a little buddy would be good for you. Do you like him?"

"I do! He's adorable, what is he?"

"Pug-beagle mix. Puggle is the word on the street. I got him at the shelter."

Her grin was unstoppable. "Perfect. I love him. Thank you."

She kissed him on the lips, lingering a little longer than she should, not that he was complaining, before pulling away and starting for the house, "I have a surprise for you too."

Jordie smiled as he picked up his bags to follow her. "I thought the surprise was gonna be you naked when I got home."

She smiled back at him. "This dress comes off very quickly."

It was the first time he actually noticed what she was wearing, and she was right, the thin little dress would come off in seconds. Flipping up the back of her skirt, he saw she had no panties on and whistled at her as she grinned. "This is true and I see nothing underneath."

She grinned back at him, holding the door before kissing the dog's head. "Easy access. And duh, I didn't want my brother seeing me naked."

He chuckled, but when her dark, lust-filled eyes met his and the curve of her lips taunted him, he wasn't sure how long he could wait to get under that skirt. Walking past her, he paused in the doorway to kiss her once more before whispering against her lips, "I missed you."

286

She smiled, her nose moving against his until the puppy reached up to lick her jaw. Laughing, she pulled away and he decided that his surprise was a mood killer.

"I missed you too," she declared. "But what's his name?"

Jordie threw his bags down by the couch and turned to look at her as she came toward him, cuddling the puppy. "Don't know. Your choice."

She looked the pup over and then looked up at him. "Well, since we are hockey family, it only makes sense that his name is Pucky."

Family. Man, how that word made him breathless…but *Pucky*?

"Pucky?" he said, his brow rising. "How about Puck? Just drop that girlie 'Y.'"

Kacey giggled. "Puck isn't as cute though."

"He's manly man dog," he said, pointing to him, and the puppy licked his finger, not proving his point. "He *will be* a manly man dog."

"Fine," she said, looking him over. "What about Gretzky?"

"Hell yeah, that's a winner," he said, nodding his head as he scratched the pup behind his ear. "Gretzky, welcome home."

Kacey beamed up at him as she reached over, kissing his lips. Wrapping his arms around her, he kissed her hard, his hands lifting the skirt of her dress to feel her totally naked ass. Groaning against her lips, he pulled away, meeting her lust-filled eyes. Taking ahold of each of her ass cheeks, his voice was rough, his cock pulsating in his jeans as he said, "Put Gretzky down and let's go to the bedroom."

Pulling back more, she held one finger up. "But you haven't seen my surprise."

His eyes were pleading as he asked, "Can I do you first and then see it without hurting your feelings or making you mad?"

She scoffed. "No and no. It will take two seconds," she added when his head fell back, his cock pressed against her soft center.

"I want you now though," he begged and she laughed.

"Two seconds. It's on the counter," she said, pushing him away, but he wasn't going anywhere without another kiss. Dropping his mouth to hers, he kissed her once more and, as he went to deepen the kiss, she pulled away, breathless.

"Please," she asked, Gretzky wiggling in her arms. "Go see. Don't seduce me yet."

He scoffed. "I don't have to seduce you. I just have to look at you and your clothes melt off."

Laughing, she pushed him away before she bent over, placing Gretzky on the floor, muttering, "Cocky ass."

He grinned as he reached under her skirt, cupping her wet pussy, which caused her to cry out as she stood straight up and smacked his hand. "Pig!"

His eyes softened as he pulled her into his arms, kissing her nose. "Aw, you haven't called me that in a long time."

She rolled her eyes, wrapping her arms around his neck. "You're killing me, Jordie Thomas."

He shrugged. "Sorry, I want you. I can't concentrate on anything else but getting that dress off you."

Her head fell to the side, her eyes pleading as she asked ever so sweetly, "Please?"

He grinned. "That isn't fair," he muttered against her lips, squeezing her ass in his hands. "I want you, but you're so cute when you are begging me to do something."

She smiled, her nose moving along his jaw. "I'll beg for all kinds of things if you do this for me."

"You don't ever have to beg, baby. I'll do just about anything for you," he promised, kissing her nose before letting her go as she grinned up at him.

"I know, you're too good to me," she said to his retreating back and he scoffed.

"I could always do better," he said, looking over his shoulder at her.

"So could I," she agreed and he narrowed his eyes.

But before he could say anything, he saw that the kitchen island was covered in cupcakes.

His favorite cupcakes from Audrey Jane's.

Turning, he grinned at her as she came over to stand to the side of the island.

"How'd you know these are my favorite?" he asked, reaching for one, but she stopped him.

"Audrey told me. But do you see what they say?" she asked and his brows touched because all he saw were his favorite cupcakes, and his first thought was that he was gonna eat them off Kacey. Instead, he looked back down and realized that they did say something.

We are having a baby!

Blinking, his heart stopped as his jaw dropped and he reread the whole thing again.

We are having a baby!

No, he read that right. But he must be losing his mind because he was pretty sure it said they were having a baby. How? She had the IUD in, and he would be the first to admit he was a beast of a man, but twice his boys got past that to impregnate her? That seemed a little unbelievable. But when he looked up, Kacey was holding a pregnancy test and he could see from around the counter that it said positive. His heart still hadn't started beating again and his breath was nowhere to be found.

His throat was thick with emotion as she mocked him, giving him jazz hands as she cheered, "Surprise?"

"Really?" he asked around the lump in his throat.

She nodded, her lip coming between her teeth. "Yeah."

"Are you sure?"

She nodded again. "I took nine pregnancy tests, all positive, and then I went to the doctor. They confirmed it."

He blinked a few times, his heart pounding against his chest. "So this is real?"

She looked away. "Yeah, I thought you'd be a little happier."

He scoffed. "A little happier? Are you crazy?"

She looked up, defeated, and he could see the tears in her eyes before she shrugged. "Guess I was wrong."

"Yeah, you were," he said, wanting to laugh at her assumptions. Coming around the counter, he took her in his arms, wrapping her up tightly before pressing his nose to hers, his eyes boring into hers.

"Because I'm so fucking happy, I'm speechless."

Relief flooded Kacey as she looked into his dark, emotion-filled eyes. When he'd only questioned her, she'd immediately thought he didn't want it. She had been toying with that idea for the last couple of days, along with the notion that he wouldn't be able to handle it. But his face was bright, the biggest grin on his lips, his eyes wide and locked on hers. He didn't look like he couldn't handle it or that he didn't want it.

He looked really fucking happy.

Grinning hard as she twirled her finger in his beard, love choked her as she croaked out, "Really?"

"God, yes, baby," he whispered, his lips so close to hers. "You know I want this."

"But with everything that's going on—"

He pressed his lips to hers, cutting off her sentence before he lifted her up in his arms, carrying her through the house, only tripping over Gretzky twice before ending in their room. Laying her down, he kissed her once more, but soon their new puppy interrupted them by licking both their faces. Kissing her nose, he pulled away, picking Gretzky up and putting him outside.

"Give me an hour, buddy," he said before shutting the door and looking back at the bed, his eyes sparkling with love and desire. Sitting up, Kacey lifted her dress up and over her head, her body burning for his as he slowly undressed, his eyes never leaving hers. Licking her lips, she opened her legs and he groaned out before dropping his pants and kicking them to the side. Coming to the bed, he cupped the back of her neck as she took ahold of his cock, the velvetiness of his skin smooth against her palms. Kissing his belly, she then kissed his hips before running her tongue along the tip of him, his ass cheek clenching underneath her touch.

When she took him in her mouth, he groaned, the sound making the desire swirl deeper in her gut as she sucked him to the back of her throat and then back out again. Holding his cock with one hand, she squeezed his butt cheek with the other as she moved up and down his swollen cock. His hands tangled in her hair, pulling it just a bit to make her breathless. His moans urged her to go faster, the pulling of her hair turned her on, and the taste of him made her want more. Moving faster along his cock, her nails bit into his ass. She then let go of him to slide her hand between her legs, swirling her finger along her clit, needing her own release.

"Fuck yeah," he rasped out, his hand squeezing her hair. "Look up at me," he demanded. She did as he asked, her eyes meeting his as she flicked her clit, his cock in the back of her throat, gagging her but pleasing her at the same time. Holding her face, he licked his lips as she sucked the tip of him, her fingers moving quickly between her two wet lips. When she came, she jerked forward, his cock going to the back of her throat, and he groaned out, his cock pulsating in her mouth.

As he continued to hold her face, he moved himself in and out of her mouth while her orgasm racked her body, the aftershocks almost as good as the actual orgasm. As his cock hit the back of her throat, hard, she gagged a bit, but that didn't stop him. He kept going, his eyes darkening with each thrust until he stilled, his hot come spilling down the back of her throat as he groaned loudly, her name falling off his lips in the most delicious way. She held his hips, sucking him dry, his body jerking and twitching as he bent over, gasping for breath.

Removing his cock from her mouth, she fell back against the mattress, her eyes on his and, man, he was beautiful. Sweat glistened on his body, his thick arms, and his shoulders. Little beads of sweat ran down his abs, his eyes were still closed, his breathing was labored, and she wanted nothing more than to cry out in joy at that moment. This man was her everything. Her forever. But their future still hung in the balance. It could all go wrong... But when he opened his eyes, they locked on hers and she'd never felt more beautiful under anyone's gaze than his and nothing mattered but him.

Covering her body with his, he kissed her jaw and her neck before taking both of her breasts in his hands, squeezing them together and licking each of her nipples, going back and forth in a back-arching way. When he let them go, she whimpered because she could feel her orgasm building again. His eyes were on her belly, his hands cupping her hips as he trailed kisses along it. Closing her eyes, she willed her tears to stay at bay before she opened them when his finger traced her belly button.

"This is really happening?" he asked, looking up at her, and she bit her lip as she nodded. Smiling, he pressed his lips to her belly once more, stilling as he sucked in a deep breath. Glancing up at her, he whispered, "I'm sort of scared."

Her heart sank as she slowly nodded, lacing her fingers in his hair. "Me too."

He smiled as he kissed her again. And without really thinking about it, she whispered, "You'll be a great daddy, Jordie."

He moved his nose along her belly before laying his head softly on it. "I can't wait."

She wanted to smile, but her heart wouldn't allow her. He was already invested; she could see it in his eyes. He believed this baby would come in nine months, while she was worried that she might lose it. It had been like that since she found out. When she got past the three-day mark, she cried for hours. And now, she was just waiting. But why wait when she had a man like this, holding her and looking at her like she was giving him the world.

"Me either," she whispered and he hugged her tightly. "Such a surprise though, huh?"

He grinned as he nodded. "Yeah, I guess my boys are strong."

She smiled as she looked away, covering her face. "Actually, I didn't have an IUD in. I forgot to go get it put back in after the first miscarriage."

He paused and then scoffed. "That's funny, it's like it was meant to be."

"That's what Lacey said."

He grinned. "So she knows?"

She nodded, looking back at him as she moved her fingers through his hair. "Yeah, but I don't want to tell anyone else yet."

His brows came together. "Why?"

She looked away, biting her lip, but he smacked her thigh lightly. "Don't look away. Why don't you want to tell anyone? I'm five seconds from making a Facebook post."

She scoffed. "You're such a Facebook whore."

He made a face as she looked back at him. "Maybe, but that's not the discussion right now. Why don't you want to tell anyone?"

She worked her lip, her eyes locked with his, and she hoped he'd just know so she wouldn't have to say it, but he looked at her expectantly. Letting out a long breath, she said, "I could lose it. I don't want to say anything till the second trimester."

His furrow deepened as he shook his head before sitting up to look down at her. His eyes were intense, serious, as he said, "No, baby. This child, our child is going to be born, and we are going to love it and raise it, I promise you. I feel it, this one is gonna make it. We are together, we are happy, it isn't going anywhere."

"You can't promise that, Jordie," she said, a tear running down the side of her face, and she had to look away again before she fully started crying.

Covering her body with his, he fell between her legs before cupping her face. "You listen to me, Kacey King. I probably can't promise, but I will."

"Don't put that pressure on me, Jordie. I already feel like a failure for losing the first one," she admitted. And as soon as the words left her lips, she realized that she still wasn't over the loss of the baby she'd carried for three short days.

"Don't you dare," he demanded. "You have no control over that, baby. I understand that, and no matter what, I love you. So please, don't stress over this. We are supposed to be happy together, so fucking happy."

Covering his hands with hers, she nodded. "You're right, I just don't want to add to any anxiety you're having right now."

He shot her a goofy grin and shrugged. "What anxiety? All I feel is happiness, because I'm gonna be a daddy and you're gonna be the mommy." Smiling, she felt her tears come faster down her face as he pressed his nose to hers. "Now be happy," he demanded.

"I am," she promised, and the side of his mouth curved up as he let go of her face to take her by the back of her knee, opening her wider. She didn't realize what he was doing, but he soon entered her with one thrust, taking her breath away. Wide-eyed, she looked up at him as he lifted himself off her, pushing deeper inside her, his fingers biting into her skin as he pulled out and then thrust back in. He held her gaze steadily. The motion was one they both knew well, but it still felt like the first time as he moved in and out of her body.

Reaching up, she cupped his jaw, her thumb getting lost in his beard as he turned in her hand, biting her palm. She hissed out a breath and his eyes cut to hers before he thrust into her, his lips pressing into her palm as she cried out. As he looked down at her, she honestly felt like she was flying on a cloud while the world praised how gorgeous she was.

A world made up of only Jordie.

He leaned into her hand, his eyes filling with tears as he whispered, "I love you, Kacey."

Her heart skipped a beat like a schoolgirl's as her mouth curved up and she ran her thumb along his bottom lip. "I love you too."

Kissing her palm once more, he held her gaze as he slowly made love to her. All she could think was that she had it all.

A man.

A dog.

A baby on the way.

But she just prayed that she'd be able to keep it all.

Chapter
TWENTY-FIVE

"**M**y girlfriend's pregnant."

Julie looked up from her pad and smiled. "Is she now?"

"Yup," he said proudly, his grin unstoppable.

It had been like that for the last week. Ever since he saw the cupcakes that spelled out that he was going to be a daddy, he couldn't stop smiling. Even through a training session that he was pretty sure she got from the devil, two games where they lost, and knowing his mom was going to be there that night, Jordie kept smiling.

"So this was planned then?"

He shook his head. "Nope, complete surprise."

"Is she excited?"

Looking down, he nodded, but he knew he was sort of lying. Kacey was happy, excited even, but the fear of miscarriage weighed heavy on her heart. She had told him more than once she didn't want to fail him, and that gutted him. She gave him a chance when no one else would even think to, so it was easy to say that she couldn't fail him. She just couldn't.

"She's scared of having another miscarriage," he answered and Julie slowly nodded, her eyes on him. "She thinks she's gonna fail me again—her words, not mine."

"It's hard when that kind of thing happens, especially since she was completely alone before."

He nodded. "She won't be ever again, though."

"Good, but do you feel the same? Are you worried?"

He lifted his shoulder and leaned back in his chair, lacing his hands together behind his head. "I'm not thinking about it, honestly. All I care about is her being happy and healthy. I don't think she'll lose this one. I feel that we are in a good place, we are happy and ready for this."

She smiled. "That's good, I'm glad it's not stressing you out. You don't need the stress."

He couldn't agree more, but slowly he said, "Yeah."

"Oh my, Jordie. That was a loaded *yeah*."

He smiled, leaning on his thighs. In the short time he had been coming to Julie's practice, he found that they just clicked. She was an older lady, sweet and really listened, but she also didn't hold back when she felt he needed to know something. Clearing his throat, he looked up and said, "My mom is in town. I'm supposed to see her tonight for dinner."

Her eyes widened for only a second before she slowly nodded. "You don't talk about her much."

"Because she's a wack-job."

"Yes, well, I guess you aren't looking forward to this dinner?"

He shook his head. "No. I don't want to go. She doesn't care about me, probably doesn't even love me."

"Then why are you going?" she asked and he shook his head, biting his lip.

"For some pathetic reason, I want her to care, to love me."

"Because she's your mom."

"Yeah, and I have no one— Well, no, I have Kacey and her family, but I really want that blood connection with someone, and I don't have it."

"I understand that," she said slowly, the tip of her pen at her lip. "But, Jordie, she's done nothing good for you, and I can see it in your body language, she really affects you. Can you share why you are so tensed up?"

Closing his eyes, he leaned on his hands as he pulled in a breath through his nose and let it out of his mouth. "Since I was a kid, she's always put me on the back burner. The only person who mattered was her husband of the month. When I was molested, she didn't believe me until the dude admitted it, and then she asked if I'd enticed him. The guy was superloaded, and she saw her meal ticket going out the door," he added when her eyes widened. "She just has never done right by me. She doesn't even know that I've been in rehab, or recovery. She hasn't asked. She is demanding that I meet her new soon-to-be husband, but she doesn't even want to meet Kacey. She just doesn't care."

She slowly nodded. "But you're going?"

"I have to. I have to give her one last chance, and if she throws it in my face, then at least I tried."

Letting out a long breath, she looked down, writing something before reaching over to hand it to him. "That is my number. If tonight after dinner you feel like you can't handle something, call me if you need me. I'm gonna schedule you in for tomorrow too," she said then, typing something on her phone, and his brows pulled together.

"Why?"

She looked up from her phone and said, "Because this is something that can trigger a relapse, and you've done so well, Jordie. We can't let her do that."

Looking down at the floor, he already knew this.

So why was he going?

As Jordie drove home, he repeatedly asked himself his previous question. He wasn't sure if it was a good idea, and honestly, she didn't even deserve a chance to be in his life. Sucking in a breath, he thought about his own child and how he was already so in love with it and he didn't even know what it was. Why didn't she feel the same? Why wasn't he enough? It wasn't fair, really. Her actions had affected him in so many ways, and he hadn't ever analyzed how she made him feel.

For years, he'd begged for attention. And when the molestation happened, he was scared to even talk to another man for years. All the husbands that came through called him a mute, and maybe he was. But she never hugged him, kissed him, or told him she loved him. She ignored him and that rejection still stung. For years, he talked to no one, became a recluse, but then he met Robbie. Robbie got him out of his house, his family loved him, and Jordie was happy again. But then that was all taken away from him. Did his mother care?

Not even a little bit.

Then during his adult life, she wandered in and out of it. Only hitting him up for money when she was between husbands. And he would give it to her. He didn't understand the hold she had on him, but it was downright sickening. He had to stand up to her, had to be a man because he was about to be a father. He had to set an example for his child and not allow anyone to walk all over him. Because Lord knows, Stacey walked, ran, and stomped all over Jordie, and he let her.

But not anymore.

Pulling into the driveway, he drove into the garage next to Kacey's car and reached for the Snickers he had bought her, before getting out of the car. Climbing the stairs, he threw the door open and smiled as Kacey's face lit up.

"There's my sexy mommy-to-be. Look, I brought you a snack to give our child a sugar high." But just as quickly as her face had lit up, her eyes went wide and her jaw dropped. Confused, he asked, "What?"

And then he realized why.

Sitting on their couch were her parents, brother, and sister-in-law with Mena in her lap. Since telling him of the pregnancy, she'd sworn him to secrecy and he'd gone along with her. She was really nervous about everyone freaking out if she miscarried and wanted to wait. While he was bursting at the seams to tell someone, he honored what she'd asked. Anything to help keep her calm, but he guessed the cat was out of the bag.

As everyone gaped at him, Gretzky didn't seem to care and was hopping and biting at his ankles for attention. But Jordie didn't move. His eyes went from Kacey to her family and back again as Regina slowly rose.

"You're pregnant?" Regina gasped. Jordie met Karson's gaze and he was glaring as Karl slowly stood, his wide eyes going from Kacey to Jordie and then back.

Lacey, on the other hand, was bouncing in her seat as she cried out, "Oh, thank God! I was having such a hard time keeping that in."

"You knew?" Karson shouted and she shrugged.

"Yeah, I knew before Jordie did," she said innocently. "I'm her best friend."

"And I'm her brother!"

"Well, shit," Jordie said slowly and Kacey covered her face.

"Well, shit is right," she said, rubbing her face before dropping her hands. "Did you not see their cars?"

He shook his head. "I was thinking, didn't even notice."

"So it's true?" Regina asked, coming to the doorway, Karl flanking her.

Jordie looked to Kacey and she looked back at him, nodding her head. "Yeah. I'm pregnant."

"Surprise," Jordie said, waving his jazz hands in the air, but no one seemed to be entertained.

The silence stretched as everyone looked at everyone else. Jordie's heart was pounding while Kacey worked her lip, nervousness in every single one of her features. Finally though, Regina shrieked before wrapping her arms tightly around Kacey, kissing her hard on the face before blubbering all over her. Karson wrapped his arm around Lacey and shook his head, a grin playing on his lips.

"Could have told me, asshole."

Jordie shrugged. "She wouldn't let me, wanted to wait till she was out of the first trimester."

"Oh yes, don't want to get everyone excited and then lose the baby. The horror!" Regina cried, and he didn't miss the grimace on Lacey's face or on Kacey's. "But that won't happen to you, baby. It's gonna be fine. Ah, my baby is pregnant!" she said, kissing Kacey again, but Kacey's face was like stone, her eyes watering. He wanted to go to her, pull her into his arms, and reassure her. But before he could, Karl came to him, shaking his hand hard. "I should kill you for not making an honest woman out of her before knocking her up."

Jordie laughed. "Complete surprise, but I'm working on it," he said with a wink, and Karl rolled his eyes.

"You don't know what happens when two people screw like gorillas? You know where babies come from, right?"

Jordie chortled with laughter as he nodded his head. "I do, but she was supposed to have an—"

"Nope, don't care, just be good to her," Karl said, cutting him off, and he smiled. "Congratulations, son, you'll be a great dad."

Jordie smiled. "Thanks, Karl."

Squeezing his arm, he said, "Come outside with me?"

Jordie eyed him. "You aren't going to kill me, are you?"

Karl laughed before directing him out the back door, and when he saw Karson following, his heart stuttered a bit because, together, they could kill him quicker. With a pounding heart, he turned as Karson shut the door and Karl asked, "You good?"

Jordie nodded. "I don't know. Depends if you two are about to jump me."

Karl laughed. "No, dumbass, I'm talking about your mom."

"Oh," Jordie said, his breath coming out in a whoosh. "Yeah, I'm fine."

He nodded slowly. "You sure?"

"I'm good, I promise."

"Okay, well, if it gets bad, you call me," Karl demanded.

"And don't let Kacey hit her," Karson added. "She doesn't need that kind of stress while she's pregnant."

"I know," Jordie agreed, his hands tucking into his pockets. "Really, guys, I'm good."

"You'll call though? If it goes bad?" Karson asked, his arms folding over his chest.

"Yeah," he promised. "I'll call."

But he prayed he wouldn't need to.

Eventually, everyone left, leaving Jordie and Kacey alone. But instead of talking to him, she went straight to the bathroom to get ready. As she stood at the bathroom counter doing her makeup, he could tell she was as nervous as he was. Or maybe she was mad. She hadn't wanted anyone to know, and he had kind of messed that up. Since her hand was shaking, she kept having to redo her makeup, which he found cute. Especially, her cry of anger.

"Motherfucking whore bag!" she yelled, dropping her hand as a black streak appeared on her cheek.

"Just draw another one on the other side, you'll be hot," he suggested and she glared.

"No," she said, her movements jerky as she washed it off, her anger-filled eyes locked on him. "I can't believe you told my family."

"Um, I didn't really tell them. I've been greeting you as my hot momma all week."

She reached down, picking up her Snickers before taking a huge bite, and said, "Whatever. They know, it's whatever," she said, but even she was eating with more force than needed.

"I'm sorry," he said softly, but she shook her head.

"No, it's fine. I just don't want to let anyone down, and now that my mom knows, she's gonna baby me. And if I lose this one, she's gonna feel bad because she said that shit about miscarriage. Ugh! It will be such a mess."

Coming off where he'd been sitting on the toilet lid, he went to her, wrapping his arms around her waist and kissing her neck. "It won't happen."

She shook her head though. "You don't know that."

"No, but I can hope so," he suggested, meeting her gaze in the mirror. "And so can you."

Letting out a long breath, she closed her eyes, leaning into him. "I'm trying."

"I know," he said softly, kissing her jaw. "It's all going to be fine."

"Yes," she agreed. "Yes, it will. I have to believe that."

"Yes, you do," he practically begged as he slowly kissed her cheek. "We've lived so long without each other. Now we have each other, and things are going to go in our favor. I haven't completely changed who I was for nothing. It was for you and for the children you're going to give me."

She smiled, leaning her cheek into his lips. "You are a good man, Jordie Thomas."

Holding her gaze, he said, "Because of the woman who loves me and stands beside me."

"Always," she whispered, her eyes heavy with emotion. Her hands then came up to his, holding them as her eyes searched his. "Are you okay?" she asked after a few seconds and he nodded. He knew everyone meant well, but it was getting annoying being asked the same thing over and over again.

"Yeah. I'm good."

"We don't have to go," she suggested and he nodded.

"I know, but I want to."

Her eyes opened. "You want to?"

Looking back at her intently, he nodded. "I want to be honest. I want her to know what she is losing."

Her brow quirked. "So you aren't giving her the chance to be in your life?"

He shook his head. "I can't. She doesn't deserve it."

"You got that right," she agreed and she patted his hands. He let her go, allowing her to get ready as he took his seat back on the toilet.

"Good thing is, we get a free meal," he said and her lips curved.

"'Cause you're hurting for money."

He smiled. "Hey, we are having a baby, gotta start saving. We play the most expensive sport, which means the baby will, plus college. And then if it's a girl, a wedding... Ugh, yeah, I need to start playing really good so I can get a raise."

"You're insane," she said, rolling her eyes, but then she looked over at him in the mirror as she removed the black streak. "It may help, y'know? Tell her that you don't want her in your life any longer and not to call, nicely of course. Unlike me who wants to kick her in the vag and cuss her out." He laughed as she continued, "And maybe it will soothe some of your pain because you'll never have to see or talk to her again."

He shook his head. "It won't be that easy."

"Sure it will," she decided. "Because she can't manipulate both of us."

He smiled. "This is true."

"So, no worries," she said happily. "But if shit gets shady, I'm gonna Spartan kick her."

Jordie shook his head, his chest bubbling with laughter as she shrugged in an innocent way, but Kacey was far from innocent. She was a whole lot of things, but innocent was not one of them. She was insanely protective though, and he believed every word that left her sweet lips. The great thing though—even though he sort of felt like he was drowning in the abyss of the unknown—was that Kacey was his.

And she'd stand by him no matter what.

He was going to need her when he faced down his mother.

He just hoped he came back in one piece.

The second Kacey locked eyes with Stacey Thomas, she hated her.

It wasn't as if she had liked her before, because she didn't. But still, pure hatred burned deep in her soul as she watched Jordie's mother wave her hands up in the air before hugging him tightly, kissing his cheek as if she was a good mother instead of the poor excuse for a human being she actually was. Jordie went through the motions but they were stiff, and she could tell from a mile away that he didn't want her touching him. That it almost pained him because they both knew she didn't want to hug or kiss him. She didn't even love him, or maybe she did, somewhere deep in that black heart of hers. But if she did, she had a poor way of showing it.

And that made Kacey hate her even more. If that were possible.

OVERTIME

Her dumb-ass fiancé stood behind her, his mouth gaping, his eyes big as he took in the wide girth of Jordie. That was one thing about him that made Kacey's heart skip a beat; wherever Jordie stood, he took up the whole room. He was such a big presence, and it left her dumbfounded that his mother didn't care more for him. He was such a beautiful person, a good man, but it was fine. Her loss, and Kacey's gain.

"This is Phil Quest, Jordie, my fiancé. He's a huge fan," she gushed, bringing Phil forward, and Jordie shook his hand, hard.

In that instant, Kacey knew why they were there. Phil was a fan, and for Stacey to look good in front of him and suck all his money out of his account, she had to act like the doting mother. Too bad everyone saw through her—well, maybe not Phil, but he was obviously a dumbass.

So sad, she thought as she slowly shook her head, just as Jordie turned to her.

"This is Kacey," he said, taking her hand in his and kissing her knuckles. She smiled as he turned back to his mother, a hopeful look on his face as he said, "My girlfriend."

Stacey looked Kacey up and down, a stuck-up look on her face, her eyes narrowing as she shook her hand. She didn't look like Jordie, she was light to his dark, so Kacey figured he must take after the father he didn't know. "How nice. Are you ready to sit down? I have to get back to the hotel soon, I'm worn out. Phil had me all over Nashville. He used to live here a long time back, says he wants to move back. Wouldn't that be nice if we lived close by?"

Jordie looked back at Kacey, and she could see the utter horror on his face. Smiling, she squeezed his hand as she shook her head, hoping he realized that his mother's rejection of her didn't hurt her feelings. That woman was nothing to her, and she needed to be nothing to Jordie. But Kacey understood his need for his mother. She couldn't imagine her mother not loving her or even caring about her everyday life. She called every day just to check in.

But Jordie's mom couldn't even do that once a month.

"It's nice to meet you, by the way, Kacey," Phil said then, stealing her attention as he reached out to shake her hand. "You've got yourself a lovely lady, Jordie."

Jordie smiled as Kacey shook Phil's hand, but before she could thank him, Stacey said, "For how long though? Jordie doesn't stay with ladies long, no matter how lovely they are."

Jordie bit the inside of his cheek as Kacey glared. "I'm not going anywhere."

Stacey looked back at her, a condescending look on her face. "Bet you aren't the first or the last to say that."

"No, I am," she said very confidently. "Jordie doesn't make promises he can't keep, and anyone who had been with him in the past knew the score. As

300

do I. He's in this for the long haul."

Stacey's eyes narrowed more, her mouth setting in a line. "Sure."

Kacey went to say more, but Jordie shook his head, his eyes pleading with hers. Dropping his lips to her ear, he whispered, "It won't change what she thinks."

"That's fine, but I refuse to allow her to think so lowly of you or, hell, me!"

He let out a long breath, kissing her below her ear as he said, "It doesn't matter what she thinks. Only what you think."

When she pulled away, his eyes bored into hers and she smiled. "Well, I think you're perfect."

He scoffed. "A perfect mess, right?"

"My mess," she reminded him, and his lips quirked at the sides before he leaned over, kissing her bottom lip. Pulling back, he asked, "How did I get so lucky to have a second chance with you?"

Her eyes never leaving his, she cupped his face. "You were you, and in case you didn't know, you're kinda irresistible."

He scoffed, leaning his nose to hers. It was something he'd always done, but yet, there was always a new wave of butterflies in her belly whenever he did. It was their thing, something she cherished, probably as much as she cherished him. And by God, she was not going to let this woman bring him down.

But thankfully, his eyes were bright as they held hers, his nose moving along hers before he paused and pulled away, grinning. "Oh, I know," he teased, and she laughed as he pulled her along to catch up with Stacey and Phil.

After he pulled her chair out, Kacey shot him a grin as she sat down and he sat next to her, taking her hand in his before resting it on his thigh. Before they could even pick up the menus though, Phil was firing question after question about hockey to Jordie. Kacey was sure he didn't mind though—he loved talking hockey—but it was obvious that Stacey did not care for it. She huffed and puffed the whole time, probably because the attention wasn't on her, but Kacey was sure Phil wasn't listening to her. He was too engrossed in Jordie.

"You play a sick game, man. I really enjoy watching you play." He beamed and Jordie grinned.

"Thanks. You know Kacey played in the Olympics," he said, looking over at her, and she waved him off.

"No big deal, I just brought home the gold," she joked and they laughed, while Stacey just glared.

"Where is the waiter?" she complained as Phil looked closely at her.

"Wait, are you Kacey 'Khaos' King?"

Kacey beamed at Jordie as he gave her an exaggerated eye-roll. "Why, yes, I am."

"I watched you on TV. You're amazing!"

"She is," Jordie agreed, kissing her cheek. "Stupid nickname and all."

Kacey was about to defend her nickname when the waiter stopped at their table. "Hey, y'all! Sorry for the wait," he said, bringing everyone's attention to him. "What can I get y'all to drink?"

"Oh, thank God," Stacey almost cheered. "Well, first, I want a glass of your best red. And then, Philly, you want a Jack and Coke?"

"Please," Phil said. Kacey's hand squeezed Jordie's, her eyes cutting to his as he looked to her, a little panic in his eyes.

"It's fine. It's gross anyway," she tried and he scoffed. "Kinda." He smiled as he shrugged, the waiter looking to her. "Water, please."

"Me too," Jordie added and the waiter nodded, but Stacey stopped him. "Also a round of shots. Tequila?"

Phil nodded, but Kacey shook her head. "Pregnant, no can do."

"What?" Stacey blurted out. "Pregnant?"

Jordie glanced at her, surprised, and she smiled. She was trying to protect him. She knew he was proud of his sobriety, and she was too, but having the attention on her and off him seemed like a good idea.

"Yeah, only seven weeks, but pregnant nonetheless."

"With your baby?" Stacey asked Jordie and he nodded, his arm snaking along Kacey's shoulders.

"Yup, we are really excited."

She made a face as Phil turned to her. "You'll be a grandma."

Cold day in fucking hell, Kacey thought, and Jordie's eyes said the same thing once they met hers.

"Eh, let's not get ahead of ourselves," she said, and Jordie whipped his head to her.

"What does that mean?"

"It means no telling what will happen between you two," she said, her lip curved as she moved her finger between the two of them.

"I can tell you, actually," he said with a little venom in his voice, his hand squeezing Kacey's. "We'll get married, have a baby, and live a fucking great life."

She looked to the wide-eyed waiter—*why was he still waiting?* She understood the drama was probably entertaining to an outsider, but he needed to go get the drinks. "So, just two shots then," she said to him, and he realized that she was dismissing him before Stacey stopped him.

Glaring at Kacey, Stacey's hand curled around his arm before she dragged her gaze to his. "No, three," she demanded before looking back at Kacey. "Just 'cause you can't drink doesn't mean he can't. Don't let her start controlling you, Jordie," she snapped and Kacey's eye started to twitch. She wasn't going to make it with this chick.

"Um, actually, still just two. I'm an alcoholic."

Well, there it is, Kacey thought, leaning back and looking at Jordie, bursting with pride. Was he perfect? Hell no, but he was honestly the strongest man she had ever met, and she loved him, truly. With all her heart. He wore his sobriety like a badge of honor, and he fucking should. He was amazing.

But apparently she was the only one who thought so.

Phil's jaw had dropped and Stacey started to sputter before she shrieked, "What?"

"Good for you, bro. I'll get you guys your drinks and just two shots," the waiter said and she almost asked him to take her and Jordie with him, because one look at Stacey and she knew that shit was about to hit the fan.

"Actually, can you make it just a Coke for me, and no shots?" Phil asked. "I don't want to wave it in your face."

"Thanks," Jordie said appreciatively, and Kacey decided that maybe Phil wasn't so bad.

"Oh no, I want my shot and my wine," Stacey said, and she must have missed the way everyone looked at her…or maybe she didn't. Because, with a snide look, she said, "What? I'm not an alcoholic. And what does that even mean? How do you know?"

Sitting up a bit taller, Jordie said, "I drank myself stupid, went to rehab, and haven't drunk since."

"That's dumb. I doubt there was anything wrong with you, just overreacting like always," she said, waving him off. "He does that. He used to make up the most awful stuff as a child. Then his friend got killed, and he's been trouble ever since. So pay him no mind. It's probably a stunt for attention."

Kacey's jaw actually dropped. "Attention? Are you fucking kidding me?" she shrieked when she recovered from the shock. Jordie cupped her shoulder and she glanced over at him, her eyes wide. Slowly he shook his head before leaning over and kissing her on the lips.

"I got this," he said against her lips.

But Stacey was still running her mouth. "Tell your baby momma to watch the way she speaks to me, Jordie Scott!"

"Stacey, please," Phil asked, but Jordie's eyes were on Kacey.

"She can't hurt me," he said slowly to her, but Kacey didn't believe him. She knew Stacey could, but soon, he was looking back at his mother, his shoulders firm as he held her gaze.

"It's not an attention-getting stunt. I had a problem; I'm treating it. And I'm not here to point fingers, but did it ever occur to you that maybe you were the root of my problem?"

She laughed. "Please, I never did anything to cause that."

"You're right, you didn't do anything," he said calmly, but his chest was rising and falling quickly. "You did nothing for me. You didn't love me, you didn't care for me, and you sure as hell never put me first."

"That's a lie," she snapped. "I did the best I could."

He scoffed. "No, you did what you wanted, and that's fine, Mom. I've forgiven you."

"You have?" Kacey asked, shocked, as Stacey glared.

"Yes," he said, not looking at Kacey. "At the beginning of the week, I had every intention of giving you the opportunity to be in my life. Give you a second chance to do right by me, because someone gave me a second chance and I'm a better person because of it. But I realized a few days ago, you don't deserve a second chance. That I'll never matter enough to you. And once I came to that conclusion, I decided I don't want to see or talk to you ever again."

Her glare deepened as Jordie slowly rose. "Phil, it was wonderful meeting you, and I hope you enjoy the game tomorrow."

He nodded, his brow furrowing as Kacey stood, and he said, "You're leaving? Already?"

"Yeah, I made a mistake coming. But again, it was great meeting you. Good luck."

"You too, I'm sorry that you have to leave."

"I'm not," Jordie said softly, taking Kacey's hand in his. Looking at his mother, he just shook his head. "Have a nice life."

He turned, pulling Kacey with him, and she went willingly. But when she noticed that Stacey was following them, her stomach dropped.

"Jordie, she's following us."

"I figured she would," he said, but he didn't seem as affected as she thought he would be. It worried her. Ushering her along, he went out the front door into the chill of the night. Wrapping her arms around herself, she kicked herself for not bringing her jacket. Turning, Jordie handed his ticket to the valet and asked her, "Do you want to get into the car first?"

She shook her head and said, very fiercely, "I'm standing beside you."

He nodded before removing his jacket, sliding it over her arms just as Stacey burst through the door, her face red with anger.

"How dare you embarrass me like that!" she yelled, her hands striking her hips, her face tipped up at him. "Are you a dumbass?"

"I don't think I embarrassed you. I was honest."

She faltered. "There was no reason to announce being an alcoholic! How stupid are you?"

Kacey's heart lurched in her chest and her nails bit into her palms as Jordie shook his head. "Most parents would be proud of their children for bettering themselves."

"Oh, what the hell ever! You think you're hurting me, Jordie Scott Thomas? Do you forget who gave you life? Who supported you all those years? Therapy isn't cheap, you shit, and I can't believe you'd embarrass me in front of my fiancé like that!"

"I could never forget, but you were never a mom to me," he said sternly, but she was already screaming.

"Oh, because I didn't coddle you or feed into your lies? I saw right through you. Everything that happened, you caused! You were jealous and came up with this lie about Gary, and then he was gone—"

Kacey was shaking with anger, but Jordie…he was calm. His eyes were on Stacey's as he asked, "If it was a lie, then why did he admit to it? Why is he still in jail?"

"Because of you! You caused him to do it!"

Kacey couldn't control herself. She really tried, she did, but the words left her mouth before Jordie could stop her. "You are a disgusting piece of shit. You really need to reevaluate your life if you think a four-year-old boy would be jealous enough of husband number one billion to ask to be raped, molested. You have some serious problems, and I suggest you go to therapy."

She laughed. "Don't need it. I'm not fucked up like him."

Kacey closed her eyes, her hands squeezing his as Jordie asked, "Why do you care, Mom? Why are you making this big scene when you obviously don't love me? Listen to the way you are speaking to me. The things you are accusing me of. A mother doesn't act like this."

"You're right, and I never wanted you," she seethed and Kacey's eyes squeezed tighter.

"Jordie, please, let's go," she begged, but still he didn't move.

"Well, you're in luck because I'm gone," he said before turning to wrap his arms around Kacey and leading her to the car.

"I'm not done talking to you," Stacey yelled just as Kacey's foot stepped into the car and she looked up at him.

"I can still Spartan kick her," she offered, but Jordie shook his head, no smile curving his lips as he pushed her other leg in.

"I just want to go," he said quickly before shutting the door. She could hear Stacey yelling something, but when Jordie opened his door, she heard him as he said, "Don't contact me again."

Sitting in the driver's seat, he slammed the door and gripped the wheel. Sliding her hand on his thigh, she waited as he took three deep breaths in and let them out, slow and steady. For once, she couldn't read his body language. On one hand, she thought he looked relieved. But on the other, she was worried he was two seconds from sobbing like a two-year-old. Still no words left his mouth as he put the car in drive and took off.

As Stacey disappeared in the side mirror, Kacey was glad to see her go, but she was pretty sure that she wouldn't disappear as quickly out of Jordie's heart.

Chapter
TWENTY-SIX

Nothing was said the whole way home or even when they entered the house. Jordie could do nothing but replay his mother's words over and over again. There was a lot for him to relive, but the most hurtful thing was that she was embarrassed by him instead of proud. He blamed his sad need for her approval for that being what bothered him the most. She wasn't nice to him, but then, he hadn't expected her to be.

He also hadn't expected the whole night to come crashing down like that though.

He could feel Kacey's gaze on him the whole ride home, yet she didn't say anything to him. As he walked through the house, he went to the fridge for a Gatorade before opening it and downing the whole bottle. He could feel her watching him as he reached for another and downed that bottle too. When she looked away, he knew that she knew what he wanted.

A big bottle of Jack. With a side of Jack. And some more Jack to chase it all down.

But the Gatorade was there to quench his thirst for things he didn't need or even truly want. He wanted an out, an easy fix, but he knew that there was no fucking easy fix for his mother. He couldn't understand why someone would treat her child like that, but Stacey Thomas was a whole other level of being. A different species that he didn't understand, nor want in his life. He was done, and he would make damn sure she never came near him again. Not only for him but for his unborn child.

Biting the inside of his cheek, he watched as Kacey took off his jacket and hung it on the back of the barstool before setting her clutch on the seat. When he reached for another Gatorade, he saw her face twist in worry before she looked away, he knew, to fight her tears. She didn't know what to do, what to say, and he was thankful for that. He needed to get his head straight before he talked to her, before he admitted that his mother had broken his heart and he wasn't sure how to put it back together.

She reached for him and he didn't move as she wrapped herself around him, going under his arm so that she could place her face on his chest. She smelled so good, but he couldn't hold her. Not yet. He knew if he did, he'd come undone, and he already felt so weak. He couldn't give her any more of a reason to feel sorry for him. He was the man, he was supposed to be strong, but what he wanted was to wrap his arms around her and just cry.

Pulling in a deep breath through his nose, he closed his eyes and let her hug him. He needed her strength, her love. He let his chin rest on her head as he kept his eyes shut and his breathing even. When his phone went off, he didn't move, his hands still braced against the counter, not only for support but to keep him upright. But then it went off again and again before, finally, she looked up at him.

"Someone is trying hard to get ahold of you."

He nodded, his eyes locked on the wall above her head. "It's either my therapist, your dad, or your brother."

"Do you want me to answer it?"

He shrugged. "You can. Tell them I'm alive."

But not that he was okay, because he wasn't. Far from it.

When she pulled his phone out of his pocket, he looked down and saw that the text was from her father.

Karl King: You good?
Karl King: I know you left. She posted a nasty status about you.

And then he sent a screenshot of Stacey Thomas's Facebook.

Don't you love when your kid tells you you're the reason he's fucked up? Biggest waste of my time was having that brat. Anyone that knows him knows his issues aren't mine and that I'm not in the wrong here.

While the status was just uncalled for, what blew his mind was that two people *liked* it.

What the hell was wrong with the world?

He looked away, shaking his head as she typed back quickly before setting his phone down and wrapping her arms around him again. Closing his eyes, he leaned on her head and was unsure what to do next. He knew that he had to do something, tell her something. Talk about it all, but he didn't want to. He didn't want to be reminded of having the worst mother known to man. A woman who didn't want him. Who didn't care about him. In a way, he'd set himself up for failure. He should never have gone. He knew going in that he would more than likely leave with heartache.

His assumptions had been right on.

As Kacey squeezed him, he closed his eyes again as she suggested, "Why don't we go to bed?"

He shrugged. "Sure."

He turned from her arms and left the kitchen, not even waiting for her. As he walked through their home, he wanted to take notice of all she had done. Kacey—well, Lacey and Regina—had really turned their house into a home. While there weren't as many pictures of her and Jordie as he'd like, they were working on it. Even planned to go do a little couples' shoot with Harper Titov, Elli's best friend, who did everyone's pictures. But a part of him wondered if he should even care about that.

Would she even want him when she realized how weak he was?

Going into their bedroom, he heard her moving around in the kitchen, probably cleaning up and getting Gretzky taken care of as he unbuttoned his shirt and threw it on the chair that she said was her thinking chair. He hadn't seen her sit in it yet, and it held more clothes than it ever had her butt for thinking, but who was he to say anything? Maybe he should have sat in the thinking chair and really rethought going to see his mother. Disgusted with himself, he threw off his slacks, tossing those too on the thinking chair as she entered the room, looking so damn worried that it killed him.

She didn't need this stress. She was carrying their child, and he needed to get his shit together before he lost both of them because of his stupidity. Pulling the sheets back, he went to get in before she stopped him.

"Can you unzip me?" she asked, and when he looked over at her, he noticed her little sex-kitten look. He knew what she was doing, and any other time, he would have stripped her down and plowed into her, but not tonight. Without answering her, he stepped behind her, moving her hair before unzipping her dress and then climbing into the bed. He felt her gaze on him, but he ignored it, cuddling deeper into the bed as she moved around the room, doing her thing.

When she finally climbed into bed, she hit the light and then turned to face him, the moonlight shining on her beautiful face. As he looked deep into her dark eyes, he knew he wasn't being the best man he could be for her. She was freaking out, working her lip, and he could feel the tension, the worry, rolling off her in waves. He had promised to do right by her, not only to Karson but to Karl too. Plus, he loved this girl. He didn't want her to worry.

Reaching out, he cupped her face and whispered, "I'm sorry, Kacey."

Her eyes widened as she shrugged. "What are you sorry for? It's not your fault she's a cunt. You should have let me kick her."

He wanted to smile, he did, but instead, he ran his thumb along her bottom lip. "I let you down, and I apologize for that."

Her brow rose. "So you drank?"

He shook his head, confused. "No—"

"Then you didn't let me down," she said quickly, her eyes holding his. "If anything, Jordie, I'm proud of you. You stood up for yourself, you told her about herself, and you did it with grace. You didn't lose your temper, you didn't really cuss her out or even allow me to hit her. You were amazing and I'm so proud of you. And damn it, Jordie, I love you," she reiterated, her eyes getting misty. His heart sped up in his chest. "In my eyes, you are strong, beautiful, and everything I want in a man. So don't apologize. Please, don't."

He wanted to take her words and run, but he worried she'd said them just to make him feel better. But as soon as that thought came, he knew she wouldn't do that. Kacey wasn't a sugarcoating kind of girl. If she didn't want to be honest, she just didn't say anything. He knew this, so why didn't he feel better?

Swallowing hard around the lump in his throat, he whispered, "I shouldn't have gone."

"You're right. But do you feel better, knowing you let her have it and she won't even be able to hurt you again?"

He did feel better on that aspect, but he was still embarrassed for how weak he felt, for allowing her to hurt him one more time. In the future, it wouldn't happen. When he'd walked away from her tonight, he was done. The things she said, the pure hatred in her eyes, reminded him that this was not what he wanted in his life. This woman couldn't continually put him down; she didn't own him. He had to let her go, and to his surprise, knowing that he would never have to deal with her again was a relief.

Looking up, Jordie held Kacey's face as he asked, "So you don't think I'm weak?"

She shook her head quickly, hooking her leg over his hip before snuggling closer to him, her nose touching his. "The opposite, Jordie. I think you are strong."

"But I keep allowing her to hurt me."

"*Kept*, past tense. It won't happen again," she corrected him and he nodded, his nose moving along hers.

"You're right," he whispered, and her eyes softened as she wrapped her arms around his neck, coming closer to him.

"It's good you are learning this now. Just don't forget it when we fight over the last Oreo or something equally silly that couples argue about," she teased and he smiled, his heart pounding in his chest.

"Deal," he promised. "But the last Oreo is always mine."

She scoffed. "Um, I'm carrying your child, the Oreo is mine."

He held her gaze and then gave in to her. "You're right."

"Again, see that's how I work," she said, her lips curving as she squeezed him. "But really, Jordie, she doesn't matter anymore. Let her go. I know it has to be hard, but just let go of that darkness. It can't haunt you any longer. Not with me being here."

He wouldn't admit it again, but she was right. She was his light that would guide him through the darkness. No matter how clichéd and silly that sounded, it was the truth. All he needed was Kacey by his side, and he could conquer anything.

"Okay," he whispered, his lips brushing against hers. "Then, thank you."

She smiled as she nodded. "That's better, and anytime, Jordie. I love you. The thing is, I never thought when I met you that you'd be this important to me, but you are. And I can guarantee you, you aren't going anywhere without a fight. You're in this for life."

His grin spread across his face as his hand slid up her thigh and onto her stomach. "I think this is proof of that," he teased and she smiled. "But Kacey, really, when I met you all those years ago back in Karson's dorm, I didn't know you'd be the best thing that ever happened to me."

His life had completely altered because of her, and he wouldn't change that for anything. He loved the man he was now—yeah, he felt down right now, but looking into her eyes, he knew that she'd help lift him back up. When her mouth turned up, his hands wrapped around her, pulling her even closer as their mouths met. As he kissed his woman, he realized that when he got his second chance with her, all he'd wanted was her love, but what he got was so much more.

A life worth living.

Leaning against the boards, Jordie watched as the puck sailed across the ice from Shea to Jayden before he threw it up to a waiting Baylor. The defense was on her though, blocking her pass, but they didn't get far before Shea was blasting it past them all to the goalie. The Canucks' goalie batted it away though, their defense grabbing it as the Assassins did a line change. Jordie should have been paying attention, but it was hard.

Because the seat across the rink that was for his mom was empty.

Phil sat there, in his whole Assassins getup, but his mom wasn't anywhere to be seen. Not that he was looking for her, per se, but the little boy in him thought she'd still come to see him play. He figured he was getting what he asked for and he should be happy, yet it hurt. Why did he care? She didn't add to his life, so she needed to be out of it, like Benji had said. He needed to let this go.

Especially when Coach smacked his back to go.

Going over the boards, he hauled ass across the ice to catch the puck from Karson after he skated around the net. Carrying the puck up the ice, he watched as his forwards got into position, and when he sent the puck up to Phillip, he waited at the blue line for a shot as the boys kept shooting at the goalie. He wasn't letting anything in though. Glancing up at the clock, Jordie saw they only had two minutes before the game was over, and they were down by one.

Erik sent the puck back to Karson, and he sailed it over to Jordie without even looking at him, which he expected. Taking it, he shot, hard, but it went wide, coming around to Karson. Instead of shooting it though, he sent it back and Jordie shot again, and this time it went right over the goalie's leg pad. Throwing his arms up, he pumped them in the air as Karson rushed to him, hugging him tightly.

"That's fucking right!" Karson yelled as the other guys came up, hugging him too.

"Let's win this!" Erik yelled, and everyone agreed as they skated toward the bench to smack hands with the rest of the team. As Jordie sat down, reaching for his Gatorade, he squirted it in his mouth, the adrenaline of scoring rushing through his body. He knew Kacey had to have seen it, but she was up in the boxes and it was hard to see up there sometimes. He still looked though, and as he expected, she was hopping up and down. He wanted to holler at her to sit down, but she looked so happy, her arms wrapped around Karl, whose face was bright too.

They were his family.

Squirting more in his mouth, he willed his eyes not to cut across the ice, but they did, and to his surprise, his mom was sitting there. On her phone as Phil stood, still clapping along with the rest of the fans. Looking away, he swallowed hard and shook his head. His eyes stung and he wanted to scream, but not now. If he knew one thing, it was that there was no crying in hockey unless you were lifting the Cup over your head. Even then it was kinda pussy-like, not that anyone cared.

As he threw his Gatorade back in its place, Karson's hand came down hard on Jordie's shoulder as he said, "Fuck her."

Exactly.

"Yeah," Jordie agreed, nodding his head, and he was ready to win this game. His feelings, his worries, and his hurt were all a thing of the past, because Stacey Thomas was nothing to him anymore. This moment proved it. There she was, on her phone, no cares at all for him. But then he glanced up at the box his real family sat in and saw they were all still standing, Kacey screaming her ass off. It was crazy how quickly things could change. Ten seconds ago, he'd wanted his mother's approval; now, he just wanted her to disappear. Because he had his approval. It was in the form of a beautiful, tough girl with brown eyes, who loved him with all the fierceness in the world—along with her family who had taken him in.

Stacey Thomas may have his last name, but she would never have his heart again.

Not when Kacey King owned it.

Swallowing hard, he knew he was right, he knew he was making the right choice. As he looked up, he was ready to do what he did best: win. But the minutes weren't his friends and they ran fast, thankfully with no score from the Canucks, which meant they were going into overtime.

Jordie was at his best in overtime. The feeling of losing it all if you didn't score first gave him such a rush. He loved the all-or-nothing feel of it, and he kind of associated his recovery with the feeling that overtime gave him. He either won or he lost, there was no in-between.

And damn it, Jordie Thomas always wanted to win.

But even though they lost the game after a sick wrister from one of the twins on the other team, Jordie knew he wouldn't lose in his quest for sobriety.

No matter what, he was going to win.

Kacey was almost bouncing on her heels in the parking garage as she waited for Jordie to come out. She was so proud of him, but she knew that even though he had scored, he'd be bummed they lost. It was a sick-ass shot though from one of the twins that caught Tate off guard. Still, it was a great game and he should be proud of himself. It was his first goal on home ice of the season and he was rocking it.

Even with his mom at the game.

Kacey had watched her the whole time. She only came to her seat every once in a while, but when she was there, she was looking at her phone the whole time. Kacey wanted to march down and kick her in the face, but her dad wouldn't let her. Said she wasn't worth it. She knew this, but she was pretty sure she'd feel better if she had. Turning to her father, she smiled as he leaned against

Jordie's truck, playing on his phone.

"Daddy, you don't have to wait with me. It's way past your bedtime."

He laughed sarcastically before waving her off. "I'm not leaving you alone in a parking lot. I'll catch a ride home with Karson, since your ma took Lacey and Mena home."

"Okay," she sang, leaning against the truck. "Thanks for waiting."

He smiled over at her, tucking his phone in his pocket as he reached out, wrapping his arm around her neck and bringing her in tight. "How ya doing?"

"Good," she answered, looking up at him, smiling. She loved her daddy.

"How's my grandbaby?"

"Growing, I pray," she said hopefully and he nodded.

"She'll be good," he promised and Kacey smiled, but then her smile dropped when she realized that he didn't know about the miscarriage. No one did.

Clearing her throat, she asked, "Daddy, if I told you something, would you promise not to get mad and not to tell Ma?"

He eyed her and then nodded. "Yeah."

Taking in a deep breath, she held on to his arms as she admitted, "This is my second pregnancy. The first one, I lost. That's why I'm so nervous."

His face didn't move, and she wasn't sure he was breathing as seconds passed. "When?"

"Right before the Olympics," she said quietly, and he nodded.

"Why didn't you tell me?"

"I didn't tell anyone. I just let it be. I had a medal to win, and I didn't want you guys worrying about me or telling me to wait."

He nodded once more. "That's understandable, I guess, but I would have been there for you."

"I know," she answered softly. "But I had it."

"My prideful, headstrong, bratty-ass little girl," he said fondly, shaking his head. "Okay, fine, but you let that go, you hear me?"

She nodded. "I am trying."

"Try harder," he demanded. "The stress will eat ya alive, and you don't need that."

"I know."

He then let out a long breath. "Was it Jordie's?"

"Yeah," she whispered and she felt him tense up.

"Man, that boy is lucky I love him," Karl muttered and Kacey smiled.

"He's not that person anymore."

"Oh, I know," he agreed. "'Cause if he was, he'd be dead."

Kacey laughed at that as her daddy smiled, holding her closer. He kissed her temple and whispered, "You know you're my favorite, right?"

She scoffed. "Liar."

He grinned. "You are. So is Karson."

She rolled her eyes, giggling until she heard a voice that she did not want to hear say, "Karl? Is that you?"

Her dad turned, taking Kacey with him as Stacey walked toward them with Phil beside her.

"Kacey?" she asked again, and then it must have dawned on her because she laughed. "That's right, she's your daughter."

"That's right," Karl said, squeezing her. "What are you up to?"

"Well, since Phil got glass seats, we got private parking," she said in a snooty way. "What are you doing?"

"Waiting for Jordie."

She scoffed. "That son of mine hates me apparently," she said offhandedly. "But whatever."

Even with the façade she put on, Kacey could tell she was hurting, which surprised her.

"Well, if you treated him a little better, maybe he would like you," Karl supplied and she gave him a dry look.

"You know, I should have never had kids anyway," she said, letting out a long breath. "It's fine. He'll make it."

Kacey bit the inside of her cheek, wanting to scream at her for not wanting to be in his life. For not loving him and doing right by him, but she knew it would be a waste of her breath.

"He will," Karl agreed. "I'll keep an eye on him."

"Good luck with that. He's all kinds of messed up," she laughed. "He's an 'alcoholic,'" she added with air quotes, and something snapped inside of Kacey.

"Yes, he is, and instead of making fun of him, you should be proud because he is fighting it. He has completely changed, become the person he wanted to be with no help from anyone but himself. He is amazing, he is strong, and you are a fucking bitch for not seeing that!"

"Whoa, now," Karl said, but he doubted either of them heard him.

"Listen to me, you little shit, he is worthless and he will hurt you. Mark my words. He doesn't have a loving bone in his body. He may think he does, but he'll shut you out in no time! He does it to everyone."

"No, he did it to you because you are worthless and a horrible person! He loves me and I love him. I am there for him, I am his rock, and you are nothing."

"I think everyone needs to calm down," Phil said, but Stacey threw her hand up, stopping him as she glared at Kacey.

"You nothing about me—"

"And she won't, ever, because you aren't in my life," Jordie said, stepping in front of Kacey. "Goodbye, Stacey," he said sternly as Kacey moved out from behind him to see Stacey's wide eyes.

"Oh, really? It's Mom to you, buddy," she sneered, but he shook his head.

"No, it's nothing because there is nothing else to say to one another. Goodbye," he said once more and then turned, cupping Kacey's shoulders. "Come on, baby, let me get you home."

"Jordie Scott, I am not done talking to you!" she yelled as Jordie directed Kacey to the truck and helped her in.

"Well, I think he's done talking to you," Karl said with a laugh.

Ignoring his mom, Jordie said, "Karl, I'll take you home."

"I can get a ride with Karson."

"He took Benji home," he commented before closing Kacey's door. She tried to roll down the window to hear but the car wasn't started, so she could only watch. Their voices were muffled as Stacey yelled and yelled at Jordie, but he completely ignored her, getting into the truck, with her father getting in at the same time.

"Fuck you, Jordie—" Her words were cut off as he slammed the door shut.

"Fucking bitch," Karl muttered and Jordie shrugged.

"Who? I didn't hear anything," he said simply and Kacey reached over, taking his hand. As he sent her a grin, her heart sang. She had been so worried, but it was obvious.

Jordie was going to be okay.

"You make me so fucking hot when you score," Kacey gasped as Jordie pushed her into the door, his hands sliding down her hips, holding her tightly as his mouth moved along her neck, her breasts. Lifting her shirt up and over her head, he kissed down her ribs, her belly button, as he slid her leggings and panties down her legs.

"Oh baby, you haven't seen anything yet," he muttered against her wanton center, his breath hot against her lips. Arching up, his mouth teased her as he whispered, "I fucking love your pussy."

She almost came undone, but soon his mouth was devouring her. Crying out, she threaded her fingers through his hair as he buried his face between her legs, her knees buckling, her heart coming out of her chest as she hollered out anything that came to mind.

Which was only his name.

Leaning against the door, her eyes shut as she held on to him, her body tightening as he found her clit, sucking it between his teeth, biting softly. Screaming, she thrashed beneath his mouth as he sucked it between his lips and then flicked the tip of his tongue against it so damn fast, her body clenched up and she came undone, her cries of ecstasy causing Gretzky to whimper behind their closed door. She sorta felt bad, but only for a second before Jordie was running his tongue along her dripping wet center.

"Fuck, you sound so good screaming my name," he said against her pussy, kissing it softly before kissing her hips.

If she weren't still reeling from her intense orgasm, she would have swooned at the way he kissed her belly, lingering for a moment before kissing her breasts and lifting her leg. Holding her leg, he directed his cock into her before filling her to the hilt. Letting her head fall back, she closed her eyes tightly, her body squeezing his. His breath was rough against her cheek as he pulled out and then back in, the motion so perfectly amazing that she could feel another orgasm building. His hands bit into her hips as his teeth sank into her neck, his cock so deep inside of her she never wanted him to stop.

He felt so damn good. So right, and as she opened her eyes to find him watching her, his eyes were so full of love and lust, her throat tightened with emotion. This was her man, her everything, and it still felt like a dream. Cupping his face, she leaned her forehead against his as his body slammed into hers, knocking the door into the wall, taking every breath she had.

"I love you," he whispered against her lips as her eyes drifted shut, the feeling of him so overwhelming that her body began to tense up again.

Holding on to him for dear life, she came, her body clenching his so hard, he paused, his hands gripping her side.

"Fuck, I love you so much," he groaned and then he pulled her from the door, bending her over and fucking her hard from behind. Her body hung boneless as he slammed into her, the sound filling the bedroom and probably scaring Gretzky since he was howling from behind the door. But Kacey couldn't worry about him, her boyfriend was pounding her and it was fucking amazing. As he bit into her back, he groaned hard, his body jerking into hers, filling her, as she milked him of everything he had. Pressing his chest to her back, his heart slammed against his chest, hers doing the same in her body as they both caught their breath.

Sitting up, he brought her with him, kissing her jaw as she gasped for breath.

"He shoots, he scores, twice in one night," she teased and he grinned, cupping her face.

"This was my favorite goal," he said, kissing her nose as he pulled out of her. Leaning over, he kissed her jaw again and then smacked her ass. "I think you wore me out."

"I wore you out?" she laughed as he kissed her again before stumbling to the bed.

"Yes, I'm dead tired," he said, falling onto the bed, his white ass in the air for all the world to see.

"Well, get up and go shower. You aren't sleeping in my bed with sex all over you," she said, smacking his ass hard. He hollered out as she giggled, running to the bathroom so he couldn't get her ass. But when he didn't follow her, she popped her head out to see that he was still lying in bed, his eyes closed. "Jordie! Come shower."

"I'm coming," he murmured, but she was pretty sure he wasn't.

Rolling her eyes, she sat down to use the bathroom, her body still vibrating from their lovemaking. He was honestly the best lover she had ever had, and the thought that she would get to sleep with him for the rest of her life made her giddy.

Oh, the hearts that must be breaking, she thought as she giggled before she reached for toilet paper to wipe. Smiling to herself, she hollered out, "Jordie, seriously."

"I'm coming," he moaned again and she smiled.

But just as soon as the grin had come, it was gone as she held the toilet paper up. Something had caught her attention.

That something was bright red blood.

Chapter
TWENTY-SEVEN

Panic.

That's all Kacey felt.

Her stomach dropped. Her chest heaved and vomit rushed up her throat as she wiped again to see more bright red blood.

No. No. Fucking no!

"Jordie!" she yelled, tears spilling over her cheeks as her chest seized and she swallowed hard, not allowing the vomit to surface.

This wasn't real.

This wasn't happening.

There was no way.

No, this baby was supposed to make it!

"Baby, I promise, I'm coming."

"No, Jordie, I need you now!" she yelled, and something in her voice must have told him she wasn't playing because he was in the bathroom within seconds. When he looked at what she was holding, his eyes met hers and she could see the panic in his eyes. It mirrored hers. Silence stretched between them as he looked from the blood to her face then back, unsure of what to do, she figured.

Because she had no clue what to do either.

"I'm bleeding, Jordie," she cried out, sucking in a breath and then letting it out slowly. "I'm not supposed to be bleeding!" She sounded like a two-year-old having the biggest meltdown known to man, but she wasn't thinking clearly.

This wasn't fair.

Sobbing, she looked up at him for help. He had to know what to do, because she was about to lose it. She wanted this child, she wanted it so fucking badly, but she was bleeding it out. Squeezing her thighs together, she let her face fall into her hands, praying that she could keep the baby in.

It had to work.

"Okay," he said as calmly as he could, but she knew it was taking all the will in him to stay calm. "Come on, let's call the doctor. I'm sure it's nothing, just a little hiccup. Come on, baby," he said, urging her to move, but she wouldn't budge.

"No, Jordie, I can't move. I have to keep it in me," she cried, and she felt his exhale of breath. It felt like defeat.

"Okay," he whispered before he lifted her into his arms, holding her legs tightly as he carried her out of the bathroom. "I won't let that happen."

That did her in, and soon she was crying so hard, she couldn't breathe.

"It's going to be fine, let's call the doctor," he tried again, but she wasn't listening. She couldn't. Not even when she heard him on the phone did she believe him. Especially when he said they needed to get to the ER, that her doctor would meet them there. No, all she could do was hold her thighs together tightly.

Praying to God that he'd let her have this baby. That she'd never ask for anything else for the rest of her life.

Just keep my baby alive, she begged as Jordie slowly dressed her. When she watched him put a pad in her panties before sliding them up her thighs, she closed her eyes tightly, unable to understand this. As he slowly cleaned up the blood on her thighs, he was so careful and it only made her cry harder. He was trying so hard, but she could see it in his movements, his eyes, he was barely keeping it together. He was scared, but he couldn't be as scared as she was. This was only his baby, but this was her life. Because she knew he wouldn't stay. If she couldn't have kids, he'd leave. No matter how much he loved her, she truly believed he'd find another reason to leave. He had always wanted kids, and his love for her, his need for her, was new. But a baby, no, that need had always been there.

And she may not be able to give him that.

Kacey cried the whole way to the hospital while Jordie held her close. As he carried her into the ER, she saw that Dr. Richards was waiting for them and directed them back without checking in. Or so she thought. Once Jordie laid her on the table, a nurse came in to get her info and it was beyond hard to talk to her. Jordie did most of the talking while still holding her and telling her that everything was going to be okay. She wanted to believe him, more than she wanted her next breath, but she just didn't feel it. Dr. Richards looked worried, the nurse did too—but Jordie, while he was scared and a little panicked, when his eyes met hers she could see he believed that this baby was okay.

That Kacey was okay.

"Doc, tell me she's okay," Jordie said as Dr. Richards listened to her heart while the nurse brought in an ultrasound machine and some other things. But it all seemed like a blur. She was staring at Jordie, memorizing his face as tears rushed down her cheeks.

"We are going to do a pelvic exam and check for a heartbeat, but I'm hopeful. Let me clean up and I'll get started," he said quickly as Jordie looked down at her. His shoulder fell as he cupped her face, leaning his forehead to hers.

"Baby, it's fine. Please, calm down. Stop crying, you're killing me here," he begged, but her lip still quivered, her heart breaking.

"You'll leave me," she whispered, and his brow furrowed as he watched her.

"What? Why?"

"'Cause I can't have kids."

"Kacey, don't say that," he said quickly, but she shook her head.

"No, if I lose this baby, I doubt I'll be able to keep anything, and you won't stay with me. You love kids, want your own, and I can't fucking give them to you," she cried and he took ahold of her shoulders, shaking her gently.

"Fucking no, Kacey. Stop! You have to stop this. I'm with you for you, not for what you can give me as an extra bonus. Stop. Okay? Just stop."

But her eyes fell shut as she sucked in a deep breath. "I just don't want to lose you."

"You aren't. Stop," he demanded, his voice sharp as she exhaled deeply, feeling like everything was leaving her body. Leaning forward, her face fell into his chest and he wrapped his arms around her, kissing her forehead. "Baby, I love you. I do, so much. Please, just stop thinking like this. You're all I need," he promised and she felt his words vibrating his soul.

But did he mean them?

When Dr. Richards came back into the room, she figured she was about to find out.

"All right, lie back, Kacey," he said and Jordie helped her lie down. "Oh, you still have panties on."

Jordie let her go to take them off as she lay there, staring at the ceiling, begging the good Lord above to let this be a dream. Dr. Richards moved her feet into stirrups as Jordie came back to her head, his cheek against hers as the doctor slowly parted her thighs. She wanted to keep them squeezed together, but she figured it was no use. As much as she wanted to believe that the baby made it, she could still see the bright red of her blood.

A sign that her baby was gone.

When she felt the coldness of the goo on the probe, she closed her eyes tightly as Dr. Richards said, "So what happened? Did it happen out of the blue? Was it after sex?"

"Yeah, we had sex. She went to the bathroom and then found she was bleeding."

"Okay," he said and then he moved the probe in deeper, causing her eyes to close tighter. It didn't hurt, but it sure as hell didn't tickle. As he moved it again, he paused and then tapped her knee. "Kacey, I want you to look at this."

Kacey didn't move at first, but Jordie was there, moving her hair out of her face, wiping her tears as he said, "Baby, look."

He moved out of her way and she rolled her head to the side to look at the screen. She had seen ultrasounds before and knew that on the screen was her baby. But when she saw the little flashing spot, she choked on a sob as Dr. Richards hit a button and the sound of a heartbeat filled the room.

Looking to Dr. Richards, she asked, tears gushing down her face, "My baby?"

He nodded. "Yup, it's fine. Strong heartbeat."

Kacey let out a sob as Jordie cupped her head, kissing the top. "Oh my God," she cried as Jordie held her close.

"Now, let me see what is going on here," the doctor said as he moved the probe around some more, but all she could do was stare into Jordie's eyes.

"Told you," he said triumphantly.

She grinned up at him, exhaling hard as the weight of the world rolled off her shoulders. As she wrapped her arms around his neck, he pressed his lips to her forehead while they waited for the doctor to find out what was making her bleed. It didn't take long though until he hollered out.

"Aha," he said and then lifted his head from between her legs. "Cervical polyps are the cause of your bleeding, and it looks like one of them is infected."

"Will the baby be okay?" she asked, a little frantic.

"Is she going to be okay?" Jordie asked at the same time and the doctor nodded.

"Yes, to both of those questions. We'll run a course of antibiotics and then schedule to have them removed once you've had the baby," he said before standing and tapping her knees. "You, my friend, are going to be fine now that we know what is going on. If it happens again, wait for cramping before you rush in, okay? But I think this little bit is a fighter, and we'll be welcoming him or her at full-term."

Kacey shook as she nodded, her heart still pounding in her chest. "Okay."

"And take it easy, no hanging from the chandelier sex, okay?" he said with a grin and Jordie snapped his fingers.

"Shit, that was the only kind of sex I liked. Now, what will we do?

Missionary?" he teased and that had them both laughing, except for Kacey. She was still trying to recover from losing her shit.

"Take it easy, okay?" Dr. Richards asked and she nodded.

"No problem."

"If it starts to happen a lot, then we'll reevaluate. But let's hope it doesn't."

"Yeah, for sure."

"Okay, good. You'll go back home, okay? Get some rest. Great game tonight, Jordie," the doctor said before sending them a wave and leaving the room. Sitting up, Kacey let out a long breath and then looked at Jordie. He was smiling, but his shoulders were still taut, his eyes still wild with worry.

"Well, that was intense," she said and he nodded.

"Yeah, scared me shitless. Are you okay?"

She nodded, taking his hand in hers before kissing the back of it. "I am. Thank you. You were really there for me."

His lips quirked up as he came to her, kissing her knuckles. "That's my job."

"You were really great though, thank you. That would have been much worse if I didn't have you," she admitted as she laid her head against his chest and his fingers threaded through her hair.

"I learned from the best, you know," he whispered, kissing her forehead. "You're always there for me, Kacey. I couldn't even begin to pay you back for what you do for me."

Her eyes closed as she hugged him tighter. They had such a great system, such a strong love, and she really felt that nothing could come near them. They had been through some shitty shit, and Lord knew it wasn't anywhere near over. She had months of pregnancy left, Jordie still had to get to his one year. And amidst all that, they had to keep their love strong, and Jordie had to bring home the Cup. But they'd take it one day at a time.

And each day she'd fall more in love with him.

Holding his gaze, she cupped his face as her heart exploded with love for him. "Well, good thing we have each other then."

Ten months ago, when she found herself in the ER in Colorado for a miscarriage, she never thought in her entire life that she'd be saying those words ever again.

But she was.

And she couldn't be any happier.

"Now, come on, let's get home," he suggested, helping her sit up even though she didn't need him to. "I'll stop and get you a Snickers and we'll watch that movie of yours."

She grinned. "You want to watch *Notting Hill*?"

He shrugged. "I will if you want to. I guess it's growing on me. I like it when the chick begs for the guy back. I'm taking notes, you know," he said with a wink and she laughed.

"You don't need them," she promised and he laughed.

"Eh, I don't know. I might forget to put the toilet seat down or fall asleep when you're talking or something else, no telling," he teased and she giggled as she got up, feeling more in love with him than ever before.

"I'll still love you, no speech needed."

"I'm gonna hold that one for later," he said with a wink and her heart soared.

Hell, she loved this man.

So damn much it hurt.

"So you think it's a boy?"

Jordie looked over at Karson as they walked down the streets of Chicago, heading toward lunch with some of the guys. Karl was back at the hotel, sleeping since they'd had a late-night flight in. It was the season's Fathers' Trip and Karl was there for both Jordie and Karson. It was nice with him there, especially when he was wearing a shirt with both their names and numbers. Everyone teased him that he looked like a Little League dad, but he didn't care. He was proud of his boys, as he said.

And it really meant a lot to Jordie that Karl was there for him too.

He hadn't spoken to his mother since the parking lot when he found Kacey screaming at her. He was completely okay with that too. She had made a few Facebook posts, but he didn't see them because he deleted her. Karl had though, and after cussing her out good one time, he deleted her too and cut off all contact. Jordie wanted to say he missed her, but he didn't. He was too consumed with Kacey, the pregnancy, hockey, and his road to sobriety.

And everything was going the way he wanted it to.

"I know it is," Jordie said confidently. "According to some of the books I've been reading, if the woman is carrying low, it's a boy, high, a girl, and Kacey's got a little gut at the bottom," he added, his hand moving along the bottom of his stomach. "Hell, even Ma agrees."

Karson laughed. "Ma just wants a boy to balance us out."

"Can't blame her." Jordie grinned, feeling complete. "We find out next week though."

"Gosh, that's going quick," Karson said, tucking his hands into his pockets, and Jordie couldn't agree more. It felt like they were on the fast track to having this baby. It seemed like only yesterday they were in the ER for her bleeding, but everything had been fine since. They did have one other episode, but unlike the first, Kacey was a champ. She only cried a little, while he was sure he was having a panic attack. Now though, she was picking out colors for the nursery, names, and wanting to buy everything she saw. It was great, and he couldn't be happier, but he'd be lying if he said he wasn't nervous. The books said that it was normal for dads to feel nervous, but he felt like it was more.

He was just so scared to let not only Kacey down, but also now his child.

He hadn't had any cravings lately, not that he had time for them. Between hockey, Kacey, and looking at spots for her gym that was close by the house, it had been a little crazy. But he felt great. He had even gone out with the guys to dinner and to the bar, but he didn't drink. He went for the interaction with his friends, and the people at AA were really proud. So was Kacey. She sounded really nervous when he told her though, but when he promised he hadn't drunk, she was elated.

"Is she still wanting to open that gym?"

Jordie nodded. "Yeah, she's driving me crazy with that. I wish she'd just wait. Do it after the baby comes. But she thinks if she does it now, it will be easier. You know how headstrong she is."

Karson scoffed. "Yeah, she's a pain in the ass."

"But we love her," Jordie supplied and Karson shrugged.

"Depends on the week," he said with a wink and Jordie grinned. "But since we are on the subject of loving my sister, you gonna marry her sometime soon?"

Laughing, Jordie shrugged. "We haven't talked about it."

Which was surprising, but he figured since they were both so busy, and neither was going anywhere, why rush getting married? They were already in it for at least eighteen years since they were having a baby together.

"Well, do you want to marry her?"

Jordie rolled his eyes. "Duh, dude."

"Then marry her," he demanded. "Stop pussyfooting around."

Jordie feigned shock, pointing to himself. "Are you calling me a pussy?"

"I am if you don't go into that store right there and buy my sister a ring so you can make an honest woman out of her before my niece or nephew gets here," he said, cocking his head to the Tiffany's across the street.

Jordie raised a brow. "Isn't that the Tiffany's you got Lacey's ring at?"

Karson grinned. "It is, and I think I remember this convo the same as one a little over a year ago, but you were calling me a pussy."

Jordie shot a grin back. "I think you're right."

"I am. So what you going to do?"

Jordie looked back at the Tiffany's that sparkled in the sun and then back at Karson before tucking his hands in his pockets to keep them from the chill. It was colder than he thought it would be in November in Chicago. Glancing back at the store, he smiled.

Really, what was he waiting for?

"All right, let's go," Jordie said, looking both ways before taking off across the street. Karson laughed as he followed him, but once they entered the store, Jordie's heart was in his throat.

She wouldn't say no, would she?

"Welcome! What are we shopping for?"

Jordie clammed up, sweat beading down his back, and Karson must have noticed his mini freak-out because he laughed, shaking him by his shoulders. "An engagement ring."

"Yes, for my girlfriend," Jordie said like a robot, and the saleslady, whose name was Cammie, smiled.

"Nervous?" she asked and he shrugged his shoulders.

"I guess so, don't know why though," Jordie admitted and she smiled.

"It's a huge commitment and our rings aren't cheap. Are you sure?"

He nodded. "Yeah, I'm just worried she'll say no."

"I would," Karson teased as he looked down at the tray of sparkling rings. "But I doubt she will. You did knock her up."

Cammie's smile widened as Jordie nodded. "I did."

"Well, come on then. What's your budget?"

"I don't have one," he said, and it was as if fireworks of dollar signs went off in the depths of her blue eyes.

"Well, this is going to be awesome," she said as she passed by some smaller rings to the bigger ones.

But before she could even bring out a group of rings, he found it.

It was perfect and completely her. She had big hands, rough ones from years of hockey, and he knew they could hold a big diamond. And boy, was this one huge. Just a single diamond solitaire, with the band made out of little diamonds. It was so sparkly and girlie, two things Kacey was not, but he knew she'd love it. "That one."

Karson looked over as Cammie's eyes met the ring he was pointing to. He could see her hesitation and figured the ring must not be that expensive. But when she got it out and handed it to Jordie, even though the price tag was higher than Jordie thought he'd spend, he knew he was right. This was the ring.

"She'll love it," Karson said, looking over Jordie's arm. "It's so girlie, she'll have to love it."

Jordie chuckled. "That's exactly what I thought."

Slapping him on the shoulder, Karson said, "Well, you got the ring. Now, ya gotta figure out how you're gonna propose. And, believe me, dude, these chicks nowadays want a production. Pinterest, dude, get on Pinterest. That's what Lacey tells me all the time. I can't figure out how to use it though."

Jordie scoffed as he shrugged. He may have to think of how he was going to ask her, but first, he had to ask her daddy.

OVERTIME

And pray that Karl trusted him enough to love his daughter for the rest of his life.

After a hard-fought game where the Assassins came out on top by one lucky goal by Baylor Moore, Jordie felt on top of the world as he walked with the rest of the team and the dads to the restaurant they'd be eating at. Usually, they did dinner the next night, but since the game was early and they had won, they wanted to do it that night. As he walked with Karl and Karson, the ring he had bought Kacey only hours ago weighed a ton in his pocket.

If he was this nervous just to ask Karl, how was he going to ask Kacey?

He knew it was because they both could say no. He still wasn't a hundred percent. He had a lot of growing left to do, and maybe he should wait. But then, what for? He could die at any time, and he refused to die without Kacey having his last name. He loved her and knew she loved him; he just had to make it official. When his phone went off in his pocket, he pulled it out to see that it was a text from Kacey.

> *Kacey: I like the name Mordecai.*
> *He gagged before shaking his head.*
> *Jordie: How about hell no.*
> *Kacey:* ☺ *It's cute.*
> *Jordie: It's demonic.*
> *Kacey: lol.*
> *Kacey: How about Kale?*
> *Jordie: He isn't lettuce, no.*
> *Kacey: It could be a she, and if so, I'm thinking Kelsey or Kammie.*
> *Jordie: It's a boy and how about we stop with the K names?*
> *Kacey: Then it's Mordecai.*
> *Jordie: No way. I love you though, and I'll call you once we get back to the hotel.*
> *Kacey: Love you and have fun!*

He smiled as he tucked his phone back in his pocket as Karson looked over at him. "She thinks we are naming the baby Mordecai."

Karson made a face. "Mena and Mordecai? Is she insane?"

"It's a girl, guys," Karl said then and grinned as they both looked over at him, shocked. "I just know it."

"No, it's a boy," Jordie insisted, but Karl was shaking his head.

326

"Sorry, buddy. It's a girl, better start picking girl names."

Karson chuckled. "He was right about Mena."

"I don't care. I know what my woman is having," Jordie said, feigning annoyance, which had everyone laughing.

"That woman is my daughter, and you are wrong, it's a girl."

Jordie scoffed. "Sorry, old man, it's a boy."

"I got a hundred bucks it's a girl," Karl said, holding out his hand.

Jordie didn't even hesitate, taking his hand, and squeezing it. "It's a boy."

"You'll see," Karl said, chuckling as he leaned back in his chair just as dinner started. The Assassins' father-son dinners were always full of laughs. Most of the dads had played in the league before and the old stories were comical and touching. These men were their future, and soon Jordie would be at his son's father-son dinner telling him stories of his glory days.

When Karl excused himself, Jordie threw his napkin down and Karson scoffed. "You're gonna ask him in the pisser?"

"Fuck off," he said, rushing to catch Karl. When he reached for him right as he got to the bathroom, he said, "Hey, I wanted to talk to you."

Karl eyed him speciously. "For what?"

"Just need to."

He shook his head. "Fine, give me a second to drain my snake," he said, turning to go back in, but then he paused, laughing as he turned. "What? Are you going to ask me to marry Kacey?"

Jordie could only blink at him as Karl's laughter died down. He held his gaze and then crossed his arms as Jordie said, "Yeah, I had a speech and everything, actually."

Holding his gaze, he nodded. "Fine. On with it."

"You don't want to piss first?"

"No," he said sternly, sending chills down Jordie's spine.

"Um, fine, well," Jordie stumbled and then shook his head, deciding to go with his heart. "I love Kacey, you know this, and I want nothing more than to marry her and spend the rest of my life with her," he said slowly, his heart pounding in his chest. "I'm not perfect, I have issues, and sometimes, that's hard to deal with. But she makes me a better person. She loves my issues away and she cares. I can promise you, I'll never hurt her. I'll only love her and take care of her the way you'd want me to. The way she deserves."

Karl held his gaze for a long time and then nodded. "Okay."

"Okay?"

"Yeah, you don't drive a Prius, so you're already a better choice than that one idiot."

Jordie laughed as Karl grinned. "What, you thought I was gonna say no?"

Jordie shrugged and he nodded, holding his gaze. "Yeah, I don't deserve her!"

"Well, no shit, but you got her and she loves you. And I love you, son. You're great for her and you've done really fucking good with your life. I think you two will be very happy for the rest of your life."

With his throat thick with emotion, he slowly nodded. "You think?"

"I know," he answered, reaching out to cup Jordie's shoulder. "Don't doubt yourself, Jordie. You have really done great things with your life and I, for one, am very proud of you and would be honored to have you as my son-in-law."

Swallowing hard, he smiled, holding his hand out. "Thank you."

Karl pushed it away and then pulled him in for a tight, backslapping hug. "I'm very proud of you, son."

"Thanks, Da—Karl."

Pulling back, Karl gripped his shoulders. "Well, as long as she says yes, I'll be your dad and I'll expect you to own up to that."

Jordie smiled shyly. "I already do."

Wrapping his arm around his shoulders, he squeezed him. "Well, then you're halfway there, just need her to agree to it."

"No pressure, right?"

Karl chuckled. "None at all," he added with a wink. "She could say no and reject you, which would leave you broken and trying to take care of a new baby, and then you might start drinking, and shit would be bad. But no, no pressure," he teased and Jordie smiled.

"Man, you're the best dad in the world," he said sarcastically but laughing since, of course, he had thought all that crazy already. He knew it could happen, but he wouldn't start drinking again. He was done with that. He was more than an alcoholic; he was a good man. One who was gonna marry Kacey and have a family for once.

"I have a mug, you know," Karl informed him. "Kacey gave it to me, and I'll make sure you get one too once my new granddaughter is born," he said with a wink.

Jordie laughed, thinking that nothing could get better than this. He had his family, he had his woman, and he was about to have a baby. Life was good. No, great.

But glancing back at his soon-to-be dad, he laughed, "I can't wait. Make sure it's blue for my son."

Chapter
TWENTY-EIGHT

"**S**o apparently, I can't go without my medicine yet."

Oh God, Kacey thought as she drove down I-24 to get to Radnor State Park for her couples' shoot with Jordie. He was meeting her since he had therapy today while she checked out a few places for her gym. Still no luck though, but her issues with that would need to wait. Lacey was having a crisis.

"Do I even want to know why you have come to this assumption?"

Lacey exhaled a long breath over the phone. "I stopped taking it like a week ago and things were fine. But then I woke up in a cold sweat last night and rushed to Mena's room, tearing off her sleeper and checking her for breast cancer. It was insane, and Karson is trying to help, but I'm just screaming at him, Mena is screaming and, ugh, it was horrible."

Kacey's heart broke for her. "Oh, Lacey."

"Oh, I know," she said softly. "I took my meds today and I apologized to Karson this morning, and Mena, though I don't she understands, but yeah," she said, and Kacey could hear the tears in her voice. "I just feel weak, almost, and pathetic. I have to stop this."

"You do. Have you thought about going to therapy? Maybe the ABC group isn't enough?"

"Yeah, we talked about it this morning. I called Jordie too and he gave me his chick."

"Julie is wonderful," Kacey informed her. "I think you'd like her."

"I'm gonna call her. I just wish I weren't so fucked in the head."

"You had a pretty traumatic thing happen at such a young age with no help, Lacey. Unlike other people, you know there is a problem and you're gonna get help."

"Thanks," she said softly. "Do you think I'm crazy?"

"Just a bit, but I still love you," she teased and Lacey laughed.

"Sure you do," Lacey teased back, her laughter coming from deep within and that made Kacey happy. She didn't like Lacey all messed up, it scared her. "How are you feeling?"

"Good," she beamed. "I'm actually heading to Jordie and my couples' shoot at the park. Maybe I should have waited till I was big. I just look fat."

"Fat is the last thing I'd say about you, but I think it's sweet you're doing it now. You need pictures for the house, for sure. Do it again when you're big."

Kacey shrugged. "I guess, I mean I'm in it to win it at this point. I'm wearing cute clothes, and my hair is on point, along with my makeup. Thanks for suggesting Michelle, she was amazing."

And she was. Kacey's hair was in beautiful curls, framing her face in a sweet, country girl way. Along with light makeup that brought out the brown in her eyes, she looked flawless. With black leggings, a long beige sweater, and brown riding boots, Kacey was sure she could pass as if she had grown up in the South her whole life.

"Jordie better have put on that sport coat. He thought it was dumb when he was here," Lacey laughed and Kacey glared, even though no one could see her.

"I'll skin him if he didn't," she warned and Lacey laughed harder as Kacey parked. She knew he didn't like the brown tweed jacket she had picked out, but it went with her outfit perfectly. They were going to be adorable.

"Well, don't get your hopes up. He said he's gonna wear something else."

"Oh, I should have known when he said he'd meet me here he was going to mess this up. I swear he does it because he loves seeing me angry."

Lacey giggled. "Probably."

Getting out of the car, she locked it as she started for the spot under a maple tree that Harper had instructed. She didn't see Jordie's truck, but then she wasn't looking. She was a tad bit late and needed to hurry, but as she turned to go around the car, she stopped dead in her tracks.

"Let me call you back."

"What's wrong? Why are you talking like that?"

"I just ran into Liam. Bye," she said and then hung up before putting a big smile on her face. He was sweating, and as she took in the shorts and sweatshirt, she figured he had been running. "Hey, out for a run?"

She didn't know how she'd forgotten that he loved to run out here, but then, she really didn't think of Liam much. They hadn't spoken in months, but yet, he smiled, his perfect jawline moving as he slowly nodded.

"Yeah, funny seeing you here."

She smiled. "I'm meeting Jordie here for a couple pictures for our house," she said, and she didn't miss his grimace. But she wouldn't act as if she weren't with Jordie. She was too happy to do that.

"Yeah, he posts about you all the time. I see that he tags you in everything," he said and Kacey nodded as a grin pulled at her lips.

"Yes, my boyfriend is a Facebook whore now. It's kind of embarrassing."

He shrugged. "I think it's great. I'm happy that it's working out for you two."

"Thanks," she said, shocked. The way things had ended, she would have been sure he was five seconds from getting a voodoo doll and practicing on her.

"So you two aren't married yet?"

Her hands came up to her belly as she smiled. "Not yet, but we are expecting."

He grinned as he looked down, her little belly between her two hands. "You look beautiful, Kacey. I'm really happy for you."

"Thank you. And you?"

"I got engaged three weeks ago," he said with a grin and she scoffed.

"Well, I guess both of us weren't really in it, huh?"

He shrugged. "I guess not, but I am sorry for how it all ended. That was rude of me, what I said. I was just mad."

"It's cool. I forgave you a long time ago," she said, reaching out to cup his elbow. "I'm just glad you are happy."

"Me too, for you too," he said and she grinned up at him.

"Okay, well, it was great seeing you. I won't wish you luck tomorrow at the game 'cause I want you to lose," she said with a wink, sidestepping out of his way. "But I gotta go do these pictures."

He laughed as he waved to her. "It was great seeing you. Good luck."

She smiled as thanks before heading toward where she was supposed to meet them. That was actually okay. She had thought it would be awkward, but she was glad that she could see Liam and have it be cool. Rushing toward the spot, she saw Harper first, her hair purple this time and shaved up the side as she took various pictures. What surprised her was that Elli was there, a camera around her neck, both of them taking pictures of Jordie as he stood like a model. While he was wearing the brown tweed jacket, he was not wearing anything else she had bought for him. Instead of the nice shirt with a tie and brown slacks, he was wearing a blue button-up shirt with no tie and the first few buttons open. His black slacks complemented his brown dress shoes, but still. It wasn't what she had picked out. Even if he did look downright sinful, he still drove her insane.

When he tucked a hand into his pocket, looking at the camera, the fingers of his other hand resting lightly on the rim of his sunglasses, she couldn't help it, she snorted with laughter.

She caught his attention and he grinned as he came toward her. Elli and Harper turned and smiled too as he took her in his arms, dipping her back and kissing her hard against the lips. Cupping her ass, his lips moved along hers as he righted them. The smell of coconuts intoxicated her and made her dizzy as he pulled away, grinning down at her.

"Man, I love your hair like this," he said, drinking her in as he cupped her face. "You look gorgeous."

She grinned back as she wrapped her arms loosely around his neck. "Well, thank you, and so do you. Yet, this isn't the outfit I picked out," she reminded him and he smiled sheepishly.

"This is true, but my ass looks better in these pants," he countered and she glared. He was right, but still.

"Jordie, we are supermatchy now except you have a blue shirt and I have beige."

"Doesn't that mean we are super in love?" he asked and she rolled her eyes.

"No, it means we are trying too hard."

His brows rose before he shook his head. "No, it means we are in love," he said, nuzzling his nose against hers. "Why are you late?"

She smiled sheepishly. "Well, first, traffic. Second, guess who I ran into?"

"Doucheface?"

She rolled her eyes. "If you mean Liam, yes."

"Yes, doucheface. Mountain of dicks…I could go on," he supplied as she glared.

"No need, he got engaged."

Jordie laughed. "What a loser," he said, shaking his head. "Couldn't get you to marry him, so he settles for the first thing he sees?"

"They could be in love."

"And I could love wearing tutus and dancing around like an idiot."

She paused. "You do like doing that. I have pictures from last week with Shelli and Posey. Your hair was in pigtails, and you had flowers in your beard."

He glared. "I told you, we don't speak of that."

"Oh, my bad," she laughed and he glared some more.

"Now, hush and let's do this."

Still laughing, she took his hand, lacing her fingers with his as he dragged her toward where Elli and Harper were clicking away. "Oh, you brought your guitar?" she asked when she saw it leaning against the tree.

"Yeah, I wanted to do some shots playing and stuff since it has been such a huge part of my recovery. I brought hockey sticks too, but then Elli was saying we should go to the rink and do some pictures too," he suggested and she smiled.

"Mr. Prop Man," she teased, kissing his nose. "But that is a great idea. With our skates on, it would be adorable. Where were you when we were deciding this?" she asked Elli with a grin.

Elli smiled as she shrugged, her camera in her hand as she looked at them sweetly. "No one asked me till yesterday, but I'm excited to be here. I miss taking pictures."

Elli had run a photography business for a very long time before becoming the owner of the Assassins and selling her business to Harper, her best friend. She still did some work, but mostly on her kids. She was very talented and Kacey was excited she was there, but she didn't understand why Harper was too. They didn't need two photographers.

"Cool, I was telling Lacey on the phone, maybe we should have waited though, since we'll probably take pregnancy pictures when I'm big," she said, more to Jordie than Elli and Harper.

"But this will be good for just you two, plus you don't even look pregnant, so no one will know," Harper said, pushing her hair out of her face. The wind was blowing, a chill in the air, but Kacey was still stuck on the idea of not looking pregnant. She thought she was huge.

"I don't?" she asked, looking down at her little protruding stomach. "I thought I was."

"Oh, to me you just look a little pudgy."

"Pudgy?" Kacey asked and then she looked up at Jordie, who was shaking his head.

"Thank you, now she's going to think she's pudgy," he said and Harper smiled.

"Listen, I'd take pudgy over fat and pregnant any time of the day," Harper said and Elli nodded.

"I was huge, all the damn time," Elli complained, shaking her head. "You look adorable, so let's do this. I want to go to the rink and finish off there."

Kacey really didn't feel like taking pictures since she looked "pudgy." But soon, Jordie was pulling her along, grinning at her as Elli and Harper directed them, catching them in sweet little moments. It was so natural for them, and they didn't need too much direction. Their love was just so inescapable and rolled off them in waves. Add in the fact that the scenery was gorgeous: the rolling hills of Tennessee, the picturesque view of the lake, and the beautiful colors of the orange and red leaves on the trees, and she knew the pictures were gonna be amazing. Especially the ones with her hunk of sexy, man-meat boyfriend in them. When he picked her up, like a prince carrying a princess, she beamed up at him as he looked at the camera, ever the model. She giggled as he put her on her feet, dipping her back and kissing her deeply.

Man, she loved him.

"Gosh, y'all are adorable!" Elli cheered as she hopped on her toes.

Harper nodded as she looked through her viewfinder on her camera. "Y'all are. I'm getting some great shots."

"Great," Jordie said, his arms around Kacey's waist, his head resting on her shoulder.

Elli snapped a picture and grinned. "Why don't we do some with the guitar, Jordie?"

He nodded as he let her go to get it and Kacey grinned. "Are these only of you and her, or can I join in?" she asked, speaking of his guitar.

He shot her a look as he put the strap over his head and ran his fingers along the strings. "Hush, you," he said and then he started playing, like really playing.

"What are you doing?"

"Shh," he said again and she smiled, confused. She loved watching him play, but weren't they supposed to be taking pictures? She understood authenticity, but really? It was getting cold out there. But then he started singing, his eyes locked on hers, and she froze.

What was he up to?

As he sang, "God Gave Me You" by Blake Shelton, her heart started to speed up in her chest. It was a beautiful song, and the way he sang it made her feel like it was written for her. And she loved it, she did. But why was he doing this in front of an audience? She couldn't cry in front of them!

Looking back at Elli and Harper, she found that they were taking pictures, big grins on their faces as Jordie came toe-to-toe with her, the music vibrating her soul while he sang with all the gusto of Blake Shelton himself. When a single tear rolled down her face—because, really, how could she not cry when he was playing, obviously for her—he smiled, playing the last note with a little flair, like he always did. She loved that, but when he pushed the guitar back behind him and reached in his pocket, her heart jumped up into her throat.

"Jordie?"

He just grinned as he dropped to one knee, holding the little Tiffany's blue box in his hand as he looked up at her. "As the song said, Kacey, God gave me you to make me better, to help me love life, and to be a better person not only for Him, but for you. I do all these things because of you, because of all the love and support you give me. I have wanted to marry you since the moment I saw you, but I was too scared to think that I could have the happily ever after everyone talked about. I thought it wasn't in my cards, I thought that it was unattainable, but you proved me wrong. You give me that happily ever after every day. And there isn't a day that passes that I don't fall even more in love with you," he said, his voice breaking with the last word. Her lip started to wobble as her vision blurred from the tears in her eyes. They hadn't even spoken of marriage or anything—she'd just assumed they'd do it sooner or later. But apparently sooner was here because Jordie slowly opened the box, his eyes on hers as he whispered, "You are my best friend, my lover, my heart and soul. I couldn't live the life I wanted without you, and it would be my honor if you'd marry me." He sucked in a deep breath as the tears rushed down her face, probably ruining her makeup, but she didn't care. Her eyes were set on this gorgeous man who was slowly opening the box, his eyes still on hers and his heart in his eyes. She didn't even see the ring, all she saw was him as he asked, "So Kacey Marie King, will you do me a favor and help me write my happily ever after by being my wife?"

Her lip started to wobble, and out of the corner of her eye, something caught her attention. When she glanced over, she saw that Lacey, Karson, Mena, her mom, and dad were standing there. Of course, her mom and Lacey were crying as they waited for her answer. Looking back down at Jordie, her heart was in her throat and she was rendered speechless. She had pictured the moment when Jordie would propose, and she had honestly thought he would throw the ring at her and tell her, "Let's do this." It was his style, but that was old Jordie. New Jordie wanted her to know how much she meant to him. He made sure her family was there, that there were photographers to document the moment they'd tell their little one about when it was older, but most of all, he spoke from his heart.

His big, beautiful heart.

"Yes, Jordie. God, yes," she said finally, and he exhaled the breath he was holding before she wrapped her arms around him, kissing him hard as the tears rolled down her face. Hugging her tightly, he stood up and kissed her over and over again, her heart flying as he leaned his head against hers.

"I'm gonna make you the happiest woman ever. I'm gonna take your breath away daily and make you smile. But I'll probably fuck up every once in the while—"

"And I'll still love you," she whispered, her lips moving against his. "I'll always love you."

He sucked in a breath, letting it out again before kissing her nose. Leaning back, he took the ring out of the box and slid it down her ring finger. It was a little loose, but she couldn't get over how big and sparkly it was. It was perfect. He was perfect.

Cupping his face, she beamed up at him as she bounced on her toes. "Thank you."

He scoffed. "Please, I should be thanking you," he said roughly, his voice breaking with emotion. "I wouldn't be where I am right now if it weren't for your support. This ring, this love I give you, will never be enough. You deserve the world."

Leaning her head to his, she looked deep into his eyes as she moved her nose along his. "And you give it to me, Jordie. Every day."

Smirking at her, he held her gaze and said, "And to think it's only the beginning."

"I don't ever want it to end," she whispered and his grip on her tightened.

"It never will," he promised, and as everyone surrounded them, congratulating them and hugging them, she couldn't stop staring at him.

Her evermore.

It was a girl.

A sweet, perfect little girl that from the 4-D ultrasound appeared as if she may look like Jordie. One thing was sure, she had some hockey shoulders. The tech said it looked like she had hair, which he knew would be dark like theirs. Jordie had hoped that it was a boy, but knowing that it was a girl, something inside him just felt right. As he watched the different angles of his child, he silently promised to love her more than life itself. To be there, to protect her, and to support her, no matter what.

Just like he did Kacey.

Ever since he proposed, things had been absolutely perfect. They had already fallen into an easy routine, but now, it just felt better, more complete. She was so happy, floating around as baby books and wedding magazines found new places in their home. The pictures from the shoot they had were already blown up and on the wall. His favorite being the one of him on one knee asking for her hand, her hands covering her mouth as the tears rushed down her beautiful face with her family behind them, all smiling, all so happy for them.

It was a striking moment, but seeing his baby was something he would never forget. If he was this in love with her now, Lord help the world when she got here.

Daddy's little girl.

Kacey beamed up at him and he grinned down at her, but then he realized what this meant.

"Damn it!"

Kacey looked over at Jordie in shock, her brow furrowing as she glared. "What the hell! She's healthy. That's what we wanted. You should be happy," she complained as the ultrasound tech eyed him cautiously.

Realizing what it sounded like, he held his hands up. "No, wait, okay, sorry! I didn't mean it like that. I'm so happy, Kacey, I promise. But I owe your dad a hundred bucks now," he complained and still she glared.

"Really? You bet my father on the sex of our child?"

He shrugged. "What? I thought it was a boy."

"I told you it was a girl!" she said and he smiled.

"And I couldn't be happier," he said softly, kissing her temple. "My two girls that hold my heart."

She rolled her eyes as a grin pulled at her lips, both their gazes going back to the screen where their daughter moved around in Kacey's growing belly. He'd never thought he could love her more. But watching each day as her body changed, her belly getting bigger, and knowing that she was carrying his child, the admiration, the love, was overwhelming. She was blowing his mind daily, and when he'd felt the baby move a few days before, he'd had to hold in his tears as Kacey grinned at him.

If this was just the start of his happily ever after, he was convinced he would die of bliss.

Pure, unadulterated bliss.

"Kaleigh?"

"With a K?" Jordie asked as they walked, their hands threaded together, into their favorite Mexican restaurant. He had noticed that she was craving guacamole like mad. Thankfully, he loved the stuff and didn't mind. He did mind though when she wanted to mix the cheese sauce, salsa, and guacamole together and stuff it down her throat. That was crossing the line, but she didn't care and it made her happy. So he went with it—after making sure he had his own bowl of his favorite dips for his chips.

"Of course," she said happily as they went to the table. "Or maybe Kassandra, Kassidy, Kristen? Kate? Krissy?"

He rolled his eyes as he lowered himself into the booth and glanced over at her. "You're killing me. Why don't we do a different name?"

"Like what?" she asked, getting a huge pile of salsa on her chip before devouring it.

Leaning back in the booth, he thought for a moment. "I don't know? I've always liked the name Delilah," he suggested and her nose wrinkled.

"Delilah?"

He shrugged. "Yeah."

"Why?"

"I don't know. I really like that song, 'Hey There Delilah,'" he started to sing, but she rolled her eyes.

"And we are moving on," she said impatiently. "How about Kara?"

"Kacey, no, I don't want a K name!" he laughed and she glared.

"But it's tradition in my family."

"Um, no, Mena Jane is not a K name."

She glared. "Fine, give me something then?"

He thought for a moment, "Billie Jean?"

"No."

"Roxanne?"

"I'm going to hit you."

"Diana?"

"We are not Michael Jackson, for one. And for two, if you can't come up with something other than song names, then I'm picking the name!" she scolded him and he smiled.

"Fine, give me a second," he said before the waitress came to get their order. Once he gave her his order, he went to a baby name site and looked through it. "Okay, how about Charlotte?"

"No way, that's old ladyish," she said, still stuffing her face, this time with guacamole.

"Okay, how about Alana?"

"No."

"Aurora?"

"How about Belle?" she countered and he glared.

"Brat."

"Dork."

He smiled as he scrolled through the names. "Oh, I like Ella," he said hopefully, and when she didn't shoot him down, he smiled. "Ella Mae Thomas."

"Mae?"

"After your mom," he suggested and she smiled.

"Maybe," she answered, typing something in her phone. "I've got it on the possible list. Give me some more."

Dropping his phone to the table, he smiled. "This is fun."

She beamed. "It is, but just wait. After dinner, we are going shopping."

Letting his head fall back in a dramatic fashion, he groaned loudly. "I don't want to!"

She kicked him under the table, grinning as he laughed, picking his phone back up. Scrolling again, he said, "Hazel?"

"Hell no," she shot down with a full mouth, and he scoffed as he scrolled some more. "So, I think I found a place for the gym."

He looked up, his phone falling to the table. Before he could say anything though, he noticed that she had guacamole all over her chin. Chuckling, he reached over, wiping her chin before she smiled sheepishly and he asked, "Where at?"

"Actually down the road from Audrey Jane's," she said and Jordie smiled.

"What, stalk the place for overweight people?"

She gave him an annoyed look. "I was actually thinking that maybe I could do a thing—buy five classes, get a cupcake."

"Doesn't that counteract your mission?"

"No, everyone has to cheat sometimes or they'll binge. Plus, Audrey has a couple healthy...okay, *one* healthy cupcake."

"No one wants a cupcake that's healthy."

"Well, duh, but they could go and try."

Jordie laughed. "Yeah, okay. When can we go look at it?"

"Tomorrow, if you're not busy."

"I'm never busy for you," he said with a wink before looking down at his phone. "How about Raleigh?"

"I like Kaleigh more," she said and he rolled his eyes as he kept scrolling. As he said every girl name he liked and she shot it down, he decided he might as well accept that this was going to be hell.

"Are you excited it's a girl?"

He looked up, grinning. "I'm just excited that she is healthy, that I am marrying you, and that we are happy."

She shot him a grin as she leaned on her hand. "When are we getting married?"

He shrugged. "Whenever you want. Do you want a big wedding or a small?"

She thought for a moment. "Well, I've been watching *Say Yes to the Dress* a lot, and I think I want to do the whole big wedding production thing."

His mouth pulled up at the side. "I think you spent too much time trying to act like a boy and now you are making up for it."

She shrugged, her eyes falling to the ring he had given her. It fit her large, beautiful hands perfectly now and shined, even in the dim restaurant. "Probably, but I want my dad to give me away and all that sweet shit."

"Sounds good to me. Just set a day, and I'll show up."

"Probably not in what I pick out for you," she scolded and he nodded.

"Probably not," he agreed before he paused. "How about Avery Mae?"

She tested the name a few times and shrugged. "I don't like Mae with that, but I like Avery."

"Cool," he said as she typed it out on her phone. As he looked for another name, his phone signaled a text, and he was surprised when it was from Natasha. He hadn't heard from her in months and not for lack of trying. He had sent her a few texts, checking in, but she was always very short with him, one-word answers or sometimes not even answering him. Clicking on the text, he felt Kacey looking at him as he read it.

Natasha: I'm in town.

Licking his lips free of dip, he typed back quickly.

Jordie: Cool, what for?
Natasha: Medical conference at Vanderbilt.
Jordie: Cool. I haven't heard from you lately.

"Who's that?" Kacey asked and he smiled.
"Just a friend," he answered. "Just a second, babe."

Natasha: Yeah, been busy, but I want to see you.
Jordie: Well, I'll have to see when I can. Season's in full swing and I have a lot going on.
Natasha: What you mean is that your girlfriend won't let you out of her sight.

He rolled his eyes.

Jordie: You mean my fiancée? And she would, she's not crazy.
Natasha: She looks it and sounds like a bitch.

His brows came together in confusion, as Kacey asked, "What's wrong?"

He didn't answer her, looking around, and then spotting Natasha rising from behind a booth across the restaurant. She looked beautiful of course, but that was Natasha. She was a hot chick, just not the chick he wanted. Brushing her dark hair off her shoulders, she was wearing a killer black dress that showed every curve of her body and a whole lot of leg, strappy heels completing the outfit in a way that would have had him in knots before. But now, he felt nothing.

She was a friend.

"Who's that?" Kacey asked, smacking his arm as Natasha made her way to their table. Natasha's eyes locked on his, mischief and anger in the depths of her brown eyes as she strutted toward him. Something in her eyes though told him that this wasn't going to be good, and when she opened her mouth, his assumption was correct.

"I'm the chick he was fucking to forget you."

Well. Fuck.

Chapter
TWENTY-NINE

"**E**xcuse me?"

Kacey's eyes widened as she cut a look at Jordie, heat creeping up her throat.

"Oh, did you not hear me?" the gorgeous chick, who had obviously just stepped out of a magazine and into her favorite Mexican restaurant, said, her eyes dark and malicious. "I said that I'm the chick he was fucking when he was trying to forget you." She said it like Kacey was dumb or didn't understand, but she fully understood. She just didn't understand why she was coming to their table with that.

"I mean, there is no need for that. Natasha, what's your problem?" Jordie said as he set his phone down, his brows furrowed.

Kacey tore her gaze from his and back to Natasha's, since she was staring at her almost as if she were sizing her up. "I heard you good and well. But why would I care?"

Natasha laughed, and even her laugh was a soft, raspy sound that one would hear in a porno. "Because he loves me."

Kacey's eyes widened more as she whipped her gaze to him, but he scoffed. "No, I don't, and I told you that plenty of times."

"So you know her?" Kacey demanded and he shrugged.

"Yeah, I hooked up with her in New Orleans," he said simply, and she swore her blood pressure rose even more.

"Remember, when you were texting him every five seconds, begging him to be with you?"

Kacey's head whipped back to Natasha, her eyes narrowing. "I never begged, and you don't know me or my relationship with him. You were just a night of fucking."

"Oh, it was more than a night, and we've kept in touch ever since. So obviously I meant something to him if I was going to rehab to visit him."

Kacey swore her eyes couldn't widen any more. Looking across the table at a gaping Jordie, she glared. "What!" she roared, and Jordie shook his head.

"You are my friend, Natasha, or were. Because the way you are acting is not okay. I don't love you. I never have, or will."

"She went to rehab to see you?" Kacey asked incredulously.

"Oh yeah, girl. All those nights he needed someone to talk to, he called me and we'd talk for hours. I know everything about you two's relationship and his alcoholism. And I helped him through that while you had no clue about anything."

Kacey's heart was pounding in her chest because, surely, this wasn't happening. Jordie couldn't reach out to her, but he could to the porn star who was standing in front of their table.

"He does love me. He's just fighting his feelings, not realizing how good we are together and how he's breaking my heart not wanting to be with me," Natasha said then, her eyes falling on Jordie. "I know I haven't been in contact, but it just hurts. You really mean something to me."

Kacey was sure she was having a panic attack as her heart jumped up and down in her throat, her belly turning. He trusted this person he didn't even know—someone who started out as just a fuck—over her?

"I never meant to hurt you, and I've told you that many times. We are friends, Natasha. Stop trying to start shit."

Unbelievable.

She meant something to him.

Kacey could see it in his eyes. He might not love her, but he cared about her, and that bothered her more. Why was she special enough to get that piece of him Kacey wanted so desperately, to help, to be there for him? And why hadn't he said anything about her?

"You love me!" she yelled like a crazy-faced bitch and Kacey couldn't take it anymore.

"Natasha," Jordie said calmly, his hands coming up. "Calm down. You know that's not true. I told you that a long time ago."

"No, I know you do. You don't share things like what you told me. You don't tell me how it hurts to not drink, how you missed having sex with me, and then you come here, get back with her, and then drop me like a bad habit."

Jordie was shaking his head. "I was fucked up back then. I'm not that guy anymore, you know that."

"Sure, but I helped you. I was there for you when she wasn't," she said, pointing at Kacey. "Who talked you through her losing her shit on you because she lost your baby so long ago? Not her, but me!"

Oh. Oh wow, Kacey thought as she slowly scooted out of the booth.

"Because you are my friend, Natasha!" Jordie yelled, his temper getting the best of him, but he must have noticed Kacey moving because he reached out, taking her arm. "What are you doing?"

"Oh, leaving, so you and your friend can catch up," she sneered, but he wouldn't let her go.

"No, she's leaving," he said, looking back up at Natasha. "Go, you're doing nothing but causing issues."

"Oh, what, I'm going to make your precious Kacey cry? If she meant an ounce to you, you wouldn't have tried to forget her every second you got."

Kacey hadn't even realized that she was on the verge of tears until Natasha said that.

"That's not true, and you know it. Stop this. Kacey, stay here," he demanded, but she shook her head before ripping her arm from him.

"Don't push me away now that I'm telling the truth."

"You aren't. You're trying to cause problems because you don't like not getting what you want. You aren't going to get me, Natasha. Just stop."

"You never told me to stop before."

"Because I, for one, was a fucked-up mess, and, two, I wasn't with Kacey."

"Yes, key words 'not with her.' And you were good then," she said and Kacey wasn't sure if Natasha was trying to convince herself or Jordie, but she was pretty sure that was a damn lie.

"Are you serious? I had one foot in the grave with a bottle in my hand, and I must have been pretty fucked up to have dealt with you for as long as I did. Because now that I am stone-cold sober, you are fucking annoying."

Oh, there went his temper.

"I can't even believe I'm wasting my time on you," she sneered as Kacey stood, fixing her shirt over her belly until Natasha started laughing. "Oh my God, you knocked her up?" she laughed. "Really, Jordie? What, you are going to be a husband and a daddy now? Do you really think you are ready for that?"

"Um, yeah," Jordie snapped. "This is what I've always wanted."

"Well, you're doing it with the wrong person, that's for damn sure. Because if she's the one who drove you to drinking before, don't you think she'd do it again?"

Kacey didn't know what came over her. All she saw was rage, her heart pounding, her blood boiling as her arm just pulled back and her fist connected with the hard surface of Natasha's nose. Underneath her knuckles, she could

343

feel bones crack, but then she swore everything went black because surely she didn't just hit Jordie's ex-lover.

"Holy shit," Jordie yelled before hopping up and blocking Kacey as Natasha tried to go after her.

"You stupid bitch, you broke my nose!"

"Damn right, I did! I would never do that to him, you stupid slut. Because, unlike you, I mean more than just a fuck. I'm a lifetime kind of chick, the one he is going to love forever, while he didn't even mention you!" Kacey screamed as the waitress and two other waiters came over to see the commotion.

"*Señor*, we need you to leave before we call the cops," one of the men said, but all Kacey saw was the blood running down Natasha's lips as she held her nose. Kacey felt like everything was moving at high-speed. Her heart was pounding, her body was shaking, and she felt like she was a rabid dog locked in a cage. The cage being Jordie's arms.

"Call them! I'm filing a report against this bitch!" Natasha yelled, but Jordie was throwing money on the table before escorting Kacey out of the restaurant. When the chill of the November night hit her in the face, she wished it would cool her down, but she still wanted to go in there and rip that bitch limb from limb.

"Stay here," he demanded, shaking his head. "I can't believe you hit her."

"I can't believe you fucking kept her from me! That you went to her instead of me," she yelled and he held his hands out.

"Baby, really? Do you know she did that to piss you off so we would fight? Use your big brain, Kacey. She didn't mean anything to me, and you know that. She was my friend," he said, his eyes pleading. "Now stay here so I can go calm her down so that my fiancée doesn't end up in jail."

And she knew he was right, but that nasty sensation of rejection was blinking in front of her face, and she hated the way it made her feel. Yeah, that was what Natasha had planned and it had worked, but that didn't mean Kacey wouldn't be upset.

"It doesn't matter, Jordie, you chose her to help you get through your recovery. I was the backup batter."

He glared. "Are you fucking kidding me? Yeah, I chose her for the beginning, but I chose you, need you, for the rest of my recovery. For the rest of my life!" he yelled, his face turning red. "Now, put your damn pride away and tuck the jealous in a bit and let me go talk her down before she does something rash."

But Kacey wasn't listening. Her heart felt every bit of the rejection and, yeah, her pride was dented that that bitch had been there for him when she wasn't. That he chose her. And call her green with envy, but that pissed her off. She'd wanted to help him, she'd wanted to be there for him, and he chose that bitch over her. It wasn't right.

"No, I'm leaving," she snapped, turning and heading to the street to get a cab. They didn't drive around much on this road, but hopefully she'd get lucky.

"Kacey, stop. Don't be so damn dramatic!" he yelled, trying to stop her, but she smacked him with her purse.

"Dramatic! You broke my heart, Jordie. Back then, I gave you another chance and I let you take my heart again, just to learn that every time something happened, something bad, you went to her?"

He shook his head. "No, the last time I talked to her was a few days before we got back together. I haven't spoken to her much since."

"But did you tell me about her? About your friend?" she snapped back. "No, you hid her because you knew that it would hurt me."

"No, I didn't tell you because I didn't think about it, because she doesn't matter! All that fucking matters is you, Kacey. You're it!"

But she shook her head, unable to accept what he was saying. "Go inside and calm your friend."

"No, not till you promise you'll be out here when I come back."

Looking back at him, she could hear and feel her heartbeat in her ears. "I can promise you I won't be here when you come back," she said, her eyes in slits.

"Kacey," he said, but she cut him off.

"Go, Jordie," she demanded and he shook his head.

"You are being childish, Kacey, seriously."

"Childish, huh? Well, you're a dick," she sneered, her arms crossing over her chest. He stood there for a second, and she could feel his anger coming off him like thunder. But she was mad too, and hurt. The pain was almost as bad as when he'd cut off all communication with her. In a way, he replaced her with that bitch, and that wasn't okay. When she glanced to the side, she saw a taxi coming toward them and she threw her hands up in relief. She had to get away from him before she did something drastic.

Like, break up with him.

"Don't get in that taxi, Kacey," he demanded but she scoffed as she pulled the door open and got in, slamming the door despite his yelling at her to get out of the cab.

"Go, please," she said, looking away before rattling off her address.

"Boyfriend troubles?" the cabbie asked as he drove off, and Kacey shrugged as her hands cupped her growing belly. Her ring caught the light of the sun and her eyes clouded with tears. She was supposed to be happy, excited for her future with Jordie, but she felt like everything she'd thought was good was a lie. That the foundation of their relationship was built on dishonesties. For the longest time, she had thought it was the help of AA and therapy that had gotten Jordie through his problems at the beginning, but instead it had been Natasha.

Someone he cared for.

Someone he hid from her.

Someone who wasn't Kacey.

Wiping away her tears, she guessed the other shoe had finally dropped.

Screaming out in frustration as the taxi pulled away, he turned just as Natasha came out, a napkin under her nose as she glared at him. But he didn't care. He could give two shits that her nose could be broken or that she was mad, because he was furious.

"How dare you?" he sneered and she shrugged.

"You are making a mistake," she said nasally. "You love me."

"No, I do not!" he yelled. "I don't fucking love you, not even a little bit. I love that woman, the one that just got a cab to go home because of the shit you started. Do you know how fragile pregnant women are? Oh wait, no, you don't, because you don't have kids or even want them because you don't get close enough to anyone to even start to have a relationship."

"I got close to you!"

"But I don't want you!" he yelled back, his heart pounding as his mind reeled with ways to handle Kacey. She was overly emotional all the time, with good reason, and he knew he was in deep shit. She was right; he should have told her about Natasha, but honestly, he never even thought of her. He was so happy with Kacey that he didn't need Natasha anymore. He knew that sounded horrible and maybe made him an ass, but he only needed Kacey.

Natasha's eyes widened as she slowly shook her head. "You don't mean that."

What the hell was up with all these crazy people? First Liam, then his mom, who was straight from crazy town, and now Natasha? When was he going to catch a break? If it wasn't fighting his alcohol issue, it was batting away crazy people who wanted to fuck with the one great thing in his life. The one thing that mattered more than the next drink, or the people from crazy town. His everything.

Stepping toward her, he took her by her shoulders. "Listen to me, Natasha. I don't love you, I never said I'd love you, and I never will. That woman though, that woman I love. More than I could even try to put into words. You know how much she means to me. Please stop this," he begged, but Natasha shook her head.

"I miss you."

He let his head fall back and he couldn't believe it. She had been such a cool chick, a wonderful fuck, and an okay person, but when did she take a detour to Crazyville and why was she doing this? Shaking his head, he said, "Natasha, don't. Because I will never be yours. I'm Kacey's. Only Kacey's." Her lips trembled as she looked away and he asked, "Please don't call the cops on her. Let that be your apology to me."

"Who said I'm apologizing?"

He expected that from her. She was prideful, just like Kacey, but unlike Kacey, she didn't forgive easily. Nor did she let go of a grudge. Though she also knew that what she'd just done was unacceptable. "You will because you know that you shouldn't have done that," he answered and she shrugged. She worked her lip, tears falling from her eyes, and in another time, another place, a drunk mind frame probably, she would have been it for him. But she wasn't, and as much as it hurt her, it did upset him. He had cared about her. After this though, he wasn't sure he could ever speak to her again.

"I do love you, Jordie," she said then, her eyes meeting his. As she dropped the napkin, he knew that her nose was broken, which made him flinch. That woman of his had a temper and a mean right hook.

Squeezing her shoulders, he said, "Do yourself a favor and stop. Find someone else who can return that love. But first, go get your nose taken care of. Forward me the bill if there is one."

She shook her head as she covered her nose. "I can't believe she hit me."

"I can," he said slowly. "She loves me, and real love brings out the irrational part in people. Now I have to go home and convince her she has nothing to worry about. I doubt you'll wish me luck," he teased and she shrugged.

"I won't."

"Didn't think so," he said, fishing his keys out of his pocket. This was one of those moments when what Benji said rang true. Natasha didn't add to his life; she messed it up, so she was out of it. "This is goodbye, Natasha. Don't contact me, and I won't contact you."

She swallowed hard, wiping her face as she stood a little taller. Her nose was already bruising on her pretty face, but that wouldn't hold her back. She was flawless no matter what, but he still didn't understand how she could do this. Then his previous statement came back to him. She was in love with him, which made her irrational, and he felt horrible for hurting her feelings, but he had never lied or promised her anything. His heart was always Kacey's.

He just had to hope Kacey remembered that.

Slowly nodding, Natasha looked away as she whispered, "Sounds good."

"Good luck," he said before turning.

"You too," she called out to him and he waved a thanks.

Because he was going need it.

Walking in the back door, he found Kacey right away.

Sitting on the barstool, she was demolishing a pint of Ben & Jerry's, *Notting Hill* on the kitchen TV.

"You and this dumbass movie," he joked, but she didn't even knowledge him.

"Go pack your shit up and leave," she called and he scoffed.

"I'm not going anywhere," he said and she glared at him over her shoulder.

"Yes, you are, out that damn door," she yelled, turning off the TV and getting off the barstool. "Our whole relationship is a lie."

Confused, he held his hands out. "What the fuck are you talking about? How is it a lie? I love you. That's pretty well-known and true."

"No, you never told me about her, that she was what helped you get through rehab. You lied to me!"

"Um, no, I didn't. But really, why does it matter who helped me as long as I got through it and became the man you needed?"

"It matters because you didn't let me in! I wanted to help you."

He set her with a look as she chucked her Ben & Jerry's in the sink, the spoon making a loud noise, before she turned to look at him. She was blisteringly mad and he got that, but really?

"Do you know how stupid that is? You're mad, no, not even mad, *jealous* because someone else helped me and it wasn't you. But the thing is, you're helping me now. Just by loving me, you help."

Her eyes widened as heat crept up her neck. "No, I'm not jealous! I'm broken."

"Broken?" he asked, completely confused. "Please, enlighten me because I really don't understand how the fuck you're broken."

She glared at his display of aloofness. "You hid her because she meant something to you. She was probably your backup plan if I didn't give you a second chance."

He pointed at her. "Wrong. If I couldn't have you, I wasn't going to be with anyone," he said simply before crossing his large arms over his chest.

"I don't believe you for a second. That girl was just your type. A huge slut!" she shot at him and he rolled his eyes.

"*Was* my type," he said slowly before shaking his head. "Don't know if you know this, but my type is a crazy pregnant lady who has a wicked right hook and eats more Ben & Jerry's than a fat kid eats cake," he said, but this time she shook her head.

"No, if I were your type, you would have let me in."

Totally exasperated, he glared. "Kacey, I couldn't even look you in the eye after what I did to you, let alone open up to you. I was fucked up, remember? And you said you wouldn't throw my past in my face. Natasha is my past."

"That was before your past came barreling into my life, stabbing me in the chest with the rejection all over again."

"What rejection?" he yelled. "I'm with you. I sleep with you! I impregnated you! I am marrying you!" he said, each sentence louder and with more meaning.

"The hell you are!" she snapped, and she might as well have hit him.

"Oh, really?" he roared. "What, you aren't marrying me now?"

"I don't know what I am doing! I am so damn mad at you I could scream!"

"You are screaming, crazy," he said matter-of-factly, and her face went red. He understood she was upset, but she was being downright dumb.

"You need to go! Get your shit and go!" She seethed, and for some reason, that bothered him. He got that they were arguing, even that he was an idiot for withholding that piece of information from her, but he would not accept that she wanted him gone. Bullshit.

He glared, striking his hands to his hips. "If I'm getting my shit, saddle up, baby, 'cause you're coming with me."

"I am not!" she yelled and he went toe-to-toe with her.

"Yes, you are, because you are mine. This baby is mine too. I am not going anywhere without the person who completes me. Get over this shit and kiss me!"

But she pushed him away, her eyes filling with tears. "If I completed you, then you would have come to me instead of going to her."

Roaring out a sound of distress, his arms shook as he let his head fall back. "Oh my God, Kacey, I wasn't in my right mind back then. I was fucked up. We both know this. Why are you acting like this?"

When he looked back down at her, she was glaring, tears rushing down her beautiful, angry face. "Because it hurts. It hurts to know that I couldn't be there for you, to help you, that you pushed me away and clung to her."

"So it's your pride, your jealousy, that has you acting like this? Wanting to throw everything away for something that I did so long ago?"

She glowered. "You know how bad it hurt me when you didn't want me to help you, and instead of being truthful with me, you lied about her. Hid her."

"I never even thought about her because I don't fucking care about her. Yes, we talked a lot, but that's all it was. I didn't even sleep with her but that one weekend. Even when she pestered me to do it when I was in rehab, I never did. I didn't want her! I wanted you!"

"But you went to her."

"Because I had no choice. I wasn't coming to you until I was at least somewhat of a decent dude. Until I was the man you deserved. Now, stop this and come here, hug this out. Your blood pressure is probably through the roof, and I hate when you're mad at me."

But her tears rushed down her face, her eyes full of hurt and rejection, and he didn't understand. She said she forgave his past. Why was she acting like this?

"No. Go."

He held her gaze for a long time, the tension so thick he almost choked. She needed time to calm down. He had no problem giving that to her, but not until he proved his point.

"Fine, I'll go, maybe for a drink since, apparently, I'm still that guy."

Was it childish? Yes, but she was on a whole other level of crazy and he needed to knock her down.

Her eyes narrowed. "You wouldn't dare."

"Maybe I will. You are willing to throw away this relationship, not care about how hard I've worked to be the man you deserve. Instead, you're flipping your shit over someone who means nothing to me and telling me to go."

"You know that's not true, and you better not! I'm losing my shit because you didn't want me—"

"Because I didn't fucking deserve you, Kacey! Shit, when are you going to get that through your head!" he roared, causing her to flinch in surprise. "I had to fix me, and it doesn't matter who the fuck I had to help me get there as long as I got there. But you don't see that, all you see is your pride and jealousy. But what the ever-loving fuck ever, I'll leave, give you a chance to clear your head. Call me when you want me to come home," he said before stomping away from her and slamming the door for good measure.

But as his foot hit the bottom stair and she didn't come to stop him, his heart stopped.

Why didn't she follow him?

He walked extra slowly to his truck, looking back at their house, fully expecting her to come out, but she didn't. Reaching his truck, he looked back and let out a long breath, his heart pounding in his chest. He could see her in the kitchen, collapsed against the island, her body shaking, and he worried what this could do to their daughter. She needed to calm down, but was she actually going to let him leave?

Pulling his phone out, he texted her.

> Jordie: *You're not going to stop me?*
> Kacey: *No. You need to go.*
> Jordie: *Did we break up?*
> Kacey: *I don't know.*
> Jordie: *?????*

Kacey: I just need a second to think.

A second?
A fucking second?
This frustrating woman was going to drive him to his demise.

Chapter THIRTY

Getting in his truck, Jordie slammed the door hard and pulled out of the driveway, his tires spinning against the asphalt before he sped down the road, headed God knows where. He knew he could go to Karson's or even Karl's, but for some reason, he drove past their houses. He did take notice of the few bars he passed, but he wouldn't give them a second glance. He didn't want a drink; he wanted Kacey to get her head out of her ass and get it together. Before he realized what he was doing, he was passing by the arena and found himself pulling into the condos that Benji lived in. Parking his truck near Benji's, he got out and went up the stairs, then banged on his door.

Pulling it open, Benji's eyes widened in surprise. "Jordie?"

"Sorry I came without calling, but me and Kacey just got in a huge fight, and she's fucking crazy."

Benji threw the door open and turned. "Want something to drink?"

"Jack and Coke?" Jordie asked hopefully.

"I got you on the Coke," he said before grabbing two cans as Jordie fell back on his plush black couch. Looking at the TV, he saw that *Game of Thrones* was on, and he was starting to think that Benji was a tad bit obsessed.

Handing Jordie a Coke, Benji sat down in his recliner, shutting off the TV and saying, "So, tell me what happened."

He did and Benji listened, not asking questions or anything. He let Jordie get everything out and it felt good. If he had gone to Karson and Karl, they would have questioned him, made sure he hadn't hurt Kacey, which he hadn't and he never would intentionally. She would always be their first priority, and he understood that. She was the baby, but she was wrong. He knew that.

"I mean, you can't control what she feels. But, dude, you did do her dirty before," Benji said and Jordie's jaw dropped.

Maybe he wasn't right.

"But she's wrong to freak out like this."

"Sure, but you are wrong too. You knew from the beginning that she wanted to be there to help you. You didn't go to her, for good reason, I agree with you there, but you went to someone else. Someone you never told her about."

"I get you," he said and he did, but Jordie still didn't feel that he was in the wrong. "But she doesn't matter the way Kacey does. I really never thought about that."

"But Kacey doesn't see that. She sees it as she wasn't the one that fixed you, in a sense, and that bothers her."

"That's selfish! As long as I'm fixed, why does it matter?"

"Because as much as men are prideful, so are women, and Kacey is very prideful. I know that, and I don't even know her that well. She takes pride in everything she does, and she loves you so much that she wanted to be the one to be there for you completely. Instead, Natasha was, and that bothers her."

"Okay," he said, nodding his head because Benji was right. "But is it enough to break up with me for?"

"No," Benji said simply. "But to her it might seem to be."

Looking down at the ground, he sucked in a deep breath. "I won't let her."

"That's all you, dude. But I don't think she is over the past. Or maybe she is, but this just opened the wound all over again and now you have to figure out how to close it back up."

"But how?"

Benji shrugged. "You know her best, Jordie. She's your chick and only you know how to fix this."

He thought that over for a long time, tracing the rim of his can with his finger. His life was one big mess that he was continually cleaning up, but she had promised she would always stay by him to do that. Now, she was freaking out over something that really didn't matter. It was his past, and she had to accept that or they wouldn't work.

And not working wasn't an option.

Glancing over at Benji, he shook his head. "Why are you single, dude? You are one of those listening kind of guys that girls eat up."

Benji smiled. "I watch *Game of Thrones*, I'm an alcoholic, and I play hockey. Not really a winning combo."

He eyed him. "It works for me when my woman isn't acting insane."

He shrugged. "One day. It's a battle every day, but I'm a warrior and I'm gonna make it. Just like you. You'll fix this, because that's been the theme of your life since you left rehab. Fixing yourself. And you won't stop, you won't give up, until she forgives you."

"You're right," he said softly.

"I remember one time with Ava. She was big and pregnant," he said with a fond smile. "Like two weeks out. And I went out with the boys, got shit-faced, and came home, ready to get some. She lost her shit, threw all my stuff on the front lawn, kicked me in the gut, and told me I was dead to her. When I woke up in my own vomit, she was sitting on the porch, watching me, and I looked up into those sparkling blue eyes and I came undone," he said sadly, shaking his head. "I promised I'd never do it again, and I didn't. Except for that one time, the one time she was killed and I lived. So yeah, this fight sucks, and you feel like you're losing. But really, at least you have the chance to walk in there and tell her that you're sorry and that you'll never do it again. I don't."

Jordie's eyes were wide, his mouth gaping. "I mean, shit, dude. I think you almost made me cry."

He sucked in a breath as Benji nodded. "Yeah, dude, my life sucks, but yours doesn't. And if I were you, I'd give her some time to calm down before I approached her again. I remember one time I didn't leave the toilet seat down and she fell in. She hit me with a frying pan."

Jordie snorted. "Damn. She was a violent one."

"Yup, the ones who love the most usually are."

"True that, brother," Jordie agreed, seeing Kacey hit Natasha all over again, the way she wanted to kill his mother, and the way she'd looked at him with the fierceness of a thousand armies. Kacey didn't play, she loved. And he had hurt her. There was no other option but to fix it. As he watched while Benji sat with a sad smile on his face, it was easy to see that Benji missed his family very much. Jordie felt for him. He was sure that's how he would be if Kacey didn't get her head out of her ass and forgive him. He couldn't imagine living a life without her. Or their child.

It just wouldn't work.

He loved her.

And he wasn't going anywhere without her.

"Are you stupid, Kacey?"

Kacey rolled her eyes as she leaned against her hand, Lacey on the line hollering at her. Instead of chasing after Jordie like she knew she should have, she let him leave mad, and it rocked her to the core. She hated fighting with him, but she was hurting and she hated feeling like she was worthless. Like she wasn't enough to help him.

"First, you hit some random chick when you're pregnant. And then you send Jordie away for something that, I'm sorry, is dumb. He never cheated on you, never deceived you or even lied. He just didn't share information about someone who didn't matter to him."

Shocked, she yelled, "I mean, shit, Lacey, whose side are you on?"

"His!" she yelled. "You said you let go of his past, but it's obvious you haven't."

"I have!"

"No, you haven't. If you had, you wouldn't be holding him to this."

"No, I'm not doing that. I just don't like that someone else helped him when I should have been the one."

"Oh my jeez, you prideful jerk. It doesn't matter who helped, as long as they did!" she yelled and Kacey bit the inside of her cheek. Jordie had said the same thing. "He needed help, he got it, case closed. It doesn't matter who held his hand, smacked his ass and called him Sally. All that matters is him getting through this, coming to you, and being the man you need," she said, and it rocked Kacey's soul. "You gave him a second chance for a reason, because you believe in him, because you love him. So get your head out of your ass and call him and apologize!"

She dropped her head as the tears leaked out the sides of her eyes. "I mean, I get that, but I wanted to be there for him."

"And you are! Just at a different stage of his life. The part I'd rather be in because, let's be honest, you two wouldn't be together if you were trying to help him through his issues, Kacey. So you didn't get your way. Who cares? You're gonna throw away a love you've been praying for and begging to come your way because you are being selfish and insane, just because you weren't the one to push him along in rehab?"

Kacey paused, leaning on her hand as she repeated the words Lacey had just said. In her head, it didn't sound that bad or selfish, but hearing it from Lacey didn't sit well. "When you say it like that, it sounds bad."

"Because it is bad!" she yelled and Kacey rolled her eyes. "You are being dumb and childish and, yeah, I get that he was sort of wrong for not telling you about Natasha. But Kacey, he finally got you back, he was happy, and I believe wholeheartedly that he didn't think about it. His main focus is you."

"I just don't get why he wanted her to help."

"Because maybe she didn't matter and it was easy to confide in someone he knew meant nothing to him rather than admit his issues, his problems, and his fears to someone he loved. Like you, he is very prideful and, Kacey, he doesn't want to show you his weakness. He wants you to see him as this strong, amazing man who could take on the world, or better yet, addiction."

Lacey was right, but Kacey's heart still hurt. Or her pride. One of the two. "It just makes me so mad, so hurt. I feel like I did before, when I didn't feel like I was enough."

"If you weren't enough, why would he have gone through hell and back when other people say fuck it and turn back to their addiction? No, he fought and still is fighting just to be the man you want. Kacey, he loves you."

And she loved him. So why was she letting this rejection, this hurt, just drown her? She felt like she wasn't enough to help him, and she knew that was dumb. She knew that Lacey was right, hell, that even Jordie had been right. But she'd let her pride get in the way. She just didn't want to be second best to some porn star; she wanted to be first. She wanted to be his salvation.

But now all she had done was drive a wedge between them.

The last thing they needed.

They had been through so much pain, so much heartache, so many things that caused soul-deep fear, but they'd come out on top. Together. But what if she had done what he did in the beginning and had pushed him away?

"You didn't, Kacey. Really. Don't you see that he isn't going anywhere?" Lacey asked softly, and she hadn't realized that she'd said it out loud. "I don't think you know how much you mean to him, and this little fight won't break you two up. He'd fight you tooth and nail before he lets you get away."

She smiled but then pressed her lips together. "I need to call him, but he threw it in my face that he could go drink since I apparently think he is the man he used to be."

"Oh my God, you two are insane. Really," she groaned.

"Do you think he would do that?"

"What do you think?"

"No," she said confidently.

"Then shut up and call him and apologize. He doesn't need this crap, and neither do you," she said sternly and Kacey couldn't agree more.

Before she could say that though, Lacey hung up on her, frustrated. Kacey wanted to be mad that she'd taken Jordie's side, but the more she thought about it, the more she knew she was being an idiot.

But instead of calling him, she stared at her phone. She didn't like admitting when she was wrong, but it was obvious she'd overreacted. The whole thing was such a sore spot for her. For so long, she'd wanted to be the one to fix him, but this other bitch had, and that wasn't fair. She loved him more than anyone, she knew him, and as soon as she thought it through, she realized how selfish and repulsive it sounded. She wasn't that person, she was the person who wanted Jordie to succeed. And if someone else helped him do it, oh well. At least she knew in her heart that she would have loved him through it.

But you're the one he's with, she said to herself.

So why did it matter? Why did she allow this girl to come in and fuck with her mind? Because she was insecure about the whole thing. She wasn't enough for him hold on to before, so why would he now later in life? Was love enough? She wanted to believe so, but she'd been waiting for that damn other shoe to drop. He was too good to be true now. He was everything she wanted, and she didn't want anyone to experience him like she did. Knowing that Natasha probably had really dug a thorn in her side.

But she couldn't be jealous and happy at the same time.

She had to pick one, she had to let go of her issues with whom he allowed to help him through rehab, their past, and really trust their love. She was the one he chose to change for, she was the one he rushed to move in with, to get pregnant, and to marry. So why did anyone else matter? All that mattered was them, but yet, she had let her ego take over.

And because of that, she had to apologize.

Biting the inside of her cheek, she hit her messages and then his name.

> *Kacey: Come home, please.*
> *Jordie: Already am. Watching as you go back and forth with yourself when you know you just want to let go of this stupid pride and anger and tell me you love me.*

At that moment, she felt him behind her, yet she didn't turn.

> *Kacey: I do love you.*
> *Jordie: I know.*
> *Kacey: I'm a brat too.*

She heard him scoff and she smiled.

> *Jordie: That's for damn sure.*
> *Jordie: But I love that about you.*

"I love everything about you, Kacey, because the best thing in life is finding someone who knows your flaws, mistakes, difficulties, and still thinks you are badass and loves you."

She sucked in a deep breath before turning to meet his gaze. Her face was tear-streaked, her heart ached, and she felt so damn small. How could she have been so stupid? He loved her. It was shining in his eyes. She was his world, as he was hers.

Swallowing hard, she said, "I shouldn't have said what I did."

"It's part of that mistakes and flaws thing. You are prideful to a fault, Kacey. I know this and it doesn't bother me because, at the end of the day, I'm not going anywhere."

She slowly nodded, her eyes holding his. "It just bothers me so badly that I'm not the one who, when you look back on all of it, will be able to say that I had been there for you."

His brows came together as he took a step toward her. "But you are, Kacey. Yeah, you didn't hold my hand, tell me I could do it. But the idea of spending the rest of my existence with you was enough for me to fix what was wrong."

"But I wanted to be there."

"And you were, in my heart, but, Kacey, you couldn't fix me, still can't fix me. I have to repair me, but you can support me, you can love me. And because of that, I'll do what needs to be done to be the man that I want to be. For you." Biting her lip, she slowly nodded as he held her gaze. His chest was rising and falling, his eyes burning into hers. "The thing is, Kacey, I'm a broken man who is slowly but surely mending myself back together, and I couldn't do it without you. I'm an alcoholic who is standing in front of the woman he loves, asking her to put the past in the past and love him for every single flaw he has because, believe me, I have a lot. But one thing is for sure, I'll love you with everything inside me and more."

"Oh, Jordie," she said, tears flooding her eyes as she shook her head. He left her breathless, unable to even fathom how he still loved her. She was an asshole, but yet, he had quoted *Notting Hill* for her and it rattled her to the core. This man, this beautiful human, would do anything to make her happy, and she had been more concerned with being the person who helped him, rather than the person who loved him. How selfish and pathetic! Giving him a shy smile, she laced her fingers with his, stepping closer to him, their toes touching as she looked up at him. "That's a hell of a speech. Unneeded, but one hell of one."

He grinned. "I told you I was taking notes," he said with a wink.

She smiled. "I don't like fighting with you."

"I don't either," he whispered, his lips dusting along hers. "And I'm sorry for keeping Natasha from you. I was wrong for that."

"But I was wrong for freaking out the way I did," she admitted. She bit into her lip as she met his beautiful dark gaze. "I'm sorry, Jordie. The past is in the past from this moment forward, like it should have been. And from now on, I'll focus on making our story a happy one."

"A happily ever after, then?" he asked, his eyes dark as they bored into hers.

"The happiest."

"Good, 'cause you know that I used to think that wouldn't happen for me," he muttered and she smiled.

"Then I guess you weren't with the right person?"

He nodded. "Nope, I wasn't. I had to repair what was broken."

"What a job you did."

He nodded. "With your help. Someone had to hand me the hammer and nails."

"I was thinking more screws and drills."

Heat flashed in his eyes and she giggled before saying, "Freaking pig."

He chuckled before wrapping his arms around her tightly. "Brat."

Smiling hard, she leaned her head to his as he slowly wiped away her tears, his gaze holding hers. Cupping her face, he said, "Are you ready to stop being crazy and love me?"

"I never stopped loving you, nor will I ever stop being crazy when it comes to you."

He grinned. "Don't worry, I'm crazy too."

"And horny," she mentioned and he nodded.

"All the damn time," he said, cupping her ass. "But this is it, Kacey. No going back. We are in it to win it. And if you ever tell me to leave this house again without you, you'll regret it."

She smiled, her eyes sparkling with amusement. "Gonna off me?"

"Damn right. If I can't have you, no one can."

"Crazy town," she muttered and he laughed.

"Love does crazy things to people."

"You got that right," she said and her hand still hurt from punching that chick. Looking up at him, she grinned. "But I'm not going anywhere, Jordie. Call me your number two, I'm there," she said proudly, but he shook his head.

"You mean my number one," he said sternly. "Because you, Kacey Marie King soon-to-be Thomas, are my one and only," he said roughly before his mouth dropped to hers and her heart soared. As their mouths moved together, their souls becoming one, she knew that she wasn't going anywhere without a fight. That between her and Jordie, it would be a knock-down-drag-out fight before either of them got away from the other. She wouldn't want it any other way, either. She had one hell of a story to write, and that story would be the best she had ever written.

As long as Jordie was by her side, helping her write it.

Epilogue

"When a crayon breaks, it's still usable. You can still color with it, and that's how I've looked at my life the last year."

Jordie looked out at the group and smiled. Karl held Regina in the crook of his arm, pride shining in his eyes, with Karson and Lacey beside them, Mena in her arms, waving her arms and trying to get down to ruin something. Elli and Shea were there too, along with Benji, who was smiling like a proud father.

But the only person he saw was Kacey, holding their sweet baby girl, Ella Mae, in her arms, tears rushing down her cheeks as she beamed up at him. She had just given birth to her three days before, and he knew that she should be home, but she wouldn't miss this for the world.

Clearing his throat, he looked down as he sucked in a breath. "I was at the lowest of lows. Broken in black and white, wanting to scream in color, but I couldn't find my voice. I was nothing, a waste of space. I broke the heart of the woman I loved, I hurt my friends and my family, but then someone took a chance on me. Someone looked me in the eye and told me I needed help. And I took it, even though I didn't want it at the time," he said, his eyes meeting Elli's, and hers filled with tears. "The last year has been not only hell, but also the best year of my life. I'm healthy. I'm strong. I'm happy. I'm loved. I'm a best friend, a friend, a son, and a fiancé. And now a father."

Swallowing hard, he looked up, meeting Kacey's tearful gaze, and said, "I couldn't have reached this day, my three hundred and sixty-fifth day sober, without those people who define me, my therapist, and this group. You all love me, push me, and know that I can get through this addiction, and I can beat it."

Everyone smiled up at him, his therapist Julie grinned, Portia from rehab was there too, along with all his group members. The support was unbelievable and heartwarming, but the look of pure admiration and pride that shone in Kacey's eyes was what left him breathless.

He wanted to say that the last nine months had been easy—the happiest of times—but they had been a whirlwind. The Assassins lost the finals for the Stanley Cup and it sucked, but they had gotten far and were setting their sights on the following year. His mom hadn't contacted him, neither had Natasha, and he was okay with that. He had two ladies in his life that took over everything, and he really didn't have time to deal with anyone else.

Kacey opened her gym down the road from Audrey Jane's and was doing well, and she was itching to get back to training the way she had. But due to complications with her pregnancy, she was unable to just yet. During her seventh month, she was put on bed rest because she had gone into premature labor. Thankfully, the doctor got her taken care of and she went full-term, Ella coming out healthy and perfect. But the fear it caused was real, and it had rocked Jordie to the core. Though, like he knew they would, they got through it. Together. And Jordie had decided that they would continue to do that as long as they had each other.

No matter what, even if their backs were against the wall with the only option to score and win, they'd succeed. Even if it took extra minutes. Jordie and Kacey would always win in overtime.

Sucking in a deep breath, his mouth turned up as he moved his hand along his forearm, flinching at the pain of the brand-new tattoo he had gotten the night before. Looking down, he grinned at the script that spelled out his daughter's name before looking back up as he went on. "I told someone once that they couldn't fix me, that I had to do it, and I am. Through this process, I've learned to not only love myself, but to love God, to trust in Him that I can do this. That I will beat this because I am strong and I have His light in my soul." He paused, his heart so full of love as he watched Kacey wipe her face, before Karl wrapped his arms around her, kissing her temple. "My fiancée told me to never be ashamed of my story, my addiction, because telling it and owning up to it will inspire someone else. So here I stand, an alcoholic, a fiancé, a father, and I'm winning. Because each day I wake up farther away from the addiction and closer to the life I want. The life I am proud of. The life I love." He paused again, choking on the emotion. "Here is to the next three hundred and sixty-five days. May they be full of happiness, but also hard times, because I want to grow; I don't want this to be easy. I want to earn my win, and I will as long as I have that woman beside me through it all," he said, pointing to Kacey. She hiccupped a sob as she leaned into her daddy and everyone clapped and aww'd for him. His chest was bursting with love for her, his forever, and he couldn't take his eyes off her as she dissolved into tears next to her father. He wanted to rush to her, hug her, but he had to accept his chip. Then he'd love on her and make her feel exactly what he did. When Julie and Portia stood, coming toward him, they both hugged him tightly and he whispered thanks to both of them. They had both been such a big part of his recovery, and he was lucky to have them. When he'd asked what he could do to repay them, both of them said that his being healthy was their payment.

They were good women.

"Usually, we present you with your year chip, but I think Julie will agree with me when I say that Kacey should give it to you."

Jordie grinned as he looked back at her, to urge her to come up, but she was already walking around the group, eager to give him his chip. Grinning, she took it from Portia and thanked both of them before looking up at him. Her heart was in her eyes, and it had been since the moment he had asked her to marry him. Had it been easy? No. Would it ever be? Hell no. But they would get through it together.

"Jordie Scott Thomas, you are the most amazing man, inside and out. I know you've quoted me a few times, but I want to quote you," she said, her voice breaking as she gazed up at him. Their sweet baby girl was cuddled in her arms, small and perfect all wrapped in a purple Assassins blanket. "You said that the most amazing thing in life is finding someone who would love you for every flaw, every mistake, and every weakness. And while I do love you for all those things, I also love you for your strength, your tenacity, but most of all, your ability to love. You say I've changed your life, Jordie, but really, you've changed mine. And I couldn't be prouder of you than I am at this very moment," she said, big, wet tears rolling down her face as she slowly reached out, handing him his chip. "You deserve this."

He took it in his hand and then snaked his arms around her, dropping his lips only a breath away from hers. "But I don't deserve you."

"But you got me," she whispered, her eyes glittering with their future.

"And I won't ever let you go."

Because you don't let go of your leading scorer in overtime—that would be stupid. Jordie Thomas was a lot of things, but he wasn't stupid when it came to the game. In the last year, he'd found his life was one big game—sometimes winning, sometimes losing, always fighting for the chance to score, and each day bettering himself in order to win. Everyone needed that one person to help them win.

And Kacey was his MVP.

The End

A NOTE FROM
TONI ALEO

It's not a secret that I battle depression, or even that I've battled addiction. Mine being in the form of food. Have I won? No. Will I? I hope so.

All I have is my hope and faith that I can be the person I want to be.

I miss my mom—that's very well-known—and this may be very personal, but this book was my way of giving her her happily ever after. My mother was an alcoholic; she battled depression and her sickness with alcohol until the moment her liver gave out. She was fifty-three years old. I was only twenty-nine. Losing your mother is not an easy thing, I know that. But when my mom lost her mom to cancer back when I was seventeen, she shut down, she stopped being the mother I knew and turned into this person that I didn't like much. Now, she cleaned up so many times but fell back just as quickly. But no matter what, she loved me. She loved me so hard it hurt and she loved my babies. That's the stuff I remember. Not the screaming and begging for her to be my mom, not the smashing of bottles on the pavement to keep her from drinking. No, it was that when she looked at me, I knew she loved me. Even at the end, I knew I was my mom's world.

I just wasn't enough to clean up for.

And that's where a lot of my depression and my addiction to food have come into play. I've always loved food—I mean, who doesn't?—but it really was a sickness. Until one day, I looked at myself in the mirror and knew I couldn't do what my mom did to me. I couldn't put my husband and children through the pain that I was feeling because I didn't want to be healthy. I had to stop. And I did, but it's a battle. A battle that I fight every day and will continue to fight, not only for myself, but for my babies and my husband.

Now, I know you're sitting there thinking why the hell is she sharing this personal stuff with me, so let me explain. If I can touch one person, help one person to clean up their ways and be the person they want to be, then, damn it, I'm doing what I set out to do. This book is my healing. My HEART and SOUL are in each word on these pages. Especially when Jordie is talking. This is how I wanted my mom's story to play out. To clean up and be happy. Since she didn't get that on this earth with me, Jordie will. And I know she's in Heaven, smiling, saying, "That's my baby."

So please, if you need help, get it. My message box is always open, and I'm not shy. I'm an open book and I'm proud of my struggles, my triumphs, my failures, and my success. I work hard for what I want, and most of all, I depend on my faith. You can too. You can do it. I know you can.

For anyone who has helped me along the way, I thank you. I couldn't do anything without you. But this section isn't about thanking you. It's honestly about thanking my mom. Because without watching her story, I wouldn't have changed how I live.

So thank you, Mom. I love you. I miss you, and the hole in my heart will never be filled until I see you in Heaven.

In other words, just keep fighting, everyone. Please. Don't give up on you. Fight for what you want.

The end result is complete bliss.

Thank you for reading Jordie's story, and I hope maybe it had an effect on you in order for you to alter yours a bit in a positive way.

Thank you and God bless.

UPCOMING FROM
TONI ALEO

You Got Me – Spring Grove novel
Hooked by Love – Bellevue Bullies
Rushing the Goal – Assassins Series

Make sure to check out these titles and more on Toni's website:
www.tonialeo.com

Or connect with Toni on Facebook, Twitter, Instagram, and more!

Also, make sure to join the mailing list for up-to-date news from the desk of
Toni Aleo:
http://eepurl.com/u28FL